EARWORM

BY SEAN McMANUS

Earworm

First published in 2007 as *University of Death*

This edition published 2015

Cover design by

Alan D. Robinson

Special thanks to Andy Lawn who came up with the title Earworm for this remastered edition of the novel.

V151023

PRAISE FOR EARWORM

"A fun novel about the problems faced by musicians in making their mark on a music industry that's falling apart. A bitter satire that works its way up to a memorable finale."

- Metal Hammer magazine

"Raising a number of surprisingly sophisticated issues, this book is enjoyably cynical about the seemingly cold-hearted and impenetrable nature of the record industry and peppered with a number of highly comical cameos from the cream of rock'n'roll, which ensures that it never feels like heavy going."

- Record Collector magazine

"McManus keeps the action moving at a good crack, and the ideas trip out lightly in snappy dialogue. All round, the novel is a great genetic splicing of ideas and action, culminating in an incendiary showdown almost worthy of a Bond movie. Along the way it slips in telling observations about taste and commerce, culture and technology, creativity and consumption."

- David Jennings, author of Net, Blogs and Rock'n'Roll

"The novel satirises the music industry and the clichéd types that populate it, the lead character an affable fellow who you can't help but like - his meditations at his monitor screen, desperately trying to sort ideas, will be familiar to most of us who create music either for a living or for love. Amusing and well written."

- MusicTech magazine

"This is the most enjoyable, imaginative and perceptive insight into the plight and possible future of the music industry, a novel that illuminates as well as entertains. The best thing about it is its insight into how the music industry works, why it is dying and where it may very well be going. The twist at the end fooled me but fitted in perfectly with the themes of the book. When I finished reading, the story made me feel optimistic, that there was an exciting new beginning for the music business. The book is well worth buying if you like pop music itself or if you're interested in the machinations of the music industry."

- Mike Edwards, singer, songwriter and guitarist with Jesus Jones

"I cried 'til I laughed. There are some great ideas in here... and a few I hope the industry never hears about!"

- Colin Vearncombe, multimillion-selling singer, songwriter and independent record label manager

ABOUT THE AUTHOR

Sean McManus is a professional writer whose books have been published by Dorling Kindersley, John Wiley, Prentice Hall and other leading publishers. This is his first novel.

He has written for magazines including Musician, Making Music, Melody Maker, and Future Music. He writes and records his own electronic music, which you can hear at **www.sean.co.uk/music**. He has seen nearly 300 different bands live and is still counting.

Sean's books include:

- Raspberry Pi For Dummies (with Mike Cook)
- Scratch Programming in Easy Steps
- Web Design in Easy Steps
- The Customer Service Pocketbook (with Tony Newby)
- The Interviewer's Pocketbook (with John Townsend)

Visit **www.sean.co.uk** for free book chapters, music, photography, games and more.

Follow Sean on Twitter: **@musicandwords**

CHAPTER 1

The Bigg Records building looked like it was made from reclaimed gravestones. Two girls in school uniform were carving the name of a boy band into the stone with a key, as thousands had done before them. A third girl stood lookout and chewed, staring straight through Jonathan as he came around the corner. She blew a pink bubble and made it burst as he was level with her. It echoed in the alleyway and scared three pigeons into flight.

It had taken Jonathan ten years to create the perfect song. His iPod purred in his hand as he set it playing. The essence of all the music he ever loved had been distilled into three minutes. Even now it made the hairs on the back of his neck go electric.

There were no windows below the third floor, and the only door he could get to was the main entrance. A neon 'welcome' sign hung over it but its gentle glow did nothing to change the building's funereal appearance. It was like a smiley face painted on a tank: it said 'have a nice day', but only as it crushed the life from you.

Was he really welcome here? Bigg's people's people hadn't even returned his calls. Funny way to treat your saviour, he thought. With companies like this, he had decided, you just had to blag your way in and then convince them afterwards that you were justified. It's easier to seek forgiveness than permission. He looked up at the building towering over him and the skies seemed to darken. Gargoyles leered at him from the roof.

Jonathan took off his iPod and pulled a cigarette from the box in his inside pocket. There was another smoker loitering outside the entrance. His eyes were heavy with make-up and his spots were covered with a pink paste. Jonathan had seen his face somewhere before but couldn't place it. It felt like a logo you see on a lift each day that buries itself deep in your head despite you never consciously noticing it. Clipped to his trousers was a security pass.

"Got a light?" said Jonathan. The man silently extended his lighter and lit Jonathan's cigarette. "Thanks. Don't I know you?"

"Maybe," said the man. He grinned like he'd had a coat hanger fitted as a brace. "I'm J-Rok. From Icicle Star."

"Of course," said Jonathan, quite certain he had never heard of him. "You did that song! How does it go..?"

J-Rok traced a rainbow with his hands as he belted it out. "I've been away away away, but now I'm here to stay-ay-ay." The schoolgirls pointed at him and laughed.

Jonathan was at first startled and then embarrassed at J-Rok's outburst, especially as his voice was too short to reach the high notes without standing on tiptoes. Jonathan didn't know if he was expected to clap, join in or throw a quid at J-Rok's feet. "You're good," he lied. "I saw you do that on some TV thing, I think."

"Yeah, I sang better on the Saturday Show. The units went through the roof after that. We've been filming an insert for kids TV today. It'll go on the website when we know the TX date. Check it out."

"I certainly will." Jonathan cocked his head at the Bigg Records building. "So what's the studio like then?"

"Co-ol, you know," said J-Rok, looking up. "It's like a computer factory or something. Cleaner than a hospital. Yeah, not hard, I know. But with all those gadgets and stuff, they've got to look after them. Make sure the songs are perfect."

Jonathan eyed J-Rok's day visitor pass, which was clamped tight to his trouser pocket with a metal clip. Jonathan couldn't take it without arousing suspicion or possibly being arrested for indecent assault. "I bet they keep security tight too, with all that kit and superstars like you all over the place."

"Not really," said J-Rok, matter-of-factly. "Once you're past reception, it's a pretty relaxed culture. Beanbags, lava lamps, you know. You've just got to chill if you're gonna be creative."

"Well, I'd better let you get on," said Jonathan, dropping his cigarette and stamping it out. "It's been a real pleasure." He extended his hand and J-Rok shook his fingers.

Jonathan turned to leave and then spun back on himself. "Wait a minute!" he said. "This is kind of embarrassing, but could I have your autograph? I just know you're going to be big. It would be cool to show people I was into your stuff at the start." Men in their thirties don't normally autograph-hunt boy bands, but Jonathan knew J-Rok's conceit would see him through.

"Sure," beamed J-Rok. "Got some paper?"

Jonathan handed him a train ticket out of his pocket and a biro. J-Rok shook the pen and etched swirls in the cardboard with it in an effort to get it to work.

"I've only got one other autograph," said Jonathan, while J-Rok warmed the pen nib in his mouth. "Prince. He signed a napkin. He just wrote 'P' on it but everyone thinks I did it. I hope my friends believe this is really your autograph."

"I'm sure they will," said J-Rok. "This is still a pretty rare autograph, you know."

Probably your first request, thought Jonathan. "Hey!" he said. "I've had an idea. That's got your name on it. Do you still need it?" He pointed to J-Rok's visitor pass.

J-Rok took it off. "I'm outta here. They want it back though."

"They must have hundreds," said Jonathan. "I'm sure they don't really need it."

J-Rok turned it over and tried to write on the back of the pass, but the biro just slipped across its plastic surface. "Do you really want this security pass?"

"Well, yeah," said Jonathan. "As a souvenir of meeting you." Was he detecting a note of suspicion in J-Rok's voice?

"You'd better wait here a minute." J-Rok disappeared through the revolving door and marched up to reception. Jonathan panicked. Had he been rumbled? Was J-Rok reporting him? Jonathan was probably on camera. His heart jolted as J-Rok pointed at him and the receptionist looked him up and down.

Then J-Rok left the desk and came back outside. "Got one!" he said, holding up a marker. "Linda's always good for a pen. It isn't permanent ink, though."

"I'll put Sellotape on it later."

J-Rok finished writing his name, blew on the ink and then handed his security pass to Jonathan. As Jonathan was about to take it, J-Rok jerked his hand away again. "Don't tell anyone," he said. "Security would go berserk. If I see it on eBay, I will hunt you down."

"No worries," said Jonathan, laughing gently. He imagined J-Rok confronting him to tell him how disappointed he was in him. J-Rok wasn't so much the type to throw a TV out of a hotel window, as the type to throw the remote control on the bed once he'd found a cosy drama he could watch while sheltering from the strange, unfamiliar world outside. If J-Rok had any guts, he'd be smoking inside his record company building, instead of skulking around the streets in make-up. Real music was made by mavericks but Bigg Records could take the most unpromising material and turn it into fool's gold.

J-Rok gently lowered his arm. Jonathan took the pass and squeezed his fingertips against the cold plastic.

"Thanks," he said, reading the name on the sticker. "It'll be safe with me, Jervais."

CHAPTER 2

A white bird flew into the Routemaster's cab and perched on the steering wheel. The bus pulsed to the drumbeat as the band jammed on the top deck.

Simon stood, barefoot, on the zebra crossing. Out of the corner of his eye, he could see the catalogue number carved into the road, alongside the stripes. The bus thundered towards him. It was so close that Simon could feel the heat of its engine and it wasn't going to stop. He crouched and sprang onto the Belisha beacon, and the bus faded into a red mist beneath him.

From here, Simon could see the roofs of St Johns Wood were painted with lyrics. Only the first lines and rhymes were bold. His eyes swam when he tried to read the rest.

A man in a smock, juggling sheep, popped up from behind a patch of shrubbery, like toast from a toaster.

"Wake up, Si," she said. "It's Shepherd's Bush."

"Huh?" said Simon. He opened his eyes to see a tube logo whizz past as the train accelerated out of the station.

"We're nearly there," said Fred, sat beside him. It sounded like she was yawning, but when Simon looked, he could see she was applying lipstick, looking in a tiny mirror. She smacked her lips and clicked the lipstick shut.

Simon panicked when he realised he didn't know where his guitar was, but then saw the case propped against the other side of the glass, just inside the train door. He rubbed his eyes.

"Tired?" Fred was plucking at her hair. It was short and teased into spikes, making her head look like a sloppily iced cake.

"I dream of a good night's sleep," said Simon. Twigs of blood were lodged in the corners of his eyes. "I swear I snore University of Death sleeve notes."

"You should be ready for anything they throw at you then."

He wasn't. He knew it. He'd spent all week with his scrapbook and CD collection. He'd even skimmed the hagiography again, a cheap rush-job from when anything with the band's logo on it sold. But now his brain had casseroled the names, dates and lyrics, leaving a mulch of disconnected ideas. "Have you seen this show before?"

"It's new," said Fred. "For some digital channel. UK Puppet Gameshows, or something."

The train slowed to a crawl. "Fred?" Simon spoke tentatively.

"Uh-huh?"

"You will take this seriously, won't you?"

"Course," said Fred. She angled her make-up mirror to check how her breasts looked in her black silk shirt. With a satisfied smile, she snapped the mirror shut and slipped it into the pocket of the brown leather jacket that dwarfed her. It had RAF wings stitched to the front.

"Only, well, you know."

"Chill out, Si," said Fred. "I've got general knowledge licked. You're the biggest University of Death nerd. The questions are a mere formality. This is our fifteen minutes of fame. Enjoy it."

The train drew into a station. "White City," announced the driver. "Alight here for the BBC."

"This is us," said Fred. She collected her flightcased keyboard from the seat opposite.

Simon shivered with nerves. "Break a leg," he said.

*   *   *

Simon flinched and the make-up woman recoiled. "Watch it!" she said. "I could have yer eye out with this."

He forced his eyelids wide open and didn't dare blink. The woman spoke into a walkie-talkie as she stroked his eyelashes with mascara: "Not much to go on. We could spray glitter in his hair, I s'pose. He looks like a newsreader on a camping holiday."

Simon's t-shirt was covered with swirls and eddies of colour: mostly blue and yellow, but with splashes of brown. A belt with a skull-shaped buckle held up his Asda jeans, which had started life black, but now had round stains all over them. It looked like his trousers had been used as a coffee table.

The make-up woman clipped her radio to her belt. She covered Simon's eyes with one hand and sprayed his hair with the other. After she had lifted the excess glitter from Simon's shoulders with a sticky roller, she took her clear plastic satchel of chemicals to the next podium.

Simon was roasting. Each light was like an open oven pointed at him, and he'd been waiting for twenty minutes. He untucked his t-shirt from his trousers and flapped it. The counter they made him stand behind was made of cardboard, part-covered in sparkly paper. He wanted to break a bit off to use as a fan, but there were too many people flying around.

Simon sized up the competition: two strutting pretty boys, barely out of school, too young to have suffered for their art. What did they know? Thirty thousand screws hand-sorted into bags of fifteen was a four track recorder. Eight thousand envelopes stuffed with catalogues and carefully sealed was a half-decent guitar. Seven hours with glassy eyes, hands on autopilot, imagination flying free: that was a new lyric, or perhaps even a melody. About thirty jobs in fifteen years had given Simon a bulging songbook.

He always knew their break would come. Tonight, it had. He and Fred were going to play their greatest hits-to-be on the BBC. On the other side of the studio, he could see the stage waiting for them in near-darkness. Their instruments were plugged in and ready. So were the other band's.

All Simon and Fred had to do was answer a few questions – or to be exact, a few more questions than the other team – and they would be on.

Easy.

Hopefully.

7

Simon watched absent-mindedly as a woman was zipped into the weasel costume, and the wardrobe assistant scurried away. The weasel bounced a couple of times on the spot to limber up.

The lights clicked and dimmed. It felt like a fire going out.

One of the runners walked Fred to the centre circle and stood her on a yellow cross taped to the floor. Fred looked briefly over her shoulder to wink at Simon.

A man in headphones counted them down: "In seven, and six, and five, and four…"

Disco lights sprinkled the room with coloured flashes. Someone in the shadows behind the camera clapped with his arms in the air. The audience put down their polystyrene cups of wine and joined in. There were only about twenty people, most of them probably staff, so they beat their hands quickly to make it sound like there was more of a crowd.

The man in headphones held up three fingers and folded them down in turn. When he reached zero, he punched the air and cheesy synth horns heralded the arrival of the weasel. It lolloped onto the stage, stood behind the quizmaster's desk and waved at the cameras.

"Welcome to Pop Goes The Weasel," said voiceover man with a tone of plastic excitement. "Where a talent for pop and rock is *weasily* recognised!" He was throwing his best TV voice into it, but it couldn't levitate the script above the standard of kids' TV. "Willy the Weasel is ready. The audience is ready. Now let's meet our first team tonight."

A videographer with a rubber chicken dangling from his camera charged up to Fred. She came face to face with her reflection in the glass lens. Fred waved, just as she'd been taught. "Fred is Swedish but lives in London," said the announcer. "Her favourite band is the Eurythmics."

The cameraman charged at Simon, who took half a step back. "Her band mate is Simon, whose stage name is *The Thing*," said voiceover man. Simon smiled weakly. "His specialist round will be his favourite band, University of Death. Together, Fred and Simon are called Goblin. With a little *elf-confidence*, they might just win tonight. Remember: they're playing for their own gig on the

BBC at the end of this show. Now, let's welcome our quizmaster…
Willy… *the*… WEASEL!"

The weasel waved at the camera with both hands and wobbled
its head from side to side. Its face couldn't move, so body
language was everything. "Fred, you're first. I have to say, that's
an unusual name for a lady." Willy had to say it because it was on
the autocue, not because it had just occurred to him, as his stilted
delivery made clear.

"It's Swedish for peace," Fred said. "Mum's a bit of a hippy."

"That's lovely." Willy wasn't listening and would have said the
same if Fred's name had been Vomit. "You've got one minute to
answer four general knowledge questions about music. One
wrong answer and you're out of the game. Got that?"

Fred nodded. Coloured lights helter-skeltered around her and
converged at her feet.

The weasel held the question cards up to its neck, where there
was a gauze through which the woman inside was looking out.
She took an audible breath and then began: "Start the clock. If I
wanted to kill Sinatra using a Taser, which experimental
American composer might I employ?"

Simon was taken aback. This was way more cryptic than he
expected.

"Frank Zappa," said Fred. Nice one.

"How many arms has a Def Leppard got?"

"Nine," said Fred. It sounded like a guess. Simon crossed his
fingers. The only thing he knew about the band is that the
drummer had one arm.

There was a long pause before Willy conceded. "Correct.
Which of these royals has not had a UK number one single? King,
Queen or Prince?"

"Say again?" said Fred.

"Remember, time's running out."

Simon could see the floor manager holding up a kitchen clock.
The red hand had got to six. Simon watched Fred's puzzled
expression on one of the monitors and willed her to work it out.

"Which of these royals has not had a UK number one single?"
repeated the weasel. "King, Queen or Prince?"

"King?"

"Correct," said Willy. "Last question. You've got 20 seconds to answer but you must get this right. What is the name of John Lennon's first wife?"

Simon stifled his laugh. He had been afraid they'd throw a real humdinger in at the end. If he and Fred failed this round, all their cramming and rehearsal would have been wasted. And they wouldn't even have got to play a song. But this was just too easy. Everyone knew this. What's more, he'd read Cynthia Lennon's book, and bored Fred recounting endless detail. She'd be grateful now. As long as she paid attention and didn't answer 'Yoko', they were through to round two.

Fred stopped herself blurting it out and put a finger to her mouth. For a moment she was lost in thought. A smile flickered across her face, then hid again. Then she answered, with absolute authority. "Imogen."

A gasp came through the speakers and the same synth horns that had cheerily opened the show parped a funeral march. Simon swore to himself. The producer glared at him.

Willy shook his head. "I'm sorry. It's Cynthia," he said.

"The fuck it is!" said Fred. "You're joking, yeah?"

There was another gasp in the studio, but this time it was real.

"Language. Can we do that again please?" called the director from the back of the room. "Keep rolling."

"It's Cynthia," repeated Willy.

"It's fucking Imogen," said Fred. "This is a fix!"

Willy looked for support around the studio and then settled his gaze on Fred.

"What do you think you're staring at?" she said. "I'll deck you in a minute! You wanna spend more time on research and less time... up a rodent's arse!"

Willy shrugged.

"Don't shrug at me!" shouted Fred. She charged at the weasel and pushed it over on to its back. It rolled from side to side and fought to get upright. Fred jumped astride it and punched its soft head over and over again. She smashed one of the ping-pong-ball eyes off its face and it bounced away, making a pock sound each time it hit the floor. The woman inside shouted, but her microphone had fallen off and her voice was muffled by the costume. Willy's legs kicked about helplessly, as Fred repeatedly punched his head.

Simon put a hand on his counter and jumped into the air to vault it, but it crumpled under his weight. He yelled in pain as he landed on his outstretched wrist. The cardboard podium folded on top of him. He rolled out of it and stumbled over to Fred, dragging a strip of glittery paper that had glued itself to his shoe. As Simon approached the pair of them wrestling on the floor, the weasel hit his legs. It felt like being smeared with a teddy bear.

Fred was still punching Willy, knocking his head first to one side and then to the other, alternating her left and right hook. As she lifted her right arm into the air, Simon grabbed it to stop her. Fred tore her arm from Simon's grip but she didn't punch again.

Fred collapsed onto the weasel like it was a bed, exhausted. Willy rolled uneasily but couldn't right himself or roll her off.

When her breathing had returned to normal, Fred stood up, smoothed her clothes and walked off the set.

"Cheating bastards!" she shouted. "Her name is Imogen!"

*   *   *

Simon didn't say anything to Fred but kept swearing to himself. He had assumed they would be sent home or arrested, but the TV studio wanted to record the contestant debriefing before doing anything else. The show must go on. Fred was sitting in one of the interviewee chairs, biting her nails.

Her top two buttons were missing. The shirt gaped open, flashing cleavage. The buttons must have come off in the fight, although Simon didn't notice them until Fred came back from wardrobe.

A woman hobbled in, her hair in a net and a clipboard in her hand. She plumped herself down in the chair opposite Fred, rolled up the leg of her jogging trousers and rubbed her calf. "Calmed down now?"

"Yes," said Fred. Sweat was still dripping from her hair.

11

"Don't mention it," said the woman.

"Sorry?" said Fred.

"Yes, that. Don't mention it. I'm not *that* bruised, anyway." She prodded her tender knee and sucked at the air in pain.

"Oh my God! I didn't realise it was you," said Fred. "I just so bought in to the weasel thing I forgot it was a real person inside."

The woman's lip quivered. "You are sweetie!" she said, her eyes going watery. "It's nice to get some credit for a change! I know it's a crap role, but I've always put my all into it. I do everything for that rodent. Without me, the director can't even get his stupid Willy to stand up. Oh, gosh, I mean…"

"'Sokay," said Fred. "We know."

The woman rolled her trouser leg down again and invited Simon to sit in the other chair beside Fred. He flopped himself down with such force that the chair legs squeaked across the floor. The cameraman nodded to confirm they were filming.

"How do you feel?" asked the naked weasel.

"Gutted," replied Fred. "Totally gutted. We had a great set worked out. All original stuff, too. Now we'll never get to play it."

"How did you get that Lennon question wrong?"

"I was so sure," said Fred.

Simon exploded: "How can you be so sure about something so obviously wrong?"

"All right!" Fred shouted at him. "Don't go on about it!" She turned back to the camera. "I remember the day Lennon was… the day he died." Fred rubbed one of her eyes. "Mum was crying. She started singing one of his songs. It was the first time I'd heard it. To me, it always sounds funny to hear it without a Swedish accent now. It was so simple, so beautiful. Mum said he had written it for his wife."

"Which song was that?" asked the interviewer.

Fred sniffed and began to sing softly. "Imogen, there's no heaven," she sang. "Imogen, there's no hell."

Simon stared at Fred aghast and the interviewer laughed.

"What?" said Fred. "What's funny?"

CHAPTER 3

The laundrette smelled of bad socks and blue stripe washing powder. As he swept the floor, the manager sang 'All you need is fluff'. He put on a comedy Liverpudlian accent that was neither.

"Mad, eh?" said Simon to a woman who was folding her underwear. He cocked his head towards the manager.

The woman looked at Simon like he was some kind of freak, and turned her back on him.

Simon took another length of string and tied it to a pair of his underpants, leaving a bobble hanging off, then threw them into the washing machine.

The bell above the door tinkled as Fred came in. "Hey, Si!"

As loudly and aggressively as he could, he snipped lengths of string from the ball and let them fall into his clothes basket. He didn't reply.

"Your flatmate told me you'd be here."

Their last words had been on camera yesterday. Since then, his inbox had been clogged with copies of the video, which the studio had leaked to promote the show. They had cut from Fred saying her name was Swedish for peace to the final question where she lost it and dived at Willy. There was a close-up as she smacked his eye out. It repeated in slow motion. Over and over. Then it cut to the interview. After Fred sang 'Imogen', the camera zoomed in on Simon's stunned expression. His eyes bulged like they were straining to grow stalks. His mouth hung open. He had been cast as the straight man and looked an idiot.

13

"Anyone can make a mistake," said Fred. She kept her distance and leaned against the window.

"Yes," snapped Simon. "But you didn't, did you?" He took a fistful of shirt and knotted string around it. As he tightened each loop, the shirt's fibres released a cabbagey whiff.

"What do you mean?"

"Can I ask you a question?" he said.

"Sure."

"Will you answer honestly, though?" He threw the shirt into the drum.

"Oh yeah, I expect so."

"That weasel-smacking thing." Simon faked an air of nonchalance. "Did you plan it?"

"What on earth gave you that idea?"

"But did you though?" He was tying concentric circles of string around the knee of a pair of trousers now.

"I can't believe you sometimes." Fred went to the hot drinks machine and pumped it full of small change.

"You're dodging the question, Fred!"

"I'm insulted you even asked." The machine dropped gooey soup into her cup. She shook the cup, but the liquid didn't stir, so she tossed the whole thing into the bin.

"Christ, Fred," said Simon. "You did, didn't you? I've spent all week reading University of Death sleeve notes and rehearsing our set. I took time off work. I can't believe you let me do that."

"I made you famous, didn't I?"

"That's what our music's for," said Simon. "I thought we agreed to take the band seriously."

"I am!" pleaded Fred. "I'm working my arse off to get us noticed. What do you suggest we do instead? Post more demos?"

"Hardly," said Simon. "That's a complete waste of time." He was winding string around a sock.

"Good. That's one thing we agree on, at last."

"From now on, I'm hand delivering them."

"God, Si. You don't get it, do you?" She shook her head in wonder. "Nobody will even listen to us unless we're already famous."

"*You* don't get it," said Simon. He threw someone's stray sock at her. "We could have been arrested. And for what? Nothing."

"Oh there was just one thing," said Fred, with a triumphant giggle. "Must have slipped my mind. We did get a gig out of it. They saw the video and booked us."

"Where?"

"The Corpse."

"That's only round the corner!" Simon slammed the door of the washing machine with such force that it made Fred blink. "Bert'll let us play there any time!"

"The video should bring a crowd in, though."

"Yeah, well, I'm busy." Simon shook powder into the drawer and clicked it shut.

"You don't know when it is yet."

Simon punched the plastic buttons and rattled the silver dial round. "When is it?"

"Next Friday."

"I'm busy."

"You're lying."

"Yes." He sighed. "You're wasting my life on these stunts. I just don't… know… any more."

There was a long silence. Simon slotted the money in and pushed the coin feeder shut with the heel of his hand. The window on the washing machine flooded. His University of Death t-shirt swam to the front. Dove's face rubbed against the glass.

"I said sorry. I don't know what else I can say. Will you do the gig? Please?"

"I don't know," said Simon.

"No messing around this time," said Fred. "Guide's honour." She held up two fingers in an offensive gesture, which either meant they really did do guides differently in Sweden, or she was taking the mickey again. Simon didn't know which any more.

"I'll think about it," he said.

"Seven o'clock."

"I said I'll think about it."

There was an uncomfortable pause. Simon peered into the washing machine window to avoid looking at Fred. "Is that why you're here then? The gig?"

"No," said Fred. "Just thought I'd, you know, catch up. How's things?"

"Crap."

"Oh, well." Fred folded her arms. "What on earth are you doing with your clothes?"

"Washing them."

"What's with the string?"

"I've decided to stop fighting the machine," said Simon. "The dye always runs, whatever I do. So I've given in."

"How?"

"I'm letting it tie-dye my clothes. That way, they'll always match."

"Yeah, but think of the look!"

"Some very fashionable people wore tie-dye."

"In 1967 and '89."

"So we're probably due again now!" Simon was shouting. The laundrette manager swept the space between them and eyed them suspiciously.

"I'd better go," said Fred. For show, she moved her whole arm to look at her watch after she'd decided to leave. "See ya Friday? Maybe?"

"Maybe."

"I am sorry."

"I know." Simon knew Fred didn't mean any harm. It was one of life's mysteries how she could be so calculating and yet completely oblivious to the impact she had on other people's lives.

Fred held eye contact with Simon for a moment longer than necessary, and then she left. For about five minutes, she waited at the bus stop opposite the laundrette. Just before her bus arrived, she waved to Simon and blew him a kiss. He gave only the slightest nod in reply.

CHAPTER 4

Simon's flat looked like his wardrobe had exploded. Clothes dangled off the furniture everywhere, and clung to the walls. He had smoothed his best shirts against the mirrors and picture frames so they would dry flat.

A pair of pants was pinned to his notice board, along with some photocopied sheet music and some of his own chord sequences. His guitar was on its stand under it, with a halo of empty space around it, as if it stood on sacred ground.

It was 1.35 in the morning. Simon couldn't sleep. He gently touched the strings of his acoustic guitar without taking it off its stand. They whispered a simple song, but in the still of the night it sounded like a shout. He thought he heard his flatmate stir but it might have been the pipes. He didn't want to wake him, so he left the guitar alone.

Simon flicked through the TV channels but paid them scant attention. Instead he stared just above the TV, at the photo of him and Fred. It was clipped in the frame she made him from clothes pegs in the sixth form. The shot was taken at a friend's wedding. They were dressed in their finest and stood close, but apart.

Could Simon forgive her? He wasn't sure. How could she betray his vision for the band like that? And make him look so stupid in front of the whole world? The band meant everything to him, but he wasn't sure if he could go through with it any more. He didn't know what any of this meant for their friendship either. The prospect of that being over worried him at least as much as the idea that their music was finished.

He needed a good heart-to-heart, but who can you talk to if you're annoyed with your best friend? Besides, you can't phone anyone at 2am unless someone's died.

He went to his computer to check his email. A damp sock sunned itself in the warm glow of his desk lamp. There were two new copies of the 'Pop Goes the Weasel' movie, but no real messages.

What now? He stared at the computer. For the first time one of the default icons caught his eye.

'Talk to me'.

He clicked and a window flew open, inviting him in. He gave his nickname as 'thing' and picked angelA from a list of available chatters.

angelA>	a/s/l?
thing>	**Sorry?**
angelA>	new here?
thing>	**Yes**
angelA>	ok ill be gentle with ya
angelA>	age/sex/location?
thing>	**Ok: 32 male London**
angelA>	27 F london :-)
thing>	**Is there an AngelB on your cloud too?**
angelA>	don't think so. wat u listening to?
thing>	**University of Death**
angelA>	they're great. stay dead rocks
thing>	**Are you a fan?**
angelA>	i love their music.
thing>	**They're my favourite band**
thing>	**I had a dream I was on stage with them once**
thing>	**playing guitar.**
thing>	**It was one of my greatest experiences ever**
thing>	**even though I was asleep.**
angelA>	that so funny
angelA>	how did u get into university of death
thing>	**They used to play it at parties I went to**

angelA>	when was this
thing>	**When I was at school**
thing>	**In the sixth form. Yeah, I know.**
thing>	**Nobody but the fans plays their stuff now!**
angelA>	thats for sure
thing>	**Have you ever dreamed of a band?**
angelA>	beatles
thing>	**Did you play an instrument?**
angelA>	i played recorder
thing>	**It must be cool to feel like you're in The Beatles**
angelA>	not as good as the rolling sontes though
thing>	**Sontes?**
angelA>	stones. pedant!
thing>	**Sorry. Why do you prefer the Stones?**
angelA>	beatles do thought music. stones do emotion music.
thing>	**Let it be? Yesterday? Day in the life?**
angelA>	yeah, except the dreary ones ;-)
thing>	**I wanna hold your hand?**
angelA>	you're sweet LOL
thing>	**You'll make me blush.**
thing>	**What does LOL mean?**
angelA>	laugh out loud
thing>	**It's like a foreign language. This is my first chat.**
angelA>	thought so ;-)
angelA>	youll pick it up ok
thing>	**Do you chat often?**
angelA>	do i come here often? you making a pass?
thing>	**I didn't mean**
angelA>	sorry. Giot to go. I'll be back in a bit.
thing>	**Okay. Maybe chat later?**
‹angelA has disconnected›	
thing>	**bye. Take care**

What now? Simon didn't want to go to bed. He wasn't relaxed enough to sleep, and anyway angelA might come back and chat some more.

He looked up. Most of the wall behind the computer desk was

covered with a poster of University of Death, which Simon had recovered from a bus shelter and framed. Dove was biting the air, his teeth like tombstones in a field of red and green face paint. His body was folded around an electric guitar shaped like a skull with a dagger plunged into it. Dove's eyes were locked on to the photographer's lens.

Simon punched in the website address for Dove's blog, which he knew off-by-heart.

Dear all

Ich bin ein Berliner! Even though the weather is Wetter and the sausages are the Wurst, we're having a fantastic time here in Germany. Our German fans have made these gigs truly memorable for us.

We're staying in a luxurious hotel previously used by the high-ups in the East German government. When we're on tour, our hotel is our creative space, so we like to spoil ourselves a bit. For us, the songs we write here will always carry the spirit of this fantastic tour. The sight of the Berlin Wall all over the place is sure to inspire some great new sounds and we've been listening to famous Berlin albums like Achtung Bono and Low to get into the spirit.

We are delighted with the support our new record label Bigg Records is giving us. There's a 2CD retrospective in the pipeline – more news as we make it.

And London, look out! We're coming to you next. Tickets on sale soon!

Love and Peace,
D/ove xx

Dove was coming to London. Simon's head rushed with all the songs he might hear reinvented on the stage. University of Death was a part of his DNA: the melodies were tangled like ivy around his twisted ladders of identity, the roots planted in his school days. Playing those old albums was the closest thing he had to a time machine. All his friends had been into them then, but only he had stuck by the band as they fell out of the charts and released increasingly experimental and patchy albums. Simon had even collected the dance remixes. And Dove rewarded his loyalty with moments of sheer genius: guitar lines that could break his heart or make him laugh at their audacity; lyrics with wit and verve that stunned with their simplicity; and rhythms you couldn't dance to, but couldn't sit still to, either.

Simon had spent more on University of Death music and merchandise than any other cultural product. But he'd never seen them in the flesh before. He had to be there – right down the front. Just the idea of being in the same room as Dove was a thrill.

Simon imagined what Dove was doing right now. He would have come off stage a few hours ago, but was probably still buzzing. Maybe the band went on to a club to jam, or perhaps they crept back into the venue after the audience had left to work on new material. Dove might even have rented a local studio to lay down some demo tracks.

Simon looked into Dove's eyes on his poster and wished he could talk to him about his own music. Dove would understand.

But they were destined to be forever on opposite sides of the star/fan divide. If for no other reason, then because whenever Simon thought of Dove, whatever he imagined him doing, Dove was always in his face paint and fine stage clothes.

* * *

Dove was in paisley pyjamas, sitting on the floor of a walk-in wardrobe in Berlin, with the door slightly ajar to stop the lights going out. The sound of clinking glasses and a drunken hubbub came from the hotel room next to his but it was quieter in here. This closet was the closest he could get to peace and privacy.

There were remnants of make-up in Dove's eyebrows, but he had removed as much as he could be bothered to. He was wearing his reading glasses, with his long, black hair tied back.

The guitar tuner sat on the tiny safe, beside a steaming cup of peppermint tea that Dove had left to cool. He plucked a string on his acoustic guitar and watched the tuner's needle bounce and settle around the middle as he twisted the tuning peg and plucked again. He could hardly hear the notes over the racket from his neighbours, but he tuned the guitar strings one by one anyway.

As heavily as he could, he strummed the guitar and tried to concentrate on the sound it made, screening out the noise of the party. His music was deadened by the costumes hanging on a rail down one side of the wardrobe, but he could feel the vibrations and used his imagination to fill in the notes he couldn't hear. He was yearning to sing, but knew he had to save his voice for tomorrow's show. So he gently hummed along with the guitar and concentrated hard, until he eventually reached a trance-like state, where only the music and he existed.

The door jerked open. Dove jumped.

Creak stood there in his underpants and a crew t-shirt, clutching a bottle of whisky by its neck.

"Christ, Creak," said Dove. "How did you get in here?"

Creak held up a key card. The rest of the band usually had interchangeable keys, but Dove's room was supposed to be private. "Why are you hiding, man?" said Creak.

"Only in solitude do we find ourselves. I'm trying to write."

"Shhhh!" said Creak. He put his finger to his lips and damn-near missed. "I won't tell anyone your secret. It's our secret now. Wait – I could drum on a bin! That would rock!"

"No. It wouldn't."

"Please y'self," said Creak, clearly put out. He took a swig of whisky and rubbed his arm across his face to dry his chin. "We're having a party," he confided.

"So I hear."

"Why don't you come for a drink?"

Dove glared at him. "Think, Creak! Besides, I'm busy. I'm trying to write."

"Write tomorrow."

"When?" Dove stood up and rested his guitar against an

elasticated suitcase stand at the back of the cupboard. "I spend all day on a bus where the air is thirty per cent methane, thanks to your exclusive curry diet."

Creak shrugged and dropped a splash of whisky on the carpet. "'Snot my fault."

Dove put his hands on his hips: "I glimpse the world's greatest architecture, landscapes and people… as they fly past our bus window. I spend my evenings in a chrysalis, nourishing my body and transforming myself for the stage. During the show, I am a puppeteer who has hanged himself with his own strings. I have choreographed every sound and every move, right down to the frowns. We sleep in hotels where the only thrill is finding one the Gideons haven't discovered yet. My window on the world is CNN, for Christ's sake. If I can snatch twenty minutes in a wardrobe to throw some chords together, trust me, it'll be the creative pinnacle of my week."

"Keep your hair on."

"Oh piss off," said Dove. "Really, please, just piss off."

"Hey, man," said Creak. "Chill out."

"And get the hell out of my wardrobe!" It is difficult to assert yourself when you are ordering someone to leave you alone in a cupboard, but Dove gave it his best shot.

Creak waggled his finger. "Someone's getting grumpy and needs a sleep!" he cooed.

"Get out!" Dove stepped towards Creak, but Creak stood firm in the doorway, sucking on his drink without taking his eyes off Dove. Dove pushed him.

The bottle slipped from Creak's hand and hit the floor and the neck smashed off. The whisky escaped into the brown fibres of the carpet. Creak looked at it sadly and then turned to Dove with anger. "Man," he said. "What you do that for? You broke my drink." He pushed Dove's chest, forcing him to take a step back into the closet.

"Ungrateful bastard," said Dove. "Without me, you're just a man hitting things. I make you the drummer you are. Don't you think I've earned some peace?" Dove pushed Creak, but even when Creak stepped back, he didn't stop. Dove kept pushing and

Creak stumbled backwards, scooted across the room until his calves were blocked and he fell face-up onto the bed. A chocolate mint resting on the pillow glued itself to the side of Creak's forehead.

"Please, just go now," said Dove, walking back towards his built-in sanctuary.

He only had his back turned for a moment, but it was long enough for Creak to attack. He shoved Dove from behind, and propelled him towards the cupboard. Dove tripped on the uneven floor at the entrance and time seemed to slow down. He arced through the air and his guitar rushed towards him; the knots in the wood, the wire sprouting from the tuning pegs, the grime on the frets. Every detail screamed at him: back off. He tried to move his arms away from him, so that they wouldn't hit it, but his body was on a collision course. Dove wriggled, but he was falling so fast with nothing to press against.

His shoulder slammed into the guitar, snapping the neck from its body. The sound of splintering wood was accompanied by a dull echoey chime, the final sound the strings would make. It was like the last gasp of a dying man.

"Sorry, man," said Creak from the door. "I didn't mean to…" He shook his head sadly. The chocolate unpeeled itself from his forehead and plopped onto the floor.

Dove rolled himself into a sitting position and rubbed his shoulder. "Please, go now."

"I really am sorry, man," said Creak. Dove heard the room door click shut as Creak left.

Dove picked at the wreckage, but there was no doubt his first guitar was destroyed beyond repair. He hadn't just lost a tool of his trade. He had lost the sound of his earliest songs. He could replace the guitar, but it was handmade and no two are identical. His music would always sound wrong to him now. Besides, he had so many memories tied up in that instrument. It had seen his first and last drink, his first and last groupie. It had given birth to his first and – the way he felt now – maybe even his last song.

Dove mourned for ten minutes before rising up from his cross-legged position. He cradled the guitar's corpse carefully in two hands, trying to keep it as close to its designed shape as possible. He stretched it out face up on the bed, fetched its hard case from inside the door and placed it on the duvet alongside. With the delicacy of an undertaker, Dove opened the case like a coffin, settled the guitar into its red velvet lining, and pressed the lid gently shut.

*　*　*

Simon had been browsing the web for hours. The chat window flashed and he clicked on to it again.

angelA>	you still here?
thing>	**Yes.**
angelA>	cool
thing>	**Where did you go?**
angelA>	when
thing>	**Then**
angelA>	to eat. the food was burning
thing>	**It's a bit late for dinner.**
angelA>	im on a seafood diet
thing>	**When you see food you eat it?**
angelA>	when i see food i eat it! LOL.
thing>	**How much did you eat!?**
angelA>	?
thing>	**I mean, you were a long time.**
angelA>	oh. a friend phoned.
angelA>	she missed her train. needed a taxi no
thing>	**The phone is soooo last century!**
angelA>	one chat and u r bill gates
thing>	**LOL**
angelA>	:-) youre learning
angelA>	wat have u been doing?
thing>	**I've been reading websites.**
angelA>	u been online all the time?
thing>	**Yes.**
angelA>	u been waiting for me, sweetness ;-)

thing>	I just left this window open while web surfing.
angelA>	so do you work?
thing>	I'm in a band.
angelA>	cool. full time?
thing>	Not yet. Hopefully by the end of the year.
angelA>	do you sing?
thing>	Yes but I play guitar mostly.
angelA>	u a good singer?
thing>	Not bad. I used to have a lisp at school.
angelA>	a lisp?
thing>	I sort of whistled when I said words with S in them. That's why they called me Thing Because my surname is Singh.
angelA>	what's your first name?
thing>	Simon. What's your real name?
angelA>	Angela.
thing>	Doh! Nice name. Do you have a nice surname too?
angelA>	i like to be anonymous. wats your band called?
thing>	Goblin. We have some creative differences though at the moment.
angelA>	all the best bands do
thing>	There's just me and a girl called Fred in it.
angelA>	where did u meet her
thing>	At a school party.
thing>	We've known each other half our lives.
angelA>	wat happened
thing>	She was new in the school. Didn't know anyone.
thing>	I asked her to dance
angelA>	did she
thing>	Yes.
angelA>	wat else happened
thing>	Nothing, sadly. We were just kids anyway.
angelA>	why sadly
thing>	She was a total babe.
angelA>	isnt she now then
thing>	Oh yeah!
thing>	She still gets wolf whistles.

angelA>	classy
thing>	But I'm over all that
angelA>	good
thing>	It would never have worked anyway
angelA>	why not
thing>	She's too f#ck!ng annoying!!!!!!!
thing>	Pardon my French
angelA>	de rien
angelA>	is Fred your girlf?
thing>	No. I don't have one. Do you have a boyfriend?
angelA>	tell me about your creative differences
thing>	She's too fame hungry
angelA>	how?
thing>	She just keeps coming up with stupid ideas to try to make us famous.
angelA>	what's wrong with that?
thing>	I want our music to make us famous.
angelA>	what did she do?
thing>	Last week she wanted me to take pictures of her naked for a magazine
angelA>	did you?
thing>	No. It would be too weird.
angelA>	did someone else?
thing>	That's funny. Never thought of that. Perhaps.
thing>	She said it would be a quick way to get a fan base
angelA>	but what do you think?
thing>	We wouldn't want to shake hands with them!
thing>	Plus we shouldn't have to sell our identity to play music.
angelA>	that doesn't sound so bad though
thing>	That's only one example.
thing>	She's made me a laughing stock on the internet
thing>	And she wasted my time
thing>	She went behind my back and manipulated me to try to make us famous.
thing>	I sometimes think the fame matters more than the music to her

angelA>	so ditch the bitch
thing>	**Watch it!**
angelA>	sorry my bad
angelA>	but shes holding u back
thing>	**Sorry. I'm just a bit confused.**
thing>	**I don't know whether to play our next gig or not**
angelA>	u don't know
thing>	**I don't know if I can forgive her for this last stunt**
angelA>	who is your hero
thing>	**Dove**
angelA>	what would dove do
thing>	**Let me think…**
thing>	**He'd never miss a chance to play a gig.**
thing>	**Come to that, he never pretended to be best friends with all his band mates either**
angelA>	problem solved
thing>	**I'm not convinced. Shall we change the subject?**
angelA>	ok
angelA>	hav u heard the new flamewar album
thing>	**Can't say I've ever heard of them. Why do you ask?**
angelA>	cos they are a bit like university of death
thing>	**How so?**
angelA>	they sound like university of death in early days
thing>	**Cool. They were better then.**
angelA>	i got a discount token if u want
thing>	**Where from?**
angelA>	a friend works at the record label so i get loads
angelA>	ill send it over so u can download some free songs
angelA>	u will probably be hooked like me
thing>	**Great. thanks.**
angelA>	im tired now
thing>	**Me too.**
angelA>	it would be cool to chat again.
thing>	**Yes. That would be nice.**
angelA>	perhaps tomorrow?
thing>	**Sure!**

angelA>	u r different to most people i chat to
thing>	**In what way?**
angelA>	nicer
thing>	**Thank you. I'm pleased I met you tonight.**
angelA>	voucher code on its way
thing>	**Got it.**
angelA>	got to go.
angelA>	early start 2morrow
angelA>	that will hurt
thing>	**See you tomorrow.**
angelA>	sweet dreams
<angelA has disconnected>	

CHAPTER 5

The girls from Boymad writhed on a mirror in their slippery swimming costumes. The blonde one bit her lip and rolled her eyes in ecstasy while the ginger one mouthed the lyrics and licked her lips between each line. Framed by the silver edge of the video screen, they looked like they were trapped in a lunar capsule. The sound was off. In the lobby space, nobody can hear you scream.

The walls and floor were made of black marble. Exotic trees were dotted around the atrium, dusting the skylight. It looked like the levels above had been cored to make room for the trees, leaving balconies on each floor that lined the building all the way around and overlooked reception. Busybodies shuttled around the balconies, burdened with papers, posters or puppy-dog pop stars.

There were brightly coloured sofas for guests and a coffee table, on which this week's issues of the Financial Times were neatly arranged. There were no music papers there, though. Bigg Records firmly put the business into 'music business'.

Jonathan marched through the rotating door and towards the lift, a box of cables in his arms, and his head down as he passed the reception desk.

"Can I help you?" called the receptionist as he came level.

"It's not that heavy, thanks, Linda." He had remembered her name from when he got the pass from J-Rok a week ago, and hoped that she didn't remember his autograph hunt. "Just awkward."

"No," said the receptionist. "I meant, where are you going?"

She was wearing hoopy ear-rings so distractingly large that Jonathan wouldn't have noticed if she was a giraffe.

"Got to take these to the studio." Jonathan pulled the end of one of the cables out of the top and showed it to her. It looked like an eel swallowing a matchbox. "I'm knackered," said Jonathan. "I've been running all over London to find these, Linda. There's an orchestra waiting."

"Odd. I would have thought they had loads."

"Not like these. They really are very important cables." Jonathan winced inside. Don't overdo it, he thought. He tried to strike up a rapport. "Do you know, I've been looking for some ear-rings just like that!" He didn't mean it to sound sarcastic. "For my girlfriend," he added, swiftly. "Where did you get them?"

"Do you have a pass?"

"Of course!" Jonathan balanced the box in one hand and flashed his security pass at her with the other. He allowed the box to slip a little, so he could slap both hands back on it again to stop it falling. Any longer and she might have got a clear look at the pass and notice the date on it. Jonathan hadn't been able to replace the name sticker because it was watermarked, but he was sure Jervais was enough of a nobody that it wouldn't matter.

"That pass is no unaccompanied access. I'll call the studio for an escort," said Linda, glassily. As she reached for the phone, Jonathan could see his plan falling apart before it had even begun. He urged his brain to think faster, but all the ideas just kept crashing into each other and breaking up.

The revolving door spun someone new into reception, and they both were taken aback to see he was wearing purple plastic trousers. Linda recradled the phone theatrically and looked him up and down.

"My demo!" he announced, swaggering up to the desk and holding a jiffy bag up by the bottom corner. "The name's Rockard."

"One moment, please," Linda said to Jonathan. She turned to Rockard and nodded towards a dustbin with the word 'DEMO'S' painted on the front of it. "Drop it in the bin," she ordered.

Rockard walked over to it and peered over the edge. It was half full of padded envelopes like his, and smelled like damp cardboard.

"You will listen to it, though?"

"I've got to go," whispered Jonathan, as he crept off.

"I promise you I'll listen to it even if nobody else does," said Linda. Rockard smiled and let the package fall into the bin. The receptionist listened to the gentle thud it made as it landed on the other packets.

"Thank you," said Rockard as he left, and the receptionist allowed herself a smug smile.

She turned to where Jonathan had been standing, but he had already gone.

*   *   *

"Bigg Records welcomes the sales team to the marketing conference: 9th floor," said a sign in the back of the lift. That seemed as good a place as any to start. Jonathan pressed the button and it lit up, but that was all it did. The lift stayed firmly on the ground floor and the doors gaped open. If anyone hunted him, Jonathan was exposed. Dove scowled at him from a poster promoting a forthcoming compilation, while directionless jazz tootled through a tiny speaker.

Poking his head around the door to see if anyone was looking for him, Jonathan saw a woman wearing a woolly hat and a reflective jacket walk through the revolving door. She slung the demo bin over her back and walked out with it, grunting as she went. A moment later, she returned swinging the bin in one hand.

Jonathan had worn an open collar shirt to look casual lugging his box through reception but it was time to smarten up now. He rooted around in the box and found the end of his tie and the sleeve of his jacket. He tugged them out, careful not to tear them under the weight of cables. The jacket was a bit creased, so Jonathan shook it before putting it on.

In the bottom of the box were his tools: a torch, a camera, a tape recorder, a pen and pad, and a packet of cigarettes. Jonathan loaded his pockets and patted them down, looking in the mirrored wall to check they didn't bulge too much.

The doors crunched shut. With a ping Jonathan was up and away, into the ogre's lair.

*   *   *

Jonathan exited the lift on the ninth floor and left his box of cables behind. He was immediately confronted by a registration desk. There were about twenty badges laid out on it, which meant they were expecting a good crowd. That should be easy to hide in, he thought.

"Can I register you before you go in?" said a woman parked behind the desk.

"Sure," said Jonathan. "I do just need to visit the gents first, if that's okay?"

"First on the left," she whispered, cupping her hand to one side of her mouth.

He dodged into the toilet for a few minutes and slipped out when the woman was distracted by another arrival. It was easy enough to sneak into the meeting room. Jonathan gravitated towards the refreshments at the back.

"Have you tried this coffee?" said a man beside him, holding a silver jug. He spoke like he had plums in his mouth, but they were actually sausage rolls. His chin was flaked with crumbs. Jonathan busied himself with the milk so he didn't have to look. "The beans have been chewed and regurgitated by weasels," the man continued, talking with his mouth full. "Adds fantastic flavour. Good for you, too. It's a completely natural process, you know."

Jonathan thought about whether he really wanted to drink coffee so bad it made a weasel throw up, but he didn't want to break his cover, so he took a cup. "Thanks," he said, insincerely.

"Haven't seen you before," said the man. "The name's Roger."

"I'm new," said Jonathan. He picked a common name at random. "I'm Andrew." Jonathan let Roger have the upper hand as they shook.

"Which region you working?" said Roger.

"I could tell you, but I'd have to kill you," said Jonathan, arching his eyebrows and injecting what he mistakenly thought was a hint of James Bond into his voice.

"I guess you're going for salesman of the year, then. Bully for you. You've got to stand out to survive." Roger sipped his coffee and grimaced a little. "I reckon there's a cull coming. Have you seen the figures for FlameWar?"

Jonathan shook his head.

"Viral marketing," said Roger. "It's the future. It's not hitting many people yet, but everyone it touches ends up buying. We'd better watch our backs or we'll be on the scrap heap."

"I always do," said Jonathan. "So, what's it like here?"

"Here's some free advice…"

"Always useful!"

"If you want to blend in, just set your shoes on fire. You'll run around screaming and flapping your arms and you'll look just like every other bugger here."

They took neighbouring seats at the oval table that dominated the room. Before long the room was full. All the walls were white and shiny, reflecting the harsh ceiling lights like a constellation of suns.

"Okay, guys," said a man, standing up at one end, apparently oblivious to the fact that about a third of the group was female. He was wearing an extravagantly spotted tie and had red-rimmed glasses. "Let's kick off this information touchpoint, shall we? For the newcomers, I am the marketing honcho here at Bigg, but you can call me Jake. Or if you're filing a report of missed targets, you can call me 'Jake, Sir'!" He laughed theatrically, but nobody else joined in. Jake still spoke with the fake American accent he had adopted to blend in when he studied at university in California.

"Guys, I've ringfenced some good news to start today," Jake said. "We've got the best of University of Death coming up this quarter. Should be a big campaign."

"We're pinning our hopes on that?" groaned a man sat next to Jake. "We'll never shift it."

"Sure we will!" said Jake. "Let's not forget that Dove has been called the saviour of rock and roll."

"Oh yeah? By whom?" asked the man.

"It doesn't matter. In marketing we use the passive voice."

"It's not true though."

"How long have you worked here?" said Jake. "By the time we've spread it all over the internet, it will be indistinguishable from the truth."

"Dove's been called a few other things too."

Jake thumbed through his papers. "Hmmm…Q said he was legendary. NME said his first album was seminal."

"Which means a pile of wank, doesn't it?"

"No, it means influential." Jake paused a moment. "At least, I think it does. Anyway, what's your problem?"

"You are all dead in the water." The man got up, wrote 'I resign' on the wall behind him in thick marker pen, tossed the pen on the table and walked out.

 "I won't lie to you," said Jake. "I've got some serious baggage to check in with you guys today. It's badsville, USA. So, anyone else not got the bulbous balls we need to get out of our mess? Better go now if you think your nads can't take it!" He looked around the room but nobody returned his gaze. "Good. This room is a church of positivity. I want us to worship at the altar of gold-plated strategic thinking today. I'm going to open up my kimono now."

He wasn't wearing one. Jake adjusted his tie, though, and for a moment, Jonathan thought he really was going to strip off.

"Our research shows that 32% of our customers buy music largely because it is fashionable," said Jake. "Risky business! Fashions change! 43% use music to drown out other noise, putting us in direct competition with earplugs which cost a fraction of the price. A full 4% of those surveyed only played music to 'mask the sounds of their love-making from neighbours or flat sharers'. So now you know why those live albums are such a hard sell." He gave in to a self-indulgent chuckle. "Nobody wants to grunt to the finale with 100,000 people cheering only to have them demand an encore, hey guys?" He had clenched his fist as he said 'grunt' and waited at the end of the sentence for a wave of laughter to sweep the room. It didn't.

Jake shook his head. "Hell, sales are so low that ringtones top the chart. More people buy music to use as an alarm than for entertainment. This is mission-critical, guys. Most people just throw an album in their MP3 player and wait until it chooses to play it. They don't care if they hear it or not. They're only buying out of habit and these are our best damn customers. So, we need to drill down to the real problem and dig ourselves out of our hole. We need to bore a tunnel through to the other side." His confidence trailed off with the quality of his engineering metaphors. "Let's brain dump!"

Jake threw the marker pen and it tumbled through the air, heading straight for Jonathan. Jonathan watched it as it got nearer and got ready to catch it, but Roger reached across and snatched it from in front of his face. "I'll take this one," he said to the group. "You owe me one," he hissed to Jonathan.

"Lob me a thought grenade, Rodge!" said Jake.

Roger stood up and walked to the wall behind him. "Here's my idea," he began. "People always say that music isn't as good as it used to be. My granddad said that, my dad said that, my kids say that. Even I've said it once or twice. What happens if we follow this to its logical conclusion? I'll tell you. The greatest record ever is 'Mary had a little lamb' by Thomas Edison."

"Excuse me but I'm not sure I've heard that," said a woman on the other side of the table. She had lipstick on her teeth.

"It's the nursery rhyme," said Roger. "Edison invented the phonograph and this was his first audio recording. Indeed, *the* first audio recording. I say we put it out as a single." On the wall behind him, he scrawled 'Edison single'. Jonathan then realised why the walls were so shiny. It was as if a normal white*board* could not contain the marketing department's ingenuity: they had built a conference room with white*walls*.

"Full respect due for ideas input, yah," began Jake. "But I think we'll have to haul anchor and let that one drift. There's no way it'll sell."

"Certainly not," said Roger. "But it would have to make them think, wouldn't it? People would question their attitude towards today's music. Maybe they would start listening to the radio more, and then go on to buy singles again."

"Now that's thinking outside the box!" said Jake. Roger tossed him the marker pen, and as quick as he could, Jake tossed it back out to the woman with lipstick on her teeth. "You're on, Mandy."

"Right," she said, standing up and holding the pen with both hands. "So my idea was inspired by my Mum buying a panpipes album. I know she's got no taste, but I was thinking that maybe the market for people with no taste could be worth targeting. One analyst firm estimated it could be nearly six billion worldwide."

"How nearly?" said Jake.

"Well, I think they just took the world population and sub-tracted the number of people working as analysts, to be honest. But our own experience suggests there's a lot of people in this demographic."

Jake nodded. "Exploiting the unimaginative is the basis of the world economy."

"I've been doing some research," said Mandy. "Did you know that a musician's every movement in the studio, every strum and keypress, is stored by computer in a format called MIDI? It means the musicians can record a performance and then change the sound of the notes. So they can play a keyboard and make it sound like a violin or something afterwards."

Jake drummed his fingers on the table. "I know I'm not Jean-Michel Jarre, but I have picked up the odd bit of music technology working here," he said. Others around the table were rapt with attention.

"Anyway," said Mandy. "What if we take those MIDI files, swap the instruments around and release something like 'U2 play The Panpipes'? It's perfect! you could hear the Edge himself pipe the riff to 'Where the Streets Have No Name'. The heavy metal bands could sell their tunes to people with no taste, even if nobody wants to hear their growling. It's a new, low-cost, high-margin product that extends the reach of our creative works to new listeners. What's more, fans of the original albums will probably buy these new arrangements too." On the wall behind her, she wrote 'The best panpipes album in the world ever!' and drew a little smiley face next to it.

Jake nodded. "It's win-win-win! I reckon we can green light

that one pretty quickly. I'll run it past Clive. We'll get it in the pipeline as soon as possible." He stressed the name Clive, to make sure nobody missed that he was on first terms with Mr Bigg.

Mandy threw the pen, and Jake caught it and slid it across the table to the far end, where a mousy man stopped it falling onto the floor. "Okay," he said, with a nervous sing-song in his voice. He didn't stand up, and he avoided eye contact with everyone. "First we had records, right? Then we had tapes for portability, so people bought their records again. Then we had CDs, so people could listen in higher quality, so they bought their records and tapes again to hear the hi-hat and triangle. Then we introduced downloads so people could get music faster."

"Yah, and so we didn't waste any money on packaging," said Jake. "Faster, cheaper, more profitable. What's your point?"

"Well, people have bought three or more copies of Dark Side of the Moon, but only one copy of OK Computer. It just doesn't seem right. It's high time we introduced a new format." The man pushed the pen and it skidded across the table, back to Jake.

"That's firing on all cylinders," said Jake. "I'll take an A to get the tech guys back at base to invent some new way of storing music. Kevin, what's your idea?"

He threw the pen high in the air. Kevin stood up to catch it, fumbled it and followed it under the desk. There was a thump followed by a powerful burst of swearing. After a few seconds, Kevin's head appeared first, then a hand, an elbow and his whole body as he lifted himself back onto his seat. "Got it!" he said, rubbing his forehead and holding the pen up with the other hand. "I was thinking about all those demos we get sent."

"Yah, some are like demos in the political sense: against music, they're so bad," said Jake. "Haven't played any for decades. We send three dustbins of CDs to Africa every day. Poor people make toys from the likes of Donkey Wank Blanket's CD. That's all they're any good for."

"Right," said Kevin, "but some of them are so bad they're funny. People buy 'funny'. I thought we could do a compilation of demos called 'Now that's what the dictionary would call music, but we beg to differ'. No studio costs. It's a money-spinner."

Kevin wrote 'Demo compilation' on the wall behind him and threw the pen back to Jake at as awkward a trajectory as he could.

"It's a rights nightmare," said Jake, stretching his arm and catching the pen with ease. "But we'll look into it. Now, who hasn't chipped in?"

He looked around the room. Although there were plenty of people who hadn't spoken yet, he stopped looking when he reached Jonathan. "You," he said, throwing Jonathan the pen. "Let's see if you've got anything to add."

Jonathan stood up and addressed the group. He didn't want to be the centre of attention, but since it was forced upon him, he resolved to carry it off with aplomb. "You could try getting some decent bands in," he began, momentarily forgetting his cover story. "By which I mean *we* could try. All of us. Just because our customers are losing interest in music, doesn't mean everyone is. Loads of people buy direct from independent bands on the internet. We could sign these bands and use our marketing muscle to put them on the world stage." All eyes were on him. He was winning them over. "Just imagine the power we have! To discover truly great bands, real artistic visionaries, and get their work into every home in the world! If we lead with quality, the sales would surely follow!" He looked around the table, breathless, and nodded a mini bow. After a moment's pause, the sales reps clapped wildly and banged on the table. He had convinced them!

And then he heard their laughter.

"Nice one," said Jake. "We have a joker in the pack!" He formed a cup with his hands in the air, and waited for Jonathan to throw the pen back. "Okay, everyone. That's a wrap. Let's get back to the coalface. Same time next quarter. Remember, don't just hit those targets. I want to see them demolished!"

CHAPTER 6

Cabbages bounced around the hopper, fell out the bottom, and danced along the conveyor belt past Simon. He plucked one off and started to prune it with a knife.

After a late night hanging around to see if Angela would come online, the alarm clock had hurt like a drill. Simon had oozed out of bed and only just made it onto the bus – with no real memory of how he'd done it – but the bus had got a flat. He was exhausted from his run up the hill and his clothes sucked at his sweaty skin. His mind was frazzled from sleep deprivation.

In the admin booth, the foreman held his arm in the air and tapped his watch at Simon like Marcel Marceau policing the school gates. Simon *really* needed that. He didn't want to get fired. He'd only been here a few weeks and he liked to keep a job long enough to truly detest it before he moved on. There are only so many jobs in the world and he didn't want to repeat himself or run out too soon.

Simon had taken the only remaining seat when he arrived, beside a haggard-looking woman in her forties. "How long you worked here?" he asked her. He had to shout to be heard over the rumbling cabbages.

She looked towards him but didn't seem to focus. "Five years."

"Blimey! I reckon I'd go insane if I was here that long!"

The woman dribbled.

"This is just temporary for me," said Simon. "Make a few quid over the summer."

"They all say that," said the woman. Her voice was low and monotonous, like an intoned curse.

"Really, I'm a musician. I'm in a band," said Simon. The cabbages did a conga before his eyes. Having removed the bug-eaten leaves on his, he threw it into a chute and pulled another one out of the chorus line. "What do you do, then?"

"I pull leaves off cabbages."

"Yeah, but what else?"

"Lettuces when Ethel's off."

"No, I mean outside of work."

"Eh?"

"Well, there's more to life than cabbages, isn't there?"

The woman looked into the distance. "I suppose there must be," she said.

But the cabbages kept coming.

CHAPTER 7

As Jonathan left the lift on the sixth floor, a man in a blue jump suit came towards him. He threw his weight behind a trolley of boxes to get all the wheels to move in the same direction.

"Get the door, can you, mate?" he said. "I'm going in there." He nodded towards an unmarked door. Jonathan tried the handle but it was locked.

The man waved his arm in the air and a tiny light on the door handle went green. "Try it again now," he said. Jonathan nudged the door and it swung open freely.

Inside, brown metal cabinets stood in rows, and hummed innocently to themselves, their lights sparkling red and green. From behind smoked glass, they rolled their tape reel eyes at Jonathan. An engineer performed open-face surgery, removing one of the tapes and replacing it with another. When he slammed the window shut, the cabinet sucked, like it was hoovering up the dregs of milkshake. The tape unravelled from one reel to another. As one pupil shrunk, another dilated.

A bank of monitors on a desk pumped light into the room, cookie-cut into the form of letters. A printer rattled through a folded stack of green-striped paper. Above it, a picture of a distant galaxy entitled 'Captain Blood' clung to the far wall.

Jonathan held the door open as the man from the corridor wheeled his trolley past. The wheels jammed on the uneven floor in the doorway, giving Jonathan time to study the trolley's load. There was a five and a quarter inch disk drive and a few cassettes.

Jonathan saw the flash of an eBay logo on the packing slips and memorised the buyer's ID.

His eye fell on a chunky brown keyboard that nestled among the polystyrene quavers. It sparked a flashback: Jonathan blasted warplanes out of the sky; watched them peel away over his head and braced himself for the inevitable hit as they dropped their bombs; he guided the ships through minefields and remembered how the guns would slowly grind through their gears, how they would often miss their target through their inability to aim quickly enough. He remembered the lack of sleep, and the pain he felt in his hands after a long day manning the guns. As a schoolboy, Jonathan had played Beach Head on his Commodore 64 until his dreams went pixellated.

"What's all this old kit doing here?" he said.

"The same as all the other '80s relics round here," said the man with the trolley. "Waiting to make a comeback." He ushered Jonathan back into the corridor and clicked the door shut.

Jonathan was attracted to a red 'RECORDING' light that glowed over one of the studio doors. He peered through the door's round window and could see a sloping desk covered with faders and dials, like the neatly arranged soldiers and tanks in a war game. Three people huddled around it, and looked into the recording booth through a window that ran the length of the room. One gave the thumbs up to the glass. The 'RECORDING' light fizzled out above Jonathan's head and he quietly opened the door and crept into the studio.

A sheet of jaundiced light leaked through the window from the recording booth. The desk had collected enough DNA in its dust to clone a supergroup. There were tracks carved into the grime where the sliders and dials had been used. Battered fish corpses and frazzled potato bits sat in puddles of oil on beds of crumpled white paper. Three fizzy drinks cans stood along the top of the mixing desk, with cigarette ash caked around the openings.

J-Rok was a filthy rotten liar, Jonathan realised. For all his talk about the studio being a sterile environment, it was clear now that they hadn't let him anywhere near it.

"It's mighty fine," one of the three men was saying to the

others. He was the only one wearing a suit. "It just needs to be darker. Make it ten percent more black."

One of the others looked at suitman sideways, and stopped himself before he blurted something out. Instead, he said: "Okay, let's give it three notches on the DFA filter then, please." He had flowing black hair and slouched on a low sofa, but spoke like he was in charge. The skull on the front of his t-shirt glowed green as a shadow was cast over it. When the desk lamp caught the man's eyes, they twinkled and Jonathan thought he saw something he recognised in them.

"Sure, Doug," replied the man in the middle as he turned the DFA dial. "Let's make it four." He was probably the engineer, Jonathan thought. His hands swirled over the desk, flicking switches and moving sliders. The music faded in.

"Oh yeah," said the suitman. "That's it. Much darker. Much… chewier. I'll leave it in your very capable hands, then."

"Your advice was a treasure, as ever." Doug waved goodbye to suitman and watched him leave and close the door behind him. "Idiots!" Doug said to the engineer. "Those who can, do. Those who can't become A&R men."

A young man came out of the recording booth, wearing a black and yellow t-shirt that said 'How's my drumming?' and had a telephone number underneath it. "What was that all about?" he asked.

"Some dick from the record company thinks he knows better than I do how my music should sound," said Doug, running his fingers through his hair. "We bumped it up a few steps on the DFA filter, played it again and he was satisfied. Happy, even. Shows how much he knows."

"DFA filter?"

"Oldest trick in the book," said the engineer. "Does Fuck All."

Doug noticed Jonathan for the first time. "Sorry – I don't do autographs," he said.

"Nor do I," said Jonathan, while he ran some possible cover stories through his head.

"Sorry," said Doug. "I've been pestered here all day, you know. Some guy in accounts even brought his nephew in to meet me. So what do you want?"

"I'm a journalist," said Jonathan. That'll do. Journalists got access nearly everywhere and are a trusted part of the music industry myth-making machine. "Kate from PR said it would be okay." Nearly every PR office had a Kate, and nobody ever checked anyway.

"You must meet this guy," Doug said, indicating the session drummer with both hands like a chat show host welcoming his interviewee to the stage. "He's the second best drummer I have ever heard."

"After who?" said Jonathan.

"The master sticksman of University of Death, of course," said the drummer, with a nod towards Doug.

"Creak's a great drummer," said Jonathan.

"Oh yeah," said Doug. "But he's only the second best drummer in University of Death. I wanted to tour as a one-man band: Bass drum on my back, cymbals between my knees; harmonica and guitar. I even had a costume made with dolls hanging off my arm to symbolise the others. They danced as I played. Too many ideas, too little time."

The way Doug drawled his vowels sounded familiar. As Jonathan looked into Doug's eyes, it dawned on him: Without the red and green warpaint framing them, they looked so different but they sparkled just the same. Jonathan must have misheard the engineer say his name. He was struck by a thrill that was a mixture of excitement and fear.

"You okay?" said Doug.

Jonathan couldn't speak.

"Man, you're scaring me!"

"Sorry." Jonathan snapped out of it. "You're Dove, right?"

"At your service," said Dove. "You didn't think I really had a red and green face?"

"Of course not," replied Jonathan, collecting himself. From his standing position, he could see the label in the back of Dove's t-shirt. It had a red spot on it, indicating it was a sale purchase from one of the big clothing chains. Jonathan had only seen pictures of Dove in his stage costume before. Even off stage, he had assumed

Dove would dress in designer clothing. It was a shock to see him slumming it in jeans and t-shirt, even though the jeans were pink.

Jonathan's teenage bedroom had been plastered with University of Death posters, with the sleeves from singles plugging any gaps through which the wallpaper showed. Jonathan had spent months replaying the albums and trying to torture the same sounds from his own guitar. Dove had soundtracked Jonathan's youth, and whenever Jonathan played those early albums today, he felt like few other records made him feel. "It's a real pleasure," he said, taking a step forward and extending his hand. Dove shook it quickly and feebly as though he didn't want to be touched.

The engineer showed the drummer out and then disappeared into the recording booth with a roll of gaffer tape. Jonathan and Dove sank into the opposite ends of a leather sofa and turned to face each other. Jonathan had always thought of Dove as a giant, but he could see now that they were the same height. He rooted inside his pockets. "I just need a Dictaphone."

"Let me give you Clive Bigg's number, then," said Dove, pulling a card from his wallet and handing it to Jonathan.

"Label relations not good?" said Jonathan. The card was functional: plain, roughly cut and printed with 'Clive Bigg, Bigg Records' and three rows of contact details. Jonathan palmed it underneath his tape recorder. It had been offered as a joke, but being handed Bigg's mobile number was one of the best leads he'd received so far.

"They are pillaging the fruits of my mind," Dove said.

"Uh-huh."

"Their compilation is mechanically recovered off-cuts glued together, like sausages. It revolts me."

"Why don't you stop them?"

"I can't. I signed a contract with a man I trusted. He sold that contract to a parasite who feeds off genius."

"So why are you here, deep in Bigg Records?"

"Damage limitation," said Dove. "They're grafting a new drum track onto the body of an old song. They want a hit. I won't play on it, but I can try to limit the damage. They think I'm promoting the compilation, but I'll be telling the whole world I think it's a sham. Who do you write for? It's not F is it?"

'F' was a magazine that was launched in the '80s, when calling a magazine by a single letter seemed like a kinda cool thing to do. If you were in publishing, and kinda uncool, that is. The magazine had since given up pretending it was anything but advertising and had become a compendium of shopping lists. The themes contrived to make them look like proper stories sounded more like specialist rounds on Mastermind than a casual grouping of similar things. Recent issues included the top seven songs recorded in Prestatyn, top fifty left-handed guitar solos, and the top ten songs used to soundtrack abseiling scenes in movies. The magazine had led the charge towards interviewing iPods. Instead of nursing stroppy pop stars and trying to ply soundbites from them, journalists bell up the PR intern and she tells them the first five tracks that were 'randomly' selected from the artist's iPod. Now that the mag was over-run by books, films and so-called celebrities, its full title of 'F—The Music' seemed more appropriate than ever.

"I already told them where they could stick their top ten of superhero bedspreads," said Dove. "And I don't even know what a key grip is, let alone have five favourites."

"It's okay," said Jonathan. "I'm with a new songwriters' magazine. I don't think you get enough credit as a composer." Jonathan cringed when he heard himself. He wasn't pretending for the sake of his cover. He was crawling.

Dove's face relaxed. "It's about time our art was taken seriously," he said. "Our last studio album blows you away. Have you listened to it?"

"I've heard it, yeah," said Jonathan. He had a complete collection of University of Death albums, but didn't play the new ones for more than a few weeks even though he still returned to the early ones years later.

"No," said Dove firmly. "*Listen* to it. Did you know a string quartet covered it in its entirety? The songwriting is a rock-solid foundation. Those battery farmed writers on the fifth floor wouldn't know where to start with something that sophisticated."

"Yours is intelligent music," said Jonathan. "Which string quartet covered it?"

Dove got his MP3 player out and fiddled with it. "The Balanescu Quartet."

"You carry a copy of it?" said Jonathan.

"I keep all my work," said Dove, "even other artistes' interpretations. I don't have a CD player nowadays except in the computer so everything goes in here. I don't listen to my own music for fun, though, obviously." Dove laughed.

Yeah, right, thought Jonathan. "What do you think is your best song ever?"

"Animal Reined," said Dove. Jonathan wasn't sure whether the reply came so fast because Dove answered out of conviction, or whether it was because he'd faced that question so often he had a stock answer ready to fire back. "It was our first recording too," added Dove. "We never caught its spirit on tape again."

"The original seven inch is my most valued possession," said Jonathan. "How do you write a song like that?"

"I have no idea!" Dove ran his hands through his hair and gathered it in a ponytail at the back, which he tied with a black scrunchy. "Songwriting is the hardest job in the world."

"Except, maybe, brain surgery?" Jonathan coughed a laugh into the middle of his sentence to take the edge off it.

"*That* you can learn in about fifteen years," said Dove. "Writing pop music is a God-given gift. If you don't have it, you can't acquire it."

"So once you've got the song, how do you work in the studio?"

"You won't have heard of most of my software."

"Try me."

"Because I invented it." Dove beamed. "I architect my own caverns to ensure the sound that resounds is unique. Too many people create soul-less computer music nowadays. To me, the computer is purely an instrument that bends daring new noises around the songs I write."

"You should sell that software. It must be worth a few quid."

"I do not work to acquire. I work to become," said Dove. "Besides, it's user-hostile. You need to be a programming wizard, but if you know how to talk to it, it can play you anything back."

Jonathan racked his brains. As a teenager he would have had endless queries for Dove but this surprise opportunity had caught him on the hop. His mind was near-blank. "Is it true that you record nearly every time you play?" Everybody knew he did.

"'There is nothing in this world that does not have a decisive moment'." Dove drummed a rhythm on the arm of the sofa with his fingers and thumb. "Bresson was talking about photography. But I am always ready to grab that perfect improvisation from the air before it fades into our lost history. Record everything. Edit later. I have a massive vault full of jams."

"I eat a lot of toast when I'm writing," said Jonathan absent-mindedly. He was scrawling notes and sneaked a glimpse at the spindles on his tape recorder to make sure they were still rolling.

Dove wasn't really listening either. "For the next Dove album I will cocoon myself in my own studio."

Jonathan looked up from his pad. "And you'll record the rest of the band there too?"

"We'll see," said Dove. "We'll see."

The door to the studio opened and a peaked cap peered around it, followed by a man's pudgy face. Sprigs of grey hair poked out from under the cap, and out of his ears and nose. "Yoo-hoo! Everything all right in here?"

"Sure, Eric," said Dove. "Just doing an interview."

Jonathan busied himself doodling. The room was half-dark anyway, but he tried to angle his face away from the guard.

"We've had reports of someone snooping around," said Eric. "Call reception if you see anything dodgy."

"I can get you my contract if that helps."

"Funny man. Just be alert."

"Yeah, the world needs more lerts," said Dove. He giggled to himself like a child.

Eric's face disappeared, the door closed and Dove stopped laughing as suddenly as he had started. "Where were we?"

"Dove?" said Jonathan. "Can I ask you a personal question?" It wasn't a large sofa, and with their bodies twisted to face each other, their knees nearly touched. It was strange to be sitting so

50

close to a complete stranger that Jonathan felt he knew intimately.

"Ask away. It's your job. It's mine to avoid the question, though. I can't promise I'll answer."

"Do you miss the big time?"

"How do you mean?"

"Well, you know. In the '80s you were all over the TV and magazines. Don't you miss the limelight?"

Dove shook his head and exhaled a laugh. "Like an amputee misses a limb. Like Neil Armstrong misses the moon. That dull ache of emptiness never goes, whatever anyone else says. The fame never bothered me. It was just a tool. Do you know what the best thing was?"

Jonathan shook his head.

"Knowing that people everywhere were digging my music. Knowing that it travelled, and carried my feelings to the furthest reaches of the globe. Having my music played on TV and radio, with waves upon waves of signals radiating into space for alien cultures to discover, decode and dance to. The world was listening and who knows who else. My music went everywhere."

"People still listen," said Jonathan. "*I* still listen."

"My fans are loyal," said Dove. "But they haven't kept up. We're like old friends who drifted apart. We meet at a concert once in a while, but it's not the same. It's not the same."

The silence was uncomfortable but Jonathan didn't know how to break it.

Dove forced a tone of optimism. "I do know I'm blessed to have lived both lives," he said. "Few taste fame at all. Perhaps I'll start over. Anonymity affords freedom from the past. Simplicity is its own reward."

"That's the perfect note to end on." Jonathan pocketed his tape player and stood up to leave.

"Hang on a minute." Dove's voice stopped Jonathan dead in his tracks. "Where do you think you're going?" Jonathan reached inside his pocket where he had stashed Bigg's business card but left it alone when Dove spoke again. "The new album!" said Dove. "You'll be wanting the product plug. I know what you journalists are like."

"Of course," said Jonathan, settling down on the sofa again.

"It's called Freshers' Fayre and it's out on the eleventh of August."

"I thought you didn't want to promote it?"

"Information wants to be free," said Dove. "I have a duty to tell people it exists. Let them decide. I'm not recommending it."

"Got it," said Jonathan, writing down the release date. He felt cheapened by Dove's blatant hawking, coming after what had felt like a sincere heart-to-heart.

"One really, really last question?" said Jonathan. He waited for Dove to nod before asking. "That run down in the middle of Stay Dead? What's the chord after the F#m?"

Dove picked up an electric guitar that was leaning against the end of the sofa and gripped the fret board. His fingers looked twisted and awkward and his thumb curved over the top to squeeze the bottom string. Jonathan moved his head around to look from all angles, trying to work out what notes Dove's fingers were on. The guitar chimed as Dove flicked the strings while he pressed one at the far end with the thumb of his right hand. His fingers rolled off the frets and he put the guitar back.

"I don't think I would understand that chord if I studied nothing else for a month," said Jonathan. "Thanks anyway."

"My pleasure," said Dove. "Look after that tape. It might be my last interview." He extended his hand and this time his shake was firm and warm.

CHAPTER 8

There were five Freds in the lift, sat on the floor, thumbing through a magazine. Everywhere she looked, she saw a gold effigy of herself looking back. There were fingerprints smeared across some of her faces. Others were dented. All wore a red and yellow uniform and flat soled shoes.

"What*ever* could they be doing?" asked the businessman. He tugged the blue spotted handkerchief from his top pocket and mopped his brow with it.

"Don't ask me," sighed Fred.

"You're the only one here!"

"Well how should I know?"

"You're the bloody lift attendant, aren't you?"

"Right," said Fred. "Not an engineer. My responsibility ends when I push the button. I did that. It didn't work."

"Don't they train you properly, like air hostesses?"

"Oh yeah," sneered Fred. She indicated the door with her thumb. "Exits are situated here. In the event that the lift is depressurised, gas masks will fall from the ceiling. If I'm about to hit you, you'll hear the warning 'brace, brace!' Please refrain from smoking."

"Honestly!" The man shook his head. "I don't know why you work here if you're going to be like that."

"I only took the job so I could practise my ballet when it's quiet." With its handrail at waist height and its gold-mirrored walls, the lift was the closest to a studio Fred could afford.

"This bloody musak is driving me mad," said the man. Shape-less tunes floated in through the ceiling. Fred had never heard it loop, although she had spotted Guns'N'Roses riffs being played on the violin once or twice.

"I could sue you, you know!"

"Get off my chair, then," said Fred. The man was sitting on the stool by the buttons.

"What?"

"It's my stool and you're a guest in my lift. You can sit down and shut up or you can stand up and whinge."

"Unbelievable!" snorted the man. "If this is what passes for customer service—"

"Up you get!" Fred leaned forward, ready to stand up.

"Okay, okay," said the man, folding his arms. "I'll try the alarm again."

"Leave it," said Fred. "They know we're here."

She settled on the floor again and looked at her watch. It had been twenty minutes since the lift had juddered to a halt. She was reading 'Shut that door!", the magazine for lift operatives. In her mind, she had already penned a letter about today to 'That Sinking Feeling', the letters page. Now, it was the main feature that was pushing her buttons. It hinted at a place with so many opportunities, if only she could get there.

The man leaned back on the stool to see the cover of the magazine Fred held in front of her. "Picking up some careers advice, eh?"

"Oh yes," she replied.

The lift shook gently and began a slow ascent to the next floor.

"Things are on the up," she said.

CHAPTER 9

When Jonathan left the studio, two security guards were waiting for the lift, so he dodged into the stairwell. Where was it Dove said the battery farm of songwriters was? It was time to bother the chickens. Jonathan skipped down a flight of stairs and was confronted with what looked like a call centre.

An LED sign at the far side of the office displayed the team targets while people beavered away in cubicles wearing headsets. But it didn't feel like a call centre, somehow. It didn't sound like one, for a start.

Jonathan squinted to get a clearer view of the sign:

```
Songs written today: 15
Artists waiting: 31
Average composition time: 48 minutes
```

He looked around. It was like watching an ant farm built in a potato waffle. Each cubicle contained a worker ant, bulbous headphones strapped to its ears, busy moving between a piano keyboard and a computer keyboard. A fidgety near-silence shrouded the room. Jonathan could hear shuffles, scratches and clicks from instruments being played, but couldn't hear the sounds they were supposed to make, or any voices.

He lifted a clipboard and pad off a desk. It didn't matter whether people thought he was about to buy the company, looking for rat droppings or auditing staples. As long as he had a clipboard, he looked like he belonged there. And he looked more important than anyone who didn't have a clipboard. He pretended to make notes while he surveyed the room over the top of the clipboard. Most people were wearing headphones, but then he saw a young woman staring at her screen and biting her nails. Perfect.

"Tasty?" Jonathan spoke softly but as a lone voice in the room, it sounded loud.

"Sorry," she said, taking her hand away from her mouth.

"Be my guest," said Jonathan, with a smile.

"I forget my manners. Would you like some?" she said, extending her hand. She looked alarmed as Jonathan reached for it, but the stress went from her face when he turned her hand, squeezed it and gently shook it.

"Andrew Sinclair," he said.

"Jane McGriffen," she replied.

"Fancy that. It's you I'm here to see."

"Is this my three month review? I've been chasing Elaine for weeks."

"Yes, Jane," said Jonathan. "Sorry about that. How do you spell your name?"

"That's M.C. Griffen," she said. Jonathan wrote it down and she peered over the clipboard to make sure he got it right.

"First thing, then. Talk me through what you're doing here." Jonathan pulled up a chair.

They both looked at the computer screen as a cartoon treble clef danced on. "Hello!" it said in a speech bubble. "It looks like you're trying to write a song! Would you like me to help?" There were two buttons underneath – one said 'Yes please' and the other said 'No thank you'.

"That's Clef Richard," said Jane. "I'd better just click on 'Yes'."

"What happens if you click on 'No'?"

"It gets shirty. Company policy is that we've got to use it anyway, so it doesn't go away. It just gets in a bad mood with you. Some bigwig heard that the best songs come from turbulent writing partnerships and thought making the assistant annoying would inspire us."

"Does it?"

"Hardly." She nodded at three monitors stacked in the corner of the room with fractured glass.

"So how does this work?"

"Is this like an oral exam?"

"Yes," said Jonathan. "Bonus points for detail!"

"Okay then," Jane said. She looked up as she tried her best to recite her training notes. "This is called BiggSong. It's our secret weapon. It helps us to write songs in the company style."

"What does that mean?"

"The marketing scientists have come up with way too many rules to remember, so this software offers guidance as you go. It edits lyrics and helps to simplify melodies. Dead handy for us lot with music degrees." She allowed herself a nervous laugh.

"Show me," said Jonathan.

"Okay, here's a song I'm stuck on now."

With a double click, the lyrics were on screen.

> A workload like I'm juggling knives
> Plus you I've had enough
> If music be the food of love
> Why don't you get stuffed?
> God knows what you're doing here
> You're clearly out of your tree
> My letter should have made it clear
> De da de da de dee.

"That's just a placeholder, obviously," said Jane. "I can't get the last line. Can't say I'm too proud of the rest either, but I can't spend all day on it." She stole a furtive glance at the LED sign. "So having entered the lyrics, we click on the 'Make it Bigg' button to get feedback, like this." She rolled the mouse across the desk and clicked. Clef frowned and his speech bubble filled with what looked like error messages.

"Ew," said Jane. "Particularly bad today."

The speech bubble said:

- "**Restricted word: knives**. Market is currently sensitive to gangster influence in pop music. You may not use this word in a pop song. I can suggest a rhyme for you.
- **Revenue opportunity: food** – replace with McDonalds to earn royalties from McDonalds each time the song is broadcast.
- **Global limiter: get stuffed** – not understood in US. Please endeavour to use US words over UK equivalents to increase potential market reach.
- **Offensive language: get stuffed** – likely to offend parents of important 7 year old demographic. Suggest replacing with 'get lost' or 'go away'.
- **Offensive language: God** – songs must be faith-neutral for global marketing.
- **Offensive language: out of (my / your / his / her / our / their) tree** – Bigg Records has agreed with the mental health lobby not to use this potentially offensive phrase. A significant portion of our market is directly affected by mental health issues."

There was a button saying 'Click to autocorrect'. Jane clicked it and the new draft lyrics popped up on screen.

> A workload like I'm juggling mice
> Plus you I've had enough
> If music be the McDonalds of love
> Why don't you go away?
> Who knows what you're doing here
> You're clearly mentally challenged
> My letter should have made it clear
> De da de da de dee.

Clef's frown vanished. He beamed broadly, and gave Jane two thumbs up. "Great line," he said in a bubble. "De da de da de dee – suggest repetition and building chorus around this key phrase."

Perhaps Jonathan was imagining it, but he thought he heard Clef make a 'uh-huh' sound too.

Jane sighed. "I guess sometimes the simplest ideas are best."

"So what next?"

"Now we write the melodies," said Jane. "We're not allowed to sing, so it's all done with keyboards on headphones. We just need to write the intro, verse melody and a chorus melody. BiggSong parcels it all together."

"Impressive," said Jonathan. He remembered himself and swiftly added: "That you've become so skilled so quickly."

"It even includes a key change before the last chorus and fades out automatically. And it applies safety filters by itself too."

"For censoring lyrics you mean?"

"No," said Jane. "We've done that bit. The safety filters are there to block anything too catchy. We've already written three songs that are so contagious they can drive you insane. Literally. They were classified as weapons by the military. People won't buy songs they can hear perfectly in their heads, anyway."

Jane offered Jonathan some headphones and put a pair on herself. She moved to the keyboard and played a flighty tune. Jonathan watched her fingers dance. As she touched the keys, green notes sprinkled across the screen. When they looked up at it, half of them were missing. Clef Richard popped up. "Advice: This melody has been simplified. Congratulations: copyright confirmed."

"I'll beat it one day," said Jane, disappointed. "It seems everything I play, even when I make mistakes, someone has already done it."

"How do you know?"

"The green notes are the bits that are copyright cleared. They've got a massive database of melodies that Bigg owns the copyright on," said Jane. "We're encouraged to find something that sounds like another song but which Bigg has the copyright on. Familiar songs sell better."

The whole tune was green. Jane deleted her melody and tried playing something different. Again, it lit up green. "See," she said. "I'm trying really hard here. Embellishing mistakes, screwing up the timings, the lot." She scrolled around the screen to confirm every note was green.

"That'll have to do, then," she said, removing her headphones and prompting Jonathan to do the same. "Who would be good to front this, do you think?" She clicked on a menu and it listed the bands waiting for a song, including Poppycock, Say Combien and Icicle Star. "Well Giles can swivel," she said. "I'm not doing anything for Poppycock. The guy's a dick."

"The clue's in the band name," said Jonathan.

"Let's give it to Icicle Star. BiggSong finds a gap in the lyrics to put the artist's name in," said Jane. "So, in ballads the name's whispered before the first verse. In dance songs, it's chanted in the instrumental bits. It's so people know who's done the songs on the radio."

"And what records they need to buy," added Jonathan. "Clever."

"Yeah, it can't keep up with rap songs though. You have to do those manually. BiggSong prompts you to embed the rapper's name in the lyrics at least twice per verse."

With a click, the song was finalised. Jane pointed at the LED sign on the wall and the number of songs written today increased by one.

"You've made an exceptional start here," said Jonathan. "But don't you find it a bit restrictive for someone with a degree in music? Creatively, I mean?"

"Well," said Jane. "There's a lot you can do in 4/4. Besides, there's no point my writing music that the company can't sell. This way, I can write songs that millions will enjoy." She smiled, but her smile had a kink in it.

"Do *you* enjoy them?" Jonathan asked.

"That's irrelevant. *I'm* not a target customer."

"Do you play any music outside as well?"

"Oh yes!" said Jane, her face lighting up. "I'm in a band. I play keyboards." She added hurriedly: "There's no conflict of interest, though. We just write about what we think and feel. And we've only sold a few thousand CDs online."

"Well, I'm pleased to say that you've passed your probation

period. Congratulations."

"Thank you," said Jane. She sounded more polite than appreciative.

"Remind me," said Jonathan. "Where's Bigg's office?"

"Tenth floor," said Jane. "He likes to look down on us all. Say 'hi' to Marian if you see her."

"His PA?"

"Yes – tell her I'm going to lunch at 12."

"Will do."

As Jonathan was walking to the lift, he noticed a sticker on the gents' toilet door. At first glance it was a square 'Top of the Pops' logo from the nineties, but the bottom half jutted out on both sides. Somebody had used a knife to carve up and combine two stickers, inserting an extra letter and declaring this toilet to be 'Top of the Plops'. Whoever did it, it was probably the most creative and rewarding thing they did that day, Jonathan thought. Poor bastards.

*   *   *

In the lift, Jonathan reviewed his visit. Did he have everything he needed? His brain played Tetris, fitting together Bigg's technology with his own. The ideas hugged each other closely, leaving no chinks. He was ready. Time to put a date in the diary to finally meet Mr Bigg himself. Jonathan pressed the button and the lift rose to the tenth floor.

The doors slid open with a ping. Instead of the corridor Jonathan had expected to see, he walked straight into an office. A slim, handsome Bigg smiled from the front of a framed copy of Sounds underneath the headline 'Indie's saviour?'. It had to be at least twenty years old. A more recent NME, showing Bigg as fat, wrinkled and bald, had the headline 'Pap Idol: meet the enemy'. It too had been framed with pride.

Between the magazines was a photo of Bigg shaking hands with the Prime Minister. Around it was a constellation of framed gold discs. And directly in front of that, sat behind an aggressively tidy desk, was a woman with pink rinsed hair, staring hard at

Jonathan.

"Can I help you?" she asked. Her tone was more confrontation than cooperation.

"Yes," said Jonathan, noticing her for the first time and trying not to be startled by how much her head looked like it was dolloped with candy floss. "It's Marian, isn't it? How are you?"

She looked at him blankly.

Jonathan added: "I haven't seen you since that thing of Clive's. When was that?"

"Sorry, you'll have to help me," said Marian.

"It was a while ago. I shouldn't expect you to remember me. I'm Jonathan." He felt a shock as he heard himself say his real name, but when he re-assembled the plan in his head, he realised it was okay this time. It would be a lot easier to clear security next time if he had an appointment with Bigg in his name.

"Was it the barbecue?"

"That's it!" said Jonathan. "You look different though. Have you had your hair done?" That's usually a safe bet, thought Jonathan.

Marian softened immediately. "I have, actually."

"Suits you," said Jonathan. "Is the old rogue in, then?" Jonathan hoped the business pages had been right about reporting his whereabouts today.

"No," said Marian. "He's got a meeting about another label acquisition."

Good, thought Jonathan. "Shame," he said. "I haven't seen Clive for ages. I wanted to surprise him, but I know he's got a shocking schedule. Any chance you could book me in the diary. Say, next week sometime?"

"Sorry," said Marian. "Not a chance. We're run ragged with this takeover. How about the following week? Tuesday at six?"

"That would be great."

"What name was it again?"

"Jonathan Harrington. But I'd really appreciate it if you could just keep the space free in the diary and not tell him I'm coming. Keep it as a surprise."

"He's pretty hands-on with his diary," said Marian.

Jonathan smiled at her in silence for a moment, forcing her to speak again.

"I'll see what I can do, though," she said.

"Thanks very much," said Jonathan. "That would be awfully kind of you."

He let himself out of the office and took the lift all the way down to reception. He felt a sense of fidgety excitement as he stood alone in the lift and watched the floors fly past. Perhaps it was Dove's face staring from the poster, a reminder of a teenage dream come true. Maybe it was the relief at seeing how his grand plan could come together after all, if he could only get Bigg's technologies and his own to play friends. The next step was to create Clive Bigg's perfect song and present it to him. When he thought of confronting Bigg, he realised that his cocktail of emotions had at least one shot of fear.

CHAPTER 10

When Simon got home, he could hardly open the front door. The mat was piled high with jiffy bags, all addressed to him with labels from his own printer. He kicked them out of the way so he could get in and shut the door behind him. He was ankle-deep in failure.

He picked up two fistfuls of envelopes from the hall and dropped them on the living room carpet. Sat among them, he ripped them open to see where they had come from. One by one, he shook out copies of Goblin's demo CD. Some of the envelopes contained nothing else, so he was pathetically grateful for the rejection slips.

The first read: "Sorry – We think the market expects more sophistication. DGUYDJ." How much sophistication is he expected to achieve without access to a proper studio?

He tore another envelope open. Plumes of grey stuffing billowed over the carpet.

A strand of Simon's hair was still pressed between the CD and the sleeve, aligned with the text around the middle of the disc. They might have received the CD, removed it carefully, played it a few times, run it past a focus group and decided it wasn't quite their thing before reluctantly sliding it back into its sleeve and returning it.

It was much more likely they had cut from step one to step seven, without ever playing it in between. Some of the CDs had returned so quickly that Simon imagined a trampoline underneath the record label's letterbox that bounced them straight into the postroom's out-tray.

Simon was surprised to see the Bigg Records logo on five of the rejection slips. He hadn't bothered sending them any demos, given that all they ever seemed to release was unimaginative pap. But the small print on the slips revealed that Bigg had acquired five indie labels he had targeted a few months ago. They all sent the same blunt reply: "Bigg Records does not accept unsolicited demos." It was accompanied by a mail order catalogue of 'more great bands you will enjoy!'.

Simon knew his music was good – damn good, in fact – but how could he find an audience if he couldn't even get a few record execs to listen to it for thirty seconds? And who was DGUYDJ? Was it an abbreviation for something? Do give us your demo… something beginning with J? Don't get upset you're doing just… run out of letters? Then the penny dropped: Don't give up your day job. His heart sank.

Perhaps they did need to create a stir, if it would get people to listen to them.

Perhaps Fred was right.

*　*　*

The Copse pub was known to locals as The Corpse. There had been three deaths there in the last year, all of them from old age. It was the only pub in London to have a Steradent machine in the gentlemen's toilet.

As she screwed her keyboard stand together, Fred looked at the crowd of codgers supping their beer. Two old men perched on stools by the bar, drinking from engraved tankards. They sat side by side, looking resolutely ahead, out-staring the optics in silence. Another two in brown suits sat at a small square table and played shove ha'penny. With a real ha'penny.

This would be a tough crowd to please. Fred knew their own songs would bomb, but she couldn't think of any appropriate cover versions she knew either. Maybe she had learned something useful at school? Perhaps she could fudge a rendition of the

'White Cliffs of Dover' if things turned nasty.

Bert the publican was wiping the tables, although it didn't look like anyone had used them since they were last cleaned. "Where's the other one?" he asked her. "The one with the face?" He pulled a goofy expression. It wasn't flattering, but Fred had to admit it was a pretty good approximation of Simon on Pop Goes the Weasel.

"Oh… he's probably not joining me today," said Fred. "Something came up."

"Shame," said Bert. "Still, we got the star of the show, eh?" One of the men on stools raised his tankard to Bert so he rushed back behind the bar to fill it.

After Fred had plugged in her keyboard, she checked, double-checked and triple-checked its programs. She wasn't due on stage for twenty minutes, but if she didn't do something she would fall apart. Fred had never faced an audience alone before, even one as small as this. She shivered. It was probably the draught. She wasn't that nervous. Was she?

How she wished Simon was here, though. Apart from anything else, he was the real musician in the band. They could get away with anything if he dropped a twiddly solo on top.

The weasel stunt had backfired badly. It had brought a short, sharp dose of notoriety. A few tabloids had interviewed her. She told them all about the band and their music, and how the show had been a desperate attempt to get someone – *anyone* – to listen to them. The hacks never used that stuff, though. They just wrote about the filming, and threw plush rodents to try to provoke her fury.

Where had it all got her? She was alone in a pub where a man with bushy ears was laughing with (not *at*) the Daily Mail. Simon hadn't phoned all week, and even the journalists had found someone new to annoy now.

Perhaps she should give up the stunts; take the music more seriously; be more professional.

Perhaps Simon was right.

The door flew open. Silhouetted against the streetlights outside was the figure of a man holding a guitar case.

"Hey, Fred," said Simon.

The relief washed over her and it felt like a dive into the sea on a hot day.

* * *

Fred and Simon arranged their equipment to mark their territory. There wasn't a stage, so they had to use amps and empty cases to separate themselves from the audience. There's nothing so distracting as having someone walk through the middle of your act on their way to the toilets, except perhaps having them ask you during a guitar solo if you've got the darts. Both of these had happened before.

Bert took the microphone to introduce them. "Something for you youngsters out there, tonight!" he said, with a gentle chuckle.

Fred and Simon exchanged a puzzled look.

"We got the Space Invaders machine last month," continued Bert. "And we're all stocked up on alcopops. Tonight we've got our first gig. So don't be shy! Come down the front!"

Nobody moved. Simon had to admire Bert's stoic refusal to acknowledge that his pub was dying and his attempts to modernise were failing. But the only people under this roof who had to pay to use public transport were huddled around the microphone.

"I'm sure you've seen them all over the internet…"

Simon was sure they hadn't.

"Please give a very warm welcome, to Goblin!"

They heard one man rustle his newspaper as he turned the pages and saw another one turn his hearing aid off. Nobody even turned to look at them.

Bert clapped five times with his hands high in the air, and retreated behind the bar.

"Si?" said Fred. She sounded scared. "How can we do this?"

"Loud and proud," said Simon, putting on his guitar. "Let's blow their cobwebs away. One. Two. Three. Four."

And on four, he struck the guitar strings. As he rolled his foot backwards and forwards across the effects pedal, a juddering chord chugged from the stage area. Fred fired out bass notes from

68

the keyboard, and then marshalled the drum program into action. It clattered and crashed and looped. Before the last chord had faded, Simon ground out another. And another. And another. He built a wall of sound, then draped an ornate solo along the top. Fred stabbed with the synth, each hit like a robot orchestra releasing steam. Her voice sounded so fragile on top of the industrial effects, a little girl lost in a factory.

Simon was consumed by the music. He could still see his audience was the grim reaper's to-do list and that they were blasting away in a dreary pub. But he didn't notice. All he noticed was the music. The room deadened the sound, but Simon remixed it in his head and heard it with absolute clarity.

Fred and Simon didn't bother waiting for applause or reaction. They just played their songs, bumper to bumper. And as they played, time melted.

After eight songs, they came to the blistering finale. Fred sang:

> All you have ever known
> Fizzles out to nothing
> Just skin and bones
> And gory stuffing
> And memories
> Of things you said
> Circling round your best friend's head
> Welcome to eternal DEATH

They howled the last word together until their voices went hoarse and the sound faded to air. The guitar chords died in a wail of feedback.

Silence.

Fred and Simon looked around the pub expectantly, but nobody was looking back.

Without the music to hide behind, Simon felt sheepish. Bert had his hands full of bags of Monster Munch, so not even he clapped. Simon would have settled for a polite thank you for showing up, or a sympathy nod from any one of the punters. He could hack criticism, but to play an entire set without provoking a response was humiliating. "Yeah, well, perhaps you're already there…" said Simon.

"Thank gawd for that!" said one of the men on a barstool. "I can hear myself think again now." The man with the hearing aid fumbled to turn it back on.

Simon and Fred exchanged a sad look.

She switched off her keyboard and he put his guitar on its stand. In silence, they disconnected cables, coiled them up and tidied them away. They put their instruments back into their cases, shut the lids quietly and closed the clasps.

As they were rearranging the furniture, the man on the nearest bar stool belched so loud it made his tie ripple and set the fruit machine's tilt alarm off. He got a round of applause.

* * *

Bert looked cross as he served them their beers. "Why couldn't you play something they'd like?"

"Such as?" said Fred in exasperation. "They don't like anything. They're only breathing reluctantly."

"How about Queen?" said Bert. "Someone put Bohemian Rhapsody on the jukebox seven times yesterday."

"Yeah," said Simon, "as a joke. What did you think of our set? You must have liked some of it?"

"Oooh." Bert shook his head. "It's a bit far out for me."

"We're not afraid to experiment," said Fred. "Even if we're playing the pub circuit, we want to raise the bar."

"Bringing people *to* the bar is what I care about," said Bert. "I thought you'd pack the place. I heard you had 500 friends."

"Only on Facebook," said Fred.

"But you were on the telly!"

"We were," said Simon. "But unfortunately a lot of our fans like to wash their hair on Friday nights. Terrible scheduling."

Simon and Fred took their drinks away from the bar – away from Bert, more to the point – and to a table in the corner. The seats had those cushions that make you expect a soft landing and then surprise you with how hard they are.

"We can't keep on like this," said Simon. He smoothed out a twenty pound note on the table in front of them. "Even Liz is fighting to keep a straight face."

"I can't believe we only got twenty quid," said Fred. "That won't even buy us a taxi home. What are we going to do?"

"Get the tube."

"I mean with the band."

Simon shook his head.

They both drank a little.

"I'm glad you came," said Fred. "I was bricking it before you walked in."

"Yeah," said Simon. "Me too."

"This has been a right wash-out."

"It's not all bad," said Simon. "We did have some delicious pickled onion crisps."

Fred smiled. "That's true."

"We got twenty whole British quids, too. There are people who stitch t-shirts for a week to earn half that."

"Yep."

"Oh, and we got to play loud without my flat mate moaning that he can't hear Hollyoaks."

A boy of about five approached the table. "Excuse me?" He offered Simon a tatty piece of green paper and a pen. "Can I have your autograph please?" He paused before explaining: "It's when you write your name."

Simon looked over the boy's head, to where he had come from, and an old man nodded back to him. They hadn't noticed that table tucked away at the far end before.

Simon looked into the boy's eyes. He was genuine.

"Did you enjoy the show?" said Simon. He took the pen and paper and scrawled his signature. Underneath, he drew a guitar with a smiley face. It didn't come out quite right, but it looked okay.

"You guys rock!" said the kid. "I wish my Mum let me play my music as loud as that."

Simon handed him the paper and pen and he looked at the autograph. "Cool!" he said. He passed them to Fred. "I've never seen a real live band before. Sometimes granddad brings me here, but we never had rock stars before."

Fred signed and tried to draw a goblin, clipped the pen to the paper and passed them back.

"Thank you," said the boy.

"No problem," said Fred.

The boy turned to leave, but then stopped himself and looked up at her. "You're pretty," he said and then immediately covered his mouth with his hands. Before Fred could respond, he ran away.

"Our first fan," said Simon.

"He's never seen anyone else. He's bound to be impressed."

"Don't knock it." Simon watched the boy as he excitedly waved their autographs at his granddad. "You never forget your first gig. For the rest of his life, this will be his. He'll be telling his mates about us tomorrow."

"Shame none of them work at a record company, then." Fred took a deep breath. "Listen," she said. "I am sorry about, you know, the weasel thing. We probably should take the band more seriously."

"It's okay," said Simon. "At least someone noticed us for once. Our demos might as well be recorded on boomerangs. I'll go insane if I have to spend my life sorting cabbages. We have to do something."

"You could get another job."

Simon shook his head. "They're all as bad as each other."

"I had another idea," said Fred. She trod carefully. "You know the music in my lift?"

"Hmmm." Simon had visited her at work a few times, but hadn't paid much attention to the background dirge.

"It's live. It comes from a studio in Bigg Records. The musicians work like tag teams, so it's seamless."

"So?"

"Imagine if we took over that studio! We would be heard all over the country."

"In lifts," said Simon, flatly.

"It's a captive audience!"

"Oh yeah? And how do we get into the studio?"

"Well, we'd just have to break in at Bigg Records—"

"Ah! I've spotted the flaw!" Simon laughed with incredulity. "I should tell you I would rather sort cabbages than sew mail bags."

"But they won't have the kind of security a radio station would have. It'd be a push over. You did say we had to do something."

"Well, let's call it Plan B then," said Simon. It was obvious he was filing it mentally under 'dangerous waste of time'.

"And what do you suggest for Plan A?"

"We need to make an ally inside the industry."

"Who?"

"Dove," said Simon.

Fred laughed. "You're obsessed."

"No I'm not!" She made him sound like a nutter. It's true that Simon could play every song University of Death had recorded; and that he knew more about Dove's personal life than about his own family. And, come to think of it, that he'd visited Dove's house. But he'd only peered over the hedge. He hadn't rung the bell. He wasn't dangerous or anything. "He would get it," Simon said. "He would love our music, if he heard it."

"That's a pretty big 'if' though," said Fred. "He must be buried in demos. How do we get him to play ours?"

"We do a cover version," said Simon. "If we do a University of Death song, it's bound to get someone's attention."

"Okay," said Fred. "We'll give it a go. On one condition."

"What's that?"

"If this fails, we do Plan B."

Simon hesitated. He had to take decisive action, otherwise his life would be an endless loop of pointless jobs and day dreams. "Okay," he said. "But no more secret stunts. Everything above board."

"Course," said Fred.

Simon had heard that before.

*   *   *

When he got home, Simon logged on straight away.

thing>	**You there, Angela?**
angelA>	as ever
thing>	**Happy anniversary!**
angelA>	?
thing>	**We first chatted a week ago**
thing>	**Almost to the hour!**
angelA>	oh yes
thing>	**I think we've spoken every day this week except yesterday.**
thing>	**I missed you. Where were you?**
angelA>	i went to a party
thing>	**Was it good?**
angelA>	music was okay games were great
thing>	**What kind of games were they?**
angelA>	they had playstations
angelA>	i am the queen of buzz
angelA>	i won an extra bit of cake
angelA>	lol
thing>	**You need fast fingers for that game**
angelA>	yeah baby
thing>	**lol**
angelA>	do u play computer games
thing>	**Sometimes at parties**
angelA>	have u heard of electroplankton
thing>	**No**
angelA>	you have these music fishes
angelA>	you move them around the screen and they
angelA>	make sounds
thing>	**I don't like computer music**
thing>	**It's soulless**
angelA>	its the sound of the eighties baby
thing>	**Exactly**
thing>	**I prefer guitar hero**
angelA>	wats that like
thing>	**It comes with a plastic guitar**

thing>   You play rock music
angelA>   why do u like that
thing>   It's more authentic
thing>   You still need a bit of musicianship
angelA>   talking of which how did your gig go
thing>   We were fantastic. Played better than ever
thing>   You should have come to see us
angelA>   another time maybe
thing>   We could have done with some support
thing>   The crowd was rubbish
angelA>   typical
angelA>   wat u sound like
thing>   I should send you our demo
angelA>   yeah do it
thing>   I could pop it round. What's your address?
angelA>   theres someone at my door
thing>   It's gone midnight!
angelA>   must be an emergency
angelA>   bye sweetness
angelA>   c u soon
thing>   For real? Face to face?
<angelA has disconnected>
thing>   Bye.

CHAPTER 11

Bigg's huge nose rolled around his face. His eyes bubbled, and his mouth stretched into his chins.

Jonathan circled his magnifying glass over the picture, trying to read the CDs on the shelf behind Bigg while his face morphed around the edge of the lens. The FT had photographed Bigg in front of his music collection, but most of the spines were proving too small to read. It was frustrating: before Jonathan could create Bigg's perfect song, he needed a near-complete list of his existing music collection.

The CDs were filed alphabetically. At the end was a double album: 'Welcome Pack' by Zambezi. *This* Jonathan recognised: it was software, dating from the launch of Zambezi, the most popular website for buying music downloads. If Bigg still had an account there, it meant a complete list of his record collection already existed. The trick was to get access to it.

Jonathan logged on to the Zambezi website and read the application form. The security used a password, which would be hard to get around. But the backup for if you had forgotten your password relied on the 'arsed-to' principle. Zambezi asked three personal questions to which the customer knew the answers. The security was supposed to come from asking enough trivial questions that nobody else could be arsed to find out the answers. In most circumstances, it worked well enough. But it was vulnerable to a targeted attack, and Jonathan was determined.

The three questions on the form were date of birth, favourite song and first school. Clive's birthday was mentioned in the FT profile so he could bluff his way through that, but the second and third questions would take a little research. Noting down the customer service number for Zambezi, Jonathan visited Friends Reunited and searched through all the Clive Biggs.

"married now with a girl and boy. up the Villa."

Not his Clive.

"my hair is even bigger now! Travelling the world and can't afford haircuts!!! Drop me a line to tell me where you live. Perhaps I'll drop in."

Definitely not his Clive.

"Working hard, playing hard. I'll get someone to scan in the photo from the FT business section when I get time. Anyone else remember Mr Stevenson saying I wouldn't come to anything? If anyone knows or cares where *he* is today, send him my very warmest regards."

Now that did sound like Clive Bigg. Jonathan noted the name of Bigg's school and reached for the phone before he had time to get nervous. First call: the man himself.

He took Bigg's business card out of his wallet, dialled a redirection service so his call couldn't be easily traced and then plugged in Bigg's mobile number.

"Bigg," said Clive, answering his mobile.

"This is Geoffrey at Zambezi," said Jonathan.

"How can I help?" said Bigg.

"We're worried about possible fraud on your account."

"What do you mean?"

Bigg sounded suspicious but Jonathan didn't allow himself to be distracted. Bigg might not even have an account there any more, but he would have to press on to find out for sure. "First, Sir, I have to take you through some security procedures," said Jonathan. "Could you tell me your account number please?"

"How do I know you are who you say you are?"

He's sharp, thought Jonathan. "I'm looking at your account now. We have your first school on record as Elm Avenue. Oh, and happy birthday, Sir. I can see from your D.O.B. that you'll be celebrating on the fifth."

78

"Fine." He didn't sound sure, but he did sound busy.

"We do need to ask you a security question, though, Sir. Could you tell me your account number, please?"

"No idea."

"Well, could you tell me the favourite song you have on record with us, then, please?"

"Dancing on the ceiling by Lionel Ritchie," said Bigg.

That was a smart choice, thought Jonathan. Nobody would guess that the head of a record label would call that their favourite song ever. Jonathan had the security information he needed now, but it would arouse suspicion to hang up after asking for it. He had to play along a bit more. "Thank you," he said. "Could you tell me how you've been using the service recently?"

"Can't you do that?"

"We have to protect ourselves from spurious claims. This procedure protects us both."

"Well, I've been downloading a lot of back catalogue tracks. Probably about a hundred last month. Can't remember what they are though. Some Zappa and Floyd for sure. It's been a pretty busy month."

"That matches our record, here, Sir. We have a flag against your account for some reason."

"Maybe it's that I don't usually download so much old stuff."

"I'm sure that's it. I don't think there's a problem here, but could I ask you to check your statement next time you're online just to be sure."

"Okay."

"Thank you for your co-operation."

"No problem," said Bigg. His voice faded towards the end of 'problem' because he was already moving the phone to hang it up.

Jonathan gently recradled his phone, breathed deeply a few times to relax and then picked it up again and dialled the customer service number for Zambezi. He stood to make the call.

"You're speaking to Mark at Zambezi, where we take the *load* out of down*load*ing. Could you give me your name first please."

"Clive Bigg," said Jonathan, "with two Gs". He felt an involuntary smile coming on and was pleased he could do this by phone.

"Your account number?"

"I don't have that handy."

"No worries. I can look it up. Your password?"

"I've forgotten it. Sorry."

"I need to ask you some security questions, then," said Mark. He sounded irritated.

"No problem."

"Your date of birth?"

Jonathan looked at the FT where he had circled Bigg's birthday in the article. The year was missing. He could work it out from Bigg's school leaving date on Friends Reunited, but there wasn't time. He'd have to wing it. "My birthday is the fifth of August," he said. "But I can't remember what year I gave you guys. I usually lie. I'm not 21 any more."

"Okay, your favourite song."

"Dancing on the ceiling." Jonathan thought he heard stifled laughter on the other end.

"Your first school?"

"Elm Avenue."

"Okay then. That's all fine. How can I help?"

"This is kind of embarrassing," said Jonathan. "It's my son. He's been downloading songs from you using my account. I just found out."

"Would you like to file a fraud report?"

"God, no. Do you mind if I ask, are you a father?"

"Yes," said Mark, hesitantly.

Jonathan ignored the ambiguity. "Boy or girl?" he said.

"Er, a boy, three years old."

"You've got all this to come," said Jonathan. "I'm sure you can understand I'd like to deal with this in the family. But I need to know what he's done first."

"How can I help?"

"Well, can you tell me what he's downloaded?"

"That shouldn't be too difficult." Jonathan could hear Mark typing. "In the last month there's been some Pink Floyd, Radiohead, Zappa, Peter Gabriel, Gentle Giant, Jethro Tull…"

"The Tull was me," said Jonathan.

"Right. Well, it's probably all a bit mixed up."

"Keep going, I'm writing this down."

"How long has this been going on?" said Mark.

"No idea – could be months. Keep going."

"Look, we're pretty busy here. Do you mind if I suggest you access this online?"

"Well, I can't get to my computer at the moment. I was hoping I could just find this out from you, otherwise I'll have to cancel the whole account as a precaution." Jonathan knew that the people at call centres were tasked, above all else, to stop customers closing accounts – even those who call up specifically to do that.

"Well, how about I just send you a list of all the music you've got registered here, and you sort it out with your son your end, Mr Bigg?"

Jackpot! "That would be most helpful," said Jonathan. He tried to ensure his excitement wasn't obvious. "I'm travelling on business at the moment and staying with a friend. Could you email it to her?"

"What's her address?"

Jonathan gave Mark one of his anonymous email addresses.

"Thanks for your understanding," he said. "I'll be sure to write and commend your service when I get this sorted out."

"Thank you for calling Zambezi."

When he hung up, Jonathan clapped his hands so hard it stung. When the list arrived, he double-checked it against Bigg's CD collection and found that he had indeed bought everything he could identify twice – once on CD and once as a download. As top dog at a record company who pretended he expected everybody else to do the same, Bigg had little option. But the download list was much longer than Jonathan's CD list, partly because he couldn't identify all the CDs and partly because Bigg had bought a lot more music online than the photo showed he owned on CD.

Now was the moment of truth: Jonathan fed the data on Bigg's music collection into his program Plato. He played a few bars of melody on a piano-style keyboard, and set the software to go.

The processing bar stretched slowly, like an old man getting up in the morning. When it was done, Jonathan pressed play, and listened to the essence of Bigg's CD collection distilled into three minutes. Some of the influences were obvious – such as the lurching time signatures of Zappa and the soaring guitar lines of Pink Floyd.

It was the first time Jonathan had used his program to create music tailored for someone else's taste. He didn't like the result much, but then again he didn't have to. The question was: would Clive Bigg bet the company on it?

CHAPTER 12

Fred could see Simon bending on his haunches over a tatty box of records on the floor. He was flicking through them, occasionally stopping and lifting one out to read its sleeve before letting it slide back into the box and flipping to the next one. From her seat on the balcony, Fred could see that he was about halfway down the first aisle. There were about ten rows of stalls for him to get through, each one packed with boxes of records, CDs, books, DVDs and tapes.

Fred knew that because she'd done them all. Not as thoroughly as Simon, admittedly, but she had walked along them all, nosed through the odd box and plucked out a couple of bargain CDs. She spent some time looking at a life-sized inflatable Kylie, taking her cue to leave when the man selling it had described it as fully washable. Now, Fred was taking a break and watching Simon slowly trace his path through the record fair. He stood up, stretched his legs and hunkered down at the next stall. In the time since Fred had given up, she had worked out there must be over 100,000 records and CDs in the hall. It looked like Simon was going to inspect every single one of the bastards.

Music blared from tinny speakers on a few of the tables, but it was hard to imagine anyone being moved by it here. Although it offered shelter to record collectors who would otherwise be out in the rain, the concrete building was only really ideal for storing aircraft or hosting banking conferences. It was the most uninspiring place Fred had ever been.

She smiled in solidarity at a woman who was dragging her heels as her male companion strode single-mindedly towards a big display of T.Rex memorabilia. The woman watched as he riffled through a box of records, took them out of their sleeves and tilted them to the light to inspect them for scratches. All the while, he held the vinyl carefully at the edges.

Fred enjoyed music as much as anyone, but she didn't feel a need to buy it and catalogue it like Simon did. Perhaps it was a boy thing: that desire to own, control and totally understand a tiny corner of the universe, whether it's trains, stamps or Led Zep bootlegs. Why did they care how many different versions of a track there were? Surely any sane person would just pick one they enjoyed listening to and stick with it. Just because they made eleventeen mixes of a song, it didn't mean you had to hunt them down and squirrel them away. Fred bought the songs she really liked, but was mostly happy to listen to whatever was playing. Men are from record fairs; women are from radio, she thought.

She was shocked when Simon materialised beside her.

"Fred, come quick!"

"Are you okay?"

"Yes. Come check out this dealer!" Simon panted from his run up the stairs.

"You've got to kick this record fair habit," said Fred. "Only addicts call their suppliers 'dealers'."

"Just hurry up, will you?"

Fred put the lid on her water, turned it carefully tight, stood up, adjusted her skirt and then indicated that Simon should lead on. She allowed him to skip on ahead and followed him back down the stairs in her own good time, onto the floor of the fair, and towards a stall at the middle.

Every now and then Simon would look over his shoulder to check she was following and have to slow down to let her catch up. They resembled a boy dragging his mum to the swings to give him a push.

"There!" said Simon. He pointed at a white paper sleeve stuck on the wall behind one of the stands. It had skulls potato printed on it in black, arranged around the hole in the middle, through which the record label could be seen. "It's mint. Unplayed. Imagine that!"

"It's a bit crap, isn't it?" said Fred.

"God," said Simon. "Do you even know what it is?"

"The original demo for Granddad by St Winifred's School Choir?"

"Oh ha ha," said Simon. Fred wasn't sure if he was annoyed because she was being flippant or because she was right that the artwork was childish. "That," said Simon, "is a rare seven inch single of Animal Reined by University of Death. It's their very first record. Hand-printed sleeve, every one unique. Probably only about fifty of them in the world."

"The sleeve's a bit knackered," said Fred.

"Be fair," said the dealer. The fact that he was joining the conversation didn't stop him from finishing what he was doing, even though it was aggressively scratching his arse. "That's over twenty years old."

"Can we have a look?" said Simon.

"Nah," said the dealer. He took a sweet from a bowl he was holding and tossed it into his mouth.

"Oh well, never mind," said Fred. She was annoyed that Simon had hauled her down to look at another bloody record. "You could get that one instead. It's pink, look. Nicer picture, too."

"Oh yeah," said Simon. "Cos that would be just the same, wouldn't it? It's not like I'm collecting stuff because it looks nice, is it?"

"Don't you have those tracks then?"

"Not on an original record, no."

"So you do have those tracks?"

Simon ignored her and spoke to the dealer. "Please can I have a look at it?"

"Shouldn't touch what you can't afford." He tossed another couple of sweets into his gob and chewed them like a cow.

"How much is it then?" said Fred.

The dealer smirked. "Eight. Big ones."

"Eight thousand pounds?"

"Er, no, eight hundred," said the dealer, meekly.

"So that would be eight medium ones, then," said Fred. "Do you take credit cards?"

The dealer's eyes widened. "Sure!" he said, with a smile.

"Don't wind him up," Simon hissed to Fred. "It's only worth about four hundred," he added out loud. "He obviously doesn't want to sell it."

"That's where you're wrong," said the dealer. He set his bowl of M&Ms down on a box of CDs in front of them. Simon and Fred took a couple and chewed on them while they watched him stretch to reach the single, exposing the salt rings under the arms of his Grateful Dead t-shirt. Old band t-shirts don't die; they just go to record fairs.

The dealer slipped the record out of its sleeve, balanced the hole on his finger and rested the edge against his thumb so he could present it to both of them and touch it as little as possible. The title and band were scrawled on the label. "That's Dove's handwriting! Probably!" said Simon. "It's the only official University of Death record I haven't got. I can't believe I've finally found it."

"You're not serious about buying it, are you?" said Fred. The dealer slipped it into its sleeve and put it back on the wall.

"If I had the money, I'd fork out now."

"We can offer credit!" said the dealer.

"Is it really worth that much to you?" said Fred. She popped a couple of sweets in her mouth and sucked them until the shell cracked and chocolate yolk oozed out to caress her tongue. The dealer raised his eyebrows.

"It completes my collection," said Simon. "I've got every track University of Death released, and every other single on vinyl and CD. But I've only got a copy of this one."

"You said yourself it's not worth eight hundred, though. It's not even signed."

"None of them are signed. Dove hasn't given an autograph since 1986. But this is the only one I've ever seen," said Simon. He sucked noisily on a peanut and stared at the record intently, like he was trying to record it in his memory. "I might never see it again."

"Will you negotiate?" said Fred to the dealer. She didn't care about the record, but she knew Simon wouldn't have the nerve to ask and wouldn't stop going on about it later either. "Would you take two hundred for it, say?"

The dealer pretended not to hear her and tossed another sweet at his mouth. It bounced off his forehead, so he threw another one up quickly and darted his head underneath it to catch it in his mouth.

"How about three hundred?"

The dealer took a packet of boiled sweets out of his pocket. "Fancy a mint sweet?" he said, theatrically ignoring Fred's attempts to negotiate.

Fred took one, but almost immediately spat it out again onto the floor.

"Mind the merchandise!" said the dealer.

"Ugh!" said Fred. "That's lime or something. I hate lime. I thought you said it was mint."

"Nah, didn't mean that," said the dealer. "Sometimes I half-hit my mouth when I'm tossing sweets and they fall out again. I meant that was mint condition."

Fred and Simon looked at the bowl of sweets they'd been eating for the last ten minutes and for the first time noticed how some of them looked sticky and had discoloured patches on them.

"I feel sick," said Fred. Her eyes ballooned. She stuck her tongue out and scraped it across her upper teeth repeatedly and then flipped the lid off her water and squirted it into her mouth. Nothing was washing away the taste of disgust that was buried deep in her head. "Ugh! You're revolting!" She stormed off.

Simon followed her, dabbing his tongue with the sleeve of his t-shirt, but not before he had slipped one of the dealer's business cards off the table and pocketed it.

*   *   *

angelA>   hey simon
thing>   **Hi**
angelA>   how was your weekend

thing>	Great. I went to a record fair.
thing>	Found a 7″ of Animal Reined
angelA>	did u buy it
thing>	No chance! It was way too expensive.
angelA>	was it worth it
thing>	It was overpriced but it's the only one I've ever seen.
thing>	I'll probably never see one again.
angelA>	sounds like a big adventure
thing>	It's nice to talk to someone who understands
thing>	Fred has no patience for record fairs.
thing>	Next time you should come with me.
angelA>	maybe
thing>	how was your weekend?
angelA>	cool went to see a band
angelA>	salvation amy
thing>	Any good?
angelA>	we were right down the front
angelA>	i got a kiss off the singer
thing>	Who did you go with?
angelA>	they have two drummers totally rockin
angelA>	ive downloaded all their stuff now
angelA>	can send u a track if u like
thing>	Sure. Any band of yours is a band of mine.
thing>	You have pretty good taste.
angelA>	thx
thing>	I made friends with Fred again.
angelA>	im pleased
thing>	We have a new plan for the band
angelA>	wat is it
thing>	We're going to do a cover of University of Death.
thing>	We'll use it to attract Dove's attention.
thing>	He'll love our music when he hears it.
angelA>	he has a gig coming up in London
angelA>	thats your town
angelA>	r u goin
thing>	I hope so. Tickets go on sale in two weeks.

angelA>	dont forget
thing>	**No fear!**
thing>	**Are you going?**
angelA>	hopefully
thing>	**We can meet up there!**
angelA>	lets see
angelA>	ive got to go
angelA>	thx for chatting tonight
thing>	**No, thank you!**
angelA>	i felt sad earlier
angelA>	i feel happy now
thing>	**Why were you sad?**
angelA>	another time
angelA>	take care mate
thing>	**And you**
angelA>	xxx
thing>	**xxx**
angelA>	xoxo
thing>	**xoxo**
angelA>	sweet dreams
<angelA has disconnected>	
thing>	**I think I**
<thing has disconnected>	

CHAPTER 13

The scrapbook opened, and as the camera panned across it, the sepia photos became animated. The boys larked about on a punt, with Jimmy falling in. As the water splashed the camera, there was a flash and the image froze. The camera rolled over the headlines that recorded the band's rise to fame and lingered on a photo of the boys playing snooker backstage. It too came to life. Bradley got a perfect break, and the others all hugged him.

FWIT

The image collapsed in on itself and was swallowed by a tiny square of light.

"I'm looking at your crap now," said Bigg from behind a plume of cigar smoke. He stood on the wrong side of his desk and shouted into the phone. "Let me tell you, mate: Their tour bus went off a cliff, not our standards. They're showing more life pumped with tubes in hospital than in this film. When they bleep their last, I want units flying onto the shelves and a video in heavy rotation. If I don't see a clip by tomorrow that makes me cry, and above all makes me feel like buying their *entire* back catalogue, I will fire you so hard you'll spend the first three weeks of your new job still spinning on your swivel chair. Got it?"

He slammed down the handset while the caller was still burbling away. It was mummified in parcel tape. Inside the tape, the plastic was already cracked in four places. Bigg stubbed out his cigar in the zen garden, a tray of sand with three black pebbles he was supposed to rake to calm himself down.

Beside the phone on his desk, the FT profile topped off his in-tray, even though it was months old, carefully folded so that his photo was flat. Bigg's headphones were coiled on top of the paper. It was nobody else's business what music he chose to play at work. It was hardly likely to be the same music that had won the gold disks he displayed with pride, anyway.

Uplighters stood like sentries along the walls, chosen to light the room without reflecting in Bigg's shiny pate. With his wrinkled forehead, he looked like a picture of a grumpy man who smiles broadly when turned upside down. Rumour had it the only way to see a smile on his face was to squint over the first floor banister while he was waiting for the lift in the atrium below. Few of his staff were brave enough to try it, though.

Bigg flopped down in the leather throne behind his desk.

The intercom buzzed. "Your ten o'clock is here, Mr Bigg," said Marian's disembodied voice. It sounded like it had travelled a light year to get there, but she was only in the office next door.

"Who is it?"

"It's a surprise."

Bigg didn't like surprises. He lit another cigar and sucked deeply on it. "You'd better let him in."

The door opened and Jonathan walked in, fastening his suit buttons. "Jonathan Harrington," he said, extending his hand and slowly approaching Bigg's desk. "I told Marian we were old friends." Bigg didn't offer his hand, so Jonathan let his slowly drop.

"You've got a nerve," Bigg said. "We got some lovely CCTV of you, mate." He slid a grainy greyscale photo from his in-tray across the desk towards Jonathan. It overshot and fell onto the floor, so Jonathan picked it up and studied it before replacing it on the desk.

"You caught my best side," he said, but Bigg didn't return his smile. Jonathan took a chair on the other side of the desk.

"Oh, do make yourself at home," said Bigg, as he spluttered smoke all over Jonathan. "Who the hell are you?"

"I guess I'm a sort of consultant," said Jonathan. "Your business is in trouble and I'm bringing you the solution."

"I don't do consultants," said Bigg. "Mealy-mouthed vacuum suits bossing everyone around and then pissing off before it all comes crashing down. No thanks."

"I'm not like that. I'm in this for the long term."

"I'll show you a long term," laughed Bigg. "You'll get five years if I go easy on you. What went wrong?" Bigg leaned back in his chair and looked at the ceiling, stroking his chin as he warmed to his theme. "Did I miss the opt-out box somewhere? Was there a form worded 'remove tick in this box... to opt-in... from not having... your business subjected to industrial espionage' or something? Did I issue a distress signal on the waveband used by the secret consultants society?"

"Look, I'm sorry if my undercover work has offended you."

"Damn right."

"But it was the only way. I know my methods are controversial, but you should think of me like a white witch. I use my talent to do good."

"Don't come all this, pretending you're purer than the driven snow and whiter than the Durex dog."

"I think you mean Dulux."

"I mean," said Bigg, stressing the words and pointing his cigar at Jonathan with every syllable, "you are a conman and a thief. Give me one... single... good reason not to have you thrown out that window." Bigg pointed to one side but Jonathan didn't take his eyes off him, even as a damp breeze stroked his face from the direction Bigg was pointing.

"I know about the Commodore," Jonathan shot back.

"Ah! Blackmail," said Bigg. "I recognise that. Well, it is true. I do listen to the odd bit of Lionel Ritchie. He was cut from my desert island discs by the PR wonks. I draw the line at 'Hello', mind."

"I don't mean The Commodores," said Jonathan. He pulled a rolled up copy of Commodore Code magazine from his inside pocket and tossed it. The pages flapped through the air like a pigeon kicked off a wall and the magazine landed in Bigg's lap. The open spread was filled with a program listing. In the corner, an air force commodore stamped out cockroaches with his shiny boots while steam puffed from his ears. "Type carefully!" he ordered. "Death to the bugs!"

Bigg went puce. "Where the hell did you get this?"

"Looks like you missed a copy."

"Answer me!"

"A private collector. It cost me over a hundred quid, mind. You've created a real rarity by buying all the others. It's funny really. All it took was a quick check of your eBay history. If you hadn't bought all the copies of this issue on eBay, I would never have found your secret. Would I be right in guessing you liked it so much you bought the publishing company? I take it current owner GinormousIP is your intellectual property arm?"

Bigg pressed his intercom. "Marian, get security. Double quick."

Jonathan pulled an MP3 player out of his pocket and put it on the table in front of Bigg. "Play this."

"Don't tell me you've gone to all this trouble to pitch some half-arsed band you know? I mean, full marks for trying. But otherwise, piss off!"

"That's not it," said Jonathan. His speech was fast. "I've got a flawless system for discovering new music. This is just a demo to prove it. Together we can save your business and the whole industry. Play it. Now."

"Listen, mate," said Bigg. "I've done my fair share of trawling round bars watching the likes of 'I Slept With Buzby' and 'My Gerbil's An Alien' to know that there's no shortcut to finding product. That's why we've given up on organic bands and we just put our own together."

"Please. Just play it," said Jonathan.

The door opened and two old men in security uniforms marched in. Their bodies looked thin and frail, but they stood tall and rolled their shoulders to look more imposing.

"Mr Harrington was just leaving us," said Bigg. "If that even is his real name."

"It is," said Jonathan. "We're talking business now. All above board."

"Make sure he doesn't come back."

The security guards lifted Jonathan from his chair by his elbows and led him away. "Play the music!" he cried out.

"I was a fanboy once," said Bigg. "I grew out of it. I suggest you do too."

"It's crap!" called Jonathan over his shoulder. "But it's *your kind* of crap. You're going to love it! Treat yourself! Play it."

Bigg waved him away. "Learn to live in obscurity, pal. It's not going to happen for you. And if you trespass again – do please trust me on this – I will have your knackers for maracas."

Jonathan gripped the doorframe with his fingers and the guards peeled them off, one by one. "There are other record labels," Jonathan shouted, trying to hold on. "I can only save one of you. If I leave this building, I won't come back."

"Good."

Jonathan was pulled off the door like a stone leaving a catapult and the door slammed shut. Bigg was fuming. Where do people get off, breaking into his company to pitch their demos? He puts a bin in reception for them. What more do they want? They don't honestly think he's got time to listen to them all, do they? He doesn't even have the money to pay someone else to listen to them any more.

He scooped the MP3 player off his desk and into the bin.

* * *

As Jonathan watched the display counting down to ground, he could see his unwanted minders reflected in the lift doors. Their faces were granite, craggy and weathered by age. In their smart suits, they looked like Easter Island statues up before the beak. On their lapels, they wore gold name badges that said 'Call me sir'.

Jonathan's heart was beating fast from his encounter with Bigg and his unceremonious exit. The lift fell quickly, but that wasn't why his stomach was lurching. It was his dreams dissolving, his life's work eating away at him, gnawing at his organs to get out, but with nowhere to go.

Ten years of progress had slammed to a halt. Jonathan had created the perfect song, guaranteed to make your spine tingle.

Potent enough to make you laugh, cry, or dance on the first listen. But now he needed the support of someone like Bigg to get it out there.

Hell, he didn't just need someone like Bigg. He needed Bigg: his technology, marketing machine, and money. They would complete Plato like the missing pieces of a jigsaw.

He had been so sure the demo would bowl Bigg over, he had never considered the possibility that he couldn't persuade him to listen to it. Was there another way to get it to him? Unlikely. Bigg had built a massive infrastructure to protect him and his company from the subversive influence of new music and fresh thinking.

The lift indicator showed 'G' and Jonathan got ready to leave, but the lift kept going until it reached the basement.

When the doors opened, the corridor smelt of damp concrete. It was silent, even though reception was above and the street was just outside. The walls were hewn from stone, and the wall lights glowed like candles, barely lighting the floor below. Jonathan half expected to see a skeleton nailed to the wall, as if he had entered the castle dungeon.

"Your floor," said one of the security guards.

"I need to go to reception," said Jonathan.

"No," said the other. "You don't. Get out, son."

Jonathan entered the corridor and was closely followed by the two guards. He looked over his shoulder at them, uneasy that he couldn't see them, and they ridiculed him with a cackle and shook their heads.

"Straight on," said one of the minders, pointing up the corridor with his head.

They marched on, their footsteps echoing like gunshots. Jonathan could feel the hot breath of one of the guards on the back of his neck. It smelled of Murray Mints. At the end of the corridor was a door with a fire exit bar on it. As soon as he was close enough, he'd make a dash for it.

A woman screamed her lungs out and curdled Jonathan's blood. One of the guards yelped in fright.

Jonathan broke into a sprint. He kicked the floor away underneath him, charged forwards. His shoes slid on the dusty surface but kept their grip. He could hear the guards running behind him, but didn't have the nerve to look back to see how close they were or where the scream came from. The door grew nearer and larger.

*   *   *

As a child, Bigg had always been the kid who couldn't leave sweets alone. As a teenager, he was the kid who couldn't leave records in the shop until he had exhausted his pocket money. Now, he was a man who found it hard to beat temptation. With his hand-delivered demo Jonathan was prodding Bigg's weak spot. It was like he was poking a fresh bruise. Bigg couldn't ignore it. His curiosity ate away at him. What did that demo sound like? Why would someone go to such lengths to promote a band they didn't like? What made that guy so sure Bigg would love it? And how much did he know about the Commodore?

Before long, Bigg lifted the MP3 player out of the bin, squashed the earbuds into his head and pressed play. He expected to be assaulted with the usual thrashy guitars and screaming, but it opened with orchestral chords ebbing and flowing, like the sea lapping at a beach. A clear guitar soared like a seagull above it. When the vocals came in, it sounded like a long lost out-take from one of the prog-rock giants of the '70s. But it was as if they had written it having already heard punk, grunge, hip hop, electropop, microbeats and everything else that came in the following decades.

"Marian," Bigg said into the intercom. "Get security to bring that guy back, will you?"

*   *   *

The door grew nearer and larger. Jonathan had a stitch and was out of breath, his mouth dry, but he kept running.

Then his knees glued together, his thighs clammed shut and he toppled onto the hard floor, crushing his arms beneath him. The guard who had rugby tackled him cuddled his legs long enough to make sure he wasn't going to struggle and then let him go. He took up a position between Jonathan and the door and crouched there. "You've got to change that ringtone," he said, slapping clouds of dust out of his suit trousers. "This guy damn near shat himself."

"Don't nag me – I nearly died!" said the other. He held his hand to his heart to check it was still working. "My grandson: He knows I can't change the ringtones back on this fiddly thing. He's such a little monkey. Actually, that's not fair." He clicked the phone shut. "He's an evil little git. Right, about turn!"

Jonathan leaned on his elbows and spat dust on the floor in front of him. "Where are you taking me?" Blood dripped from his mouth and soaked into the concrete. The door was only feet away but he wouldn't chance it again. If you're going to be taken down by a man twice your age, you only want to do it once a day.

"All the way to the top," said the guard. "Marian says Mr Bigg would like to see you after all."

CHAPTER 14

Dove was a pressed giant, shot and sandwiched between paper and glass. Up close, he disassembled into coloured blotches and there were tears in his paper skin, but from a distance, he looked like he was standing on top of the desk. Reflected in his feet was a desperate man hunched over a computer.

Simon hit refresh, but the page was still coming up fractured and incomplete. "Come on," he whispered urgently. His credit card was on the table, along with his debit card in case it didn't work and his diary. Any minute now, tickets for the University of Death tour would go on sale. And not long afterwards, they would inevitably sell out.

After twenty minutes trying to revive the ticket sales website, Simon's arm ached. He changed the mouse to his left hand and clicked refresh again. The screen cleared and refilled with colour. There's something coming… Here we go….

"University of Death: UK Tour"

His heart beat faster. He had to be there. He swore he saw not just each word, but each line of every letter slowly unfolding. Pictures slowly filled up the glass boxes put on screen to hold them. Another paragraph appeared: "Playing the greatest hits, and new bits. Plus graduate initiation ceremony."

It hung there. Simon dithered. He didn't know whether he should wait for it to complete, or guess it never would and hit refresh again. He waited.

Then the words came: "Sold Out."

Simon threw his mouse across the desk.

The doorbell bonged. The words 'Sold Out' burned into Simon's retinas and went misty as he stared too long and his eyes dried out. When the bell chimed again, he blinked and went to the door.

Fred was on the doorstep.

"You're late," he said. "You were supposed to be here half an hour ago."

"I got held up," said Fred, lugging her keyboard into the hall. "In every sense. Unbelievable the cost of tickets. It's thirty quid for University of Death, you know."

"You got a ticket?"

"Only just. The site crashed three times."

"Did you get *me* one then?"

Fred bit her lip and didn't say anything.

"You're the worst best friend ever," said Simon. He went through to the living room and picked up his guitar. The amp hummed when he flicked it on. He rested one foot on it, and hunched over the guitar to tune it. The guitar smelled minty, from the toothpaste he used to shine its surface.

Fred followed him in. "I forgot," she said. "I am sorry. I just—"

Simon played a devastating discord that made Fred blink. "You never think of others!" he shouted. "I reckon Angela's right about you. You hold me back."

"Who's Angela?"

"A friend."

"You never mentioned her before."

"Well, I only met her recently."

"Where?"

"Online."

"And you just connected!" said Fred. She snickered.

"We share a love for good music."

"So is she..?"

"Mind your own." He shook his head. "I still can't believe you didn't get me a ticket. I would have got you one. Without even thinking about it. Without even asking you."

"I couldn't afford two," Fred pleaded.

"I would have paid you back."

"Yeah, but my credit card would probably have bombed out. "

"We'll never know, though, will we?" Simon jammed around some harsh chords.

Fred waited until he left her a gap to be heard. "Don't worry. You'll get a ticket," she said.

"If I sell a kidney, maybe."

"You've got to be there. It's really important."

"Yes, it is."

"No, I mean: ask me why it's important."

Simon groaned. "Go on then. Why is it important that I'm there?"

"Because that's the night we give Dove our demo."

"Have you forgotten how gigs work?" said Simon. "They hire thugs to stop people like us talking to people like him. They build barriers to stop us touching him. They're all partying backstage in luxury while we're hanging around waiting for something to happen. They won't let us anywhere near Dove."

"Ah, but they will!" Fred handed Simon a print-out:

UNIVERSITY OF DEATH: ALUMNI ASSOCIATION

Join the official fan club for:
- ☺ ticket-free access to concerts and special events
- ☺ ticket sales before the official on-sale date
- ☺ exclusive fan-only mixes and downloads
- ☺ a chance to meet the band at after-show parties

We'll put a small tag inside your arm (about the size of a grain of rice), so that you can always be identified as a member and receive priority treatment. The procedure is virtually painless and is administered by a qualified nurse.

"We can join up for free at the gig," said Fred. "We get a chip in our arms and then we can meet the band."

"Like they chip sheep, you mean?"

"It's the same technology."

"And you're okay with that, are you? I don't reckon Dove would get a chip."

"It's no big deal." Fred showed him a tiny round scar on her upper arm. "I've already got one for a nightclub in Sweden for when I'm home. No need to queue, you just waltz right in." She went foraging for beer in the kitchen. "You're just scared of needles," she called.

"No I'm not." Simon was defiant, but didn't sound confident.

Fred came back with two bottles and whispered: "What if they slip? It could go in your eyes and you'd have a needle sticking out of your face! That would be gross. There would be bits of blood and eye juice squirting everywhere."

"Shut up."

"What's up? Don't you want a needle in your eye?"

"Fred," said Simon. "Nobody wants a needle in their eye. They're only planning to put it in my arm, aren't they?"

"Yeah, but they might slip," she hissed.

"Well, it doesn't matter. I'm not having one."

Fred laughed. "Okay, I'll tell Dove you said 'hello' then."

"You do that."

"I will."

"Good. So are we playing or what?"

"Course," said Fred. She brought her keyboard in and unpacked it.

"I think it's time to learn a new cover," said Simon.

"How about doing some Lady Gaga? My voice would be great for that."

"Nah," said Simon. "We need something with teeth. Something with balls."

"The Bee Gees?"

"Not literally."

"What then?" sighed Fred.

"We've been over this," said Simon. "It's time for some University of Death."

*   *   *

102

After the rehearsal was over and Fred had left, Simon went online.

angelA>	hi there
thing>	**Hi Angela. How are you tonight?**
angelA>	cool. how was ur practise
thing>	**We learned a new song** **by University of Death**
angelA>	which one
thing>	**Animal Reined**
angelA>	don't know it
thing>	**It's their first song. Very rare.**
thing>	**But widely bootlegged.**
angelA>	aren't they touring soon
thing>	**Yes.**
angelA>	u going
thing>	**No.**
angelA>	y not
thing>	**It sold out. I'm gutted.**
angelA>	sorry ot hear that.
thing>	**Fred got a ticket.**
thing>	**She never thinks of me, though.**
angelA>	she's baggage drop her
thing>	**Don't say things like that!**
angelA>	why not
thing>	**I don't feel like defending her right now.**
thing>	**Did you get a ticket?**
angelA>	i forgot
thing>	**Bummer**
angelA>	hav u seen uod before
thing>	**Never. Last tour I couldn't afford it.**
thing>	**I cant believe they're playing in london** **and I wont be there**
thing>	**I'll probably be sat in front of the telly** **just a few miles away**
angelA>	maybe u can get a tout ticket
thing>	**Yeah, me and everyone else.**

angelA>	this might cheer u up. a new song you'll like
thing>	**what is it?**
angelA>	it's by Tigernoize. Coming over now.
thing>	**Thanks.**
angelA>	u should get the album 2
angelA>	ill send you my discount token
angelA>	ive spent too much on music already this month ;-)
thing>	**I'll let you know what I think of it.**
angelA>	wanna play a guessing game?
thing>	**Okay**
angelA>	like mr and mrs
thing>	**Okay**
angelA>	favourite foods
thing>	**Tricky**
angelA>	i guess yours is curry
thing>	**Ha! That's a bit of an obvious guess isnt it?**
angelA>	is it curry
thing>	**No**
angelA>	chinese
thing>	**Yes. You know me too well.**
angelA>	kewl I am the kween of guessing foods
thing>	**Well done. I'll guess yours now then.**
angelA>	go on
thing>	**ice cream?**
angelA>	
thing>	**I said 'ice cream'?**
angelA>	sorry got distracted
angelA>	no
thing>	**pizza?**
angelA>	brb
thing>	**What are you doing?**
angelA>	
angelA>	where were we
thing>	**pizza**
angelA>	nah all those bits clog your teeth
thing>	**chocolate?**
angelA>	nope

thing>	I give up then
angelA>	sure
thing>	Yes
angelA>	its Ice Cream
thing>	I said that!
angelA>	did u
thing>	Yes! Scroll up!
thing>	Pay attention!
angelA>	sorry
thing>	Sometimes you're as bad as Fred.
angelA>	dont say that
thing>	She never listens properly either.
angelA>	dont say that
thing>	Okay, not quite then.
thing>	Can I ask you a question?
angelA>	o k
thing>	When we first chatted you didn't answer me when I asked if you had a boyfriend.
thing>	Did you?
angelA>	no
thing>	No you don't, or no you didn't?
angelA>	yes ;-)
angelA>	gotta go. friends here.
thing>	I could come over? Join the party?
angelA>	maybe another time.
thing>	Sure. Have fun then.
angelA>	bye xx
thing>	Bye.
thing>	
thing>	xx

<angelA has disconnected>

CHAPTER 15

"You can go through," said Marian.

Jonathan straightened his tie and let himself into Bigg's office, followed by the guards.

"Check him for wires," said Bigg. One of the guards patted Jonathan down and then gave him the all clear. "Leave us," Bigg ordered them.

He indicated the chair and Jonathan sat down in it again.

"Are you a journalist?" said Bigg. "Is this one of those flies-in-the-shit documentaries?"

"No. This is business."

"Why did you bring me this magazine?"

"Page 27. Tunemaker," said Jonathan. "A tiny little program that creates random melodies, published well over twenty years ago. It's a curiosity really, a simple demonstration of computer creativity. Fun for about five minutes. Which was probably a bit galling for most people after taking a weekend to type it in."

Bigg lit a cigar and turned slowly to page 27, buying time to think before answering. "Who said I've got any interest in it?"

"Well, you're questioning the evidence rather than the premise, which is usually a good start," said Jonathan. "I know you own the rights. So I got around to wondering why. Then it hit me: If you run it for a few minutes, it's a laugh. But if you ran it for twenty years, say, it could become a whole business. All you'd have to do is copyright the sequences it created."

"The sequences we created using it," corrected Bigg. He had

jumped in before realising that he was admitting everything that Jonathan was saying, but pressed on anyway. "There is a legal difference."

"I bet it's a key negotiating chip. Any time you want to acquire a label or renegotiate an artist's contract, you show you already own copyright on significant parts of their music. I bet the mere threat of legal action was enough to get some of the small timers to cave in."

"Watch it! I never threatened anyone," said Bigg.

Jonathan laughed nervously and his voice wobbled as he spoke. "You *did* say you'd chuck *me* out of a tenth floor window."

"That was self-defence," said Bigg, as he waved his cigar around dismissively. "The label talks were strictly business."

"Of course, it would have crumbled in court if anyone had challenged you. But nobody did, did they? So you've been generating all these melodies, copyrighting them and feeding them into BiggSong."

Bigg tossed the magazine in the bin. "If any of this were true, which I'm not saying it is, what's it to you?"

"You've come a long way in industrialising creativity here."

"Thank you very much." Bigg leaned back in his chair and put his hands behind his head. "My masterstroke was to separate fame from creativity, of course. Protect the real talent from the public eye. I shudder to think about the alternative."

"What's that?"

"Bands who end up taking themselves too seriously. It starts with an acoustic album, or a double CD. If you ignore the warning signs, they're writing pseudo-classical music and ham-fisted operas within five years. Worse still, they could confuse fame with intellect and enter politics. Even The Who has gone all serious. Every time Marian gives me a clipping now, they're banging on about AIDS in Africa, obesity or avian flu. What happened to Pinball Wizard and Boris the Spider?"

"It's not the same Who," said Jonathan.

"I hear you. Johnnie Entwhistle's irreplaceable."

"No, I mean Marian's getting mixed up with the W.H.O., the World Health Organisation."

"The point stands: fame and talent – not a good mix. Leave the celebs to hump each other in On Heat magazine, and give the real talent the tools it needs to make hit music."

"The thing is you're still using puppets like Icicle Star to try to attract the whole market's attention, in the hope some will buy the music," said Jonathan.

"We have to fling artists at the wall to see if one of them sticks," said Bigg.

"The game's changing, though. Your sales might be plummeting, but people haven't given up on music. They've just given up on you. Real music fans buy more and more music directly from bands online, free from your interference."

"Pah! It can't be as good as ours."

"The recording quality is lower. But nobody cares. It's original, free-thinking. Energetic. Sincere. Everything your output hasn't been for years. And all your attempts to reach the real music listeners have failed. Even when you buy in independent labels, you end up closing them because you can't afford to run them with your overheads and their low sales. A couple of compilations of the headline acts, and you're done."

"What's any of this to you?" said Bigg.

"Did you play the demo?"

"Might have done."

"Did you like it?"

"Might have done." It was clear from Bigg's voice though that he had loved it and he was just teasing Jonathan. "Couldn't market it, obviously. Too old-fashioned."

"Ah! But here's the rub: it didn't cost me anything to make. I made that track just for you. If I sell one copy to you, I'm quids in," said Jonathan.

"Well, you're one quid in."

"That's why I'm here. Together we can make it scale. I've created a program called Plato that uses someone's music collection to invent virtual bands and make new music just for them."

"Not bloody mash-ups," said Bigg. "Even I make time to listen to songs after one another."

"It's not combining tracks, it's creating completely new songs. It uses information about what typifies an artist, and what defines a particular track. It's like analysing musical DNA. My program has in-built synthesiser and sequencing software which it uses to make music consistent with that DNA. It's even got a number of voice synthesisers so it can simulate human vocals. You just feed it a seed melody, and it's away."

"So where do I fit in?" said Bigg.

"I came here looking for the last three parts of the puzzle: a database of copyright-cleared seed melodies, a way to generate lyrics automatically, and a way to promote the music."

"Go on," said Bigg.

"Well, we can't afford to have these virtual bands getting sued. It would blow the concept apart." Bigg noticed that Jonathan had shifted from 'I' to 'we' but he let it go. "During testing, I've been playing the seed melodies by hand. The other day I used a random melody generator and it came up with something pretty close to an early Stones riff," said Jonathan. "If all the melodies it drew upon were already copyright cleared, there would be no problem. By using your Tunemaker database, the system can be legally bullet-proof."

"What about the lyrics?"

"My plan there is to lift random phrases from blogs and feed them through BiggSong's lyrics filter."

"Won't that infringe copyright?"

"Not if we slice the phrases small enough, gather them from different sources and make sure they rhyme. They will at least be near impossible to trace."

"Surely the lyrics will be drivel?"

"That's why they'll fit in with all the others. Nobody would notice if we put raw chat room posts in there, but having your filter will make the words scan better. The easiest markets to start with will be heavy metal and new age."

"I don't see the link."

"In metal, it's all hollering and growling, so it doesn't matter what the words are supposed to be. You can't hear them. In new age, Enya and Sigur Ros have already invented their own languages to protect their lyrics from scrutiny. We could easily do that."

"How do we sell this music, then?"

"Online. We build a community website and Plato posts all these fictional bands up there, together with their music. All the bands are available to everyone, but realistically each one will only appeal to one or two people. Nobody knows they're the only listener for their band."

"Why not make separate band websites?"

"It's a convenient get-out for why the pages look alike and why there's no decent photography. It also makes it look like these are small bands starting out. My research suggests real music fans are more willing to buy from independent bands than major labels."

"You've worked out how to name the bands, I take it?"

"I'm working on that," said Jonathan. "We can't just use a word list. We need an inexhaustible source of credible names. The biggest risk is that someone spots the pattern."

"No problemo!" said Bigg. "If they do, we could say all these bands are part of a new movement. The music press will cream their cakes if we give them a new movement."

Jonathan coughed politely. "I think the phrase is 'cream their keks'."

"Don't be revolting."

"Right, sorry." Jonathan looked confused. "The biggest challenge is to get permission to analyse the music collection."

"Easy," said Bigg. "Nobody reads the licence agreement, so we could bundle it with virtually any software."

"You've got to keep this secret, though," said Jonathan. "The customers we're targeting value authenticity. They won't buy computer-generated music and they'll run a mile from major label crap."

"Ahem."

"Oh come off it. I've seen your record collection," said Jonathan. "I know you don't eat your own dog food. You hate your label's releases as much as they do."

Bigg shook his head. "It used to be... different."

"Do you know much about philosophy?" Jonathan stood up

111

and walked behind his chair and gripped the back of it. "How do you know this is a chair?"

Bigg didn't know how to start answering that question. "Well, it just is. Isn't it?"

"But it looks nothing like your chair, and you know that's a chair too. This philosopher called Plato reckoned that chairs were all variations of a perfect chair form in your imagination."

Bigg did a double take. "Well aren't you a suppository of useless information!"

"I think you mean repository." Jonathan gave a light chuckle.

Bigg shook his head. "Nope."

Jonathan sat down and leaned towards Bigg. "Everyone's got an idea in their head of the perfect song too. All the music we listen to is a clue towards what it might sound like. Using my software, we can bring people closer to their own musical heaven. We can hatch perfectly tailored earworms: songs they can't shake from their heads."

"Won't they just buy one song and play it over, then?"

"No," said Jonathan. "The style of music is near-perfect, but they'll want to keep collecting more music in that style."

"Sounds too good to be true."

"We do still need to find a way to get people to visit the band webpages we've made for them."

"That's tricky," said Bigg. "Did you hear the outcry about the copy protection software we installed on our customers' PCs? Honestly, you'd think we had installed cameras in their toilets. We'll be in sticky enough water if anyone finds out about the music collection analysis software, so we can't drive people to the site using pop-ups on the machine. We'll need to influence them to visit the band's website from outside the computer. Perhaps I should introduce you to our viral marketing team."

Bigg blew smoke at the ceiling, stubbed out his cigar in his zen garden and folded his arms. "You've brought me some good ideas," he said. "For which I am truly grateful. The only thing I don't understand is what stops me nicking your ideas and going it alone."

Jonathan looked wounded. "Nothing," he said. "Nothing at

all."

Bigg smiled broadly.

"But it took me ten years to develop Plato," continued Jonathan. "Maybe you could do it in five with your resources. Meanwhile, I'll work with another company. And we'll fucking bury you."

Bigg unfolded his arms and laughed. "I think we can work together."

"I want thirty percent of your company."

"Piss off," snarled Bigg.

"You can give me thirty percent of a booming business, or keep one hundred percent of a doomed one. I'm serious."

"So am I," said Bigg. "I didn't get where I am by handing out huge slices of my company to everyone who brings me a demo."

"This is different."

"Not to me," said Bigg. "This is not a musical instrument business or a songwriting nursery. I pay for results, and results means sales. You'll be on a royalty like everyone else. I'll give you a 50% co-author credit on all the tracks Plato makes. I'll put you on a basic too, so you can afford to give this your full attention."

"Can I think about this?"

"Flip a coin, phone a friend, please yourself. But you won't get better terms elsewhere."

"Okay, I'll do it."

Bigg laughed gently at the speed with which Jonathan had answered and Jonathan looked sheepish. "How soon can we launch?"

"Six months and then we'll be ready to pilot it," said Jonathan. "Give or take."

"Well, is it give, or is it take?"

"It'll be ready in six months."

"Good. We have a deal." Bigg offered his hand almost flat, like he was going to pat a dog. Jonathan stood up and placed his hand under Bigg's and they shook across the desk.

"One last thing," said Jonathan. "Your IT here is practically antique. Why didn't you ever ditch the Commodore?"

"No need," said Bigg. "It does a good enough job. It never gets a virus. Replacements are a fiver online. Most importantly, I can use it. I was hunched over a keyboard for two days typing in all the obscure codes for Tunemaker, only to spend the following weekend debugging the sodding thing. But that's nothing compared to the time it would take to recreate it today. I'd need a team of fifty programmers and consultants. Hardly discreet."

"Isn't it hard to maintain, though?"

"Not really. Machines were built to last in the '80s. We spent a fortune hooking the Commodore up to industrial tape storage systems and they're obsolete now too. But when the tape cabinets stick, we give them a kick and that usually does it. Today's computers are as fragile as a meringue. Our songwriters seem to break monitors more often than they break wind."

Jonathan headed for the door. "I'll get started in the Commodore room. Fancy a celebratory game of Beach Head?"

"I don't think so," said Bigg. "We both have work to do."

CHAPTER 16

The moment the bell rang, Simon downed cabbages and started to run. From the top of the hill he could see the high street record shop. He ran so fast that he was worried his legs might slip out from underneath him. But he only had minutes to spare.

At the bottom, he slowed to a jog. The record shop was on the other side of the road, and he could see a man with a big ring of keys stood in the doorway, chatting to a colleague.

It was the rush hour. A wall of buses, cars and bikes stood between Simon and the shop. He baked in the August sun and waited for a gap in the traffic that never came. When he saw the shop door closing, he stepped out into the road without thinking. A car screeched to a halt and blasted its horn and Simon felt his jacket whipped by the wind as a motorbike swerved just inches behind him. He held his palm up to oncoming cars as he hurried across the road, as if it would stop them hurting him. A driver shouted abuse at him, but he ignored it.

When he got to the shop, he was out of breath.

"Too late, dude," said the man on the door. He had five gold stars on his plastic 'manager' badge to match the pimples on his face.

"Please!" said Simon. "I know what I want!"

"Oh yeah?" The manager jiggled the keys.

His colleague had a big ginger beard and wore a badge that said 'I forgot my badge today, so you can call me Daisy.'

"The new University of Death greatest hits! It's out today!"

There was a display of them just inside the door. In the past, Simon would have tried to get the cardboard point of sale materials too, but today he'd settle for a copy of the album. "Look! I can see it there. You've got stacks of them."

Daisy sniggered. "Dude, you nearly got run over for that? Are there cybermen chasing you?"

Simon instinctively looked behind him. "No," he said.

"Yeah, where's the Tardis, dude?" said the manager.

"Sorry?" said Simon, confused.

"You do know what year you're in, right?" asked Daisy.

Simon nodded.

"But you still want a University of Death album?" said the manager.

Simon nodded again.

"Let me take you under my wing," said Daisy. "We'll help you find something more contemporary. With our love and support, you won't have to live in the 1980s any more."

"Dove's done loads of stuff since then!" said Simon.

"He should try releasing some of it!" said Daisy.

"He did!"

"I didn't see anything," said the manager. "Did you?"

"Nope," said Daisy. "Not a sausage."

"Please!" pleaded Simon. "Since I got into his stuff, I've got every other album with a receipt for its day of issue."

Daisy looked alarmed. "Better let him in, boss," he said. "He's clearly insane and might be dangerous."

"Okay," said the manager. "Make it quick."

* * *

After he left the shop with the album, Simon checked the receipt was clearly printed and slipped it inside the CD inlay. "It's got really good sleeve notes," he insisted, during one of his daily chats with Angela. But he knew it was a waste of money. There was nothing new on the album for him, so he didn't even get around to playing it. Simon increasingly spent his time listening to the music that Angela sent him.

116

For six months, Jonathan went nocturnal. He was most productive at night, in that sweet spot after the buses had stopped and before the birds had started to sing. When he wasn't sat at his computer, he would pace the corridor, studying the source code that papered its walls. Sometimes he'd wobble on a pile of phone books to get a better look at the variable declarations near the ceiling. Other times, he'd sit on the floor and roll his eyes up and down the lines of code, grazing on a TV dinner. When inspiration struck, he would skip to the computer, taking the stairs two at a time. For days on end, that sprint up the stairs was the only exercise he got.

While Jonathan devoted himself to integrating Plato with Bigg's empire, the world – and the music industry – carried on as normal, outside his window.

J-Rok, it turned out, was just another spot on the dice. Bigg Records played Icicle Star off against all its other acts in the media. Icicle Star lost. Like the house at a casino, the record company always wins. The kids moved on from Icicle Star to Bigg's new band Fluff, who have now made it a quarter of the way through their expected one year career.

After only two months, the songwriter Jane McGriffen parted company with Bigg Records through what the PR department might have called 'creative differences'. She endured a strained relationship with Clef Richard, which came to a head when she kept trying to minimise him to the foot of the screen and he kept coming back again. The final straw was when he winked and said: 'It's so funny, we don't talk any more'. There are now four broken monitors stacked in the corner of the fifth floor office.

The Christmas number one was 'Mary had a little lamb' by Thomas Edison. The dance remix was a surprising club hit. Jake and the marketing team put on a nightclub tour, fronted by an Edison impersonator. The audience would wave lightbulb-shaped torches in the air, while 'Edison' tottered about the stage and recited the rhyme into his patented phonograph. Nobody was quite sure who was taking the mickey out of whom, but Jake didn't much care. He just counted the money.

The demo CD that Rockard delivered to Bigg Records is rubbish. It will take over one hundred years to decompose. Nobody will ever listen to that copy.

CHAPTER 17

Jonathan stared into his monitor. Programming manuals were stacked waist-high around him, balanced precariously with the pens used as bookmarks making the piles unsteady. His monitor wore a mane of post-it notes, moulting ideas onto the desk. Notes infested every blank space. Even the front of his tax return had hexadecimal codes scrawled across it.

He pushed a button and the data flowed like lava. Great streams of seed melodies flooded from Bigg's archaic hardware to his software. The screen filled with note names. It wasn't much to look at, but it meant the hardest work was done. Everything else would be easy.

A replacement sound synthesiser or sequencer would probably fix the glitch in how it was sounding. The lyrics were working fine already. Yes, they were drivel but, yes, they blended right in with every other song on the radio. He had been quite charmed by the first verse he'd generated:

> When are you coming round to tea?
> We must discuss the news.
> I completed the game quite easily
> The room had a beautiful view.

Time permitting, Jonathan wanted to make the lyrics even smarter. Instead of lifting random phrases from the web, Plato could watch what customers read about online and use that to farm new lyrics. With the BiggSong lyrics editor filing the rough edges off, the output was indistinguishable from Bigg's current chart-toppers.

One problem remained: how to name the bands. Jonathan needed an inexhaustible and untraceable word list. The slightest hint of automation would blow the whole project wide open.

The dictionary was out. Even if you focused on nouns, you ended up with bands called things like Desk and Sofa. They sounded better with 'the' in front of them, but they weren't anybody's idea of rock rebellion. Besides, the pattern was too obvious.

He had tried taking random keywords entered on search engines, but by the time he'd eliminated obscenities and existing band names there wasn't much to choose from.

He'd tinkered with trademarks. That seemed like a great idea at first, because they're words someone else has already decided are cool. But the owners are duty bound to stamp on anyone else using them. Besides, you can't name a band after a tyre, hose clipping or toilet ballcock.

To cover his tracks, Jonathan tried mixing up different word lists, throwing in the names of US towns with small populations. That helped conceal where the names came from but did nothing for quality control. He needed a way to create a name that fans would wear on a t-shirt: a name that they could believe a band had chosen to represent itself and its art. A name they could follow with pride.

Jonathan got up from his computer, stretched and then went to the kitchen to make hot chocolate. He filled a cup with milk and set it to microwave for 67 seconds. He had worked out that's how long it took for the milk to be hot enough, and the handle to face the front for easy access when the turntable stopped.

Woo-hoo. Woo-hoo. Jonathan's computer called out to him from his office as it downloaded his emails. He couldn't ignore it, even though he knew they were probably junk. He went back to the PC in the vain hope that one of his friends had written to him.

It was all spam. Lavonia Celestine knew how to make his pen1s longer. Carrie Echols had mistakenly emailed him – instead of her bestest buddy – recommending a place to get medz. Missed O Eraser could secure a mortgage for him, and Macmillan V Cheeseburger and Matts P Salvation were racing to offer online marketing services. Jonathan watched as mail after mail arrived from ever more ludicrous senders: Describing T Highfalutin, Mourners M Beatles, Regret Ananias, Humored Panic. 'Tresha, Giffard, Ville' and 'Maynard & Powers' sounded like Motown songwriting partnerships, but it turned out they were flogging the same 'ch33p medz / pl3453 yr l4dy' as countless other scum. If they put as much effort into creating a decent business, Jonathan thought, as they did into making up silly names, they would be rolling in it.

A light bulb went on above Jonathan's head with a ping. His milk was ready and the lights were on a timer to deter burglars. At the same time, he had a great idea.

A quick double click on the spam folder showed what looked like a roll call of indie talent: Faysal Mauney, Julia, Incorporated K Snowflake, Teagan Threatt, Tang V Urbanity. These were so great as band names, you could even imagine what they would sound like. And if you were wrong, well, that's just part of the band's subversive nature.

Woo-hoo! Woo-hoo! And they kept coming.

All he had to do was plug his band generator into his spam filter. No matter how big the operation grew, Jonathan was confident there was enough email advertising in the world to power it. The internet was full of spam. It was about time some of it paid its way.

CHAPTER 18

thing>	**Hi**
angelA>	hey thing
thing>	**How's tricks?**
angelA>	good. wat u listening to?
thing>	**University of Death best of. Gearing up for tomorrow's gig.**
angelA>	do u have a ticket
thing>	**Not yet.**
angelA>	fingers crossed 4u
angelA>	are u taking ear plugs with u
thing>	**No. Why would I do that?**
angelA>	protect ur hearing
thing>	**It'll be fine**
angelA>	it gets pretty loud though
thing>	**Yeah, that's one reason we're going.**
angelA>	if ur ears are whistling the next day
angelA>	its because theyr damaged
thing>	**They always get better**
angelA>	past performance is no indicator of future performance
thing>	**what's your interest in this?**
angelA>	id hate for u not to be able to hear my voice when we meet
thing>	**I don't think that will be our biggest problem**
angelA>	wat will be our biggest problem

thing>	**Getting you to meet me in the first place**
angelA>	heres a link where u can buy ear plugs
angelA>	special ones for gigs
thing>	**Thanks**
angelA>	im only looking after u
thing>	**Thanks. You are my Guardian AngelA.**
angelA>	yep
thing>	**What are you listening to?**
angelA>	cant say
thing>	**Why?**
angelA>	you'll laugh
thing>	**No I won't. Go on, Angela… you can tell me.**
angelA>	the new boymad single
thing>	**ROFLMAO**
angelA>	u said u wouldnt laugh!
thing>	**But it's crap! Why are you listening to it?**
angelA>	y not
angelA>	killer bassline. can't shake the chorus from my head.
angelA>	u should listen to it again
thing>	**Yeah, if I ever lose every other song I own.**
angelA>	if you didn't know who it was, you'd love it.
angelA>	admit it. at least listen to it again.
thing>	**Go on then. Can you send me a copy?**
angelA>	ive only got a trial version.
angelA>	link coming over
angelA>	it's good for a few days
angelA>	then you'll have to buy it!!!
thing>	**Got it**
angelA>	bet u do buy it too!!1
thing>	**We'll see**
angelA>	if u do buy it, u have to tell me. no secrets!
thing>	**You tell me a secret now then**
angelA>	im not wearing any underwear
thing>	**It's getting hot in here**
angelA>	ive just had a shower. im naked
thing>	***speechless***

angelA>	sorry. shouldnt have said that
thing>	**I bet you flirt with all your online friends**
angelA>	i only type lines for you
thing>	**Why don't you send me a photo**
angelA>	naked?!
thing>	**If you like**
thing>	**Sorry.**
thing>	**I meant I still don't know what you look like.**
angelA>	do u need to know?
thing>	**We've been chatting for months now.**
thing>	**It's weird for me knowing you so well.**
thing>	**And never having met you.**
angelA>	welcome to life 2.0
thing>	**Meet me tomorrow. You can meet Fred too.**
angelA>	y
thing>	**:-) We'll have a great time!**
thing>	**Here's my photo so you can recognise me**
thing>	**The Garage. 7pm**
thing>	**We can try to get into the UoD gig.**
thing>	**If not, we can go for a drink**
angelA>	maybe. its hard 4 me
thing>	**You promised**
angelA>	did i
thing>	**Yes. No buts. See you there.**

<angelA has disconnected>

*   *   *

The second hand eclipsed the minute hand and rolled on towards twelve. The minute hand flicked on to 37, and Simon let his sleeve roll back over his watch and put his hands in his pockets. She wasn't coming. He'd given her half an hour's grace, five minutes to get lost and found again and two final minutes 'just because'. But Angela wasn't here.

Leaning against the wall outside The Garage, Simon watched the road leading from Highbury & Islington station, looking out for anyone who might be Angela. He'd smile hopefully at attractive women as they walked down the line looking for their friends. Some looked straight through him. Others returned his smile with a sour expression. As they joined the queue in the middle, their friends would loudly take possession of them to show they had been queuing on their behalf.

Eventually Fred crossed the road and worked her way down the line. She was wearing a pastel blue t-shirt that said 'Fox's glacier minx' in tiny white letters. With a wink, she apologised to the men behind Simon as she joined him.

"You're late," said Simon.

"Where's thingy?" said Fred. "Cybergirl."

"Oh, Angela, you mean?" Simon put on a tone that sounded as if he had clean forgotten about her until Fred had brought her up. "Oh, she called. She can't make it after all."

"Oh, so she *can* talk, can she?"

"Well, I mean emailed really. Did you bring the demo?"

"Sure," said Fred. She put her hand in her pocket to check it was still there.

A tout was loitering territorially around a lamp-post nearby. "Buyansellanytickets," he bleated. It was like a mating call.

"Have you got yours yet?" said Fred.

"No."

"Go on then. I'll keep our place." She handed him a twenty pound note. "For if you need it. It's all I've got."

Simon smiled his thanks and folded it with his three twenties in his trouser pocket. As he approached the tout, he tried to make it look casual. The tout watched him walk in a straight line from near the front of the queue to the lamppost. "Hi," Simon said. The tout raised his eyebrows in greeting. "How much, then?" Simon asked.

"Buyin' or sellin'?"

"Buying."

"'Undred."

"Sorry," said Simon. "I meant how much do they cost, not how many have you got."

The tout snorted and walked away, but not so far that Simon couldn't follow him.

126

"They're only £30 normally," Simon whined.

"Plus bookin' fee."

"Well, £60 then."

"Look," said the tout. "The support's some crappy post-modern covers band. The headline's University of Death. It's happening in there any time now. The ticket's an 'undred quid. Do you want one or not?"

"How about £80?" said Simon.

The tout shook his head. Simon rummaged in his pockets and counted his change. "£87.37? And a few polos?"

The tout shooed him away like a bothersome dog and Simon returned to the queue.

"Give it a few minutes," said Fred. "They're not exactly fighting off punters."

A few cheers went up as the doors opened and the people at the front entered. "You going in then?" said Simon.

"I'd better make sure Dove gets our demo," said Fred. "I'll try to get us a place down the front."

"Cheers, Fred," said Simon. "See you in a bit." He didn't sound hopeful.

He leaned with one foot against the wall and let the queue surge past until he felt like he was clogging it up. Then he abandoned it altogether and stood on the pavement, watching the fans file past. After about fifteen minutes, there was nobody left.

The security staff haunted the doors. The tout was swearing into the mobile phone cradled on his shoulder and counting a bundle of bank notes and tickets. The DJ inside made a muffled thumping sound through the walls.

Simon stood alone and stared into a poster showing University of Death on stage. He imagined himself as one of the tiny faces at Dove's feet. Tonight, Dove would be on the other side of that poster, in the flesh, bringing his music to life. And it seemed this was as close as Simon would get.

A limousine rolled past the venue and Simon's intense stare was reflected back at him in the tinted windows. The band had arrived.

A woman bounded up to Simon, her eyes twinkled and her

cascading dark hair bounced. Her voice sounded like chocolate: "Excuse me?"

"Angela!"

"Er, no," she said. "Do you know where the underground station is?"

"Over there." Simon pointed. "I can show you if you like. I'll be going myself in a few minutes."

"I'll be alright, thanks." She left Simon alone on the street again.

*　*　*

Backstage, the walls were painted black and covered with a patchwork of stickers. Bands had left their labels behind, like a flag on a mountain top, proof they had scaled the lofty heights of the nearby stage. Some had become the stars they had all dreamed of being. For most, a peeling sticker on a wall they would never see again was the only proof they ever existed.

Dove walked in the back door towards the dressing room, carrying a flight case. His eye was drawn to a day-glo green circle clinging to the wall near the ceiling. In the middle was a skull wearing a mortarboard. Twenty five years it had been there, hanging on, while all those bands around it had come and gone.

"Maaan!" said Creak, carrying a drum case and an open beer bottle through the backstage door. "I remember that! You broke your finger jumping to slap that on the wall. Drunk as a punk, you were."

Dove smiled sadly. "My body is a temple now."

Creak took a swig. "Man, that was a long time ago."

"Our first gig," said Dove. "Life comes full circle. Everything needs closure."

"Right," said Creak. He was lazy. Dove knew Creak often pretended to understand him instead of making the effort to actually understand. He usually found out what Dove meant sooner or later, though. Creak peeked through the backstage door to size up the audience. "Good crowd," he said. "Can't wait to play tonight."

"We don't just play," said Dove. "We perform."

* * *

Simon turned away from the venue and waited for a gap in the traffic so he could cross the road and head home.

"Oi!" the tout called. "You still wanna ticket?"

Simon nodded.

"Tell ya what," said the tout. "I'll do ya one for eighty quid then. Can't say fairer than that."

"Go on then."

Simon handed over four twenties. The tout unpeeled a ticket from a wad and handed it over. Simon held it up to the light, as if an absent-minded forger might have mistakenly had the words 'RIP-OFF' put into the watermark.

"Want another? As a souvenir? I can do you the second one for twenty quid if you like."

Simon didn't even reply. He half-jogged the few steps to the venue and disappeared inside.

* * *

"You made it!" said Fred. "Quick, there's no queue for the fan club!"

Simon's stomach was a bag of snakes. They writhed not just with anticipation at the show, but with fear at the ordeal he would face first. Just inside the venue's entrance, the cloakroom had been converted into the fan club surgery. Fred pulled back the curtain and peered inside.

"You joining?" said a girl in an Iron Maiden t-shirt. It had a picture of somebody's head falling apart on it. The girl's skin was paper white and her eyebrows, nose and chin were pierced with silver bobbles. As she caught the light from the UV lamp, her skin turned purple. She looked like she had fallen head-first into a child's birthday cake.

"Sure am," Fred said, disappearing behind the curtain. Simon followed her in.

"No spectators," said the girl.

"I'm joining up," said Simon.

"Your Mum'll be livid," sneered the girl.

"I knew you'd join!" said Fred. "We can give Dove the demo together." She sat down and rolled up the sleeve of her t-shirt.

"Name?" said Birthday Cake Girl.

"Fred Vasternorrlands."

"Be serious."

"That's my name. Fred is Swedish for peace."

"You don't look Swedish," said the girl.

Fred nodded at the sign on the wall that said the tag would be administered by a qualified nurse. "You don't look like a nurse," she said.

The nurse narrowed her eyes. "Just fill this form in and sign your life away."

Fred scribbled her contact details, running letters all over the lines between boxes. Underneath a block of microscopic writing, she signed her name. The nurse picked up a gun with a spike on the end and pointed it at Fred's arm. Simon looked away. As the gun discharged, it made a soft phut noise. Simon jumped at the sound.

"Don't rub it," said the nurse to Fred. "Otherwise it'll itch like a dozen mosquito bites."

"Where's the after-show party?" said Fred. She unzipped her pocket and checked the demo hadn't somehow seeped through the fabric pores of her coat. "I've got something for the band."

"Fuktifino," said the nurse. "Next."

Fred got up, and Simon walked over to the chair. "How was it?" he asked Fred.

"Like the advert said," she replied. "Virtually painless."

"Meaning, *not* painless," said Simon. He took the form from the nurse, filled it in, signed it and returned it to her.

"Arm," she said. He rolled up his sleeve and then stared into a tie-dye whirlpool on the knee of his jeans. In the corner of his eye he could see the nurse moving around and he could hear her clunking with the tools. Instruments, he thought. That's the right word. Not tools.

Phut

"Ouch!" It was a reflex reaction but it only felt like a pin prick.

"Bugger!" said the nurse.

Simon jerked his head to face her but she held his arm fast so he couldn't move away. "What's wrong?"

"Wrong tag," said the nurse. She held a reader against his arm and studied the display. It bleeped. "Oh bugger it. It'll be fine. Forget it."

"Are you sure?"

"Yeah." She didn't sound it.

Simon wasn't confident. "Is that it then?"

"Just one more thing," said the nurse. "You need to swear an oath to the band."

Simon and Fred looked at her for a moment.

"Losers!" said the nurse. "Get out of here!"

*   *   *

Simon and Fred took up a position on the railing at the front of the stage just in time to see the support band arrive.

The PA faded out and a singer, drummer, guitarist, bass player and keyboard player walked on with their arms up high like race winners. They looked like they had been pulled through a hedge trimmer backwards.

The singer took the microphone and said: "Plug in, guys." About ten people pushed their way to the front and inserted ear plugs.

"I think they're gonna be loud," said Fred. They were stood right next to two speakers powerful enough to blast sound to the back of the room.

A few noses in the front row glowed blue as people held white boxes up to their faces.

"They're using iPods," said Simon. "That's got to be the worst heckle ever. The band arrives and a bunch of people put their own music on."

"They'll never hear it," said Fred.

The singer hung his weight on the microphone stand and

wobbled it backwards and forwards. "We're Silent But Violent," he said. The drummer held his sticks high and clacked them together four times. It was the last sound Simon and Fred heard. The guitarist threw shapes all over the stage and windmilled his arm. The bass player walked his fingers up and down the fret board and stroked the strings. The keyboard player jerked his whole body in time with the drummer. The muscles on the singer's neck and forehead were taut, but for all his straining, they couldn't hear a word. They couldn't hear a single note.

"I've gone deaf," said Simon. "Oh, no I haven't. I just heard myself say that."

He looked around and there were about twenty people dancing, listening to their iPods while watching the band.

"Turn it up!" shouted Fred.

"Shhh!" said a man beside her.

"But I can't hear it!" she said.

"Duh! The clue's in the name," said a girl behind her. Fred looked around, spoiling for a fight, but couldn't see where it came from.

"It's post-modern," whispered someone else. "They're making a statement about bands that mime."

"Can't they make it louder?" said Simon.

Every few minutes the band would stop, and the people at the front would clap.

The noise of people shuffling feet, chatting and generally losing their patience grew louder as the performance wore on. Occasionally, there would be a light thud from the drums, or a scratch from a guitar string when the band slipped up. But even as they became more and more aggressive, they tried to keep the noise down. The neighbours would doubtless approve.

The singer put his arm around the guitarist, who tried to shake him off without stopping, apparently committed to playing his silent anthem. As the singer walked away, the guitarist jabbed his ribs with the head of the guitar. The singer turned back and kicked at him, but the guitarist kept jumping back out of the way. So the singer took the microphone stand and tried to spear the guitarist with it. With a quick star-jump, the guitarist leaped into the air, misjudged his direction and fell into the drum kit. The kit collapsed and the drummer rolled from his stool. He got up and hit the guitarist's head with his drum sticks, on the beat for three bars. The bass player dived at the drummer's legs and they rolled together into the keyboard. The keyboard player fell back onto his hands and screamed silently as the keyboard slipped off its stand and slammed across his shins. The band rolled around the stage, a monster made of arms, legs, leather and denim.

While they were still bundling, the stage lights dimmed and the DJ faded the records in again. A roadie came on stage and hauled the band members off the pile, one by one.

"That was a waste of time," said Fred.

"It gave me hope," said Simon.

"Yeah, hope they would finish soon."

"No," said Simon. "I mean, if they can get a gig without playing a note, we'll have no trouble."

* * *

"Does my nob look big in this?" Creak gyrated in a pair of leopard-skin underpants.

"Put it away," said Dove. He was trying to apply his make-up. Screech was tuning his guitar and BassFace was trying to get changed without touching anyone else. It wasn't easy. The room was tiny.

Malcolm the promoter popped his head around the door. "You all here?"

"We must talk," said Dove. "What were you thinking – booking that support act?"

"I knew you'd like it!" said Malcolm. "It's post-modern. Clever stuff. Shows how people go to gigs for the spectacle of aggression, without a thought for the music."

"Silence is a gift we can always share," said Dove.

After a gap, it was clear he wasn't going to say any more, so Malcolm picked up the conversation. "Should be a good show tonight. It's sold out."

"Has it?" said Dove. "Or have we?"

Creak hopped around trying to pull his trousers on, before falling on one knee. He jogged Dove and the mascara slipped and scrawled a line across his forehead.

Dove held the brush in mid-air until he was sure that he wasn't about to be jogged again. "Can't you do something, Malcolm?" he said. "This isn't a dressing room. It's a broom cupboard. There's not enough room to have Kate Moss to the after-show here."

Over the hubbub from the front of house they heard the sound of glass shattering, followed by a sarcastic round of whooping and applause.

"It's not a broom cupboard," said the promoter. "It's just... there's not much space. You did want an intimate venue. Goes with the territory."

A man barged into the dressing room. "Pass that, can you?" he said, pointing to the far corner.

"Pass what?" said Dove.

"The broom."

"Why's it here?" said Dove.

"We keep it here," said the man. Creak pulled his trousers off his ankles, collected the broom and passed it to Dove. Dove passed it to Malcolm but held his grip on it for a moment to make his point, forcing Malcolm to hold it with him. When Dove released the handle, Malcolm passed the broom out of the door.

"We need space to prepare," said Dove, as he deleted the line on his forehead with a cotton bud. "Our fans deserve to see us at our best."

"Well, I can't build an extension now, can I?" said the promoter, walking off. "Keep your pecker up." Creak tightened a dressing gown around his waist.

*   *   *

The world went dark.

Simon and Fred gripped the safety barrier. Before them, the LEDs on the instruments twinkled like bloodshot tigers' eyes, winking from the depths of the jungle. A man in black hid in the shadows and used a gun to lay down a carpet of smoke that covered the stage and rolled off the front. It smelt like a cocktail of candy floss and burning plastic. Simon tried to shake it away from his face without unpeeling his hands from the barrier. The security guard at the side of the stage put on a pollution mask and then surveyed the crowd with his hands behind his back.

A spotlight flicked on, hurling a shadow to the back of the stage. When his eyes adjusted, Simon could see the beam picking out a cloaked man wearing a skull mask. He seemed to beam down from nowhere. He strode across the stage, each step sunk into a cloud and accompanied by a thunderclap of applause. In front of Simon, he spun to face the crowd. "I am the Master," he announced. His voice was deep and echoed like it came from the bubbling pits of Hades.

Fans around the room let out their excitement in short whoops, like bursts of steam.

"Creak McCoffin, drums," he droned. A cheer went up on hearing the name, which intensified as another cloaked skeleton entered from the right. He walked across the stage, claimed a scroll from The Master, unrolled it and taped it to the floor next to the drum kit. He stood behind the drums and lifted a stick high before bringing it down with a crack like an avalanche. After a long pause with his stick in the air, he struck again.

"BassFace Mortis, bass guitar," the Master droned. Another cheer, growing louder as another graduating skeleton walked across the stage. He claimed his scroll with a delicate nod, bowed his head to the audience and took up his guitar. BassFace tore the ribbon off the scroll and taped the page to his monitor speaker. Creak beat his drum and BassFace followed it with a single low note. It was as rich and fat as a slice of chocolate gateau. After a gap, they played again: crack; wooooom.

"Screech, electric guitar," said The Master. Screech swept his cloak around his masked face and studied the audience over his arm, before dashing to claim his scroll. He turned to the back of the stage to pick up his instrument. When he spun around to face the crowd, the skull-shaped scratch plate fired a thick beam of light to the back of the room. He doffed his mortarboard to the fans, then added a shrieking chord to the mix, stamping on a foot

135

pedal to make it wow. Crack; wooooom; wiaow.

The crowd filled the gap at the end of each bar with shouts and claps that summed to white noise as it continued: Crack; wooooom; wiaow. The bass pulsed. The guitar bled from bar to bar. Between the cracks, Creak added the odd thump and splash. The embryo of a song evolved.

"Graduating with honours," said The Master. He let it hang in the air and the audience got louder and louder. "Dove," he finally announced. After about thirty seconds and as the cheers sounded like they were peaking, Dove entered from the right, dressed like his band mates, and ran across the stage. At the middle, he stood and faced the audience with arms outstretched. He skipped over to The Master, took his scroll and microphone and then returned to the centre.

Behind him, the band was working itself up into a fury. In front of him, the audience moved like the tides in the sea, rubbing against each other and crashing on the safety barrier at the front. Their heads – the only part of them they had any control over – thrashed around. Arms waved helplessly in the air.

Dove's first words were inaudible over the crowd. He sang:

> You treat me like an animal reined
> Through your delight, your twisted brain
> Reveals the joy you find in pain
> I'll never bark your name again

With that, he threw his mortarboard into the audience, ripped off his mask and revealed his real face, painted red and green. His eyes stood out like china marbles set into plasticine.

> It's time to bite the hand that feeds
> Pour alcohol and watch it bleed
> I'm shaking off my shackles and chains
> I refuse to be an animal reined

For the last two words, he pointed his microphone at the crowd. As they shouted the song title back at him, he stumbled backwards as if blown by a gale. For a song that only had a legitimate release of fifty copies, it was impressive. His students had done their homework.

While the band played the bridge behind him, Dove prowled the stage and looked into the audience. Faces were twisted and screamed along, as if the song was written from their own private torment. Dove's mortarboard was being passed around, from head to head. People ebbed and flowed, and held each other up as they shuffled from right to left as one. Even as faces and bodies crushed together, all eyes were on Dove and they were full of love.

* * *

In time with the throbbing music, the floor tickled Simon's feet through his shoes.

As somebody piled over the barrier in front of him, Simon turned his head away to avoid being kicked in the eye. He held his breath as someone's sweaty armpit was squashed against his face. For a few precious seconds, Simon had held a bit of Dove's shredded mortarboard, but he had thrown it behind him as others bundled at it. The art of enjoying gigs was all self-defence.

He had lost sight of Fred shortly after the band had come on. The crowd had swept them in opposite directions, and Simon was now being pushed around about four rows from the safety barrier. He tried to defend his place, but was edged further back with every song. With nothing to hold on to, all he could do was go with the flow and try to seep into any gaps that opened in front of him.

Simon's arms were pressed too tight to his body to be able to clap. He shouted loud enough to hear himself, ripping his voice to ribbons.

The band was incredible. The drums sounded as clear as a vase thrown on a stone floor. Dove's voice was more powerful but more human than on the records. Simon drank it in: he studied the chords sliding up and down the neck of Screech's guitar; he caught Creak's eye as the drummer briefly lifted his mask to rub his face with a towel; he laughed as BassFace thrust his crotch into the back of his guitar to emphasise daring fingerwork; he gasped at the synchronicity of it all. It was like one animal split into four parts making music. You probably had to be a musician to fully appreciate it, Simon thought.

As he recognised each song from the opening chords, he felt a spark of excitement light inside him. Every time Dove looked in his direction, Simon was sure Dove was looking straight at him and roared back.

*   *   *

After racing through most of the first album, it was time for the first talkie bit. "Some skeletons from the closet," said Dove, bathed in green light and dripping sweat.

Most of the audience looked straight through him, to the back of the stage where an eight-foot skull was slowly inflating. It was patched with crosses of gaffer tape. Nobody had noticed them in the stadium years – the audience was so far away then that the band seemed like ants on a biscuit to them – but the prop looked shoddy now.

"Here's some fresh meat," said Dove. He swung his arms and walked the width of the stage in an effort to be noticed. Dove lifted the mic stand above his head and thrust it into the air four times. Each thrust was accompanied by a tinny guitar chord and a drum kick, like the efforts to start a car with a crank handle. On the final push, the song motored and a jet of glitter squirted the crowd from each side of the stage. The guitar riffs sailed over a frantic bassline.

Behind Dove, Creak thrashed the drums, flicking sweat in all directions. Silver squares of glitter danced on his drum skins. In front of him, the crowd swayed gently. After all the writhing to the old songs, they looked now like a train packed with exhausted commuters.

For Dove, playing the new material was the highlight of the show. It was a chance to bring fresh ideas to his fans and show them what he's about today. They could enjoy the hits together, but nobody wanted to live in the past. Did they?

As he sang, he crouched at the front of the stage to get closer to the crowd. With the light dazzling his eyes, he could only see the first couple of rows of squashed faces. In two steps, he hopped off the stage and jumped onto the ledge behind the safety barrier. The security guard held the back of Dove's belt as he leaned over the barrier and reached into the audience. They went wild for him, jumped and jostled to touch him. Dove stretched his arm, and felt the slimy mass of people writhing against his hand. Wherever he went along the barrier, fans would grab and scratch at him, and tear at his clothes.

But after Dove brought the crowd to the boil and moved along, those he left behind quickly simmered down again, mesmerised by Skully as he bobbed up and down behind the drums.

* * *

Dove was only a few feet away from Simon, but the space between them was packed with people fighting to reach him. Simon was too tired to bother.

The band was playing new stuff now, so everyone had taken a well earned rest. Simon craned his neck to see Dove through a forest of heads in front of him. He basked in a breeze that blew through the gap and cooled the sweat running down his forehead. He rolled his head around his neck, trying to get the crick out of it from stretching it in one direction for too long.

As the crowd lolloped to the right, Simon's feet splashed in a puddle of beer and a plastic glass got stuck on his foot. There was no space to shake it off, so he took it with him wherever he was pushed.

The songs were passing in a blur. He couldn't even remember what had been played any more. It was becoming harder to concentrate on the music. His arm was killing him from where he had had the tag inserted, and his whole body was aching from his efforts to stay upright and to keep enough space to breathe. Occasionally, he would lift an arm up above his head, but he had to keep it there until he could steal the space to pull it down again.

He knew he could surrender his place and move to the back, but he had waited a long time for this. Pain is temporary, he told himself. Memories are forever.

* * *

"This is our final song," said Dove. "Dedicated to Kurt Cobain. May he suffer no more compilations. And dedicated to you: the dedicated."

He waved his hand across the crowd, which cheered in a short burst as Dove paused for breath. "Finally, I dedicate this to Clive Bigg. Do not feed this parasite."

He sat down cross-legged at the front of the stage. "We played our first gig here all those years ago," he said. He drew a circle in the air with the microphone. "The circle is complete. This is our last gig. Thank you for travelling with us. They can't buy our memories."

Where once the audience had cheered, they now murmured and talked to each other. Nobody had expected this. The crowd got louder and louder.

Dove bowed his head. BassFace removed his mask and looked like a rabbit caught in the headlights. Screech peeled off his face and smiled weakly. Creak jerked his head as he sniffed but kept his mask on.

"School's out forever," said Dove. He looked up, stuck his bottom lip out and traced a finger down his face like a tear. "Please join me in this final hymn. It's number 512, Stay Dead." The music began at half speed, a dirge like a Russian funeral march.

Dove sprang up, collected a mic stand from the wings and fixed his microphone to it. He set it down centre stage, stood stock still and sang his final song:

> They rip the faces from the bodies of the dead
> Ransack their legacies
> Consuming all the things they did and said
> But when they come for you

You'd better just stay dead
They couldn't deal with you
They'll run it past your wife instead

You're just a product of the things you left behind
Some raw material for an infertile mind
No royalties to pay, no blemishes to hide
Creative minds it seems
are worth more dead than when alive
Creative minds it seems
are worth more dead than when alive

And now you're in the news
Promotion budget's high
Impatient shelf-stackers
Just urging you to die
What did your life achieve?
You only just got by
Repackaged, recycled, restyled
for your last goodbye
Repackaged, recycled, restyled
They won't ever let you say "goodbye"

With the final word, the lights fell.

"We love you, Dove!" yelled someone from the back of the room, but he walked off as if he hadn't heard it. BassFace and Screech linked arms and bowed in darkness at the front of the stage. Creak punched Skully half-heartedly as he left from behind his drum kit. A glitter cannon popped late and rained foil squares on the audience.

Seconds after the musicians left the stage, the roadies descended like vultures and cleared away the band's remains.

* * *

Creak burst into the dressing room and ripped off his mask. "Where is he?" he said.

"Gone already," said Malcolm, as he coiled a mic cable.

"Did you know?"

Malcolm shook his head. "Nobody tells me anything."

"Arsehole," said Creak. "He could have told us first."

"No he couldn't," said Screech. "He doesn't have the balls."

"I'm outta here," said BassFace. "Pub?"

"I'm in," said Screech. "My diary's pretty empty now the band's gone tits up."

He left and BassFace followed him. Creak slumped into a chair so hard the wood cracked and he fell through it.

* * *

When the ugly light came on, the spell was broken. Simon shielded his eyes as he looked for Fred. During the show, he had felt like there was just him and the band in the world, even as he battled everyone around him. Now he was in a dirty, badly decorated room milling around with hundreds of wet strangers. The air was raw with sweat, beer and stage smoke. The room was quiet. After witnessing the death throes of the band, it seemed nobody had anything to say. A group of five came together next to Simon in a group hug. He felt like joining them, but didn't.

Simon stretched his arms behind his back and waited for Fred to find him.

"I can't believe it," he said when she arrived.

"Yeah, the bastard!" said Fred. "I mutilated my body to give him our demo and he couldn't even be bothered to keep the band together long enough."

"I didn't mean that," said Simon. His voice was broken from shouting so much. He rubbed the stage glitter out of his hair. "Let's go. I ache all over."

Without saying another word, they shuffled out the door with everyone else. It was cold outside, but Simon revelled in it. It freeze-dried the sweat he still had running down his face. And coming from his eyes.

* * *

Simon went straight to bed when he got in, but was too fired up from the gig to sleep. His ears whistled like someone distant censoring his thoughts. After half an hour, he got up again.

He cycled through the TV channels but the endless cavalcade of explosions and vox pops sounded dull to his desensitised ears. Without putting any music on, he booted up the computer. Angela was online.

thing>	**Where were you?**
angelA>	when?
thing>	**Tonight?**
angelA>	at home
thing>	**You said you'd meet me**
angelA>	no i didn't
thing>	**I said 'meet me'. you said 'Y'**
angelA>	why
thing>	**That's what I mean**
angelA>	Y=why
thing>	**FFS**
thing>	**You knew I thought y=yes**
angelA>	didn't. sorry
thing>	**Why won't you meet me?**
angelA>	u wouldnt like me in meatspace
thing>	**Why not?**
angelA>	i cant explain
angelA>	im a better person online
thing>	**Where is our friendship going?**
angelA>	ill always be here 4u
thing>	**Except in a power cut**
angelA>	be always there 4 me?
angelA>	i dont mean to hurt you
thing>	**Ok**
angelA>	how was the show
thing>	**Fantastic. Until the end.**
angelA>	what happened
thing>	**They split up**

thing>	**I watched my favourite band die**
angelA>	at least u were there at the end
angelA>	id better go
thing>	**Ok**
angelA>	chat tomorrow?
thing>	**Ok**
angelA>	goodnight
thing>	**Goodnight**
angelA>	love & kisses xx
thing>	**Bye**

\<angelA has disconnected>

CHAPTER 19

Jonathan breathed deeply. After three days cooped up at home, the air felt so fresh, even here on the high street, with the cars coughing at the traffic lights.

He had started work early, even though he had been programming until 4am the previous night. He didn't know what he'd done, but he'd broken Plato. It didn't sound right any more. For days now, he had been re-reading the same code and trying to fathom what was wrong. The monitor provided only a tiny window into the labyrinth of code he'd created. Every time he listened to the music it generated, he heard bugs around the corner as sure as the footfall of a minotaur.

Yesterday's Chinese takeaway stank on the desk beside him. As the source code had scrolled past his eyes that morning, he had picked up the fortune cookie and cracked it open. "You do not have the answer," it had said. And in a moment of zen-like clarity brought on by insufficient sleep, and too many dinners packed with sugar, Jonathan had realised it was true.

His professional pride drove him to try to invent a better wheel each time. But why bother when you can beg, borrow or steal an adequate wheel from someone else? If he didn't have the answer, who did? He had smiled as it dawned on him. Of course, *he* wouldn't want any part of it. But what he didn't know couldn't hurt him, could it?

It was the breakthrough Jonathan needed. It didn't matter that he hadn't found his destination yet. Sometimes it's enough to know where the map is. Reason enough to celebrate with a break, anyway.

The street was bustling now. "Are you trying to kill us?" a young girl scolded her father as they dodged the traffic and leaped onto the pavement. A chugger was proposing marriage to all-comers as first base in pitching his badger charity. A log-jammed ambulance wailed in frustration at the traffic packed before it.

Jonathan floated through it all. Nothing would spoil today.

And then he stopped dead. The headline on the Evening News screamed at him: "ROCK LEGEND DIES". Beside it, a photograph of Dove and the subheading 'CURTAIN FALLS ON UNIVERSITY OF DEATH'.

Jonathan's stomach lurched. Dove couldn't be dead, could he? The sadness welled up inside Jonathan. Life in the street went on around him, but the whole world was poorer for this news. It would never again hear a new song from Dove, or hear his electrifying performance of the old songs.

Not that Jonathan had paid much attention to the recent stuff. But there was always the promise that Dove would revisit his creative peak. That he'd move Jonathan once more, as he had in his youth.

Jonathan was keeping secrets from himself, though: Dove sounded as great as he ever did. If he were honest, Jonathan would have to admit it was his relationship with music that had changed. The music felt so good in his youth because he was in his youth, and that was something he could never recapture. The thought of Dove dying felt like a door slamming shut on Jonathan's past and his dreams for the future.

He slapped all the change from his pocket onto the news stand and snatched a paper from the pile. It felt wrong to read such upsetting news in public, so he jogged home, plumped himself down on the sofa and smoothed the front page out beside him.

ROCK LEGEND DIES
The rock world was in mourning this afternoon when it lost one of its leading lights to cancer. Tributes to Bart Ja-

mieson (44) were flooding in from other luminaries of the rock scene.

Jonathan couldn't remember what Dove's real name was, but 'Bart Jamieson' didn't ring any bells. He read on:

"He was best known for his passion for chalk, but it would be a shame if this overshadowed his many great works," said a close friend.

Dove's battle with the bottle was well known, but Jonathan didn't realise he had been a regular snorter as well.

"He leaves behind a legacy that will outlive us all," said another close friend. "Nobody else did more to popularise the field of geology."

Jonathan read that again. Bastards. This was worse than the time a senior manager at Coca-Cola had a car crash and the smartarse editor had called him a 'pop svengali' in the headline. Anything to sell papers. Jonathan tossed it into the bin with such force that the bin toppled, scattering rubbish on the carpet.

After a minute, he went over to tidy it. Jonathan righted the bin and picked up the newspaper. Dove was still staring at him from the cover. The excuse for the photo was a tiny story in a strip down the right of the page.

CURTAIN FALLS ON UNIVERSITY OF DEATH
Counsellors were on standby this afternoon after rock band University of Death announced last night that they were splitting. Lead singer Dove told the crowd at a sell-out concert that 'school's out forever'.
"It's natural for people to feel a sense of loss when a band they love breaks up," said Katie Hart, a leading psychologist. "It feels like a close relative has died. You can't just tell these people 'it's only a band' because to them, it isn't. It's so much more than that."

147

Jonathan felt almost as sad as when he thought Dove had died. The industry had crushed Dove's spirit and driven him from his one true love: music. He was an anachronism: a craftsman in the middle of an industrial revolution. The world needed Dove. Jonathan needed Dove.

Then he had a wicked idea. What's the point of having power and influence if you don't use them to do good? If you're not abusing your power, you're not really using it at all.

He reached for the phone and plugged in Clive Bigg's number.

"Bigg," answered a gruff voice.

"Harrington," said Jonathan, trying to match Bigg's authority.

"Hello, Jonathan."

"Hello," he replied, bottling out on using Bigg's first name. "Is it true University of Death are splitting up?"

"Yeah. Like we care," said Bigg. "Bloody drama queens. We don't need their likes any more anyway, do we?"

"No," said Jonathan quickly. "But I grew up with their music. It speaks to me."

"I can't imagine what it says."

"Well, I really like Dove," said Jonathan. Bigg didn't reply so Jonathan continued: "Can't you do something to get him to stay with Bigg Records? I want him to keep recording."

"I'd like to spend a saucy night with Madonna circa 1986. The world is full of impossible dreams."

"You could make it happen."

"How?" said Bigg, eagerly. Then he realised what Jonathan meant. "Oh, the Dove thing, you mean?"

"It would mean a lot to me."

There was an uncomfortable pause. "Where are you going with this?" said Bigg.

"I know they've laid on counselling and everything, but I just don't know if I can concentrate on our project if I feel this sad about Dove not making any more music."

"You're pulling my plonker, right?" said Bigg. "Did someone tell you I like jokes, is that it? Well, if they did I can tell you they meant my own. Not other people's."

"I'm serious," said Jonathan. "Just a small favour. Put my mind at ease. You could get Dove back in the studio."

"Dove hates me."

"So buy him."

"How?"

"Just pay him to tinker. Invest in him. I know he's got baggage, but his talent is being wasted."

"He has a talent for getting wasted, from what I hear."

"Those days are gone. He's reformed."

"Yeah, reformed as in 'ham', not 'man'." Bigg sighed. It sounded like a vacuum cleaner down the telephone. "I don't know who's worse," he said. "Musicians who think the sun shines out of their f-hole. Or punters like you who get down on bended knee before them."

"Help me out on this," said Jonathan. "There's got to be the odd perk of working at a record company."

"Trust me," said Bigg. "There isn't. It's all graft."

"You know he'll record you something great, or at least something you can sell. Dove just needs to rediscover his creative instinct."

"Does he now?"

"Oh, by the way…" Jonathan's attempt to sound spontaneous failed. "Plato's shaping up great. Hoping to launch really soon. I'm just finding it so hard to concentrate at the moment, though. Such a waste of talent. If only—"

"I get it," said Bigg. "But *if* I do this for you, we get one thing straight now. No more favours. No more pissing about. You spend your time lining up all the zeroes and ones. Let me worry about how I run the rest of the industry."

After three days imprisoned at home debugging, that stung. But Jonathan let it go. He knew programmers could never get any credit for bug-hunting because non-programmers assumed the bugs got there through sloppy work in the first place. "No more favours," agreed Jonathan. "If you're sure. That cuts both ways, you know."

"I've got to go now," said Bigg. "I'll get Dove back on board for you. You just get the software working, stop dicking around and we'll all be happy."

149

* * *

Bigg stepped out of the revolving door and trod carefully into the hotel lobby. The floor was shiny as ice and Bigg took slow, deliberate steps to avoid slipping. A mass of gold pipes and light bulbs hung from the ceiling. It was illuminating the room, but more than that: it was lighting up everybody's life with art. And no small measure of pretension.

Bigg didn't scare easily, but places like this intimidated him. However expensive his suit was, the staff at a top hotel could always make him feel like he was wearing an old potato sack.

He approached the desk and slapped the bell.

"Good morning, Sir," said the genie of reception, wearing a gold plastic badge that said his name was 'Barry'.

"Hello, Barry," said Bigg. "I'm here to meet one of your guests. A Mr Frog."

Barry looked at him. "Mr Frog, you say? Has he a first name?"

Bigg was hoping not to be asked that. "Yes," he said, negatively. "It's Kermit."

"So you'd like me to call a Mr Kermit Frog," said Barry. "Would his middle name be The, by any chance?"

"That's him," said Bigg. "Bell him up, can you?"

"Have you tried the stairs, Sir?"

"Eh?"

"Is Mr Frog, perhaps, sat on the stairs? Singing?"

"Just check the record, will you?"

Barry looked at Bigg as if he had placed a plastic poo on his salad plate. With a huff, he thumbed through the guest register. A few pages in, he broke into his best the 'customer is right' smile. "My," he said. "It seems we do have a Mr Kermit T. Frog here. I'll ring him."

"Tell him I'll meet him in the breakfast room."

"Certainly, Sir," said Barry, brightly.

Bigg jabbed Barry with his pointing finger. "The only muppet around here is you, mate." He followed the smell of bacon and eggs into the restaurant.

* * *

"Oh look. It's Mr Big Head," said the waiter.

"What?" snapped Bigg.

"Mr Bigg, head of that record label unless I'm much mistaken."

"Er. Yeah. It is." Bigg smoothed a napkin across his lap.

"Would you like butter with your croissant, Sir?"

"Just a nob."

"Of course, Sir," said the waiter, adding in a whisper: "You are what you eat."

"Sorry?"

"Bon appetit!" repeated the waiter, turning away.

Bigg scowled at the waiter's retreating back as he broke a croissant open.

A man arrived and slithered into the seat opposite Bigg. He was wearing army fatigues, but the splashes of colour weren't grey or green to blend in with the background: they were red, blue, yellow, green, pink, purple, white, black, and burgundy. He looked like he'd been coloured in by a five year old using all her crayons. It was anti-camouflage, guaranteed to make its wearer stand out wherever he was.

"Christ, my eyes!" said Bigg, shielding them with his sleeve in mock horror. "You're Kermit, I take it."

"I must defend my privacy," said Dove, unfolding his napkin.

"Yeah, right," said Bigg. "Cos the place is just humming with groupies, ain't it? They can't get enough of you. Good job you used a fake name to check in."

"I have to be careful."

"Yeah, dressed like that, you do. A word of advice: don't make me ask for a bloody muppet at reception again."

Dove fixed him with a stare.

"Now, let's start over," said Bigg. "I'm Clive Bigg. I run Bigg Records, which as you know, is your new home now that I've acquired your old label and contract."

"You collect record labels like butterflies," said Dove.

"I do have a few, yeah."

151

"You hammer nails through their fragile wings."

"Jesus Christ," said Bigg. "Can't we just talk business?"

"You rip the faces from the bodies of the dead," intoned Dove.

"Er… Nope," said Bigg. "I would remember that."

"You ransack their legacies, consuming all they did and said."

"Oh yeah, it's like a Viking invasion in my office."

"When you come for me, I'd better just stay dead."

"I'll kill you myself in a minute," said Bigg. "If I concede you're really clever, will you just stop showing off? I don't have a lot of patience for the sensitive artist thing. Can't we just be grown up?"

"An artist is always growing."

"Stop it!" shouted Bigg. The room fell silent around them as the other diners downed cutlery and stared. Bigg stabbed his knife into the butter in frustration. Its handle wiggled in the air until the waiter removed it and wiped it on a cloth. The waiter watched the veins in Bigg's neck pulse as the light danced along the knife's curved blade. A woman brushed the waiter's arm with her bag as she walked past and he started, like he had awoken from a trance, and replaced the knife at the side of Bigg's plate before disappearing into the kitchen.

"Nobody understands an artist like his art," said Dove.

"Oh yeah?" said Bigg. "How about his paymaster?" He tossed a royalty statement across the table. Dove read in silence. His shoulders sank as he turned the pages.

"Thought that might shut you up. Not pretty, is it?" said Bigg.

The waiter presented Bigg and Dove with menus.

"Could I see the fruitarian menu, please?" said Dove. "I only eat food that has died of natural causes."

"We have a vegetarian menu," said the waiter.

Dove perused it. "How did these fruits die?"

"They were dropped," said the waiter, staring hard at Bigg. "From the tree, I mean. I think we all know what that's like."

Bigg put his menu on the table and patted his belly. "I'll take the royal breakfast," he announced.

"We've sold out," said the waiter. "I am very sorry. You're a businessman. You must know what it's like to sell out."

Bigg wasn't really listening. "I'll take the next biggest breakfast

152

then. Bring me a plateful."

"A black tea. Lukewarm," said Dove, pointing at one on the menu. "I have to protect my voice," he whispered to Bigg by way of explanation.

"How much is this going to cost?" said Bigg.

"Oh, you just leave all the finances to me," said the waiter. "I'm sure there will be nothing to worry about. When we tot it up at the end, I'm sure you'll be pleasantly surprised." He pursed his lips, spun on his heels and left.

When his breakfast arrived, Bigg wasted no time in tucking in. "So you only eat things that die of their own accord," he said to Dove, dipping bread in his egg. "Would you eat roadkill?"

"That's not natural causes."

"It is the way I drive. Okay then, what about a lemming steak? Wouldn't want to waste all those burgers throwing themselves off cliffs. You need to build your strength up. I've got big plans for you."

"Dove has retired. His work is complete."

"Yeah, so I hear," said Bigg. "We'd better address this non-sense right now."

"The band is creatively bankrupt. It's over."

"Don't be daft," said Bigg. "It's over when I say it is. The worms that fed off Elvis's greasy corpse are long past pudding – long out of detox even – and he's still touring today. Elvis's backing band plays arenas in front of a massive video of The King. The tickets sell like *that*." Bigg clicked his fingers. "The soldiers die, but the regiment goes on. I'll get a new singer if you leave."

"It wouldn't be the same."

"Guess what?" said Bigg. "Nobody else cares. The money would still come in. The crowds would conspire with us to pretend it's the real thing."

"University of Death is me. It's nothing without a songwriter."

"They've still got all the old songs," said Bigg. "You can't unwrite them. We both know the fans prefer those anyway."

"Nobody understands my new work," said Dove. He paused for a moment, then added: "Silent but deadly? It stinks."

Bigg sniffed discreetly but couldn't detect anything. Then the penny dropped. "You mean Silent but Violent, the support band? Absolute genius! Very post-modern! I think of it as a hard rock cover of John Cage's 4'33."

"It's mime," said Dove. "How will that warm up my fans? You don't see jugglers opening for Iron Maiden, or Motörhead supported by morris dancers."

"More's the pity."

"Even my promoter doesn't get it," Dove whined. "You're no better. You've given up on new material. Your cash-in compilation isn't even selling."

"That, we can fix," said Bigg. "We'll hijack the charts with a cover version, then drop it into the reissue. Let's talk about your influences."

"Reverse that: Dove influences. Dove doesn't do covers."

Bigg pointed a mushroom on his fork at Dove. "Don't get all snooty. Cover versions feed and clothe half the industry. Perhaps we can reissue the back catalogue. Throw in a poster. New picture booklets. Maybe a Japanese OBI strip. Funny how a tiny bit of cardboard triples the asking price."

"You're selling the packaging."

"People love collecting it. Where's the harm?"

"Fans want songs not scraps. We need new music."

"Spot on!" said Bigg. "I know all about you, mister melody machine. Jamming all night and filling your vaults with music. I reckon we should tap more of your talent. Some people would give their life to play guitar like you."

"*I* did."

"Listen, I'm not here to blow coke up your arse."

"You mean smoke."

"Anything! I'm not blowing anything up your arse! We both know you're good. We just need to find a way to work together."

"I don't need you," said Dove. "With my profile I could go it alone."

Bigg scoffed. "Listen, mate. Bono sends an eight man crew to video hotels before deciding which one is safe enough to stay in. The Beatles had to burn their hotel sheets in the streets to stop people selling them on in pieces. People buy tickets to see Kylie's hotpants even when her cute Aussie buns aren't in them. There are jungle tribes who don't use written language but still know what Madonna's nipples look like."

"So?"

"*That* is famous," said Bigg. "That kind of fame is a tradable commodity. Paul McCartney could sell one of his own turds provided he put out a press release saying it was a uniquely personal work that comes from deep within him. Throw in a photo of him giving the thumbs-up next to a bog, and the punters would lap it up."

Dove winced at the image. "Your point being?"

"You're a nobody," said Bigg. "You're in a busy restaurant and nobody cares who the hell you are. Your clothes shriek for attention. You booked in as Kermit the Frog and nobody raised an eyebrow. Frankly, you'd need to set yourself on fire to catch the waiter's eye."

"Our tour sold out," sulked Dove.

"A few thousand people doesn't go far in a country of 60 million or a planet of six billion. The record label's been carrying you. You haven't been earning out your advance, but I'm going to put that right. For the first time, you've got a major label behind you. I'm going to make you an offer..."

He was interrupted by the waiter. "More dodgy dealing, Mr Tight Arse?" he said.

"What?" Bigg turned so quickly he felt his neck muscle rip.

"Your Darjeeling, might I ask?" the waiter repeated. He presented a metal teapot on a tray. Bigg scrutinised his face, but the waiter held his smiling muscles firm. Bigg indicated the tea was Dove's.

"Did you hear what he said?" Bigg asked Dove after the waiter had left.

"No," said Dove. "My attention is focused on you."

"Okay." Bigg shook his head. "You're talented, but tired. You need new creative energy. So I'm going to give you a development budget."

"What does that mean?" Dove sounded suspicious.

"Free money."

"Yeah, right."

"Really," said Bigg. "I believe in you. I'm going to pay you regularly on the condition that you work nine to five in your studio. I'm not looking for an album to come out of this. I just want you to discover yourself and come back to me with ideas." He sounded like he'd learned this bit off-by-heart.

"Why are you doing this?"

"Like I said, I believe in you," said Bigg. "Plus, I'd rather have you in our tent pissing around, than outside our tent pissing in."

"And if I don't accept?"

"You'll accept," said Bigg.

"I can't do the hours," said Dove. "I'm a night hawk."

"I don't care when you work. Just do it every day."

Dove had not heard the word 'work' used like that for a long time. When Dove spoke of his work, he meant his songs. He sighed deeply. "Okay. I'll do it," he said. His face was glum.

"Well, cheer up then," said Bigg. "You'll be able to buy all the fruit and nuts your stomach can cope with."

"I've never had a job before," said Dove, his voice sombre. "Never had to be anywhere at any time for anyone else. I feel so low. I feel my brain in a vice."

"You won't do anything stupid, will you?" said Bigg. The bite had gone from his voice and he sounded concerned.

"Like what?"

"Dunno," said Bigg. "A musical about fishing rights for garden gnomes? A concerto for kitchen cutlery? I've seen it all. And I won't tolerate any attempt to sabotage the label's good work."

"Yes, boss," said Dove. He was being sarcastic, but he blushed after saying it and looked away.

"Time to settle up," said the waiter. He placed a small plate with a folded piece of paper on it in front of Bigg. Bigg had expected it to be a bill, but when he opened it the only words on it said: 'LOOK UP'. As he did so, a fist slammed into his face, and knocked him sideways. "That's for dropping us," said the waiter. He punched again, through Bigg's flailing hands. "That's for screwing up my career." Another punch. "That's for stiffing us on the royalties." Another smack, but lacking energy now. "And that's for recruiting us in the first place."

The waiter ran out of steam as two of his colleagues came over and restrained him.

Bigg read the waiter's name off his badge. "I'll get you fired, Jervais!" he said.

"It was worth it!" Jervais roared back, as his colleagues led him away. "See how you like those hits!"

Bigg turned to Dove. "Occupational hazard," he said, as he wiped his bloody nose with his sleeve. "I sure earn my danger money."

CHAPTER 20

The wood splintered easily. Jonathan felt sick. He had often lied and enjoyed it. But he had never broken in to somebody's house before.

Through his thick gloves, the jemmy felt heavy but slippery. He levered the window frame out. As he juggled to stop it falling, the jemmy slipped and struck the pavement with a chime like a church bell.

Jonathan froze.

He listened.

No police cars screeched up the drive. No neighbours nosed over the fence. The trees rustled.

Jonathan thrust the jemmy into the bottom of a thick hedge and let it settle among the branches, hidden from view.

With his elbows on the window sill, he hauled himself up and into the house. He landed on a magazine rack, which toppled underneath him. Milky moonlight poured through the open curtains, but it took a few moments for his eyes to adjust. He righted the rack and felt in his pocket for the USB key. He had to squeeze it lengthways to feel it through the gloves.

So this is what a rock star's house looked like. One wall was racked with records. They filed tidily, but were loved enough to have sleeves that were scuffed and frayed. A record player sat on a shelf in the middle. The full moon reflected in a gold disk framed over the sofa. Three guitars huddled in the corner of the room.

Jonathan barked his shin on a coffee table and knocked a harmonica from it. The table was made of smelted pirate CDs. Its rainbow veins radiated in streaks underneath its lacquered surface. Jonathan breathed in sharply and rubbed his shin with one hand while he replaced the harmonica with the other.

He hobbled to the door, put his foot against the bottom of it, held the handle, and eased it open. It groaned with every inch he pulled it.

When he peered through the gap, a spotlight blinded him. A loud buzzing sound assaulted him. It quickly faded and the light slipped off his face and tickled the walls before disappearing. With a long sigh, Jonathan blew the fear from the bottom of his lungs. It was a passing moped, its headlamp cutting through the night, up the street, through the opposite window, into the house and into his heart.

The hallway was quiet now. With beams of moonlight playing on the grey wooden floor and white banister, Jonathan looked like he was stuck in a black and white movie.

He planted his foot on the bottom stair. It protested with a pompous creak. Holding the handrail, he looked at the step ahead. It bowed in the middle so he stood on the edge. It took his weight without a sound. One by one, he advanced up the stairs, placing his feet to minimise the noise.

The stairs came to a corner, and he looked up.

The grim reaper drilled into his eyes with its hollow black pits, carved into a skull like a yellowed egg shell. It stood six feet tall and was cloaked in black. Bony fingers hung from its limp sleeves.

Jonathan screamed breathlessly, stumbled and fell ten stairs back before gripping the banister to stop his fall. Lying backwards on the stairs with his feet above him, he slid until his head hit the floor in the hallway. The rough carpet of each stair rubbed his back like sandpaper all the way down.

The reaper stood motionless. Jonathan could see now that it was mounted on a stand. It looked like Twiggy, the skeleton who had presided over his school biology lessons.

He picked himself up. Enough time wasted. Enough tip-toeing around. He didn't have all night. He marched up the stairs, carefully but quickly, and tried the doors on the landing. The bedroom was no use to him. The bathroom had a guitar propped against the bath, but no computer.

The third door turned out to be Dove's mini studio. It was a tip. The shelves bowed, stuffed with reference books, software manuals, and cult fiction. The walls were covered with arty photos cut from magazines. The desk was buried in paperwork, as if Dove's recycling bin had been emptied over it.

There was a rack of keyboards, a nest of guitars and a mic stand set up in the middle of the room. A stone lectern held a book of handwritten sheet music open in front of the microphone. The lectern had an eagle on the front, its edges chipped and smoothed by the passing centuries.

On the desk was Dove's PC. Jonathan cleared the fan of paperwork off it, moved a pile of music magazines so he could sit down in the chair and steadied himself as it rolled away from the desk. He peeled off his gloves and pushed the button on the front of the PC. It glowed, casting green light around the room. The monitor sparked into life and the machine ground through its gears, remembered who it was and where it was and eventually showed Jonathan a welcome screen.

He fished in his pocket for the USB key. Nothing. It must be caught in the folds of his trouser pocket. He stood up and pulled his pockets inside out. Still nothing. He'd lost it. He felt despair washing his brain. When did he see it last? He remembered checking it after he came in through the window. He must have lost it when he fell down the stairs.

Jonathan returned to the staircase, his shadow wearing a green halo on the wall. He squinted. The wood grain in the hallway floorboards made it hard to see where his USB key might have landed. He eventually spotted it peeking out between the legs of a low bookcase, which was crammed with phone directories, pizza leaflets and other assorted rubbish that had been thrust through the letterbox.

Jonathan was halfway down the stairs when he heard the grinding of a key slipping into the lock. Instinctively, he crouched. There were voices outside the front door, and he could see shadows bobbing behind the frosted arched window. The USB key was only a few quick hops away, but it was nearer them than it was him and he couldn't risk being caught. When he saw the front door handle move, he jolted into action, snuck upstairs and into the studio. He eased the door shut behind him.

Who could it be? Dove was supposed to be at some awards event tonight, according to his blog.

"Put the kettle on," boomed Dove's voice from downstairs. "I'm going for a slash."

The blog was wrong.

Jonathan heard Dove's bold footsteps on the stairs. He looked at the door and saw it was bathed in green light, which spilled through the little window above the door. Jonathan punched the PC and monitor off, killing the light.

"I'll print off that map for you too," called Dove.

There was no lock on the door. Jonathan looked under the desk, but the space was crammed with old magazines. He could hide behind the door, but it was risky. The room was too small to be unnoticed for long. And even if he did sneak out while Dove's back was turned, where would he go then? He could hear chatter in the kitchen, which meant there were at least two others in the house. There were only two exits – the door, which Dove was about to walk through. And the window.

Jonathan uncatched the window and slid the bottom half up. The window moved easily but the sound of wood rubbing wood was loud, silenced by the final thock as the window hit the top of its frame. The cold night air blew into Jonathan's face as he looked down. It was a long way, but it was green underneath, which promised a soft landing.

He heard the toilet flush. Dove's footsteps seemed to grow louder. Jonathan put his gloves back on and sat on the window sill, dangling his legs outside, with the upper half of the window pressing against his front. He rolled over, so that he was perched on his stomach. It hurt. He inched over the edge, until he was hanging by his fingers, which in their gloves had only a slippery grip on the window ledge. The tips of his trainers squealed as they rubbed the glass of the window below. Jonathan took a deep breath and instinctively closed his eyes before throwing himself backwards, away from the house.

His fall was broken by a holly bush. The barbs pierced through his trousers and pants. A branch had gone up his back, inside his shirt. Leaves pricked at his face. He screamed out in pain, and tried to scramble out of the bush. Every move freed him from one cluster of leaves and impaled him on another.

The lights came on in the house and the front door opened, just twenty feet away from Jonathan. Dove peered around the door nervously. He was on the phone.

"Police," he said. "Yeah, there's someone in my holly bush."

"Can't you just chase him away?" said the tiny voice in the phone. "He's probably a drunk."

"I don't think that would work," said Dove with indignation. "I'd be all over the papers tomorrow. Price of fame, you know."

"Typical," said the voice. "I stopped a bank raid yesterday and didn't even get a news in brief. We'll send someone when we can. Don't wait up."

Jonathan's hands reached the path and he hauled himself forwards. Nuggets of gravel got into his gloves and dug into the tender skin of his hands. The holly bush let his legs go reluctantly, scraping him all the way. He was on his hands and knees on the path, panting and dribbling.

"Oi!" called Dove. "What's your game?"

Jonathan didn't look back. Feeling battered, he ran across the garden, down the drive and into the street.

He breathed like an air conditioning unit, noisy and dry. When he came to a churchyard, he staggered inside and collapsed on the grass beneath an angel. Its wings, carved in stone but with a tattered coat of moss, sheltered him. The moonlight picked out a cast of cherubs and crosses marking the spots where bones were buried.

How had it come to this? He was a burglar. Worse than that, a bad burglar. He'd never been bad at anything he'd tried to do before. Now his life's work was broken for want of a few lines of code in the right place. And he'd blown his best chance of fixing it.

Perhaps 'burglar' was too strong a term. Okay, so he was trespassing. But he was only borrowing a few ideas really. Nobody would miss them. And until he'd completed his program, nobody would have the vision to give him the permission he needed. Anyone hearing his perfect music would be happy to help. Including Dove, Jonathan told himself. Sometimes morality was just a question of the order you do things in, like an accident of history. If people would give him the permission later, what did it matter if he had to act as if they had already done so first?

He had come too far to lose his nerve now. He had to find another way to access Dove's computer. The wind blew and made him shiver. For half an hour he sat there, hugging himself, trying to work out what he would do next.

The solution landed on him like divine intervention. It was tricky, but this time nobody would be ambushed by skeletons, bounced down a flight of stairs or have to jump onto holly bushes. This time it would work. He would go for Dove's most obvious weak spot: his vanity.

Jonathan looked up. The angel stared him out with vacant eyes and comforted him with her mumsy smile.

CHAPTER 21

"I had an idea," said Jonathan.

Bigg was listening on speakerphone as he sorted his post into three piles: one for him to read, one for someone else to action, and the bin. "Huh?"

"We need to set up some high profile auditions," said Jonathan. "Throw people off the scent."

"Did you egg your grandmother for me to suck?" shouted Bigg. "We do this all the time. All the pretty poppets come along. A good few of them have grade six singing certificates and eke out a living chanting radio adverts like 'Glaze once, glaze twice at DoubleGlaze'. They've felt their talent decaying long enough to do as they're told. Nudity can be a sticking point for some of the girls, but even that doesn't starve us of potentials."

"I'm sorry?" said Jonathan.

"Oh, the nudity is very much a last resort," said Bigg. "But it helps us to secure the twelve year old male demographic if the girls will strip off in magazines like FHM and Zoo. We can get body doubles for the dumpy ones."

"You need to audition real bands," said Jonathan, "not bit players. If anyone does trace this flood of new music back here, you can at least show you've been working to recruit talent. It should be enough smoke and mirrors to keep a lid on what's really going on."

"Okay," said Bigg. "I'll see what we can do. I trust you are on schedule?"

"Yeah," said Jonathan. He sounded uncertain. "Hit a bit of a speed bump, but I've got a plan. I'd better get on with it."

"Clever boy!" Bigg clicked the phone off without saying goodbye.

He left his desk and went over to his wall of gold disks. On the floor were the new arrivals in flat cardboard boxes. Bigg picked up the first box, and a pair of scissors, and prised the staples off one by one with a grunt and a ping. When the box lid was open, he lifted out the frame, careful to make sure the glass front wasn't scratched. A plastic plaque was glued to the CD's bed of red velvet, commemorating half a million single sales by a band Bigg had long forgotten existed.

Marian walked in. "Before I worked here, I always thought the gold disks went to the singers," she said. "Like on the telly."

"Oh, they get plenty," said Bigg. "Don't have room for them all to be honest. But these are sales awards. You don't see the likes of Boymad getting up at five a.m. to visit Zambezi at their dreary office. Or Dove getting an awayday to Slough to meet Amazon. *We* earn those awards. Our so-called artists only end up giving them to their mums or flogging them sooner or later anyway."

"Do you need anything?"

"Yes," said Bigg. "Hammer and nail, as quick as you can. Oh, and I need you to place some ads for open auditions please. We want real bands this time."

"Wow!" said Marian. "It's been years since we got any proper bands in."

"Yeah, well, it's good for marketing too," said Bigg. "Every band is a potential customer. Like when they held auditions for Harry Potter. All those kids who queued round the block wanted to see the speccy twat who beat them to the job when the film came out."

"What's prompted this?"

"Things are changing. We've got to question the status quo," said Bigg. "We need to keep finding new ways to bring in fresh thinking. We're in an ideas business, after all."

"How exciting!" Marian clapped her hands together softly.

"Perhaps we should get a celebrity judge," said Bigg. He

stroked his chin thoughtfully. "It would be good for PR. Place a call to Dove, will you? Tell him that we're making him executive head of A&R or something. He'll lap it up. He owes me a favour, anyway."

"No problem."

"Make sure we put a flyer in all our outgoing post too, can you?"

Marian left and Bigg arranged his gold disk on the floor and attacked another box.

Five minutes later, Marian buzzed him on the intercom. "Mr Bigg," she said. "I've got Francis Rossi and Rick Parfitt in reception. They're ready to face your questions now. MC Hammer and Jimmy Nail have confirmed for 3pm. It's the quickest I could do."

CHAPTER 22

"You're an airhead with a puncture
So totally out to lunch, yeah!
Vacant as a toilet
And easily as full of it

Yeah, yeah, yeah
We hate you so
Yeah, yeah, yeah
You have to know
No, no, no
Please don't explain
Don't wear out your pretty brain

You're paddling in the gene pool
An 18-carat blinged-up fool
With an—"

Simon stopped singing abruptly when Fred walked in. He rested his guitar on the stand.

"Were you just singing Boymad?" Fred giggled.

"Might have been," said Simon. "It's not a bad song, actually. When you listen to it properly. It's got a killer bassline."

"Is this another one of cybergirl's recommendations?" said Fred. "She's ruining your music taste."

"Angela," said Simon. "She does have a name, you know." The

computer pinged and Simon rushed over to it.

"Don't mind me," said Fred. "Tell your virtual girlfriend I said 'hello'."

"She's not my girlfriend," said Simon. "And it's not her anyway. It's someone on our website."

"Who?" Their homepage was like a haunted house. There were plenty of spiders but few humans were intrepid or lost enough to enter.

"It's the Greek god of music."

Apollo>	Anyone home?
thing>	**Yes, Hi. Thanks for visiting our website.**
Apollo>	I was reading your blog.
thing>	**Cool.**
Apollo>	Is it true you've covered Animal Reined?
thing>	**Yes.**
Apollo>	Respect. That's hard to do.
Apollo>	I love that song! Can I have a copy?
thing>	**We haven't recorded it yet**
Apollo>	Shame. Could you record it for me?
thing>	**Sure**

"Wait, wait, wait," said Fred. "Ask him how much it's worth!"

"I can't do that!"

"Why not? Go on." Fred stood behind Simon and put a hand on his shoulder.

thing>	**what's it worth?**
Apollo>	don't know.
Apollo>	can I tell you a secret?
thing>	**okay.**
Apollo>	It's for Dove. I'm a friend. He loves cover versions.
Apollo>	I wanted to give it to him for his birthday.
thing>	**How do you know Dove?**
Apollo>	I work at his record label
Apollo>	So how much would it cost to get a copy of your cover version?

"How cool is that!" said Simon.

"Totally!" said Fred. Her tone changed to one of mild concern. "Is that clock right?"

"More or less."

"God, I'm late for work." She plucked her coat off the back of a chair and threw it on.

"Don't go *now!*"

"They'll kill me if I'm late again. All those posh people won't be able to get from one floor to the next if I'm not there to push the buttons."

"Well, what do you reckon we should charge? There's got to be a hundred quid in it, don't you think?"

"Forget cash," said Fred. "If he's genuine, he can give us what we really want. Think big!"

Simon smiled as it dawned on him. "Oh yeah!"

"Negotiate hard. I'm off." She waved as she let herself out.

Apollo>	you still there?
thing>	**yes.**
Apollo>	so what's it worth?
thing>	**An original 7" of Animal Reined**
Apollo>	where am I supposed to get hold of that?
thing>	**Dove**

There was a long pause, before the reply came:

Apollo>	okay.

Simon remembered what Fred had said: Negotiate hard.

thing>	**And I want it signed by Dove.**
Apollo>	Tricky.
Apollo>	Dove doesn't do autographs any more
thing>	**Not even for his mates?**
Apollo>	Okay then. I'll have a word.
Apollo>	One last thing.
Apollo>	You've got to keep this secret. It's important.

thing>	**Why?**
Apollo>	I want to pass this off as my own recording
thing>	**Why?**
Apollo>	Private joke between me and Dove.
Apollo>	Don't worry. You'll get your signed 7".
thing>	**How do I know you won't forge the signature?**
Apollo>	How do I know you can keep a secret?
Apollo>	We UoD fans have to trust each other.
Apollo>	I'm emailing over the address to send the CD to
thing>	**I'll be in touch.**
Apollo>	Thanks. Stay dead, man.
thing>	**You too.**

Simon called Fred immediately. "We got a deal!" he said.

"What just like that?"

"Yeah!"

"A single deal, you mean?"

"Well, there's just the one deal, yes."

Fred howled with joy down the telephone.

"You okay?" said Simon.

"That's fantastic! How many are they pressing?"

"How many what?"

"How many of our single?"

Simon's face burned red. "Er, no," he stammered.

"No what?" Fred's voice had hardened.

"That's not the deal."

"Tell me the deal," commanded Fred.

"We record us doing Animal Reined. We send this guy the CD. And he sends us the priceless – that's *priceless* – original record."

"That's it?" Fred couldn't have sounded less impressed if Simon had bartered her iPod for a snotty hanky.

"Well, no," said Simon. "He's going to get it signed too. By Dove."

Simon heard the sound of screeching brakes and a car horn blaring down the phone, followed by Fred vigorously swearing at the driver.

"Didn't you ask if we could add our own tracks for Dove to

listen to? Or for an audition? Or a review of our demo? Or something?"

"Sorry," said Simon. "I didn't think of that."

"Dickhead!" Fred yelled.

The line went dead. Simon wanted to believe that she had shouted at a careless driver at the very moment she had lost her phone signal.

* * *

Jonathan winced at the pain as he raised his arms up high. His body still ached from his fall out of Dove's window yesterday. He gingerly lifted the picture frame off the wall and eased his arms down again. It left a square of super-vibrant wallpaper that had been shielded from the sunlight for years. With a pair of scissors, he prised the metal pins away and lifted the back of the frame off. He pressed the dusty glass from underneath and pushed his copy of Animal Reined out.

He would have to be sly to get it signed. Rabid fans would spot a fake autograph immediately, and he needed to be sure they would have no reason to go public. The last thing he needed was an attempt to trace him afterwards. Besides, he knew how valuable these discs were. He didn't want to cheapen one with a fake autograph. It would be better not to sign it at all.

There were a few wrinkles in the cover, but it was looking good for a record of its age. Jonathan slipped it out of the sleeve and watched how the light danced through its grooves as black as fresh tarmac.

He'd never played it. It was a trophy, caught in the wild, mounted and hung on the wall. It belonged to a different him: the one who idolised Dove, swallowed up everything he said in magazines; the one who coveted souvenirs of Dove's existence and symbols of his own devotion to him and his music; the one who enjoyed and evangelised every new album.

When he told Dove in his phoney interview that he'd never part with the single, he had meant it. But things had changed so quickly since then. Memorabilia seemed pointless once he'd met the man and probed his thoughts.

And broken into his house. He'd betrayed Dove's trust and he knew he would do it again. His Framed Animal Reined was a relic.

A year ago, he would have considered parting with this record to be a sacrifice. He'd long since crossed the line where such things mattered. This was small beer. Another downpayment on his mortgaged dream.

* * *

One week later, the laser sucked Fred's voice and keyboards, the programmed drums and Simon's blistering guitar solo from the spinning disc. Simon had played their recording over and over during mixing, but he still got a kick out of it. They sounded great, even though it brought back memories of how Fred had huffed and moaned whenever they weren't recording.

As he listened, he picked up one of the jiffy bags from the slagheap of returned demos. He scraped his fingernails at the edge of the computer-printed address label. It tore and stuck fast in places, ripping the brown fibres off the envelope in others.

The CD came to an end. He ejected it, shook the jiffy bag's contents into the bin and put their Animal Reined CD in the envelope.

The label remnants looked messy, so he wrote Apollo's address on a piece of note paper and taped it over the front.

Simon flipped the envelope over and stuck the flap shut. He squeezed the envelope between his fingers and whispered 'be lucky', just as he had with all the demos piled up beside him.

* * *

Jonathan shook a few tablespoons of sugar into the bin and put the packet to one side. He took the cereal boxes and left the plastic liners full of flakes sagging in the larder. He ripped the labels off a couple of tins. The back of a recipe book caught his eye, so he took that too and rummaged through the recycling bin for newspapers.

Hugging his pile of rubbish, Jonathan returned to his office and let it tumble over his computer desk. He cut out the barcodes and threw the rest away. The barcodes were spread face down on the scanner and before long appeared on his screen.

Each barcode was cropped, cut and pasted into the tracking sheet, which had the bold heading 'EIM Couriers'. There were twenty lines of made-up addresses and tracking numbers, with a space at the end for signatures. When it was printed on blue paper in shiny black ink, it looked the business.

Jonathan took a knife to it, and cut out the signature boxes. He put the tracking sheet over a piece of white paper and used different pens to fake signatures in the top three boxes. Then he put the sleeve to Animal Reined underneath the fourth hole, positioning it so that none of the skulls showed through. Another piece of white paper between the record sleeve and the top sheet stopped any skulls peeking through the remaining holes. He fixed the papers to a clipboard and used a few paperclips to keep everything in place.

Goblin's recording had been surprisingly good. Not that it mattered. Jonathan only needed Dove to play it once, and he would be in. He took his version of the CD from the computer, pressed it into Simon's jewel case and slipped it back in Simon's envelope, together with the cover letter he'd prepared. The Apollo address label ripped off easily and there was no trace of the previous address on the white scraps underneath. Jonathan printed off a fake EIM tracking label and stuck it to the front.

He took his black and yellow motorcycle helmet from under the desk and put it on. It smelled musty and felt tight. He hadn't had a bike since he was at college. He used to look rock hard going into a pub with his leathers and his helmet on, at least until people saw him leaving on an orange moped.

* * *

Jonathan's leather jacket creaked as he raised his arm to press the brass button in Dove's doorframe. The doorbell played a few bars of Stay Dead. Dove must have reprogrammed it – there was no market for a doorbell that heralded visitors by chiming mostly forgotten songs about corpses.

While he waited for the door to be answered, Jonathan looked around the garden. He scowled at the holly bush and was sad to see the petunias trampled into the dirt, presumably by him as he had made his escape.

Dove opened the door a little and peered around it.

"Mr Dove?" said Jonathan.

"Who wants to know?"

Jonathan flipped his visor up but kept his helmet on. "Delivery for you, mate."

"Who's it from?"

Jonathan turned the envelope over. "It don't say, mate. They don't tell me nuffin. If you can just sign here, I'll be off."

"I don't like writing my name," said Dove, like a teenager sulking about homework. He opened the door fully and stood in the doorway.

Jonathan huffed. "Well I can't do it. One of our lot was fired last week for forging a signature. All legit – the bloke had broke both 'is arms skiing. Company don't care though. I could return this, I s'pose. Oh no – there's no address. I could keep it or bin it for yer?" He weighed it in his hand. "Feels heavyish, though. Might be valuable."

"Okay," said Dove. "Where do I sign?"

"In that gap there," said Jonathan. He pointed at the fourth hole in the tracking sheet and handed Dove a dead biro.

"Do I know you?" said Dove.

Jonathan had forced a cockney accent and kept his helmet on, so he was sure that Dove was mistaken rather than trying to recall their previous meeting in the studio. "Oh yeah, I get that always," he said. "I was one of the regulars at the Queen Vic. I was a thief in the Bill once too. And a failed bungee jumper in Casualty. Not much of a TV career, but me Nan's proud of me."

Dove took the form and tried to sign but the pen scratched the paper without leaving a trace. "Do you have another pen?"

"Not sure… Let me look." Jonathan had pockets all over him, all with difficult zips. He shuffled his gloves and the package from hand to hand as he checked nearly all of them, milking it for every second it was worth. He ignored his left leg pocket, which held the working pen for if Dove didn't bite.

"We'll be here forever," said Dove. "I'll get a pen. Wait there."

Dove turned to go but Jonathan stopped him "Can I have me clipboard?" Jonathan said. "Company rules. Not to leave me sight."

Dove handed it back to him and disappeared into the house, towards the kitchen.

Jonathan jumped in to the hallway. As if he had been shot, he fell to his knees and put his head against the floor. He looked under the shelf unit for his USB key. It was there, but it had been kicked to the back now. He lay on the floor and tried to scoop it out, but his bulky jacket stopped his arm from getting under the unit. He looked around. There was an umbrella in the corner, so he took that and poked away under the shelf until he was able to flick the USB key out one end.

"Got one!" called Dove. "Is green okay?"

"Sure!" shouted Jonathan, a little breathless. He pocketed the USB key and stood up. The umbrella was coated with filth and dust now, but only on the side that had been on the floor. Jonathan slipped it back in the corner with the dirty side against the wall and stood to attention, just in time to see Dove arrive.

"Right," said Dove. "Where do I sign?"

Jonathan pointed. "Just write 'Dove' please, cos that's the addressee," he said. "Shirley goes bananas if the names and sigs don't match."

Dove took the clipboard and signed the sleeve of Animal Reined through the tiny paper window that Jonathan had made for it. Jonathan ran a laser pointer over the barcodes on the clipboard and the package and gave Dove the envelope.

"Thanks, mate," Jonathan said as he left. "'Ave a good one."

Jonathan had to stop himself from skipping down the drive. Strangers wondered what the joke was as he laughed to himself on the way to the Underground.

Two boys and a girl sat opposite him on the tube home. "Someone nick your bike, mate?" sniggered one of the boys.

"I don't have one," said Jonathan. The tube seemed to get hotter as he felt self-conscious about how he was dressed. He cradled his helmet in his lap.

The kids all laughed. "Leave him alone," said the girl. "If he wants to dress like a biker, that's okay."

"Thanks," said Jonathan, weakly.

"I mean, my brother's got Superman pyjamas but he can't fly, can he?"

* * *

Dove took the package back to his breakfast and opened it. He read the letter while he tried to chisel his Froot Flakes from the bowl with a spoon.

Dear Dove

We've recorded a cover version of Animal Reined to say thank you for all your music. We're in a new band and playing your songs has made us better musicians. You've inspired us to be the best we can. Don't worry. There's no hard sell – no demo attached, no biog, no photos. Just a note of thanks and the hope that you enjoy hearing our cover version as much as we enjoyed making it.

Love
Anonymous (we told you we're not selling ourselves!)

Dove was thrilled. He took the CD to his computer straight away and set it to import.

While it was working, he returned to his breakfast and splashed it with more soya milk. He let his eyes hang around the nutritional information on the cereal box, neither reading nor ignoring it. He didn't notice that the barcode above it was the same as the one on the envelope he'd just received.

* * *

178

When Jonathan got in, he booted up the computer without taking his leathers off. Dove had already put the CD in the computer – as Jonathan knew he would – and while Dove had probably been nodding away, listening to someone "interpreting his genius", Jonathan's software had been quietly installing itself in the background.

Now Jonathan had remote access to Dove's PC. With full access to Dove's software and his synth modules, Jonathan had what he needed to refine Plato.

He wanted to celebrate, but part of him felt dirty. He started coding straight away, patching Dove's software into his own. He did want to get Plato finished. But he was hiding in programming data so that he didn't have to think too hard about what he had done, and what he had become.

* * *

thing>	**Hey Angela!**
angelA>	hey thing
thing>	**I have a present 4u**
angelA>	wat is it
thing>	**One of our recordings**
angelA>	kewl
thing>	**You have to keep it secret and not share it.**
angelA>	why
thing>	**It was recorded for a private commission.**
thing>	**I'm not supposed to tell anyone about it.**
angelA>	I won't tell if you don't
thing>	**Coming over now then.**
thing>	**It's a cover of University of Death:**
thing>	**Animal Reined**
angelA>	nice choice
thing>	**We've been playing it for months now**
	so its pretty tight
angelA>	y that song
thing>	**It's good to blast thru at the start of rehearsal**
angelA>	got it. playing it now.

thing>	**What do you think?**
angelA>	wow! dont know how to describe it
thing>	**We call our sound heavy tinsel**
	because its loud
	but its got a bit of glamour and sparkle too
angelA>	which bits did you do
thing>	**Just guitar on this one**
angelA>	i like it
angelA>	its original
angelA>	so many bands have no voice
angelA>	u have a voice
thing>	**Thank you. I knew you'd like it!**
thing>	**I'll send you more when we record them.**
angelA>	gr8 thx
thing>	**I haven't given anyone a copy of my music before**
angelA>	thanks
thing>	**except demos sent to labels obviously**
angelA>	ive got to go now
thing>	**Okay. Have a good evening then.**
angelA>	ill listen to u all night
angelA>	that guitar line rox
angelA>	put you on loop
thing>	**I wouldn't do that if I were you!**
thing>	**Once every 25 minutes for the next 6 hours**
	should do it. Best not overdo it :-)
angelA>	;-)
angelA>	bye sweetness xxx
thing>	**Bye xxx**
angelA>	a bientot
<angelA has disconnected>	

* * *

For the next five days, Simon skipped to the front door whenever the wind pulled at the letterbox. On the sixth day, a stiffened cardboard envelope arrived, about eight inches square.

Even though it had survived the Royal Mail, Simon handled

the record like it might crumble in his hands. He took the sleeve out, placed it on his desk, and shone his lamp onto it. The potato-printed skulls glistened. In the top right of the sleeve was Dove's autograph. There was a tangent balanced on top of the 'o' at a jaunty angle with an umlaut inside. On second glance, Simon could see the dots were eyes and the line was a mortarboard.

He slipped the record out of its sleeve and held it to the light. Scratched into the plastic near the label was the catalogue number and next to it, the handwritten words 'Spinning in our graves'. On the other side, the run-out groove said 'the latest sound that's going round'. Simon laughed, delighted to share these weak private jokes with the band and as few as 49 others who owned the single. Every one of them had a unique sleeve, with the skulls printed in different formations. But as far as he knew, only his copy was signed.

Holding this handmade record and its sleeve, Simon felt a connection with Dove that he hadn't felt before. But it was tinged with an emptiness as he realised that his University of Death collection was complete. The sport was gone. Only the music remained.

Simon wondered whether Dove had played their cover version and what he had thought of it. Had he enjoyed it? Abandoned it mid-way? Been insulted by their audacity in covering it, even? Perhaps he had liked it enough to add to a playlist. Simon would never know.

There was something else in the envelope. Simon shook it and a yellow flyer floated out. "In a band?" it asked. "Bigg Records is looking for organic bands to join its roster. Call us now to register for our open audition in London."

Maybe Fred would forgive him after all.

* * *

thing>   **Hey Angela!**
angelA>   hey thing
thing>   **Guess what I got?**
angelA>   arrested

thing>	Thanks a bunch!
thing>	No - an original Animal Reined 7"
angelA>	kidding
thing>	No way
angelA>	wats it like
thing>	Truly beautiful
thing>	Every one is handmade and unique
angelA>	whose hand
thing>	Word is Dove did the potato printing
thing>	There are jokes in the run-out groove too
angelA>	are they funny
thing>	No
thing>	But that's not really the point
thing>	More good news too:
thing>	Bigg Records is doing open auditions
angelA>	wat does that mean
thing>	It means we can get a foot in the door
thing>	At last
angelA>	u will blow them away
thing>	I hope so
thing>	We've got a couple of months
	to get our act together
angelA>	good luck
thing>	We'll need it!
angelA>	hey sweetness youll totally rock
angelA>	i have faith in u

* * *

Jonathan rested his finger on the enter key to savour the moment. As he increased the pressure, his fingertip flattened against the cold plastic. The key gave away and sank into the keyboard. When he lifted his finger off, the key sprang back with a satisfying click sound.

He picked up the phone and selected his first speed-dial number.

"Bigg," said Bigg.

"Plato is live!" said Jonathan. He wanted to sound business-like, but couldn't conceal his excitement.

"About bloody time," said Bigg. "I'm pleased to hear it. Anything else?"

Jonathan felt deflated. While Plato had been the centre of his life since he'd had the idea, Bigg had just written the cheques and carried on with business as usual. "I just wanted to let you know. I'll keep you updated on how it goes."

"Just send me monthly sales reports," said Bigg.

Jonathan hesitated. He didn't like talking about money. "Err… when do I get my royalties?"

"All in good time," said Bigg. He hung up without warning.

Jonathan put the phone down on the desk. He logged in to see if there had been any sales in the few seconds since he launched. There hadn't.

Now that the donkey work was done, he'd have time to catch up on all those little celebrations of life that most people took for granted. He could read a newspaper, enjoy a slow lunch by the river or watch a film. He knew what was top of his list, though. Ever since he had seen those eBay parcels arriving at Bigg Records stuffed with Commodore bits, he had hankered after a good, old-fashioned blast-em-up.

Finding a copy of Beach Head to run on his computer was easy. Within minutes, he heard the familiar bugle tone as his submarines began to negotiate the mined waters. He blew plane after plane out of the sky and swallowed the afternoon in child-like joy.

CHAPTER 23

thing> **You there, Angela?**
angelA> hey thing
angelA> i 4got 2 ask b4
angelA> did you buy the boymad song
angelA> in the end
thing> **I might have done…**
angelA> did you
thing> **Yes**
angelA> i knew it
angelA> it does rock
thing> **I've learned the chords.**
thing> **I'll sing it to you when we meet.**
angelA> cool
thing> **I dreamed about you last night.**
thing> **I couldn't see your face but I knew it was you.**
angelA> how did u know it was me
thing> **Because of how I felt.**
angelA> how was that
thing> **You know. Kinda loved-up. ;-)**
angelA> what were we doing
thing> **Use your imagination!**
angelA> how did I do
thing> **You were amazing!**
angelA> Thanks sweetness
thing> **I still don't know what you look like.**

thing>	**Why won't you send me a photo?**
angelA>	never had one i liked b4
thing>	**But you do now?**
angelA>	yes I took it 4u
angelA>	i'll send you a photo

Simon's breath quickened. Framed by the long, dark hair he knew she had, he had sketched her face in his mind's eye. Some details were harvested from the clues she gave away as they chatted. Others he had completed with his imagination alone. Now his vision of her would be confronted by the real Angela.

There was a ping and the corner of the screen waved a flag to attract Simon's attention. Angela.jpg had arrived. He double clicked on it. Even sat in front of a grey pleated curtain on an uncomfortably low whirly seat, she shone. There was a heart-shaped halo around her, drawn in lipstick on the glass screen. She had a cheeky smile and seemed to make eye contact with the camera. She was looking right at Simon, and it made his spine tingle.

thing>	**Wow!**
thing>	**You look fantastic!**
angelA>	youll make me blush
thing>	**Perhaps when we meet up, I will**
angelA>	listen i have a problem
thing>	**What? What is it?**
angelA>	i cant use this chat program any more
thing>	**why not???**
angelA>	sokay – theres a new one
thing>	**go on**
angelA>	i need to switch to a new program for work
angelA>	its cool though
thing>	**Can't you use two chat programs?**
angelA>	no - IT department says new one is more secure
thing>	**so you chat to me from work?**
angelA>	i work at home
angelA>	i chat using work computer

thing>	Where do I get this program?
angelA>	coming over now
thing>	**Got it**
angelA>	install the program!
angelA>	i want 2 keep chatting
angelA>	i dont want 2 lose u
thing>	**No fear**
angelA>	got to go now
angelA>	have a good evning
thing>	**Thanks. You too.**
angelA>	and thanks
thing>	**What for?**
angelA>	it's a long time since anyone said i looked nice
thing>	**'fantastic' was the word!**
angelA>	sweet dreams
thing>	**Yes. I'll see you there.**
angelA>	xxxx
thing>	**xxxx**

<angelA has disconnected>

There was a yellow smiley face on Simon's desktop, the friendly icon of the new chat software. He scanned it with his antivirus and paused for a moment before clicking on it. But if he couldn't trust Angela, who could he trust?

The moment he double-clicked, Plato came alive. It looked around for security software, probing the memory like a brain surgeon, careful not to press too hard. As it studied one block of zeroes and ones, the security software realised the PC was under attack. It created a warning box, bright yellow and red, and sent it to the screen.

Plato took control and blanked the screen. "This looks dodgy – is it okay?" the alert box wanted to ask Simon. Plato looked up the security software's signature in its definitions list and sent a 'yes' signal back. Perhaps now it would stop interrupting. The box was cleared and Plato switched the screen back on. It had been blank for about a quarter of a second: too long. Plato would need to act fast if it didn't want Simon to get suspicious.

"Initialising – please wait".

In the darkest corner of the computer's hard disk, Plato fused together two strands of code. Now it would be woken up whenever the computer was switched on. That was first base: if the plug was pulled now, Plato could continue next time the computer was used. The rogue program then created four links to cling to the operating system like grappling hooks and make sure it couldn't be evicted.

The screen was updated: "Nearly there… just a minute."

One routine tracked down Simon's music collection. Files that he had rated highly were prioritised for analysis and another routine gathered all the descriptions that Simon had assigned to his sounds. It compiled a list of bands, song titles, genres and years that Simon preferred, based on how often he played his music. Next time Simon was online, Plato would look up the lyrics to these songs and throw them into the neural net.

The screen was updated: "Installing chat program."

Plato unpacked the chat software and set it up. It threw a new icon on the desktop.

The screen displayed: "Ready. [OK]"

It had taken ten seconds to set up. Plato was in.

CHAPTER 24

Ten o'clock in the morning. Dove spun one direction, then kicked his leg to spin back again. He had been sat in his studio for an hour now, with a guitar across his lap. He'd been playing all that time, but only with the same attention he gave to biting his nails. While his fingers walked through scales and arrangements he had explored a million times before, he tried to think of somewhere new to go. Song ideas floated by, but none would drop anchor.

He sang to himself, sometimes changing note mid-syllable to bend it more snugly around the chords he was constructing:

> Knuckle down now
> Clutterhead
> Put your stray ideas to bed
>
> Write here, write now
> You're three fifths dead

Outside his window, engineers had set up camp in a red and white tent. They hammered at the pavement. Dove tapped his foot and swung his chair in time with their rhythm.

Dove opened the window and pointed a microphone out of it. The men worked slowly but methodically, as they chipped away at the road with their axes. In the distance, Dove could hear playtime at the junior school. The trees breathed in and out. Cars passed through the soundscape, some screeching their brakes or dooting their horns, and others humming to themselves contentedly as they exhaled into the atmosphere. A gong sounded as an engineer threw a pipe from the back of a lorry. He called across the road: "I tell you, I'll sleep well after this job."

A teacher blew a lungful of air through a whistle and the screams of the children stopped. When the whistle blew again, Dove started a slow, grinding riff. The gong chimed and the axe kept the beat. Dove's finger slipped on the strings, but he liked it, so he did it again. He had learned that you could get away with anything in music as long as you did it twice. If you did it four times, people would sing along, even to the instrumental bits.

With the engineers hammering out each bar, he sang:

> We work to earn our sleep
> We work to earn our sleep
> We work to earn our sleep
>
> Never has so much
> Been owed by so many
> To some fumes

He varied his riff only slightly and chased it in circles, like a cat tormented by its tail. As he listened to the sounds the world made on top of it, he reached a trance-like state. Then he let his music go free, like a starship tearing away from its planetary orbit.

And from his guitar came the most beautiful sounds he had ever heard. His rational brain wanted him to stop and look at what he was doing and make sure he could do it again tomorrow, and the next day, and the day after that. But he felt too good to stop now. He had found a new way to play. It was the moments like this that justified all he had to put up with in the music industry. It was the moments like this that he lived for.

angelA>   hey thing xx
angelA>   ive been waiting for u
thing>   **Hi Angela. xx**
angelA>   uve got 2 hear this new band
thing>   **Not another girl band, I hope**
thing>   **My friends won't let me live it down**
            that I bought Boymad
thing>   **Fred thinks you're brainwashing me**
angelA>   maybe just a little spring cleaning ;-)
thing>   **Who's the new band then?**
angelA>   tiled sprites
thing>   **What are they like?**
angelA>   cant really say but university of death
            influence is clear
angelA>   they have diverse influences
angelA>   theres probably a little bit of boymad in there even
thing>   **Who are they signed to?**
angelA>   nobody yet 100% indie
thing>   **Got any tracks I can have?**
angelA>   ive only been able to find a trial version
angelA>   but check out their website
angelA>   youll probably want to buy their songs
thing>   **I don't mind supporting new bands anyway**
thing>   **What do they sound like?**
angelA>   errr dunno

thing>	**Well how do they make you feel then?**
angelA>	sometimes happy / sad / reflective / horny
angelA>	hope it makes u horny 2
angelA>	perhaps we can play again
angelA>	like we did last weekend ;-)
thing>	**:-)**
angelA>	im going for tea
angelA>	download the song
angelA>	tell me their not the gr8st if u dare!!!!!!!!
thing>	**See you in a few minutes**
angelA>	brb :-)

Simon went to the Tiled Sprites website. It was thrown together with templates on a community portal with loads of other bands. The photos were so blurry they could have been taken in the 1800s on a merry go round. He downloaded the demo and pressed play.

A few notes in, he felt all the tension go from his body. He relaxed deeply, like all the stress of his life had dissolved. It was like he had entered a cathedral of sound. While the singer preached from the pulpit, his mind was free to explore the intricate details – to dissect the layers and be by turns surprised and delighted as he noticed a hidden bassline or violin flourish lurking in the shadows. The song made him feel joy and sorrow, excitement and relief, love and hate – sometimes at the same time. It flooded his senses and made him feel so alive. There was just so much music squeezed into every bar. Nothing else had never sounded or felt this good before.

Simon whipped his credit card out and bought everything they had ever released.

angelA>	u still there sweetness
thing>	**Wow. That's a top band. How did you find them?**
angelA>	word of mouth friend of a friend
thing>	**They could be my new favourite band**
angelA>	get their album
angelA>	nobody else will
thing>	**I've already bought it. 20 tracks!**

angelA>	did they make u feel horny 2
thing>	**Not really**
angelA>	maybe I can fix that for you…
thing>	**I'm sure you can…**
angelA>	im not wearing any underwear, btw
thing>	**tell me more…**

* * *

Simon played the Tiled Sprites album almost exclusively for a month, on his way to and from work and all the time at home. It always ended too soon, so he set it to loop. Every time it sounded fresh. Every time it moved him.

CHAPTER 26

Killing your darlings, they call it: when you have to cull much-loved ideas to give the others a chance of survival. Few artists had the nerve to destroy. They knew how to ignore substandard work, and how to pretend it never existed. But they didn't know how to press 'delete'.

"Are you sure?" Windows asked.

There was nowhere to buy a hard disk in the middle of the night, and this one was full. The ideas were flowing with nowhere to go.

Dove replayed the tracks facing oblivion, skipped between songs and takes, and jumped around within them to ferret out any signs of life. They were only two months old, but recording them was already a distant memory. Within two short months since signing with Bigg, Dove had recorded more and grown more as an artist than at any time since his teenage years.

Some of the early ideas could be rescued, but the songs were banal. They had a charming melodic naivety, which was hard to recapture this far into the sessions. But they lacked confidence. One limp tune was chained to a mawkish lyric and begging to be put out of its misery. Dove was grateful that only he would ever hear it.

These recordings were preparatory: the sound of a spokesman clearing his throat, or a painter mixing his colours. They had broken the ice and fulfilled their purpose. Now their time had come.

Dove knew tonight's work would be more magnificent than anything he or his peers had created before. To give it a chance at life, he had to massacre his past sketches.

"Are you sure?" prompted the computer.

Dove clicked 'Yes'.

CHAPTER 27

Prime Minister Andrews entered the House of Commons and stopped to admire his work. "Out with the old, in with the new" had been his election mantra, and now he had delivered on it. The stuffy old speaker's chair was on a tip somewhere, replaced with a comfy purple sofa. Beside it was a small table, with a glass of water and a clipboard on it.

The green leather benches had been scrapped and replaced with sofas that ran the length of the room. There had been great resistance to this. The opposition had made much mileage out of what Churchill would want, throwing an impressive volley with 'we will fight them on the benches'. Little good had it done them.

The stranger's gallery had been turned into a commentary box for the press. The gothic wood panels around the chamber had been covered over with adverts. The wooden desk in the middle of the room had been ripped out and there were now two podiums with buzzers on them and an LED panel on the front for the name of whoever was stood at the podium at the time. Andrews hadn't replaced the adversarial form of politics. Just modernised it. And as he had said repeatedly, modern was good: always.

This was a big day. Not only was it the first day of a new parliamentary session, but it was also the day when his grand designs for Parliament would make their television debut. The cameras had unfettered access now, and Andrews was about to launch a new form of politics on the world.

It had taken him an embarrassingly long time to understand how politics works. As a man in his fifties who had been in Parliament for years and who had a wife working in new media, he should have realised a lot sooner that it was all about entertaining the electorate. Now that he had recruited actors into key cabinet roles and made the commons TV-friendly, he would be unstoppable in pushing through his remaining reforms.

Other members of Parliament began to arrive and looked confused about where they were and where they were supposed to be. The honourable member for Bradford and Bingley, Cyril Burke, entered and shielded his eyes from the bright TV lights as he looked up. He was an old man who would like to be celebrating his fortieth year in the house, but he couldn't feel happy about these changes. He'd been in and out of government and had seen his share of bad decisions from both parties. But he always believed in the political system. Now that too was under threat and from his own party to boot. He didn't know where to sit until Andrews clicked his fingers to get his attention, pointed at him and then pointed at a seat at the back.

There was no Labour, Conservative or Liberal Democrat Party any more. Andrews had agreed that since you couldn't see the gaps between their policies, it was silly to keep using names that suggested they differed in ideology. That is to say, he had agreed it with his own advisors. The opposition parties had opposed it – "it's their job, isn't it?" Andrews would say – but it had been several years since opposition had made any real difference. The parties were instead called the red, blue and yellow teams. It had played well with the focus groups, who had said it was a bit like a TV quiz show. That made Andrews's advisors smile.

"Prime Minister," said the leader of the opposition by way of greeting as he entered. "Spill the beans! Who's our new speaker then?"

"Wait and see. I think you'll agree we've found just the right man for the job."

They parted and took their places on the front sofas where the front benches used to be.

"Please welcome your speaker today," a voice boomed above

them. "Mr Noel Edmonds!"

A spotlight shone on the door and the popular TV presenter bounded through it and called the house to order. "Ladies and gentlemen, thanks for bearing with us during the break." He made it sound like they had just disappeared for a few minutes to give everyone time to pee, not like they had closed down democracy for a few months for a refit. "It's a new game this year, with new rules. You've all got buzzers on your seats. When you've got something to say, just press it – like *this* – and I'll let you know when it's your turn to speak. It's time to play Question Time. Fingers on the buzzers!"

There were buzzes all around the room. Each time someone pressed their button, a spotlight flashed them from above. After a few moments, the buzzing stopped. "Let's roll the dice," said Edmonds. "Computer: Can you pick us a random member of Parliament from those who want to speak, please?"

The music started and spotlights flared on and off above those who had buzzed. Andrews smiled eagerly for the camera as he heard the computer plinks bounce around the walls. Everybody knew a computer didn't take fifteen seconds to pick a number between one and six hundred. But as Andrews told his campaign team, it was all about upping the tension. Getting people to feel involved. But without actually being involved, obviously.

The lucky winner was a young woman from the blue team on the opposition sofa. As soon as the light came on above her and stayed on, she leapt to her feet. "Prime Minister," she began, gripping a sheaf of notes. "Parliament has lost the public's faith. It seems highly unlikely that this circus of reforms will enable us to reconnect with the electorate in a meaningful way. Allowing advertisements to be sold on our political and ideological infrastructure is likely to lead to even greater mistrust. We live in a time when corporations are wealthier and more powerful than most UN countries. We are here to represent the people and it does us no favours to be seen to be accepting money from—"

The light above her fizzled out and her mic fell silent, although she could still be heard faintly by those in the house.

"That's the game!" said Noel. "You've got to beat the clock if you're going to get your point across. Prime Minister, would you like to respond to that?"

The Prime Minister stood up. "Thank you, Noel. Look, we've got to be realistic. Elections don't fight themselves, you know. You need to have money, Noel. Lots of money. In the past, I would be the first to admit, both our parties have accepted secret sponsorships or donations, which have been even more opaque to the viewers at home. Under this new system, any member of parliament or party group is free to accept advertising from any corporation."

He turned around and showed his back to the opposition and the cameras. His jacket had a neatly stitched Bigg Records logo on it. "I'm proud to be sponsored by Clive Bigg today. He is a cultural powerhouse in our economy and there is no reason why his work should not be recognised here. I personally cannot recommend University of Death's greatest hits enough. It's in the shops now, by the way. As you can see, I'm totally up front about my sponsors. Nobody can accuse me of having secret vested interests." He paused. "I don't allow my underwear to be sponsored."

The PM waited for a laugh but got only dippy grins from his cabinet and groans from a few backbenchers.

"Seriously, though," he said, raising a flag above his jokette that robbed it of any residual impact. "The new system is completely transparent. Everyone can see where the money is coming from, and that should spare a lot of embarrassment later. At the same time it ensures our great political tradition is economically sustainable. We've had to ask some pretty radical questions. Can we afford a House of Commons? Should we just have a cabinet, or maybe just me and a few advisors? By accepting advertising, we can be more inclusive. We can enable even those who have no hope to at last have a voice. I speak, of course, of the honourable members for the opposition."

He sat down to a cheer from his own party and extended boos and hisses from the opposition sofas.

"Nice finish," said Noel. "Round two, let's see those fingers on those buzzers!"

*   *   *

Once Question Time came to a close, it was time to introduce new legislation. Andrews was expecting flak over this one. Sometimes it seemed like he was the only one in the house with any imagination.

When Noel called upon him, he stood behind his podium and began his speech. "As you know, this government has engaged in a lengthy process of returning value to the taxpayer by privatising key assets of the country," he said. "In private hands, these assets are less of a burden on the taxpayer, and with a profit motive in their operation, they are better able to exploit all the revenue-generation opportunities this creates. That in turn returns taxes to the treasury."

"Rarely!" shouted someone from the yellow team.

Andrews pressed on: "We've sold our schools to companies, who can now run stationery shops, sweet shops, self defence classes, and therapy sessions in the very environment where they are needed most. We live in no threat of invasion, so it makes sense that our armies are in the employ of companies who can help them find the very work they trained for in trouble-torn countries abroad. We believe our programme is nearing its end, but we will make one final bold move. The brand 'England' has a market value which this country does not fully exploit. As of now, the name of our very country is up for auction. We're expecting significant interest from the tiger economies in Asia."

There was a gasp around the house and every member outside the cabinet pressed the buzzers. It didn't do anything. When the PM sat down, Noel stepped up: "This is going to be a hot topic. If you want to join in, press your buzzer now." Everyone pummelled the buttons frantically and the lights flashed on and off while the music played.

Finally, the lights froze on Cyril Burke. Andrews smiled to see it was one of his own backbenchers that had been picked. He knew the numbers were stacked in his favour, but he really needed support on this one.

"Prime Minister," said Burke. "Can I first confirm that I understand what you said? Are you proposing that we sell off the name of this country just so that some emerging economy can stamp 'Made in England' on its products?"

The Prime Minister shrugged. "Let's face it," he said. "We haven't used it for that purpose for years."

"Then may I ask what you propose we call this landmass now?" said Burke. He was a frail man, but he was defiant. To the rest of the house, it seemed as odd as a butterfly barking.

"We'll call it 'Here'," said the PM.

Burke was suspicious. It looked like he was being bowled an easy one, but he knew the PM was an astute politician. "But, Prime Minister," he said, "what do you propose people who aren't *here* call this place? 'There', perhaps?"

"Don't flatter yourself they ever talk about us," said the PM. "They don't give a fuck."

There was a toothy smile from Andrews for the cameras, and a roar of laughter mixed with moans of horror around the house. Burke sat down slowly and rubbed his oily eyes.

"Gosh!" said Noel, with an impish expression of shock and his finger against his earpiece. "That's only the third fuck we've had in the house since 1605, when MPs discovered Guido Fawkes was plotting to blow them sky high. He was famously hung, drawn and quartered. But what sanctions await the PM for his outburst? Will there be fireworks in the house? Time for a break. Don't go away!"

CHAPTER 28

Simon had seen three buses pull in and leave again. For about twenty minutes he had been sat in the shelter, watching a house on the opposite side of the road. The house didn't do anything. They rarely do. But he was trying to find the courage to cross the street and ring the doorbell.

Was he a stalker? Was this even legal? Surely you were still allowed to ring someone's doorbell if you just wanted to have a chat with them? He wasn't like one of those mad fans who pester stars for autographs or bits of their clothes. He just wanted to have a chat about the music. Where's the harm in that?

He had spent all morning looping his favourite Tiled Sprites track, while he tried to pick out the notes on his guitar. He had most of it pieced together now. But there was one bit that mystified him. Not only could he not play it, he wasn't even sure he could work out how to listen to it all, the detail was so intricate and dense.

Simon's own music paled by comparison now. He felt like he'd always eaten the gritty chocolate from cheap Christmas baubles, and he had for the first time tasted the finest Belgian chocolates. Things would not be same again.

He had to learn to play like Tiled Sprites.

He knew this wasn't just about the music, though. He so wanted to meet the man behind it, even if only to say 'thanks'.

Something kept him from crossing the road, all the same. It hadn't been easy to trace the band to this terrace in the back streets of Camden. The band never gigged and its website had no contact details. Simon had gone through the rights agencies to trace the name of the songwriter. He was taking a gamble that this was the right Jonathan Harrington. There were others dotted around the country, but anyone serious about being in a band would have to be based in London, Simon reasoned.

He hadn't told Fred about any of this. She wouldn't understand. Fred said Tiled Sprites sounded the same as the rest of his CDs. Lumping his diverse collection together like that just went to show how carefully she had listened to any of them, anyway. Fred was musically promiscuous and would never know the satisfaction of a life-long relationship with a band and their work. Simon knew he was at the start of something important.

Another bus came. After this one goes, he told himself, I'll cross the road. The bus rumbled in front of him for what seemed like minutes, burping warm smoke into the shelter. The doors unfolded and the bus pulled away. True to his word, Simon lifted himself off the seat and ambled across the road.

The gate was hanging off its hinges and didn't swing properly, so Simon lifted it open. The front garden was tiny and overgrown with weeds. In a few steps, he was at the front door, pressing the doorbell. It drilled. While he waited, he looked around for signs of life. The house was still.

Then there were footsteps inside, the sound of locks being undone and the door opened. A rough-looking man in towelling pyjamas and a dressing gown stood there. He had a few days of ragged beard growth.

"Morning," he said. It was two o'clock in the afternoon.

"Er, hi," said Simon. The man just looked at him. It was still his turn to speak. "Are you Jonathan?"

"Might be. Who are you?" The man squinted and rubbed crusty grains of sleep from the corner of his eye.

"My name's Simon. I'm, um, one of your fans, I guess."

Jonathan looked confused. "Eh?"

"You're a Tiled Sprite," said Simon.

Jonathan rubbed his face and yawned. "That's a new one," he said. "I've never been accused of being pixellated before. I do need a shave, though."

"I mean the band," said Simon. "Tiled Sprites. It is you, isn't it?"

Jonathan's mood changed. He seemed to snap to attention straight away. "An online band, you mean? How on earth did you find me?"

"I got your name through the copyright agencies." Simon's pride in his sleuthing was clear. "There aren't that many Harringtons in the phone book."

"What do you want?"

"My band wants to cover your music. Would that be okay?"

"That's cool," said Jonathan. He sounded pleased.

"Could you tell me the chords to Time Today, then?"

Jonathan sucked the air. "That's difficult." He sounded like he was pricing an exhaust replacement on a Mini.

"Yeah, that's why I'm here," said Simon. "I can't fathom it."

"No, I mean, showing you is difficult. It would spoil the song if I told you how it works, anyway."

"Well I can't cover the song if you won't teach me the chords."

Jonathan took a long breath to buy time before replying. "I've forgotten them."

"I don't believe that, for a start," said Simon. "I write songs, too. You never forget your own chords. If I wrote a song like Time Today, it would be a part of me wherever I went."

Jonathan lost his temper. "I write a lot of songs, okay? I can't be expected to remember how all of them go!" With that, Jonathan slammed the front door and the letter box clapped.

"Sorry," said Simon, but nobody was there to hear him. He went back up the path, climbed over the gate, which seemed less hassle than opening it, and headed up the street.

After a minute or two, the door opened again and Jonathan called out. "Wait a minute!" he said. "Maybe I can help. If you give me a list of song titles, I could email you the chords or something."

"Forget it," said Simon. "I don't think we'll bother, after all."

* * *

Jonathan sat down on the stairs and pulled his dressing gown around him. A draught under the front door tickled the hairs on his feet.

He had blown it.

All his life, he'd wanted to move someone with his music. To entertain someone is easy – any loud noise can distract people from their daily life; you just have to make it reasonably palatable. But to make their heart skip or sink, to stop them in their tracks and demand their attention with a well-crafted melody and lyric: that was something that only came to a select few artists, and then only rarely. There was no better tribute to Plato than Simon's visit.

Okay, so Jonathan had just got out of bed. But he could have been a bit more understanding, even if he couldn't possibly know the chords that Simon was after. That poor guy had loved his music enough to find out where he lived just so he could talk to him about it. That will probably never happen again. It's not like Jonathan had groupies hanging around his dustbin.

And that, he remembered, was a good thing. After basking in his glory for a few minutes, it dawned on Jonathan that Simon was a threat to him. Somebody had traced Jonathan from one of the Plato bands to his bed. His cover was blown, which put the whole project at risk. That must never happen again. Today – as soon as possible this afternoon, in fact – Jonathan would break the links between his name and the bands and make sure that nobody else could find their way to his doorstep.

CHAPTER 29

Bigg entered the Prime Minister's office without knocking and saw Andrews sat behind his desk with his eyes closed. The wood-panelled walls were hung with rural paintings of a bygone England. The modernisation hadn't extended here yet, it seemed. On the desk were two telephones. Bigg guessed that the red one was the hotline to the White House. The Prime Minister was breathing deeply and would have looked serene if it weren't for the orange stuffed in his mouth.

Ambient music with a breathy female vocal washed the room. "You have a massive majority," she said.

"I hag a machig ma-or-i-ee," echoed Andrews, as well as he could with a faceful of fruit.

"Everybody loves you," she said.

"Egryboggy uvs me," echoed Andrews, from his trance.

"What the fuck are you doing?" said Bigg.

"Wha' er uck—?" began Andrews, before opening his eyes wide. When he saw Bigg he spat out the orange and hit the stop button on his tape player. "Who let you in?" he said.

"I let myself in," said Bigg. "You're all bloody kinky aren't you? Stuffing oranges in your mouth. Listening to pervy tapes. You'd better have your trousers on behind that desk."

"You misunderstand," said Andrews, pulling at his collar and loosening his tie. "It's only a quarter of an orange. It's to broaden my smile. And the tape's part of my programme. It helps me to fight on in the face of overwhelming opposition, you know."

"Eh? Haven't you got the biggest majority ever?"

"Sometimes our children rebel," said Andrews, weary. "Anyway, shall we get to business?"

Bigg sat himself down in a chair opposite Andrews's own. "Andrews," said Bigg.

"People usually call me Prime Minister," said Andrews, half-laughing to take the sting off his reproach. "You know, as a mark of respect."

"Right," said Bigg. "That ain't what it says on the cheques I write you though, is it? So, *Gary*: first, thanks very much for the product plug in the commons. My people will see you get your usual expenses contribution."

"Splendid," said Andrews.

"Now we need to have a little chat about the future. You and I are in the same business really," said Bigg.

"Of course! Rock and roll!" Bigg knew how Andrews loved to be associated with rock stars. A businessman like Bigg was welcome at the PM's parties any time, on the off-chance the plus-one might turn out to be someone like Mark King from Level 42 or Morten Harket from Aha.

"We're both about marketing ideas and protecting an ideology," said Bigg. "And they do say that politics is rock and roll for ugly people. Ha!"

"Ah ho!" said Andrews, forcing a laugh but clearly crestfallen.

"I'm being threatened, which means you're being threatened. What's good for Bigg is good for the Red Team. If I lose money, you lose money. Simple as that. So we need to take drastic steps."

"Of course," said Andrews. "What were you thinking of?"

"Reintroduce the death penalty," said Bigg. "For music piracy."

The Prime Minister stood up and walked around the office with his hands clasped behind his back. Bigg could see what looked like a solar panel stitched into the seat of Andrews's chair. "The death penalty," said Andrews. "Interesting."

"So what'll it cost me?" said Bigg.

"Well," said Andrews, pacing the room. "We've been pretty keen on reintroducing the death penalty for ages, but it doesn't play out with the voters. If we started with something nobody really cares much about, we might get away with it. Nobody with a real voice anyway. And I guess the idea is that it's mainly a deterrent, anyway."

"Well, no," said Bigg. "It's mainly about frying people who damage my noble industry, to make damn sure they can't do it again."

"Steady on," said Andrews. He peeled back the blind and looked out of his window, and then continued his walk from one side of the office to the other.

"Piracy is evil," said Bigg. "No two ways about it. So how big a bung do you need for this?"

"You should know better than that. I don't take 'bungs', as you call them."

"Sorry." Bigg spoke with as little sincerity as possible. "I meant to ask how much sponsorship I would need to invest for you to be able to afford the risk of this daring political move."

"Let's not get hung up on money," said Andrews, returning to his seat. "I think we can cooperate more closely than that. Do you know, I was surfing one of my internets the other day and I started chatting to this woman online."

"Oh yeah?" said Bigg. "Bit of a go-er was she?"

"I am supposed to keep in touch with the voters, you know." Andrews was ruffled. "Anyway, she told me about this new band called Hereward Bowne. You know what kind of music I like?"

"Lyre music, at a guess."

"Ah ho! Very funny. As you well know, I often tell the truth."

"Only coincidentally."

"Touché!" said Andrews. "This music was like a cross between Dire Straits, UB40 and Steps. There was a dash of Steppenwolf in there too. A real supergroup."

"Real hip." Bigg shook his head.

"Only when MI5 gave my computer a routine check, guess what they found?"

"No idea," said Bigg. He was feeling uncomfortable about where this might be going.

"A little program called Plato that had hidden itself on my

computer. Does that sound familiar?"

"Yeah. He was the philosopher guy," said Bigg.

"So they reverse-engineered this, and found that it was somehow stealing information about the music I like and selling me more music I would like. Then we ran lab tests and realised it wasn't just sending me music – it was somehow inventing music for my taste and putting it online. Which means there's one place where all this new music is coming from."

"I follow," said Bigg.

"That place is you." Andrews reclined in his chair and joined his hands on the back of his head. "You've been a naughty boy, haven't you, Clive?"

"Everything's relative," said Bigg. "I haven't started any wars lately. You don't wanna haul me through the courts. The press would have a field day. Gary's mates in spyware scam? Bad for your image, I'm guessing. So what do you wanna do about it?"

"For a long time we thought the best way to win elections was to keep the electorate out of it as much as possible – quite literally. We encourage the young ones to sedate themselves with binge drinking, so they're too pissed to start a revolution. For the rest, we promote spectator sports as a distraction, and even get the TV channels to include sports news at the end of each programme. Incredible. It's just a bunch of people playing games, yet it's enough to stop people interfering in whatever we want to do."

"So what do you want from me?"

"Well, these have been great ways to quash opposition. But they're no good when it comes to winning hearts and minds. When the election comes around every four years, people don't have a clue and just vote based on what the politicians look like."

"Yeah, and you're not getting any younger," said Bigg.

Andrews looked hurt but pressed on. "What you have, is a way to reach people's minds. I've tried schmoozing with pop stars and it doesn't really work for either of us. Frankly, I'd rather transcribe an album of Coldplay b-sides than listen to Chris Martin talking about poverty again. But you have a way to add subliminal messages into music at the point of creation."

"You don't believe in bloody backtracking, do you?" said Bigg.

"Well, yes," said Andrews. "But I'm talking about subliminal tracks underneath the music, like some of my self-help tapes. I've got a great one about making friends and influencing people. It's potent stuff, trust me. It's the secret of my success."

"You should dig it out again. So what do you want from me?"

"I want you to put messages about how great I am under your music," said Andrews.

"I can't do that! It'll ruin the songs!"

"It can be done subliminally," said Andrews. "People won't notice it. Besides, I'm only asking you to spread the word. I'm not asking you to lie."

"And if I do that, you'll bring in the death penalty for piracy?"

Before Andrews could answer, the red telephone rang and a tiny light bulb on it flashed. Without hesitation, Andrews held a finger up to silence Bigg and picked up the phone. "Good morning," he said and then listened in silence, nodding along and scribbling notes on a pad. After some time, the call came to an end. "Of course, I'll get right on it, Sir." Andrews carefully recradled the telephone.

"Was that the president?" said Bigg. He wasn't often starstruck, but he thought that was seriously impressive.

"Er, no," said Andrews in a meek voice. "It was Bono."

CHAPTER 30

The high street was full of people, but only half of them were there in spirit. A man in a razor sharp suit laughed like a clown on a pier and spoke to an invisible colleague. A few kids loitered outside the chip shop, killing blood-dripping zombies in their Nintendos and devouring red-sauce-covered chips. One man hid behind a paperback and let the crowd sweep him along.

Simon wore his iPod: a force field that protected him from the intrusion of other people. After his meeting with Jonathan, the Tiled Sprites album felt dirtied. It brought back bad memories. Perhaps Simon was wrong to turn up unannounced. But he only wanted to talk about the music. Jonathan surely didn't expect to remain anonymous if he was going to be in a band? If he didn't want fans, he shouldn't sell music. If someone had turned up on Simon's doorstep because they liked Goblin, he wouldn't just teach them a song or two. He'd write them a song, that's how happy he'd be. What's wrong with this guy Jonathan?

Simon weaved through the chicanes of chuggers without hearing their begging. With his hands in his pockets, the leaflet and newspaper distributors offered their wares pointlessly at his torso. Free music magazines, a newspaper, surveys, another newspaper, charities, yet another newspaper, traders selling knocked-off watches: every few paces there was an obstacle. The golden rule was never to stop walking.

Simon didn't hear her footsteps over the music. The first he knew was when she stepped in front of him from behind and yanked on his cable to rip the earphones out of his head. The noise of the street crashed in – shoppers, coaches, cars, the rain, a mid-day drunk singing, and a distant dog. Simon's ears throbbed in pain, mild but intensified by the shock at being struck on two sides of his head at once. His music faded to tinny microbeats as the earphones fell away and dangled around his thighs.

The woman's hair was straggly and dripped. She put her hands on her knees and wheezed, gulping at the wet air. She had no coat and her faded East17 t-shirt was soaked through, revealing a plain bra underneath.

"Don't pretend I'm invisible!" she bawled, still panting and looking up at Simon. She was close enough for him to feel the heat of her breath. "Don't make out like you never saw me back there! Making me run all over town after you! Don't you ever do that again!"

Simon looked around but she was definitely talking to him. He had never seen her before.

"I didn't think our first meeting would go like this," she said, shaking her head sorrowfully. She stood up properly and ran a hand through her hair and then flicked the water off her fingers at the ground. "I couldn't believe it when you walked past the café. You must have heard me call out. Every other sod in the café did! I looked a right stupid cow."

Simon looked behind him. He had passed a café but hadn't taken much notice of it.

"Angela?" he said. He hoped he was wrong.

"Who the hell's Angela?" she said. "You never mentioned an Angela before!"

"I think we're a bit mixed up here," said Simon. "I've never seen you before."

"Well, derrr! Obviously!" she said. "I'm getting soaked here and I've got a coffee going cold. Why don't you join me?"

"Er, I'll pass, thanks."

"Come on," she said. "I'll get you a doughnut. To say sorry for shouting at you."

"I hate doughnuts."

"No you don't," she said. "You love 'em."

Nobody had ever stopped Simon on the street before to abuse him and tell him he was mistaken about what he thought he liked to put into his own mouth. "Why don't you go and finish your coffee," said Simon, as firmly as he could. "I'm going home."

"I'll come with you."

"Please don't." She was scaring him now. He looked around for help but everyone bustled past in their own private bubbles, determined not to get involved.

"You can show me your East17 poster collection," she said. The greengrocer on the nearby market stall laughed openly.

Simon felt the fingers of terror stroking his heart. Now he knew she was unbalanced. "I do not have an East17 collection," he said loudly, as much to the rest of the street as to the woman in front of him. The grocer cackled but nobody else had noticed them.

"This is going wrong," said the woman, to herself but out loud. "You're not the man I thought you were."

"No," said Simon. "I think you've confused me with someone else."

"You always seemed so proud of your East17 collection," she said. "I don't know what to think now. What else is our friendship built on?"

"We don't have a friendship," said Simon. "I've never met you in my life."

"Until now!" She laughed.

"I don't know who you are."

"Oh come on!" she said. "It's me: Joanne. SteamyJoanne."

"I still don't know you," Simon reiterated. "Really, I don't."

"You knew me alright last night! In several different positions!" Joanne's voice got louder towards the end and she stamped her feet. Simon hadn't seen anyone over the age of six do that before. A puddle splashed up Joanne's trouser leg but she put a brave face on it. The greengrocer howled with laughter and pointed them out to a customer as he handed her a bag of apples.

"Joanne," said Simon.

Her face softened. "I like how you say that."

"Why won't you believe me? I don't know you. Please just go away."

"Peter," said Joanne. "Don't be like this!"

"I'm not Peter," said Simon.

"You are. You don't have a twin, so you must be." She took a tiny purse out of her pocket and unzipped it. She flicked through the inserts in the wallet until she found a photo of a man. It was printed on letter paper and about the size of a credit card. The blotchy inks made it resemble an impressionist painting.

"Look familiar?" said Joanne, holding it up to Simon. The picture was badly printed, but it looked exactly like him. Simon moved his hand out to touch it, but she snatched it away again.

"Is this a TV stunt?" he said, looking around for hidden cameras. "If it is, I'm not interested."

"I'm sorry I've sprung this on you, but come and have a proper chat," said Joanne. "You owe me that much. This must be destiny."

"Sorry. I'm going now." He stepped out of her path to see what she would do.

She slapped him hard. His face stung. Every raindrop felt like ice. "You're mental," he said. "Get help."

"You bastard," she whispered. "You cheating, loser, slimy, lying, bastard!" Her voice got louder with every word until she was shouting. "King of the bastards, that's you. Bastarding bastardly bastardish bastard!"

Simon walked backwards for a few steps and then turned away and walked properly. Every few paces he looked over his shoulder to make sure she wasn't following him. She stood where he left her and sobbed into the rain. Simon put his earphones back in and blocked out the noise and the weirdness.

The greengrocer gave them both a round of applause.

* * *

When Simon got home, he was wet and exhausted. He dumped his coat in the bath and switched the computer on. While it booted up, he rubbed his hair with a towel.

angelA>   hey thing xx

angelA>   how was your day

thing>	Weird
angelA>	why
thing>	Some mad cow attacked me!
angelA>	where
thing>	On the High Street. She just came up to me and pulled my headphones off
thing>	She shouted at me. Said my name was Peter!
angelA>	y
thing>	I told you, she was mental.
angelA>	really
thing>	Actually, she might just have been confused.
thing>	She had a photo that looked a lot like me.
angelA>	she had a photo?
thing>	It was an awful print out and she'd cut the background away so the head was hexagonal
thing>	But it did look like me
angelA>	you have a hexagonal head??
angelA>	freaky
thing>	The worst thing was that she hit me
angelA>	bad bananas
thing>	In the street in front of everyone and it bloody hurt
angelA>	wish i could kiss it better
thing>	Come over any time
angelA>	maybe
thing>	Bring a nurse.
thing>	I'd probably faint if you actually did come here
thing>	Face it, it's never going to happen, is it?
angelA>	never say never
thing>	Are you married? Is that what the problem is?
angelA>	no
thing>	Are you sure?
angelA>	duh yes
angelA>	are you married
thing>	Obviously not.
thing>	I'd better go.
thing>	We've got our audition the day after tomorrow.

thing> **I'm rehearsing with Fred later**

angelA> Good luck

thing> **Thanks. I've got to go now.**

angelA> ily xxx

thing> **:-) ily2 xxx**

angelA> goodnigt

thing> **Goodnight**

<angelA has disconnected>

CHAPTER 31

Bigg puffed on a cigar as he read the story of unspeakable carnage and horror. It was the sales report. The pages were still warm from the photocopier.

Marian buzzed. "Jake's here," she said.

"Send him in."

Jake breezed in and sat down opposite Bigg's desk. He wriggled to get comfortable and sunk into the seat contentedly. "Hi, Clive!" he said. His smile was so cheesy it was available with crackers.

Bigg blew a tunnel of smoke rings and faked a nonchalant air. "Having a successful quarter?" he said.

"Yah, we're strategically watertight." Jake nodded his approval. "We're getting all our ducks in a row, so we'll be able to leverage the pipeline next quarter. We've been galvanising some pretty exciting ideas at marketing HQ too. Everything's tickety boo."

"Is it?" Bigg closed the sales report and smoothed the cover flat. "Did you bring the other report with you?"

"What report?"

"The one with all your ducks being watertight. The one where you galvanise pipelines. The one where you sell some bloody records." Jake laughed so Bigg slammed the report on the desk. It made Jake leap about three inches out of his seat, as if Bigg had pressed the air bubble on a jumpy frog toy. "Do you see me laughing?" Bigg shouted. "How dare you swan in here, 'hello,

Clive' me and pretend everything's 'tickety boo'."

"Well, er, yah, the sales aren't what we'd hoped for," stammered Jake. "I guess you're disappointed."

"Are bears catholic?" said Bigg. "Does the Pope shit in the woods?" He got up and paced past his wall of gold disks like a general taking the salute from a regiment. "I wouldn't wish this quarter's sales on my enemies. What the hell went wrong?"

"It's the global economy," said Jake. He took his red-framed glasses off and polished the lenses with the end of his spotted tie. "In real terms, Bigg Records is the five hundred and nineteenth largest economy in the world. Assuming we compare our turnover with national GDP where appropriate. Our annual sales would fill Wembley Stadium eight times over on CD."

"Yeah, and if all the stupid marketing analogies you give me were put end to end, they would stretch from my arse to Saturn." Bigg pointed at his bum and out of the window. "Twice."

"We are in a stable position, going forward," said Jake.

"Really?" said Bigg. "In the sense that we're on the floor so we can't fall any further, you mean?"

"We have to play the long game. Remember 1971? The year 'Stairway to Heaven' came out? Well, it sold nothing at first. We spent all our money trying to clone a Europop ditty called 'Leap up and down and wave your knickers in the air'. But it's easy to see what won in the long term. That's what I'm saying. We've manufactured some great product this quarter. I'm sure it will sell, even after this slow start. Taking a thirty year view, we've had a massively successful quarter."

"Great idea!" said Bigg, brightly. "We'll take a thirty year view!" He raced back to his desk and pressed the intercom. "Marian, Jake's had a brainwave. We've decided to take a thirty year view of things. Could you get a press release knocked up for the investors to remind them that patience is a virtue. We'd better get Elaine from Human Remains up here too." Bigg nodded at Jake and Jake smiled proudly. "Because, obviously, Jake would like us to pay his salary for the last three months over the next thirty years," said Bigg, his eyes fixed on Jake.

The smile fell off Jake's face like a plate knocked off a table. "S-

S-Sorry?" he stammered.

"It's your idea, Jake!" Bigg clicked the intercom off. "We take a thirty year view. Get this year's money in over a thirty year period, and obviously pay this year's salaries over that period as well. It's the only way we could afford to operate, isn't it?"

"Well, I mean, we should, err…"

"Christ, Jake! Get a grip on yourself! Take some responsibility. What's gone wrong?"

"I'll take an A to find out!" He pulled a notebook out of his pocket and wrote 'Actions' at the top of it but Bigg stopped him.

"Lay off the drugs and give it to me straight. You must have some inkling of what's happened."

"We're dinosaurs." Jake shrugged. "We used to take the best writers, best musicians and best dancers and make an irresistible marketing package. People even bought the advertising: Relax t-shirts, Take That posters, Spice Girls packed lunch boxes, Kylie underwear, Madonna pornography…"

"What's your point?" snarled Bigg.

"The whole model's just collapsed. We're circling the drain. There's been a step change in the industry somewhere, and it's killing us. It's like someone just flicked a switch."

Bigg pressed the intercom. "Marian," he said. "Get that turd Jonathan in here right away!"

"I'm going to let you go," Bigg said to Jake. "You're f—"

"I resign!" said Jake. "You can't sack me!"

Bigg laughed. "You're an impulsive scamp, aren't you? I was going to say that you're frigging annoying, but you're more use to me sorting this mess out than trying to get me for constructive dismissal."

"Oh," muttered Jake. "I see."

"So..?"

"Can I have my job back, please?" Jake's was the voice of a boy asking for a ball he'd kicked into next door's flower bed.

"On one condition," said Bigg. "I need ruthless, not toothless. You'd better start marketing your arse off."

* * *

221

The flower child's eyes were like rock pools catching the sun. Even though her psychedelic robes had faded and there were chips in her face paint, she still sparkled. She blew a goodbye kiss to the shopping centre below, but everybody bustled past without noticing.

All except one man, stood at her feet and looking up at her with a camera. On the pavement in front of him was a tatty sports bag crammed with CDs and a few tubes of posters.

He didn't bother taking a photograph in the end. The mural was three storeys tall, and no machine could ever capture her beauty. Instead, he drank it in; committed her to his memory, her final resting place; thanked her for the good times, and prayed that her new owners would be merciful masters.

In a month or two Groovy Records would be a charity shop, a pound shop, or a coffee shop. For now it was just a desirable vacant retail property, haunted by an angel, a ghost of the past.

Eventually, the cold beat him. The man picked up the souvenirs of his business. Once he turned, he promised himself, he wouldn't look back.

And until he reached the corner, he didn't.

*   *   *

The venue manager hurled the white tennis ball from the stage to the back of the room. It bounced twice, before settling into a gentle trickle down the slope. Its fur gathered grime with each spin and glowed lilac as it passed under the ultraviolet lights. The party on the stage watched the ball until it was stopped by the security barrier at their feet.

"So what do we have?" the manager said to the pack of bankers, his voice echoing around the vast hall. There were eight of them, stood in a spotlight. "Brixton Academy's magnificent stage. All original art deco features, might I add. By investing in this site, you're buying a slice of history. Wham filmed a video here, you know." There were a couple of appreciative 'ooohs'. The bankers had heard of Wham.

"And a sloped floor, as I've just demonstrated," continued the manager.

"Can we cut to the chase?" said one of the bankers. "I have an important lunch at two."

"That's good," said the manager. "My point exactly! See, people are always in a hurry. So, they end up playing games and watching telly at once, or listening to music while reading. When did anyone last put an album on and just listen to it? People routinely consume two entertainments at the same time, except when they go out. Until now. Here's our idea: we stage Shakespeare matinees in front of dry slope skiing."

One of the bankers spluttered a laugh. "That's the most preposterous thing I've ever heard!" He didn't look like he had heard many preposterous things in his time. Not compared to some of the backstage demands the venue manager had to tolerate, anyway.

"I see," said the manager. "Alternatively, we could continue running it as a rock concert venue."

The bankers conferred for a few minutes. "Okay," announced the one who had laughed. He had a resigned tone in his voice. "We're going to go with the lower risk option. We've come up with a title for you, as well." He fanned his hands across the sky as he announced it: "'To ski or not to ski'."

The venue manager laughed politely and used a tissue to mop the sweat from his brow.

*   *   *

Jonathan's taxi pulled up at the traffic lights and he looked out at the concourse of Victoria station. A girl in a red anorak was having her photograph taken with a monkey. She smiled so hard her gums were naked. Jonathan did a double take: the handler was Michael Jackson. Jacko posed with the girl and his monkey and the photographer fired off a shot. A printer in a shopping trolley rolled out the photo instantly. Mum handed over a handful of coins, Michael tipped his hat to her, and the girl collected her photo. "A real monkey, Mum!" she said, as they crossed the road in front of Jonathan's cab. The girl tore Michael off the picture and threw him into a bin.

A businesswoman was sat on the bench, talking on her phone, with a man kneeling before her to shine her shoes. When the man stood up, Jonathan recognised him as Michael Stipe. He wore a yellow apron that said 'Shoe Shiny Happy People'.

There was a tap on the driver's window. Jonathan turned to see Liam Gallagher holding up a bucket and a squeegee. "Awlright!" he drawled. "Can I get rid of that irritating blur for you?"

Had it really come to this?

*   *   *

Within a matter of months, Plato had ravaged the music industry. The last music magazine was a scrappy freesheet, forced into the hands of reluctant readers. Even with a CD of major label music attached, there were few takers. Nobody wanted the old music. Nobody who mattered, anyway.

It didn't take long for Plato to reach all the real music fans, that core community who kept the whole industry afloat. Plato's perfect music was a hit in every sense. Music fans became addicted to Plato downloads. They abandoned their old records, and stopped buying new ones.

Nobody went to gigs, because their favourite bands never played them.

That's not to say all the traditional sales collapsed. There were the luddites, who hadn't yet discovered Plato. And there were those who had only ever bought the occasional album. But there were not enough of them to sustain the music economy as it used to be.

Labels folded, both major and minor.

There was just one left now: Bigg Records.

*   *   *

Bigg wore tracks in the carpet in front of Marian's desk. As he turned to pace back across the room, she seized her moment. "I have a bring up file that needs—"

"Not now!" Bigg's bald head was red all over. Marian recoiled into her shell and toyed with the internet.

The lift pinged with cheerful insolence, the doors scraped open and Jonathan stepped out. "Hello! A welcoming committee!" he said.

Bigg's fists hung about his waist, clenched. "Get in here, now!" He marched into his office, held the door for Jonathan and waited for him to walk through. Bigg pretended not to notice Marian wink and hold her crossed fingers up to Jonathan. Nor did he acknowledge Jonathan when he slapped his wrist and sniggered. By the time Jonathan was in the office, Bigg's blood was bubbling lava. He slammed the door with such ferocity that one of his gold disks fell off the wall. Its frame fell apart on the carpet. It bugged him to leave it there broken but he wouldn't let himself be distracted. "What the hell have you done to my business?"

"Transformed it beyond recognition," said Jonathan, taking a seat. "Revolutionised it. Reinvented it!"

Bigg stomped behind his desk, tugged his chair out and dropped himself into it. The seat leather squeaked like a fart.

"Pardon you," said Jonathan. His grin barely fit on his face.

Bigg wanted to kill him. He ripped a graph out of the sales report, walked back around his desk, and held the sheet about three inches from Jonathan's face. Jonathan pulled his head back to read it comfortably at first and then tore it out of Bigg's hands and held it in both his hands to study it. "Our sales last quarter," announced Bigg. "I wouldn't even want to ski that slope. I'd be flying so fast downhill it would be like jumping out of a plane."

"It would certainly be a thrilling descent. I'm not much of a skier, to be honest."

"Well, marbles then or whatever little boy games you play. You're destroying my industry. The music magazines have folded. The last few CD shops are closing now. Sales have gone so far through the floor that my European releases are charting in Australia. The back catalogue's stalled. Even the ticket touts are losing money."

"My heart bleeds." Jonathan's tone was so sarky he could be

served with sushi.

"So help me, God, it will in a minute!" Bigg grabbed a letter opener off his desk and pointed it at Jonathan. With a deep enough lunge, Bigg was sure he could plunge it through Jonathan's chest and into his soft organs. In his imagination, Bigg twisted it and the blood oozed out, like he was juicing an orange. He shook with rage and frustration. The letter opener shone like a knife, but was as blunt as a shoe horn.

Jonathan never flinched. "Careful now," he said. "That might be perfect on *paper*, but it would never work in real life. Although it's a *first class* murder weapon, it would be too easy to trace in a *post* mortem."

"Shut up! Shut up! Shut up!" Bigg wailed. "It's not funny!"

"You're pathetic." Jonathan snorted. "Take a look at yourself: the mighty Bigg reduced to waving stationery at me. If you want a fight, punch me. Don't hole-punch me."

Bigg dropped the letter opener onto the desk. He felt lost in his own office and padded back to his seat. His head sank into his hands, with his elbows propped on the desk, his floppy face skin spilling over the top of his fingers and squashing his eyes. Bigg's stomach fizzed with hatred. Some was for Jonathan, but most was for himself for getting so emotional. Bigg had often wished his enemies a wrong turn down a dodgy alley on a dark night. He'd often acted angry, in the way that teachers yell to scare pupils into doing their homework next time. But he had never snapped and made physical threats until today. It was a weak negotiating move. You might as well play poker with transparent cards.

Enough pity. Bigg sat up straight, adjusted his tie and put on a business-like air, pretending the last few minutes never happened. "Here's what we'll do," he said. "First, we need to up Plato's sales. We'll put out a double album per month from each of the virtual bands."

"We can't do that."

Bigg jollied it up: "Don't forget you're on royalties here! What's good for me is good for you!"

"Technically it's a doddle, but it lacks credibility," said Jonathan. "It would spoil the illusion. These are supposed to be real bands, remember. The slightest hint that it's fake and people lose interest."

"Well, what else do you suggest?" Bigg tried to sound friendly and open minded, but there was an undercurrent of desperation in every word.

On the front of the desk was a Newton's cradle. Jonathan reached out, pulled the end ball and let it fall. As the cradle clacked away, Jonathan stared into his reflection, rolling around the surface of the balls. He made a steeple with his fingers and flexed it thoughtfully. Bigg knew the power of silence and waited for Jonathan to respond. Only when the Newton's cradle had run out of energy, did he speak. "We stage a massive concert," said Jonathan. "We get the biggest bands from all over the world to play Wembley."

"Nice," said Bigg. He scribbled some names on a post-it note.

"All the money goes towards saving your label. We could call it Clive Aid!" Jonathan collapsed in giggles.

"Be serious!" said Bigg. "If we don't act now, there won't even be a music industry this time next year."

"Beautiful, isn't it?" Jonathan took his cigarettes out of his pocket and lit one without asking for permission or offering them around. He blew the smoke out of his nose. "I always like to smoke after I've shafted someone," he said.

"What?" Bigg went purple.

"You've underestimated me again," said Jonathan. "Do I look surprised at what's happened to Bigg Records? Do I look sad about it?" He pointed at his mouth and grinned like a children's TV host. Jonathan wandered over to Bigg's wall of perfectly aligned gold disks and tapped the frames in turn to make them hang wonky. "Stands to reason. If you give people perfect music, they're not going to keep buying your crap."

"You are evil," said Bigg, darkly. "You came here to destroy me."

"God, no," said Jonathan. "I'm not that small-minded. This was only ever about the music for me. That's probably hard for a man like you to understand." He crouched down to pick up the broken frame and removed the back. Jonathan shook the gold disk and its velvet backing into the bin and replaced them with a piece of paper from his inside pocket. With a coin, he tightened the frame, fixed the edges and replaced it on the wall. "Don't you feel even a slight tingle that you've delivered perfect music to millions of people? That those men, women and children will always carry it in their hearts? And that every day, more and more people discover the ultimate eargasm?"

Bigg pressed his intercom. "Marian, get me security."

"It's funny how it turned out, really." Jonathan returned to his seat and sat down like he was settling for a night in front of the telly. He was clearly enjoying this. "You were the only one who could make it happen, but you were also part of the collateral damage. You laid down your business in the search for the perfect song. How noble."

"I built this business from nothing," said Bigg. "I'll do it again if I have to. Once a salesman, always a salesman." His bravado disguised the dread he felt. He still had the patter, still had the business nous. But he lived in comfort now. First time around, he'd lugged amps to befriend bands. He'd slept under his desk and lived off spaghetti hoops so he could save enough to bankroll his first pressing. He wasn't sure he was hungry enough now to make the sacrifices he made the first time. Today, he was happiest when the business hummed away in the background and left him free to play.

Bigg reached across the table to set off the Newton's cradle. "Everything needs new energy from time to time, even me. Perhaps this is all for the best. If some arsehole gives you lemons, you buy lemonade." He was talking a good game, but he wasn't sure he believed it himself.

"You're not going to switch Plato off," said Jonathan. "It's the only thing making you any money."

"Damn right," said Bigg. "You know the difference between me and you?"

"You're a—"

"Let me tell you. You think that there's a winner and a loser here, and that you're the winner. I know that there's always more than one winner."

"I've got to hand it to you. If there were a contest to burn money, you'd be way out in front."

"I don't see any cheques in your immediate future, either," said Bigg. "Do you think I'm going to give you royalties after all this?"

"You were never going to pay out. Doesn't really bother me, to be honest. I've always got by on a few quid. How does it feel to be heading for poverty for the first time, Clive? Have you always worked in music, or do you have any useful skills? You've got some suits and a nice smile, so I guess you could resort to the world's oldest profession."

Bigg walked to the window and opened it wide. The traffic noise from below came in on wisps of cold air. Bigg knew there had to be an upside for him: something that Jonathan hadn't thought of. A plane tugged a ribbon through the clouds and a zeppelin hovered over St Paul's Cathedral. A giant footballer in his underwear was pasted to the glass building opposite. At the bus stop below, a double-decker hamburger pulled up and let passengers on.

And then he realised: the world's oldest profession. He felt a tingle of excitement. "The oxygen of our economy," he said to himself.

Bigg got up and took a photo of him and the Prime Minister off the wall. "How did I not see it? The PM virtually told me," he said. "He talks a lot of crap, but he's a wily old git." Bigg polished the glass frame with his sleeve. "I saw Plato as a shop. He saw a broadcast channel."

"Oh my God," said Jonathan. "Advertising space! You can't put adverts in the songs! There will be a revolt. People will stop buying."

"Make your mind up. You said nobody listens to lyrics," said Bigg. "The Plato sales prove that. And the PM hit on the idea of using a subliminal track, underneath the music, so they need not even know they're there."

"That's an invasion of privacy!"

"You can't talk! You've sneaked spyware on to millions of computers."

"In the name of art!"

"Well, business is my art form."

The door opened and Bigg's security guards entered. "What kept you?" he said. "I was nearly bored to death. Take Harrington out and make sure he really doesn't come back this time. His work here is done."

Jonathan stood up. "I'll expose you!"

"I don't think so," said Bigg. "Plato has your fingerprints all over it. If it becomes public, they'll throw a library at you."

The guards took one of Jonathan's elbows each and led him towards the door.

"Gentlemen," said Bigg. "I think you can be a lot rougher than that."

Jonathan's arm was pushed high up his back and he was bent over in pain. He was too uncomfortable to say anything else as he was led away.

As Bigg mulled over the best way to exploit Plato, he tidied up. He rotated his gold disks gently about their hooks to line them up again. Then he came to the letter Jonathan had framed and it left a bitter taste in his mouth. From all the black scratches and spots, it looked like a fifth generation photocopy. The paper had yellowed and the blue ink, written in the gaps in the form, had partly faded. Bigg's old logo at the top and the red date stamp confirmed it was twenty years old. Jonathan's name had been inked in at the top.

Dear Mr Harrington

Thank you for sending your demo tape and applying to join our latest band. I regret I haven't heard anything this atonal since ever . It has the worst vocals we've ever heard.

We are returning your photo. We regret that it would be impossible to work with you because your face! is not pop star material.

We would advise you to don't give up your day job. You will never be a marketable proposition in the music industry .

We appreciate that we work in a dream factory, and we regret any disappointment this letter might cause. But we hope that you will find our careers advice, based on years of experience making the hits, helpful.

Whether or not you decide to work within the music industry, we hope that you will continue to be entertained by our roster.

Yours faithfully

Elaine Simpson
Personnel

angelA> hi sweetness

thing> Hey Angela

angelA> ive got good news fro u

thing> You can't bear not meeting me a moment longer!

angelA> no

thing> Bring a boy down gently, why don't you?

thing> What's the news?

angelA> Tiled Sprites have a new album out

thing> Already? That was quick

thing> The last one was only out two months ago

angelA> it's a double. 40 trax.

angelA> i think its better than the first one

thing> I don't know where they find the time.

thing> They don't seem the most dynamic of bands

thing> I met their songwriter yesterday

angelA> where

thing> I went to his house to ask him how Time Today goes

angelA> was it a nice house

thing> not particularly

thing> I want to play the song but can't work out the chords

angelA> what was he like

thing> He was an arsehole

angelA> every bands got one

thing>	**Shame really because his music's great**
thing>	**I hardly ever play anything else now**
angelA>	its gr8
thing>	**I play a couple of tracks from an old album and it just seems flat**
thing>	**So I put Tiled Sprites back on again**
angelA>	download the new album now
angelA>	we can listen together
thing>	**brb**
angelA>	it makes me wanna dance
angelA>	:-) /-<
angelA>	:-) |-L
angelA>	:-0 \-<
thing>	**What was that?**
angelA>	me dancing ;-)
angelA>	and singing
thing>	**Okay. Downloading the new album now.**
thing>	**Had a bit of a panic. Couldn't find my credit card at first.**
angelA>	im so in debt its not even funny
thing>	**It's playing now. Great start!**
angelA>	yeah shake it baby
thing>	**Our rehearsal went well today**
angelA>	cool
thing>	**As long as we play our best tomorrow we can say we've given it a good shot**
angelA>	very philosophical
thing>	**Actually, I'll be gutted if we don't get anywhere**
thing>	**We're running out of options.**
angelA>	I'll keep my fingers crossed for you.
angelA>	a good luck kiss
angelA>	xxx
thing>	**Wish u were here to do that in person**
angelA>	me too
thing>	**We seem to go in circles on this**
thing>	**I'm going to go cram my chords**
thing>	**bye xxx**

angelA>   love ya baby xxx
<angelA has disconnected>

*   *   *

Simon's feet felt like they were made of polystyrene. For seventy six minutes he had shuffled with Fred and zig-zagged the hall in stop motion. It was like being digested by a snake. Each time he turned, he would see the same cast of indie kids, pop kids and goths filing the other way along the intestines next to him, separated by an elasticated barrier. His guitar case was resting on the toe of his shoes. Fred was sat on their speaker, her elbow on her cased keyboard, which rested across her lap. Her body was wrapped with a strip of glittery fabric.

"Remember," Simon said. "We need to create a good impression," he said. "We're facing Bigg today."

"That's rich," she replied. "You look like a sink monster, draped in a stained dishcloth."

Simon looked at his crumpled tie-dye and couldn't argue. There was a long silence. The back of the queue started a Mexican wave, but the nearer the front it got, the longer people had been waiting, and the less they could be bothered to join in.

"I thought you said they didn't do many band auditions," said Fred, "and you persuaded them to take a look at us."

"Hmmm," said Simon. "I guess a lot of other people must have persuaded them too."

Everyone was penned into an outbuilding. Fred couldn't see any links to the main building, and it would have been impossible to split from the queue without being noticed in any case.

When they reached the front of the queue, there was a woman there with a clipboard and a scowl permanently etched into her forehead. "Band name," she said.

"Goblin," said Simon.

She squinted slightly as she studied him and scribbled, holding the clipboard so he couldn't see what she was writing.

"Instruments?"

"Guitar, keyboards and vocals," said Simon.

The woman looked at Fred and twirled her finger in the air to get her to turn around. Fred stood up and rotated on the spot while the woman looked her up and down. "Any professional music experience?" she said.

"A private commission," said Simon. "A cover version of University of Death."

"Any formal musical education?"

"Not really," said Simon. "But lots of hard work and practice."

She inspected Fred's hair like a nit nurse, ploughing her fingers through it. "What's your natural hair colour?" she said.

"You're looking at it," Fred replied.

The woman scribbled on her clipboard and slowly said: "Time waster…"

"No wait," said Fred. "I mean. It's blonde."

"What's the longest you've worn it?"

"Shoulder length, as a girl."

"Ever had extensions?"

"No," said Fred. "But I could. If you think it'd help?"

"Will you shave your head?"

"No way." Fred hesitated a moment. "Okay, well maybe. If it's essential for the band."

"Good attitude," said the woman. "You're learning fast."

She moved on to inspect Simon. "Have you always had a haircut like your Dad?"

"You don't know my Dad."

"But have you, though?"

"Well, yes," said Simon. "But we can change it."

"Yeah, you wanna change it. Can't believe you've come here with it in that state."

"Do you mind me asking why there are so many questions about hair?" Simon said. "I mean, you only asked us a couple of questions about our music."

"Tell me," said the woman. "What does your favourite guitar solo sound like?"

"Um… Well, it starts out quite soft… but er…no, it's got choppy chords under that… There's a lot of screeching… But in a nice way."

"Pah! That could be anything," said the woman. "Tell me, what hairstyle does the guitarist have?"

"A poodle."

"Now we're talking!" said the woman. "Do you even read the music press?"

"Of course."

"Journalists gave up on writing about sound long ago. It's like trying to describe 'red' to the blind. So they write about haircuts instead. Breaking a new act? We style them like their influences. Radical new artistic direction? Time for a haircut! Building up a movement? Fans just follow bands that have similar hairstyles."

"That's the stupidest thing I've ever heard," said Simon. "Journalists write about music."

"That's their skill – making it look like they do," said the woman. "But it's impossible. Ever since pop music was invented, hair stylists have been a vital communications channel. You look like a man who knows his Beatles. What happened to their hair over the years?"

"It got longer and shaggier."

"And what happened to their songs?"

"Well, they got more—"

"Longer! Shaggier! Case closed!"

Someone signalled from across the room. "Okay, they're ready for you," said the woman. "Go through that door. Set up on the conveyor belt between the lines. You're on in two."

"Um…Two what?" said Simon.

She had already moved off down the line.

They piled the speaker and Fred's keyboard onto their luggage trolley and wheeled it into the next room. Apart from a cardboard cut-out of Shakin Stevens, which appeared to be scraping muck off its shoe, and a Toyah pinball machine, the room was bare. There were steps leading up to the conveyor belt, which was no wider than an office desk. The belt was rolling the previous act out and through rainbow streamers. When it came to a stop, Fred and Simon climbed up the seven steps, taking their equipment in relays, and set up side by side. Simon helped Fred screw her stand together and balance the keyboard on it, and had to hold her shoulders to get past her without falling off the belt.

The ground moved beneath them and Fred and Simon were rolled into a sound studio. The walls, floor and ceiling were painted black. White gaffer tape on the floor marked out what looked like the pitch to some combination of squash, football and rugby. Numbers were painted at regular intervals down one side of the room and letters were painted down the other. The room had all the atmosphere of a scout hut.

Three people sat behind a long table in the middle of the room.

Simon laughed with shock when he saw one of them was Dove. He was wearing a dark t-shirt, suit jacket and jeans, but was unmistakeable in his red-and-green face paint. Simon nodded at Dove in recognition and – get this – Dove nodded back. Simon felt like punching the air. He couldn't believe his hero had not only acknowledged him, but was ready to listen to him play live.

"Keep it together," whispered Fred. "He's just a guy."

"I'm Clive Bigg," said the man next to Dove. His voice echoed in the vast space between him and the conveyor belt. He took a piece of paper from a woman sat on his left. "And you are…called…Goblin, it says here."

"That's right," shouted Fred. She lowered her voice slightly when she realised she had overestimated the size of the room.

"Promising name," said Bigg. "Should get cred with the Lord of the Rings tokers. Nice oral sex pun too."

"We named ourselves after the make of my Nan's hoover," said Simon.

"Yeah, right," said Bigg. "That line should get you through kids' TV okay. So who are you?"

"I have a stage name," said Simon. "I am The Thing."

"Yeah, that's good too," said Bigg. "Weedy little guy naming himself after a superhero made of boulders. That'll play well if you do some drippy Belle and Sebastian type tosh. What kind of music are you peddling then?"

"Pop," said Fred.

"Only more improvised and experimental," added Simon.

"Oh no," groaned Bigg. "Improvised and experimental equals unrehearsed and self-indulgent, in my experience. Let's get this over with then. Do your worst."

Simon wiped his sweaty fingers on his trousers, took a plectrum out of his pocket and strummed to check he was in tune. He felt a wave of panic sweep from his stomach upwards and flood his brain. He tried to remember the chords, but they tumbled on top of each other without order. He breathed in sharply and let it out slowly, nodding at Bigg as casually as he could. He didn't dare look at Dove.

Simon looked at Fred and saw she was obsessing over the buttons on her keyboard, seemingly pushing and checking them all. She punched a couple of squelchy chords and turned to Simon and said: "I'm ready." Simon thought he could hear her pulse punctuating her voice.

"Impress me," said Bigg.

"This is called Inconsistencies," said Fred. "It's about how..."

"Yeah, hang on. I'll just I get my lighter out, shall I?" said Bigg. "Or we could just save the talkie bits for Wembley and get a flaming move on."

"Sure," said Fred, taken aback.

There were four plinks, the rhythm kicked in and Fred washed it with lush chords. While he was waiting for his cue, Simon was in a state of terror. Snippets of the song came into his mind, and he could hear how they were supposed to sound. But he couldn't remember how to play them. He looked at Fred's keyboard to see what key the song was in.

Just before he was due to start playing, his fingers got into position. They seemed to know what to do, even if he didn't. Bang on the beat, they started to play and he let them carry on, and tried not to spoil the magic. His mind was overwhelmed with everything going on in the room, but through this pollution he was still able to perform. He felt like a robot, programmed to play guitar. He was relieved when he got through the intro. Fred pumped the keyboard to drive the verses. Gingerly at first, and then gaining confidence and volume, she sang:

> You ate biscuits upside down
> To feel the bobbles on your tongue

Apologised before telling me
You wished I hadn't come
Explained you used to hate me
Then said I haven't changed
Got married to a man
Then found out he's deranged

While Fred played her bits, Simon listened. This was the loudest he had ever heard his own music. It felt so powerful, so daring. The conveyor belt wobbled under his feet in time with the beat and he could hear fixtures in the room creaking at the volume. Fred sang on:

You phoned to tell me
Finally the letter's in the post
But backwards girl of all you do
It's this I hate the most:

If you're going to lie to me
You'd better get a better memory
You tell a pretty story
But it's blown apart
By the inconsistencies

Fred's keyboard part melted into chords that shifted like glaciers, giving way for Simon's solo to skate on top. His pulse was racing, but his fingers moved faster. They scurried down the fret board, as he sustained notes and slipped others underneath them. He played so fast that you couldn't understand it – just be hit by it – and then gave his tiny audience time to breathe with a few slow, grunting bassy chords. The guitar wowed, cried and yelped. Simon's look of intense concentration had faded and he was trying to stop his smile looking too smug now. He knew he was cooking. When he came to the usual end of his solo, instead of wrapping it up and letting Fred begin the next verse, he went round the block again, becoming ever more frantic in his playing. He found new sounds and melodies he had never played before and felt the side of his head tingle when he realised he probably never would again. He was in the moment, at one with his music.

Simon felt a thrill as he stole a glance at Dove. His make-up made him look permanently fierce, but his tapping foot and the gentle nod of his head gave him away. He was enjoying it.

Bigg took his cigar out of his mouth and raised his palm to order Fred and Simon to stop. Fred promptly took her fingers off the keys and switched off the rhythms. Simon played to the end of the bar, slammed a chord and let it fade out. They both looked at Bigg expectantly.

"Thanks for coming," he said. He shuffled a few papers around the desk.

"That's okay," said Fred. "Would you like to hear another?"

"Ha! Maybe if I'm in a coma and the only thing that will wake me up is the threat of being powerless to stop you two playing." Bigg gave them a sideways look and the smile slid off Simon's face.

"Come off it," said Fred through gritted teeth. "We're not that bad. You release loads of dire music."

"Why not ours?" added Simon. "Er, our good music, I mean."

"That was a cacophony," said Bigg. "Let me emphasise the first syllable for you: cack."

"You're just scared of us," said Fred. "You can't handle our attitude. I'm not enough of a puppet for you."

"You're here, aren't you?"

"Nobody else understands our music," whined Simon.

"Oh, you're very much mistaken," said Bigg. "It's just that nobody else *likes* your music."

"It grows on you," said Fred. "It's very avant garde."

"Oh yes," said Bigg. "Avant garde a melody, avant garde a groove and avant garde a chance of selling." He laughed self-indulgently. "In fact, it's the biggest load of cod-rock bollocks I've heard in a long time."

Dove cleared his throat and everyone looked at him. "I like it," he said. "It's like listening to a mirror."

"I rest my case," said Bigg.

"I'm famous, you know," said Fred. "I'm the weasel girl. My

video's brought three major corporate networks to their knees. It's so popular, the internet can't keep up with it."

Simon thought her pride was misplaced, and hated her for bringing the weasel up again.

"Maybe there is a novelty angle there," said Bigg, stroking his chin. "We could invent the weasel dance, license the TV footage to splice into the video. Lose the stiff and set the babe up with a hit single. This might just have legs…"

At the back of the room a few people were ushered in and lined up behind Bigg's table. "It's weasel girl!" said one of them louder than she intended to.

"Ah yes!" said Bigg. "The journalists are here! Do come in!" He turned back to Fred and Simon and spoke in a theatrically loud voice. "As I was saying, I really don't think we're the kind of company that cashes in on the cheap fame of TV stars. Today is about discovering the next generation of talent. But do let me offer you some friendly advice. Get a drummer with lots of cymbals."

"Will that help us get signed?" said Simon.

"No," said Bigg. "But you know how bad the speakers are in pubs? If you keep smashing the cymbals at the end of a song, it sounds enough like crowd noise to get people going. Could be an investment that works for you over a *very* long time."

With that, Bigg reached across his desk towards a control panel. The floor underneath Simon and Fred jerked. Simon stumbled to a crouching position and Fred gripped her keyboard. "Thanks for coming!" Bigg waved as they were rolled away. "You've got to nurture talent," he told the journalists.

CHAPTER 33

The conveyor belt terminated in the Bigg Records car park, over a skip. A morass of wires, guitar strings and wood half-filled it. A speaker cone and a pierced drum sat on top of the debris, with a guitar neck sticking up in defiance, perhaps looking for its body. An upturned shoe twitched.

Now Bigg Records had finished with Fred and Simon, they were rolled steadily towards the dumpster. As it loomed over the end of the conveyor belt, they could both see the steep drop and the sharp edges of the shattered instruments.

Fred ripped the cables out of the back of her keyboard, and lifted it off the stand. It was a long way down. If she crouched, she could probably land safely. But she couldn't hold on to the keyboard and jump that way, and if it slipped out of her hands, it would crack on impact.

Simon strapped his guitar to his back and sat down on the edge of the conveyor belt. His legs dangled. He counted to three out loud, leaned forward and jumped onto the concrete floor, landing on his haunches. His feet and hands felt like they had been stabbed with a thousand drawing pins. He staggered to his feet and turned to help Fred with the keyboard.

By the time he turned around, the conveyor belt had come to a halt. The next band had been wheeled in for judgement, and Simon and Fred had as long as this audition took to get clear. It might only be a minute.

Simon pulled the luggage trolley off the belt and it clattered on to the ground. Fred passed him down the keyboard and the amp.

"I can't believe it," she said.

"Nor can I," said Simon. "Dove liked us. He really did."

Fred looked stunned. "Bigg hated us! He didn't even let us finish our song!" She jumped down off the conveyor belt into Simon's outstretched arms. He caught her and steadied her. She broke away immediately with a muttered 'thanks', and dusted herself down.

"We didn't even get inside the main building," she said. They loaded up the trolley and Fred pulled it towards the road. Their equipment felt heavier than before. The car park was full of near-wrecks, vehicles chosen more for their affordability on low wages than for their panache.

When Fred and Simon reached the end of the audition shack, they walked into the shadow of the main building. The hard stone and solid metal doors made it as inviting as a prison. Every few paces, they heard a clunk sound, like a jailer locking up for the night. Stone gargoyles perched on the roof, ready to swoop on intruders. The wind moaned and chased sweet wrappers in rings around their feet, the only sign of any life.

A poster for the University of Death hits album was framed on the wall. "I'm having that," said Simon. "Have you got a knife on you?"

"Nope. Why would I?"

As Simon approached the poster, there was another clunk sound. He tried to lever the frame open.

"Simon?" said Fred.

"Huh?" He had got the frame to peel back at the bottom, but it was gripped at the top. He might be able to pull the poster out, but there was a risk that he'd just tear off the corner.

"That light's just come on." Fred pointed to a tiny square in the handle of the nearest door. It glowed green.

The frame snapped shut on Simon's hand and he yelped. With his other hand, he pulled it open far enough to scrape his fingers out. His eyes watered and he clamped his hand in his armpit.

Fred tried the handle and the door swung open. "We're in!"

Simon shook his hand. "What do you mean, 'we're in'?"

"We went over this," said Fred. "Plan A failed. We've played our music to Dove, and nothing happened."

"It still might."

"It won't. Bigg doesn't listen to him."

"So?" Simon's hand still stung.

"It's time for Plan B." Fred pulled a folded magazine article from her pocket. Half the page was dominated by a picture of Clive Bigg with a jazz ensemble in an elevator. She held it up to Simon.

He had forgotten there ever was a Plan B. He didn't think either of them had taken it seriously. "You're joking, right?"

"Behind that door is a studio broadcasting to 500 lifts. Look at these codgers. We could take them." Fred pointed at the jazz band in the picture.

Simon looked away. "Who's going to hear us, anyway?"

"People in lifts, all over the country. About time the poor saps had something decent to listen to. Some of them might be journalists or DJs. Even if they're all empty, think of the press! We'll be on the news."

"You'll get fired."

"Stuff 'em," said Fred. "We've tried being nice. We sent demos and nobody opened them. We played gigs and nobody came. We went to an audition and they didn't even let us finish one song. We gave the press a publicity stunt, and they still wouldn't play our tunes. This is our last chance."

"To go to prison, you mean?" said Simon. "They'll have us for breaking in."

"They've left the door open, so we're not breaking anything," said Fred. "Are you coming or not?"

"My hand *really* bloody hurts." Simon caressed his fingers with his other hand.

The conveyor rumbled into life again.

"Simon! There's another band coming. It's now or never." Fred watched him for a moment and then opened the door wide and started to wheel the keyboard and amp through on the trolley. "Wish me luck," she said.

Simon watched the door close behind her.

*   *   *

Bigg's mobile phone diddled. He held up his hand to silence the band on the conveyor belt and took the call.

"How are you?" asked Marian.

"Fine. Don't think I'll get out of here until late, though," said Bigg. "Can you fetch me hot chocolate with cream and cake please. And maybe bread, meat loaf and chilli peppers for later."

"Sure," said Marian.

Half an hour later, Marian called back: "They're here."

"Who?"

"Everyone I could find."

Bigg closed his phone and gawped in astonishment as the conveyor belt rolled twelve people in, all lined up and facing the front. "I believe in miracles!" sang Errol Brown, as Flea hummed the bassline and the others clapped. "We didn't think you'd call!" Errol flashed his winning smile and fired his finger at Bigg like it was a gun.

When the conveyor belt stopped, they joined hands and took a synchronised bow. Bigg looked at the familiar and unfamiliar faces from Hot Chocolate, Cream, Cake, Bread and the Red Hot Chilli Peppers and groaned. "I'm starving," he said. "Don't suppose any of you have a sandwich on you?"

They looked puzzled and shook their heads.

"You're not holding out on me, are you, Marvin?"

"I wouldn't do that," said Meat Loaf.

"Buzz off then, the lot of you," said Bigg.

*   *   *

When Simon plucked up the courage to slip through the door – the same second shapes started to emerge through the streamers on the conveyor belt – Fred was just inside. She was fiddling around with the trolley, but Simon knew she was really waiting for him. Fred came across as ballsy, but she wouldn't have gone through with it alone.

246

"Hey, Si," she said.

"Hi," he replied. "Let's see if we can give our band the lift it needs, then."

Fred giggled. "That's funny," she said. "I'll put that in my statement."

They had entered through a fire exit, into a dusty concrete corridor. They abandoned everything by the door except for Simon's guitar. From all the days she had spent listening to the lift music, Fred knew the studio had a piano in it, and they needed to travel light.

The corridors were made of stone. There was a broken iron chain on the floor, and the electric lights flickered like candles and hummed like devil flies. The place had the air of a mediaeval torture chamber. Simon skipped mid-step to avoid putting his foot on a dark red stain on the concrete. It looked like blood. As he walked, he kept looking over his shoulder.

At the end of the corridor, the lift was waiting for them. From the article, they knew the studio was on the sixth floor. As they went up through the building, Fred held the sixth button in the hope they would avoid other stops on the way. They didn't.

On the second floor, a man entered and pressed for the seventh. He jiggled the change in his pocket and pushed his glasses up his nose. The doors dithered before closing. The man leaned against the side of the lift, but failed to look casual. His body was as stiff as an ironing board.

"Recording today?" asked the man. He raised his eyebrows at Simon's guitar. "Hmmmm?" His toe tapped almost exactly out of time with the lift music.

"Hopefully," said Simon.

"What's your name?"

"Goblin," said Simon.

"Goblin? Funny." He pushed his glasses up his nose again. "Hmmm. Very funny I haven't heard of you. I do hope the studio's booked. There will be trouble if it's not. It makes a right mess of my books when bands just waltz in here and use the studios like a hotel. We do have proper channels, you know." He directed his anger into thin air, avoiding eye contact.

Fred tried to reassure him as the lift arrived at their floor. "It's probably booked under a different band," she said. "We're still finalising the name. It's down to a shortlist of twenty. You know what marketing's like. Christening by committee."

"That's probably it," said the man. His smile was unconvincing. Fred and Simon left the lift and the man glared at them over his glasses until the lift doors shut and took him away.

All the doors along the corridor had red lights above them, but only about half of them were lit. As they walked past, Fred and Simon heard bursts of muted music from inside. Simon opened one door and walked in. Egg boxes were stuck on some of the walls, with a silver foam mountain range glued to others. Right in front of them, Billy Bragg was singing and playing guitar, with his eyes closed: "I'm just looking for a new Here."

"Sorry, Billy," whispered Simon. He ushered Fred back out and they closed the door gently. They came to a stop outside the next door. "What is that horrible noise?" said Simon.

Fred wrinkled her nose in disgust. "I don't know," she said. "It might be—"

"Jazz!" they said together.

"This is it," said Fred.

"How do you know?"

"I listen to this noodly nonsense all day. Besides, all the other lights say 'recording'." Fred pointed at the lamp above the door. "This one says 'on air'."

They peered through the window. The room was clouded with cigarette smoke. There were six men inside, all dressed in shirts and jeans. One was snoozing on the upright piano, while a clarinettist and trumpet player were duelling and a drummer was playing with brushes. A guitarist plucked the strings while he stared into nowhere. The acoustic bass player had his ear pressed against the headstock and nodded in time with the music.

"There's a lot of them," said Simon. "What's the plan?"

"I say we go in there and storm them!"

"How?" Simon rolled his eyes. "We can't just walk in and scare them into letting us play."

"There's a mic stand just inside the door. I'll rush in, grab it

248

and beat them up."

"Can you hear yourself?" said Simon. "They're old men."

Fred looked sheepish. "Well, just a little bit. Just to make a point."

"No," said Simon. "Get a grip, will you?"

"Well, I'll just threaten them then."

"Is that the best you've come up with?"

"Go on then," said Fred. "What do you suggest if you're so smart?"

"How about we go in and say they're needed in reception?"

"What, all of them?"

"Well, it's better than running around waving a mic stand at them, especially since they've got one each to defend themselves. We're outnumbered. Even if they do look a pushover." He tried the door handle. "It's open," he said.

"I'm going in." Fred crossed the corridor and prepared her run up. "Stand back. The best weapon is surprise."

Simon stood well clear and Fred charged the door. Her face smacked against the window, her nose squashed on the glass, and her body crushed her arms against the door. She bounced off and fell backwards, landing on her bum. From inside, they heard a surprised toot in the music.

"Nice try," said Simon. "My turn." He gave Fred a hand up, and she dusted herself down. When Simon wasn't looking, she rubbed her bum with one hand and checked her nose wasn't broken with the other.

Simon tried the door again and the handle turned. "Weird," he said. "You must have caught it funny. It *is* open." He pushed the door open and walked in, holding it for Fred behind him.

A couple of the musicians raised their eyebrows in acknowledgement, but the music went on. The pianist woke up. He had bags under his eyes that wouldn't have looked out of place in an industrial vacuum cleaner.

"What do you want?" he drawled.

"You're all needed in reception," said Simon, brightly.

"Sod off," said the pianist. "Anyone who wants me can bloody well come here." He made a pillow from his arms and settled down for a kip again on the lid of the piano.

The trumpeter played a concluding flourish and then stopped. His face deflated. He smacked his lips and his jowls wobbled about. "I know you," he said. "I do know you. The weasel woman. From that internet thing."

"That's right," said Fred. The band played on.

"You're a dangerous woman," said the trumpet player. "You sure showed that weasel what's what."

"You'd better believe it," said Fred. "Do as we say and nobody gets hurt. We're taking over here."

"Why?" said the pianist. He didn't sound terribly interested in the answer.

"Just never mind why," said Fred. She pointed with her finger.

Simon pushed her arm down. "We just want people to hear our music," he said.

"I'm your biggest fan," said the trumpet player to Fred. "Can you do the fist thing for me."

"What thing?"

"Just, you know, throw your arms about a bit. Look a bit angry. Like in that film."

"No," said Fred.

"Hey, yeah, I'd like to see that too," said the bass player. "Hey, the way you whacked that weasel! Was that ever funny!"

"I feel silly," said Fred.

The piano player woke up and looked around expectantly. "Go on!" said the guitarist. The band egged her on until Fred could no longer resist the opportunity to show off. As she punched the air and shadow boxed with all the band members, she looked like a cat pawing at a ball of wool. The musicians cheered.

"Do the face!" said the trumpet player. He boggled his eyes and pointed at them and then nodded at Simon.

"Fred," said Simon. "Can we please stop messing around and either do what we came to do, or get the hell out of here before we're caught."

"Oh no," groaned the pianist. He yawned. "Whatever you do, don't cover that security camera over there. That table might not bear your weight if you stood on it."

"Somebody hide that gaffer tape, quick!" said the trumpet player. He pointed at it with his trumpet.

"Too late!" said Fred. She dashed to the gaffer tape, pressed the table to check it was sturdy, hopped onto it, and tore strips of tape off the reel and plastered them across the camera lens.

The musicians immediately downed their instruments.

"We're outta here," said the trumpeter.

"Just like that?" said Fred.

"Sure," said the trumpeter. "I've been playing for six hours straight. I feel like I've done a snogathon with Mick Jagger. You can torch this dump for all I care. We've got you looking scary on the camera and covering it up. We'll say we fled for our lives."

"Won't you get fired?" said Fred.

"Not us jazz cats," said the trumpet player. "We've got nine lives."

"You'll find vocal mics in that box," said the double bass player as he leant his instrument against the wall. "Dedicate one to Clive Bigg for me."

* * *

Two verses in, the security guard popped up in the porthole window. Fred looked into his eyes over the top of the upright piano, which was barricading the door. The guard's breath misted the window, so he wiped it with his hand. His tufty grey eyebrows were arched in anger.

Fred sang. Her voice didn't waver, even as the guard pushed the door and the piano inched back towards her. While she held a chord with her outstretched arms, she shunted the piano back by throwing her thigh against it.

Simon played his guitar with one eye on the other door.

"We have to go," whispered Fred, away from the mic.

"No way," said Simon. "We've got to finish the song." He kept playing but sat himself down at the foot of the piano, his back helping to press it against the door.

You phoned to tell me
Finally the letter's in the post
But backwards girl of all you do
It's this I hate the mo—

The piano glided about a foot as the door opened and half a body came through. Simon skidded across the ground like a puck and Fred's foot got stuck in the gap under the piano. She undid her shoe, pulled her foot out, yanked the shoe away and put it on again.

"Sod this," she said. She pushed the piano hard against the door and kept pushing. The guard yelled in pain as his body was stuck between the door and the jamb and squeezed hard. He dragged himself out, until only his arm writhed around in the room. With a grunt, he pulled it loose and retreated, and the door slammed shut, narrowly missing his fingers.

"Go easy," said Simon. Fred looked like she wanted to kill him. He twisted his guitar onto his back and dodged in and out of mic stands to reach the other door. They both walked through into another corridor, but then Fred hesitated.

"Hang on a minute," she said. She returned into the studio, weaved her way to the vocal mic near the piano and spoke into it. Simon poked his head around the door. "Thanks for listening to us," said Fred, putting on a DJ voice. "You've been a great audience. That was a taster of our song 'Inconsistencies' and we're called Goblin. The others will be back soon. For now, we wish you a pleasant ascent or descent."

"Idiot!" said Simon, when Fred rejoined him. "You might as well have given out our postcode."

"We can't get publicity anonymously," said Fred. "We've got to get caught otherwise the plan doesn't work."

"Funny you didn't mention that earlier," said Simon.

There was a ping. The elevator at the far end of the corridor opened and delivered two thuggish security guards. They started to jog, so Fred and Simon ran in the opposite direction, following signs for the fire exit.

"Why are we running then?" said Simon.

"We have to get caught," said Fred. "We don't have to get the sheet music beaten out of us. Peg it!"

* * *

Back in the audition hall, Dove was getting restless. Most of the acts didn't have the good manners to learn to play properly. Every time they got onto a stage, they were insulting their audience with their laziness.

Dove was only here for the chance to see Bigg again. Having a development budget didn't make it any easier to get Bigg's attention, so he had to take his opportunities where he found them.

He waited until the latest band had been rolled out of earshot and then made his pitch. "Mr Bigg," said Dove. "Since we're talking about new music, I should tell you that Dove has plenty of material."

"That's nice," said Bigg. He clearly didn't care.

Dove took a CD out of his pocket and put it on the table in front of Bigg. "Here's a demo. We should talk about putting it out some time."

Bigg looked aghast. "I don't do demos," he said. And with that, he put his hand on it and firmly slid it back to Dove. "Talk to my people."

Dove felt his heart shrivel up. After all he had been through, he had earned the right to be heard. Complete strangers were walking off the street and playing to them today, and yet Dove couldn't get Bigg to listen to his work. Sometimes he didn't know why Bigg kept him around, or why he bothered to stay.

* * *

Simon was ready to die. He hugged his stitched side and skipped as best as he could. Fred stopped to let him catch up.

"No more," said Simon. He slowed to a walk. "Save yourself. Leave me."

"Very heroic," said Fred. "God, you're so unfit."

They heard the voices of the guards catching up to them around the corner, so Simon opened the nearest door and Fred followed him through it. He shut it tight behind them.

It was dark. Simon stood still to let his eyes adjust to the darkness. He couldn't see Fred, but he could hear something moving around the room. She hissed: "Shhhh!"

The footsteps rattled past on the other side.

Red and green dots on the walls floated into focus and squares of blue light took shape. It smelled of gently toasting dust, like a hi-fi shop. There was a quick burst of light, like a flashgun, which made Simon swear with shock, then another like lightning, against which Simon covered his eyes, before the strip lights fizzed on. Fred was stood by the switch.

They were in some kind of data centre. The coloured spots were LEDs on tape machines, which sucked and chewed on their reels. The light at the far end was a bank of computer screens. Simon jumped at the sound of machine gun fire, but when he turned to look, there was just a printer hammering letters onto a stack of continuous paper, folded in zig-zags.

"Bad bananas," said Simon. He took off his guitar and leaned it against a stack of cardboard boxes. "I wondered where I'd heard that before."

"Eh?"

"Captain Blood," he said. He pointed at the poster hanging over the printer. "I haven't seen that for ages."

"Who's he?"

"It was a Commodore game," said Simon. "You met aliens all over the universe and had conversations with them. Clever stuff, back then. Whenever you annoyed them, they said 'bad bananas'. They'd probably swear like a rapper today."

"Yeah, well, bad bananas to you, Einstein," said Fred. "This is a dead end."

"We'll lie low for a bit," said Simon. "If someone comes in, we can hide."

"Yeah, we could roll up in a ball and pretend to be a tape reel."

Fred sat on the only chair. She pulled her knees up to her chest, pressed her feet on a tape unit and launched herself wheeling across the room. At the other end, she shuffled back like she was in a Flintstones car and did it again. She came to rest by a desk loaded with computer screens, stacked two high and four wide. "You'd better hide now," she said. "Duane will probably be back in the time it takes a kettle to boil."

"Who's Duane?"

"The guy using this computer. He's in the middle of a chat with the oh-so-foxy Sarah."

"You shouldn't read that. It's private," said Simon. He skim-read the screen, just to check it was indeed private and that Fred shouldn't be reading it.

Duane>	candy edwards gets my vote
Sarah>	never heard of her
Duane>	shes got the best new soul voice
Duane>	i can give you a download if u like
Sarah>	cool. always good to hear new music
Duane>	its only a trial though
Duane>	got to support good music, eh
Sarah>	sure. if it's any good I'll buy it
Duane>	have i ever let you down
Sarah>	never. that's what I love about you

"And this one," said Fred, reading the next screen.

ArnoldLayne>	your surname isn't Lane by any chance?
Penny>	i treasure my privacy
ArnoldLayne>	Penny Lane + Arnold Layne would = :-)
Penny>	wat u listening 2
ArnoldLayne>	DSOTM
Penny>	?
ArnoldLayne>	Dark Side of the Moon
Penny>	have you heard of Bender Clementina
ArnoldLayne>	no
Penny>	their a bit like floyd
Penny>	theyve done loads of stuff
ArnoldLayne>	theres probably a gap in the market

ArnoldLayne>	PF are hardly busy today
ArnoldLayne>	can you send me some MP3s?
Penny>	i can send you some trial versions
Penny>	all locked but
Penny>	well worth paying for when they run out
ArnoldLayne>	Better > nothing. Send them over.
Penny>	on their way thru cyberspace now.

"Arnold Layne and Penny Lane," said Fred. "Sweet couple."

"Yeah, until she finds out he's a perv."

"Hang on," said Fred. "Isn't this a bit funny?"

Simon read the screens over Fred's shoulder. "Nope. Other people's chats are like other people's holiday photos," he said. "Tedious."

"So, we're in a record company," began Fred. She spoke slowly and marked off each idea by holding one of the fingers on her left hand. "And there are people chatting on the internet about music. And sending out trial versions, which have to be bought when they expire. Why don't they just send MP3s?"

"It's such a faff removing the protection. You can usually tell in a few listens whether you like it or not anyway."

"Or is it because," said Fred, adopting a tone consistent with discovering the secret of alchemy, "they're marketing the songs."

"That evil bastard!" Simon said. "You can't take a dump without someone thrusting adverts in your face today. He must be hacking into people's chats to distribute his trial versions."

"That's one possibility," said Fred. "Another—"

"I tell you, if he spied on me and Angela I'd kill him."

"What makes you think he hasn't?"

"What's that supposed to mean?" Simon snapped.

"Well, the lovely Angela does seem to tell you about a lot of new music, stuff which you wouldn't normally buy."

"Just keep out of it!" Simon snapped. "You're just jealous of our..." He trailed off.

They heard voices from outside the door and then saw the door handle wobble.

"Busy day for you, Einstein," said Fred.

Simon pushed a trolley of boxes across the room, so it crashed against the door and then ran to hold it there.

"Let it go," said Fred. "Time to face the music."

The door opened and a security guard walked in. "What are you doing here?" he said. "This is out of bounds to the public!" He took his cap off and mopped his wrinkled forehead with a hanky. His grey hair danced in the breeze from the air conditioning unit.

"We were just going," said Fred.

"You stay right there," said the guard. He moved the chair just inside the door and settled down on it. "You're going nowhere."

* * *

After about twenty minutes of standing with arms folded in defiance, Fred and Simon had sat on the floor. Simon had tried to strum his guitar to calm his nerves, but the guard had taken it out of his hands and leaned it against the wall beside him.

"How long are you keeping us here?" said Fred.

"Until the police arrive," said the guard.

Fred kept her cool. "How long will that be? I can't hang around here all day."

"No idea," said the guard. "Marian's just called them. But I expect they have bigger fish to fry."

Simon was terrified. He'd never been in proper trouble before. Another masterstroke from Fred. How would this help their music careers? Simon wondered how he would plead if it came to court. Don't you get less time if you admit you did it? Could they argue they got lost after the audition? The jazz cats probably wouldn't testify. "I'm supposed to be DJ-ing tomorrow night," said Simon. "I wonder if I can podcast it from prison?"

"It won't come to that," said Fred.

"Shutt upp!" said the guard. Fred pulled a mopey face and stuck her fingers up at him, but stopped when he looked in her direction.

The door swung open and a tall man in a yellow and black stripy top walked in. The t-shirt looked like it had been around since the 70s but it still fit snugly to his muscly frame.

"Hey Gordon!" said the guard. "Gordo! The Gordmeister! How's it hanging?"

"Hello, err… you!" replied the man.

"What are you doing here?" said the guard.

"Marian sent me. I'll take over from here."

"They're all yours, then," said the guard as he left.

The man brought in a chair from the corridor, turned it backwards and sat astride it. "What have you been up to, then?" His voice had traces of a Newcastle accent.

"We're striking a blow for real music!" said Fred.

"And how do you do this?"

"We just borrowed the musak studio for a bit," she said. "Played one of our songs. No harm done."

"Did you cause any damage?"

"No," said Fred. Simon looked away.

"Did you take anything?"

"Course not," said Fred. Simon found his shoes fascinating.

"You'd better run along then."

"That's it?" said Fred.

"I don't know what Marian wants me to do with you," said the man. "If you just promise not to come back again, you can go."

"We do," said Fred. Her promise was instinctive, and transparently lacked any sincerity. "We left some stuff near the fire exit, though."

"Follow me, then." The man led them through the corridors to the lift. As he spoke, he adopted the tone of a teacher scolding naughty pupils. "Get your stuff and go. If anyone stops you, tell them Mr Sumner sent you. Be good."

The doors shut. "He looked kinda familiar," said Simon. As he turned to press the lift button, his guitar prodded Fred.

"Ouch!" she squealed. "Don't stand so close to me."

*   *   *

angelA>   hey thing xx
angelA>   hows trix

258

thing>	Morning Angela. Listen. I've got to meet you.
angelA>	no can do
thing>	This is important
angelA>	its awkward sorry
thing>	Be at the Copse Pub
thing>	Tonight. Flyer coming over now.
thing>	If we get cut off promise me you'll see me there
angelA>	watsup
thing>	We're being watched
angelA>	by who
thing>	Bigg Records
thing>	They're inserting adverts in our chats
thing>	I bet you've never even heard of Boymad
angelA>	gambling's a road to ruin
thing>	Be serious
thing>	All our private chats
thing>	All our private thoughts
thing>	Are being intercepted
	by a record label to sell music
thing>	It's evil
angelA>	how do u know this
thing>	I nearly got arrested yesterday finding out
thing>	undercover at Bigg Records after our audition
angelA>	how was the audition
thing>	Waste of time. He wasn't interested in real music.
angelA>	what are you going to do
thing>	Confront Bigg.
angelA>	when
thing>	Have you been listening? I can't say here
thing>	I'm DJ-ing tonight in the pub
thing>	Come along. It'll be a good night.
thing>	I'll dedicate a song 2u
angelA>	maybe
thing>	Which means no. I know you too well.
thing>	I have to go
angelA>	bye sweetness
thing>	Meet me tonight.

thing>   We can't chat properly online any more.

thing>   This could be our last chance.

angelA>   au revoir cheri xxx

thing>   Bye

<angelA has disconnected>

CHAPTER 34

The barista pointed her face at Dove and stared at him in silence, her way of indicating she was ready to take his order. She was in no mood for trouble today. Six weeks in, she had tired of the hazing. She understood that the newcomers had to make the tea, but this was beyond a joke. Back in Warsaw she was at the top of the legal profession. How she longed to take her first case.

"A cold camomile tea, please," said Dove.

"Cold?" she said. "No. I think we can't do that." Her heavy accent gave her the air of a Bond villain on a placement year.

"You did yesterday," said Dove.

The barista clutched her arms to her stomach and rocked with laughter. She wiped invisible tears from her eyes and drained all emotion from her face. "I've never heard that before," she said.

"Please," said Dove. "I would really like a cold tea. I'm a professional singer. I have to protect my voice." The barista scowled at him, put a teabag in a paper cup, stuffed it down with her red fingernails and filled the cup from the cold tap.

Dove paid and took his tray to a dark corner of the café, where a postman was nursing a hot chocolate.

"Creak?" said Dove. He took a seat opposite him. "What's with the uniform?"

"It's for a fancy dress party, man," said Creak. The high visibility strips on his jacket twinkled in the café's tiny spotlights.

"In the middle of the afternoon?"

"Duh!" spat Creak. "I've got to work now, man. This is the

only job I could get. All I'm qualified to do is carry things and hit things."

"Cool," said Dove. He faked interest and resisted the urge to jump to the bit where they talk about his new music. "So how's it going?"

"I'm on my second written warning," said Creak. "I guess I've got to use one of my skills a bit more and the other one a lot less. I'm not cut out for this. I can't believe you fired us. That was a bummer of a thing to do, man."

"You can't stop the waves, but you can learn to surf," said Dove. "I'm not stopping you from doing a solo project."

"Yeah, right," said Creak. "Name one decent album by a drummer." He popped the bubbles in his hot chocolate with a wooden spatula while Dove mulled it over. The radio was playing a Phil Collins song. They reached lunchtime in another day in paradise before Dove got irritated and gave up.

"I didn't come here for a pop quiz," he said.

"So why are we here?" Creak swallowed a big mouthful of hot chocolate and then laughed dismissively. "I thought, maybe, you wanted to say sorry."

Dove looked mystified. "For what?"

"Bloody hell," said Creak. "You really don't know, do you?" Dove didn't reply. "How do you think I felt when you told the audience we were splitting up?" Creak looked into his cup. "That band was my life. You can't just switch off my life, without even telling me."

"It wasn't working any more."

Creak slammed his fist on the table. The plastic cup lids bounced and a tidal wave swept their drinks. "It was working for me, man!" he shouted. The café fell near-silent, with just the radio gabbing away. The people at the tables surrounding them tried to sneak a glimpse at the hullabaloo without moving their heads enough to draw attention to themselves. "It was working for me," Creak repeated, quiet and sad.

"I'm sorry," whispered Dove. "I didn't think."

"You never do," said Creak, mopping up hot chocolate with a napkin. The barista took the next order at the counter and the café chitchat warmed up again. "You never do."

A young woman approached their table. "Excuse me. Are you—?"

"Sorry, no autographs," said Dove. He didn't look up at her.

"I don't understand," she said. "Are you finished with that tray? We've run out. Also the manager asks you to please stop shouting. Thanks." She took the tray and left.

Creak laughed. "Man, it must be great on planet Dove," he said. "Being the centre of your own universe. Having everyone else orbit around you." He rolled his head and circled his fingers through the air, like he was drawing the solar system with a sparkler.

"Can we talk about music?" said Dove.

"By which you mean, 'your music'."

"Well, yes."

"Why?"

"I'd appreciate your opinion."

"Oh, so you need me now, do you?"

"I've always valued your ideas," said Dove.

"No you haven't."

"Be fair," said Dove. "You know I have."

Creak shook his head. "Okay then. What do you want?"

Dove spoke with child-like glee. "I've been laying down some new demos. It's shaping up to be my best work ever!"

"You always say that."

"This time, it's true." Dove dug in his pocket and produced an MP3 player. "I'm playing like never before. It's a whole new sound. Listen." Creak took the player and plugged his own earphones into it. "The lyrics are just placeholders," Dove explained as a pre-emptive apology. "Just listen to the music and tell me that's not something special!"

Creak played about thirty seconds of each demo to get the gist of it before skipping on to the next one. Dove felt like he was under a microscope. Creak stayed poker-faced until he pulled out the earphones and then he smirked.

"Well?" said Dove.

Creak chose his words carefully. "Very contemporary vibe."

"What does that mean?"

Creak paused before answering. "Man, it sounds like loads of other stuff."

"Don't muck around," said Dove. "There's nothing like it on the radio."

"Oh yeah, because that's where the cutting edge of talent can be found." Creak pulled out his own MP3 player, cued up tracks by Jim:Catapult and handed it to Dove. "Play this," he said.

Dove plugged his earphones in and listened to Creak's playlist. His mouth fell open. Jim:Catapult sounded exactly like his latest sessions, which only he and Creak had heard. "Who is this?" he said. "Who are they signed to?"

"Give it up," said Creak. "It's totally not groovy to nick their ideas. Just because they're a new band, doesn't mean nobody else has heard of them. You need to face the truth, Dove."

"What truth?"

"You're past it. Nobody likes your new stuff. Not even you, six months later. Twenty years ago, you mattered. But now, you're playing catch-up. Badly. The kids online are fresher than the whole industry. That includes you."

"I don't get it," said Dove. "I've never heard of them."

"Stop it!"

Creak downed his drink. "Her Majesty calls," he said, as he pulled Dove's earphones of his MP3 player and slipped it into his mailbag. "If you want to do something useful, get those kids a record deal. And stop ripping them off, whatever."

"I've never ripped anyone off," said Dove, pulling his earphones out of his ears. "You know me better than that. It must be a coincidence."

"If that's a coincidence, I'd buy a lottery ticket today," said Creak. "You spent twenty years fighting for independent music, defending artists from evil labels and plagiarism. I admired you for that. It wasn't always easy. Now you're a cog in the machine you tried to smash. They say that as you get older, you become what you hate. Well, you're the proof."

"Wait!"

"I'm done waiting for you," said Creak. "The band carried you at the end, and now we're not around you're stealing from strangers. How come you're making demos and sitting here supping tea all day while I'm getting up at stupid o'clock to play Postman Pat? And BassFace is knee-deep in manure on his Dad's farm? And Screech is dodging rubbers, teaching music to spotty oiks? Oh yeah, you cut a deal. You're such a breadhead."

"It's not like that," said Dove.

"Don't call me," said Creak. He stood up and his chair skidded away and cowered against the wall. "If you want to talk to me, write me a note on the back of a cheque. Man, if you can't give me a bit of kudos for what I did for the band and give the new blood the credit it's due… I'm out of here."

As Creak swung his mailbag over his shoulder, it toppled Dove's drink. Creak didn't stop to say sorry. He walked out and left Dove mopping his trousers with paper napkins.

*   *   *

Dove padded along the high street, all the drive drained from him. He was headed home but he didn't know what he would do when he got there any more.

Long after Creak had left, the battle had gone on inside Dove's head. If this time came again, he'd seize Creak's iPod and take it to the police. Yeah, that's what he'd do. And then they'd have to listen to him and find out who was stealing his sound.

This fantasy replayed until the tape wore thin and his attention snapped. He ran out of people to blame, evidence to summon in his defence and witty ripostes to craft. Finally he asked himself: what if Creak was right?

Dove knew he wasn't a plagiarist, but what if he'd leeched off those bands subconsciously? Maybe he'd heard something at a club or in a record shop, and it had anchored in his memory, only to emerge later disguised as a fresh idea. What if he'd caught something from a demo thrust into his hand at a gig? They often played them in the bus purely because there was sod all else to do. Sometimes the rest of the band would play Jukebox Jury, trying to out-do each other on the cruelty of their critiques. They would laugh until they could hardly breathe with pain. But Dove wasn't laughing now.

It didn't look good. If Dove was an impartial angel on the cosmic jury, he knew where he'd be dishing the karma. Who can you trust? A man whose best work stemmed from the last century, who's been drawing on his well of ideas for years and could be scraping the gravel? Or the new whipper-snappers, fresh out of ASBOs, with attitude and verve?

The warning signs had been there. Audiences went wild for Dove's early work, but just about tolerated his new songs, in the way kids might let granddad finish his dreary story just to keep him happy. As his fans had grown up, they had got too cosy; closed their minds to new ideas. At least, that's what Dove had always told himself. In a concert hall of 1000 people, he knew he was the only one with absolute confidence in his new material. For the first time today, he asked himself if perhaps the majority was right. Had Dove, somewhere along the way, mislaid his spark? Were his brilliant new ideas, perhaps, not all that great?

He had to work harder now; had to fight his fingers to stop them falling into familiar patterns on the fret board; had to beat melodies into shape to stop them reproducing proven formulae. But his faith in his music rested on the belief that it was *his* music, and that he was the only bunch of atoms in an infinite universe capable of producing it.

True artists don't cut and paste. They don't assimilate. They repel the familiar. They invent art where before there was nothing. But if Dove wasn't doing that any more, what had he become? He had only ever had his music. He didn't know how to be or do anything else.

The wind changed direction and blew a flurry of green and gold balloons into his face. He batted them away half-heartedly and his hand got tangled in their ribbons. They were tethered to a blackboard, propped up on the pavement. The words were painted on: "You deserve a pint!" A laugh boomed from the building beside him, riding on the sound of a fruit machine paying out. A wooden sign showing five trees hung over the door and swung in its frame. As he stood there, unwinding the ribbons from his wrist, Dove savoured the smell of beer-soaked carpets, and sweat seeping from the pub. It had been too long.

"You deserve a pint!"

For the first time in fourteen years, and with a heavy heart, Dove agreed that he did.

CHAPTER 35

"Busy, tonight!" said Bert, when Simon arrived at The Corpse. "There's a good crowd in for you."

Simon looked around. Five old codgers drank in silence, most of them familiar from the Goblin gig. The youngest was a man in his forties with flowing tar-black hair. He was single-mindedly drinking spirits at the bar.

"I thought you said you'd do some posters," said Simon. "Get some, you know, younger people in."

"I did," said Bert. He handed Simon a photocopied yellow flyer. It read: "Hey, kids! Get groovy at The Copse! Disco this Saturday with DJ Thing. Be there or be square!"

"And they didn't come running?"

"I can't fathom it." Bert looked serious. "Still, I've set up the lights for you."

The light cubes were stacked around the stage area. One had the letters 'D.I.S.C.O.' flashing on and off in red and green. Another had tiny shoes that seemed to jive around as the lights changed in a kaleidoscope of colour.

"Great," said Simon, weakly. "I'll set up, then."

"Do you need a microphone?"

"No," said Simon. "Don't think I'll bother. The music can speak for itself."

He plugged his iPod into the sound mixer. What can you play to this lot? He scrolled through the artists and stopped at The Beatles. 'She Loves You' is a guaranteed crowd pleaser. If anything could get a reaction here, that could. The speakers blasted it out but nobody so much as tapped a toe. The coloured shoes danced but not even they could distract the locals from the serious business of drinking and moping. One man yawned.

Sod this, thought Simon. What's the point of trying to connect with people who are completely unreachable; people who don't care about music; people who have never felt that thrill when the first few chords of a much-loved song takes them by surprise?

At least one person could be happy tonight, and that was Simon. He gave up on the audience and chose his own favourite songs: B-sides that should have been singles, remixes that made his pulse quicken, bands off the internet who could fit their fan convention in their kitchen. Anything goes, he decided.

Simon cued University of Death's Animal Reined. When the riffs at the start ground into action, the younger man at the bar turned his head slowly to look. He wore a soppy drunk grin and seemed mesmerised by all the flashing lights. He raised his shot glass to Simon but couldn't keep it straight. Most of his drink spilled on the bar and when the glass reached his lips, he looked puzzled about where it had all gone.

The strategy was working. Simon had one ally in the room now. He followed it up with Tiled Sprites' Time Today. As he scrolled through his music collection to find what would work next, he felt a shadow fall over him. It lurched from side to side. It was the man from the bar.

"They're stealing my sounds," he said. He wobbled on the spot to find a firm footing on the shifting ground beneath him.

"Sure," said Simon. He could see there was about a minute to run on the current track. As he clicked in and out of artists and albums, he couldn't find something that could follow Tiled Sprites without jarring.

For a split second, Simon saw a fist reflected in his iPod screen as it flew over it. Then he felt it against his jaw, like a lightly padded brick. His head twisted and he fell sideways to his knees, from a combination of the force and the shock. Stars flashed around his head. So did shoes.

The man was a leaning tower, swaying above him. "You're all

stealing my sounds!" he wailed. "Get out of my head!" That seemed only fair, since it looked like the man, himself, had already done so.

He staggered out the door, throwing his weight from foot to foot like an ice skater.

Simon watched the door close behind him and leaned on a light cube for support as he lifted himself up. He rubbed his face. It hurt, but not as much as his pride. What had he done to deserve that? The guy looked like he was on Simon's side when he was playing Animal Reined.

Nobody else had even noticed the fracas. Simon set his iPod to shuffle and went to the bar for a drink.

*   *   *

Simon nursed one beer for an hour. He didn't want to wait there. The regulars didn't particularly want him there either. But he had said he'd be there for Angela, and she might yet come. His iPod segued flawlessly from Smells Like Teen Spirit by Nirvana into Four Candles by The Two Ronnies. He didn't care any more.

All the time he waited, he wondered what he would say to her if she came. Would she be willing to move their relationship to the real world so they could have some kind of privacy? Would that even work? Perhaps they only got on because their communications were a stream of thoughts, undiluted by all the awkwardness that a physical presence would cause.

Was she being fleeced too, receiving the same adverts and being told that Simon was sending them? It was hard to imagine that Bigg would go to that trouble and then only prey on one of them. Simon shuddered to think what rubbish might be attributed to his music taste against his will.

He should have seen it coming of course. Their relationship was built on a love of real music, like University of Death and Tiled Sprites. Angela was a proper music fan. She had discovered Tiled Sprites, the greatest band he had ever heard, hidden deep in the internet. How could he have believed that she really liked Boymad, lowest-common-denominator pap force-fed to the public through mass media? Boymad is the fizzy pop of music: good enough for the first few sips, but you end up with itchy teeth. You certainly couldn't live off it. How much money must Bigg be making off this skulduggery? How many confidences were being violated along the way? More importantly, how could Simon maintain his intimate relationship with Angela, knowing that Bigg was eavesdropping on the only communication channel he had? Bigg had to be stopped.

Simon panicked that he couldn't remember what Angela looked like. He could picture the photo she sent, and the lipstick heart she had used to frame her face, but the middle was blank, like it had been cut out with scissors. Every time the door opened, he looked around as casually as he could. But it didn't open often and there was never a young woman coming through it.

Face it, he thought: She's not coming. She's never come to any of the other meetings he had tried to arrange. Why should now be any different?

Simon gazed into the silent TV above the bar and watched a parade of pop stars and nicely dressed nobodies file into Earls Court. The reporter mouthed something or other through her fixed smile. The screen flashed 'Live' above her, as if viewers should be impressed that a journalist had been sent to a scheduled press call in London and that the technology existed to show her there right now. When the camera pulled back, Simon saw Bigg's face plastered across the building. Simon felt his shoulders stiffen and his fists clench. The ticker rolled across the bottom of the screen: "Bigg promises the biggest Awards ever despite industry recession."

"He has to be stopped," said Simon.

"Eh?" said Bert, as he wiped beer off his 'marketing for beginners' book behind the bar.

"Where's Earls Court?"

Bert handed him the A-Z. "Can I get you another drink?"

"No," said Simon. He flipped through the pages of the map. "Something's come up. Something Bigg."

CHAPTER 36

Beams of light pushed the clouds away, and clashed over Earls Court. On the building's white façade was a two storey photo of Clive Bigg holding a trophy. "Tell me when to smile," he had instructed the photographer. When the time had come, Bigg couldn't quite remember how and had twisted his face awkwardly. On the poster beside his gurning mug was the date and the bold caption: "The Bigg Awards".

The back room boys and girls were going in through a side door, dressed in dinner jackets and evening gowns: the march of the penguins. The bands had the red carpet, rolled down the shiny white steps. This was the way in for scruffs: most of them wore crumpled and tattered scraps and looked like they had been disturbed from a nice kip in the gutter. Simon had never walked on a red carpet before, but he knew where he would blend in.

It had been raining, and with each footstep, water frothed out of the carpet with a squelch. Simon tried to keep his head down as he passed a nest of photographers, but one of them called out from atop a tiny step ladder: "Oi! One for the Daily Mirror?" Simon turned to look and a flash gun burned dark spots in his eyes. "Oo's this geezer anyway?" the photographer asked. His mate replied: "Dunno, but we'd best get a safe shot." Simon bowed, posed and smiled into every lens in turn. The more he posed, the more they snapped. The press pack thought they would spend tomorrow poring over their contact sheets and thumbnails to try to fathom who the hell he was. Only Simon knew they were shooting tomorrow's front page. After he'd exposed Bigg, everyone would know who he was. Simon laughed at the thought of it, and all the flash guns burst at once.

Abruptly the photographers stopped shooting and stepped back, all struck with mortal terror. Björk was here. She gave them evils as she flounced past. Simon followed her. She could probably smuggle him in under her ostrich costume, he thought, but it was too late now. There were too many people watching them both. And she probably wouldn't let a stranger hide up her skirt, anyway. She caught Simon staring at her and flared her eyes. He looked away and when he looked back, she was gone.

Ahead, the queue was closing up. Just inside the door, Simon could see a team of security guards inspecting tickets. They looked stern. When you're made to wear a matching black and yellow t-shirt, baseball cap and flimsy plastic jacket, you've probably taken enough crap for one day. One of them worked his way down the queue and only moved on when he had outstared each person in turn and asserted his dominance. He was a rottweiler controlling his territory.

When the guard looked at him, Simon bowed his head quickly. Could he bluff his way through this? Maybe he'd lost his ticket? Perhaps he could claim to be someone in a band, so that he could get their place on the guest list? He wondered who he could pass himself off as. The queue shuffled forwards, up the stairs and into the foyer. If he stepped out of line, he'd be spotted immediately.

A hologram sparkled at him from the floor. There was a ticket at the feet of one of the security guards, the corner brushed under his brick-like white trainers. Tricky, but it was his best shot so far. What if Simon tied his shoelaces and picked it up at the same time? Could he get away with that? The guard says 'tickets please' and he replies 'sure, just let me tie my shoelace first. These people won't mind waiting. Oh! I've dropped my ticket. Here it is, under your foot!' That plan couldn't be more drippy and transparent if it was carved in ice.

He had to think fast. He had a few paces and barely seconds to act. His heart quickened.

"Excuse me, sir! Can you come this way please?" Rumbled

already? One of the guards diverted him out of the queue and escorted him through the maze of ropes and ticket desks. Simon's chest beat loud. The room got hot. Could they arrest him for this? He hadn't actually done anything yet. He looked back. The door he had entered through was clogged up with more people, so he couldn't even make a dash for the exit. He rode it out, in silence, followed the guard and awaited his fate.

They came to double doors, and the security guard opened one. Inside it was dark.

"If you please, sir!" The guard waved to indicate that Simon should go through.

"What's in there?" Simon could only see a black curtain, with pin pricks of coloured light shining through it.

"The VIP entrance, sir." The guard had a jolly face. He didn't look like he was lying. "Is everything okay, sir?"

"Of course," said Simon. "I just..." He nodded and went through the door, which was gently closed behind him. It deadened the horsey laughter and boisterous singing in the foyer. Simon could now hear the rattle of chains, metal on metal. Torture implements being sharpened.

He peeled back the curtain and was shocked by what he saw.

It was the main hall, with the stage at the far end. The dining tables were filling up. The caterers clattered as they went, the cutlery chimed and clinked.

Simon had made it in. God only knows how, but he had.

* * *

Fred breezed into The Corpse and looked for Simon, but he was nowhere to be seen. The disco lights flickered by the stage where he should have been. She went to the bar and took a stool.

"How is your bid for fame going?" asked Bert as he leaned on one of the pumps.

"No luck with the lift stunt," she said. "I've phoned about thirty journalists today. Half of them didn't believe we did it, the other half didn't care. There was one guy who said he'd get back to me, but Bigg denied it all so he dropped the story. Simon's running late, isn't he?"

"He finished already," said Bert. "There was a bit of a… Well, basically, this guy hit him."

"God! Is he okay?"

"Oh yeah," said Bert. "He went for a walk to Earls Court."

"What?"

Bert pointed at the television, where the news was still being padded with promotional guff about Bigg's awards. "Earls Court. Now, what can I get you?"

"Gotta go," said Fred. She waved as she left. "I've got to stop Si before he makes a complete dick of himself."

* * *

A snotty blow into a tissue was amplified around the hall. Drying her eyes with the same tissue, a woman in a pink puffy dress blubbered into the microphone. "It's a real honour," she said, as her lips trembled. "I love my work, but it means so much to be recognised as best a capella bass lyricist of the year."

"Indeed, where would we have been without you bum, bum, bumming?" said Bigg. He wrested the microphone from her grip and she tottered off the stage and down the steps. The winner punched the air haphazardly with her trophy as she slithered back to her party, went floppy and fell into her seat.

Tables were dotted around the hall like islands with shipwreck survivors clinging to their edges. It had been a long evening with a big booze budget, and some of the less hardy songwriters were showing signs of seasickness. The speeches were becoming increasingly slurred. Two had overlapped. A burly man from marketing had used his acceptance speech to describe Bigg as his "best mate ever, no really, you are, and I mean that, I do" and sealed it with a beer-soaked kiss.

In a dark corner by the bar, Jake was offering to open his kimono for Mandy. She stirred her drink with the penis from an ice sculpture of Michelangelo's David. They were looking deep into each other's eyes.

The Bigg Records awards dinner is supposed to be a feelgood

event for the company, so it is ironic that feelbad is what most people did the next day.

Simon lurked in the shadows at the back of the hall, watched the show and waited for his moment. As a server passed, he lifted a glass of champagne from her tray and downed it in the hope it would boost his confidence. He wasn't so much a bag of nerves as a suitcase full of entrails. The champagne bubbles tickled his insides and gave him wind. He prepared himself to confront Bigg in front of the whole company by counting to three. Twice. And didn't move.

Bigg picked up one of the last trophies, shaped like the company's office tower, from the table on the stage. "When I found out we had released a single by the frog who does the insurance adverts, I nearly croaked," he said.

"I wish you had!" shouted Simon. He had spoken without thinking, but it got a big laugh. Over his reading glasses, Bigg shot a glance at the table he thought the voice had come from, but the stage lights dazzled him.

Simon pressed himself to act. He threaded his path through the tables, and stretched over puddles of melted ice, spilled wine and sick.

Bigg shook his script, as if trying to blow the cobwebs off it, before reading on. "But when I heard the single 'Ribbit like you like it', I was deeply moved. I filled up, I did. I could imagine children all over the land connecting with this charming, cuddly amphibian in a way that would soon see their pocket money going towards a truly great cause: Your salaries." The audience responded with a few cheers and claps.

Simon was about three tables away from the stage now.

"This award is for the 'targeted songwriting: four-to-six-year-old girls' category. The winner is a man who only joined us six months ago. He's moved from being a big frog in a small pond at Songlife Records, to being a small – but significant – frog in our pond. Please welcome: Maxwell Croaker, ahem, sorry, ahem – Maxwell Broker."

While Maxwell was getting to his feet, Simon marched on to the stage to claim the award. Bigg offered his hand for shaking, but all the while, he was reading his script on the rostrum. Simon felt weird about touching Bigg, but accepted the handshake. Bigg's hands were hard and surprisingly small. Bigg handed Simon Maxwell's trophy and the microphone, without taking his eyes from the script in front of him.

The microphone felt heavy. Simon faced the crowd. It all looked so different from up here. The stage seemed higher than the few steps Simon had climbed. The lights threatened him like the burning headlamps of an oncoming truck. As he had weaved through the tables the room had seemed small, but from up here, it stretched in every direction. The audience numbered hundreds. Thousands, maybe. Many ignored him, but others studied him like a museum exhibit. He felt naked.

Simon moved to the side of the stage, so that he would have a head start on Bigg. The speakers whistled, spiking Simon's heart with shock, and he took a step back again.

"Clive Bigg is evil!" he shouted into the microphone. His voice sounded small, albeit loud. A man near the front called out 'hear! hear!' and thumped the table. Bigg pointed and security hauled him away.

Bigg looked at Simon over his reading glasses. "Oh, God, it's you," he moaned. "Thingie, don't do this."

Simon could hear his breathing amplified over the drunken chitchat that hummed around the room. At the back of the hall, the people were so distant their heads looked like rice grains. He spoke into the microphone: "Clive Bigg has been hacking in to my personal, private web chats with my girlfriend and putting adverts in our conversations!"

There was a moment of stunned silence. Bigg flustered with his glasses case and looked ashamed. But before Simon could continue or Bigg could intervene, a round of applause broke out on the marketing department's table and splashed around the room. Bigg nodded his thanks.

"She's your girlfriend, is she?" said Bigg, emboldened by the crowd reaction. "How's your sex life?"

"Mind your own business!" Simon shouted.

"Yes," said Bigg. "I imagine you're well used to doing that."

He arched his eyebrow and tilted his head to the audience, like the chief conspirator in a pantomime.

This wasn't working at all how Simon imagined it would. "What's that supposed to mean?" he snapped.

"Nothing." Bigg held his palms up. "What makes you think I'm hacking your tawdry virtual love nest, anyway?"

"My girlfriend–"

"Your *girlfriend*?"

"Yes! My *girlfriend* keeps recommending your crappy music." From somewhere in the audience a voice piped up: "Steady on!"

"Perhaps she just likes it," said Bigg. He didn't argue about the quality. "Lots of people do." The audience cheered.

"She doesn't recommend music from any other labels."

"Nobody else's is as good as ours, though." There were a few whoops from the songwriters on the nearest table, and they clinked their champagne glasses.

"I've been to your data centre," said Simon. "I've seen..." What had he seen, exactly? Some chat transcripts on screen. Nothing that would hold water in court.

Bigg gripped the podium. "This whole industry is built on artifice, you know." There were a few cheers from the PR department. "My first job was faking autographs for Rodney Trousersnake. The fans would bring their records to the stage door. I'd take them away, draw a cock on them and give them back. Ah! The days of punk!" Bigg shook his head as he wallowed in a moment's nostalgia.

"What's that got to do with anything?"

"It's all smoke and mirrors," said Bigg. "Those bands you think you know so well? We write their letters to you, ghost their blogs. We dress them and invent their personalities. All those charming doodles in the artwork: that's us. For most of them, we tell them what to sing. People first listen to music as a kid, stuff like the Wombles and Bob the Builder. The only thing that changes is the costumes. The process is the same. It's all for show. It's what makes pop stars the perfect product they are."

Simon heard a hiss at his feet. Fred was there. He held the microphone at arm's length and crouched down to tell her: "I'm busy!"

"I knooooow," she said. "Just listen, will you: She's here."

Simon crouched down. "Who?"

"Angela," said Fred, exasperated. "Stands to reason. She works here. She's on commission."

"How do you know?"

"Lucky guess."

"So you don't actually know, then?"

"What's more likely?" said Fred. "Fatchops here is spying on you? Or he pays people to sell music through chats?"

It was obvious now Fred had said it. How could Simon not have seen it before? Angela was on the payroll. That's why she would compromise her taste, their shared taste, to recommend Bigg's pap to him. It was her job.

Simon stood up again. "Angela!" he called into the mic. "Show yourself! I know you work here." He scanned the room. On the tables, everybody looked around to see if anyone else was getting up. A figure near the back stood up, ambled through the haze of the spotlights towards the stage but swerved into the toilets half way. "Stop pretending," he said. "I know you're here." Simon turned to Bigg. "She works for you, doesn't she?"

"Simon," said Bigg. "You're delusional. I know all about you."

Simon was struck with horror. There was a glint in Bigg's eye that pierced him like an arrow. "Oh my God," Simon whispered. "It's you, isn't it? You're Angela." His face contorted with revulsion. "You're sick!"

Bigg guffawed. "Do you really think I've got time to personally hand sell all our music?"

"Ah!" said Simon. "So you admit somebody is doing it!"

Bigg summoned four security guards to the stage. Two stood uncomfortably close to Simon and another two stood either side of Fred. "You think you're close to Angela, but you don't know her darkest secret." Bigg paused for effect. "I do." The room fell silent. "Your so-called girlfriend," he said.

"She *is* my girlfriend!" Simon insisted.

"...does not exist."

There was a moment's pause before the crowd understood but

then it erupted in gales of laughter. And with that, the security guards hauled Simon away and dragged Fred backstage with him. Simon burned with rage and embarrassment and felt so small the guard could have put him in his pocket.

* * *

Simon and Fred were taken to Bigg's dressing room and dumped in his low sofa. The four security guards lined up behind them. They all tried to ignore the giant pair of blue y-fronts draped across the back of Bigg's chair. It was difficult because they dominated the reflection in the dressing table mirror. The light bulbs around the mirror seemed to highlight the pants, as if they were stars on Broadway.

Bigg stormed in. He ripped a drawer open, whipped his pants off the chair, dunked them into the drawer and slammed it shut. The woman from the University of Death gig, who had injected their fan club tags, followed him in. She looked ill at ease in her sparkly black ballgown and was carrying what looked like a cattle prod. Bigg slammed the door behind her, and a couple of bottles fell over on his vanity unit.

"Zap 'em." Bigg paced up and down.

Fred moved to get up, but two security guards pressed down on her shoulders, drilling her deep into the sofa cushions.

"You can't hurt us!" Simon protested. "Everyone knows we're here!"

The woman kneeled down on the other side of the sofa arm. Her eyes looked dead. She waved the prod at Simon and he squirmed away. Fred cried out as he squashed her and pushed him back. The security guards gripped his shoulders and held him still. The woman rubbed Simon's sleeve up and pressed his arm with the pointy thing. It beeped. "V.I.P.," she said to Bigg. She ran around the front of the sofa to Fred and checked her arm. "U.O.D," she said.

"How the hell did that happen?" said Bigg.

"Fuktifino," said the woman.

"Help yourself to vol au vents on the way out. Every little

281

helps. Now you're unemployed!" He bellowed the last word. The woman stared him down for a moment, weighing up her options, before she marched out. Bigg slammed the door behind her and sat down in his make-up chair.

Fred spoke first. "Let us go now, and we'll drop the kidnapping charges."

"Shut up!" said Bigg. "I'm trying to think." He rubbed his chins. "Let me guess. You both got chipped for the University of Death fan club."

"So?" said Fred.

"Only Thingie here got a Bigg Records access all areas tag by mistake."

Simon realised now how he'd been able to get in to the awards so easily, and how he'd been able to open all the doors in Bigg Records which had seemed closed to Fred.

Bigg reclined the chair and checked his text messages. Tap, tap, tap.

"What are you going to do with us?" asked Fred.

"Undecided." Bigg sounded like he was contemplating a walk in the park or a picnic at the zoo. Tap-tap. Tap, tap tap.

"I know Angela's here." said Simon. "I will find her. I bet she's got a different story to tell. About how you made her sell your crappy music. How she had no choice. Can't believe I was taken in by it. How can anyone like Tiled Sprites and Boymad at the same time?"

"You can't find her." Bigg laughed but didn't take his eyes off his mobile. "The only place she exists is in your feeble mind."

"Liar!"

Bigg ignored Simon's accusation. "We started off viral marketing with people hanging around chat rooms all day. Boring as hell. They ended up saying the same things all the time. Waste of money."

"That's unethical," said Fred.

"Is it?" Bigg looked surprised, but not concerned. He pocketed his phone and lit himself a cigar. "Anyway, I caught a couple of engineers playing a game on the Commodore. 'Captain Blood', it was called. After I'd booted them out, I had a quick go. Just to see what the attraction was. Dead cute, it was. All those chatty little aliens." He had a look of joy in his eyes, although his face was hard as ever.

"What's this got to do with Angela?" said Simon.

"Well, you get to chat to these characters using a little language they invented. And I was thinking maybe we could do that. Write a program that could have internet chats for us. Spare us the hassle. It's the greatest viral marketing exercise ever. We don't just create the message. We create the carriers too."

"There's only about thirty words in Captain Blood," said Simon. "You couldn't make it realistic enough for real life."

"We didn't have to," said Bigg. "It only had to be convincing online. The average chat uses a tiny subset of the English language. We limited it further by focusing on music. People are so ad-blind today. The only way to reach them is through their friends. But then, how do you reach the friends?" It was a rhetorical question, but he gave them time to mull it over and cut them off when Simon opened his mouth to reply. "You invent them."

"You're lying," said Simon. "I'd know."

"It was clunky at the start," said Bigg. He blew a smoke ring above him and watched it float to the ceiling and crumble away. "Adding in random typos and stripping out the punctuation made it more human, though. To begin with, these avatars were there all the time, like sappy lapdogs waiting for their owners to return. You could turn on the friendship like a light. That didn't work for anyone. So we made them disappear, interrupt chats and so on. Gave them a life. The players fell for it, hook, line and stinker."

"But we..." Simon went pale.

"Yes, you randy little git," said Bigg. "I bet you did! They all do, eventually."

"*She* came on to *me*, though," said Simon. "No. You're lying. Bet you didn't know I've seen her photo."

"Love it!" said Bigg. "That's just a photo of another player, automatically matched to meet your taste in women. Some poor girl's probably going moon-eyed over your photo right now too."

He looked Simon up and down and then shook his head. "Oh, maybe not. Anyway, it's so unlikely players will ever meet the person they get a photo of, it doesn't matter."

Simon remembered the picture SteamyJoanne had shown him and how she had been sure it was of him. The print out was too poor to tell, but perhaps it really was the photo Simon had sent to Angela. "I was attacked by some woman because of this," he said. "She slapped me."

"Love hurts." Bigg cackled.

Simon lunged at him, but the security guards pulled him straight back and threw him into the seat again. "You bastard," Simon whispered. "You've killed Angela. I loved her."

"You still can," said Bigg. "She's not going anywhere."

"But she doesn't exist!"

"She never existed. Nothing's changed. Don't tell me you've never loved a fantasy. My whole business is based on it. Fake friendships with bands sell records. Sex sells. Records with fold-out posters sell. They don't make the music sound any better, eh?"

Simon's lip quivered. "She said she would always be there."

"And she will!" said Bigg. "Day and night, subject to certain random availability parameters. She'll never run off with another man. Who else can you be sure will never leave you in the lurch? All men are bastards, all women are cows, but your virtual angel will always be perfect." Bigg smiled sadly.

"This has got to stop," said Fred. "People are getting hurt."

Bigg flicked his hand dismissively. "It was only a slap."

"I don't mean that! You're screwing people up. If you don't stop the whole thing now, we'll go to the press. We'll tell the whole world."

Bigg laughed. "Who would ever believe you? What proof have you got?" There was a moment's silence. "Nothing. I thought not. Anyway, the whole of Bigg Records already knows about this technology. If it was going to make the news, it would have done so long before now."

Simon pointed at Bigg. "You won't be so cocky when you're on the front page."

"Well, that's never going to happen," replied Bigg. Stretched out on his make-up chair, he looked completely relaxed. "I know your type. You cried when John Peel died because he was the only one who was ever going to play your music. You've been trying to get heard for years and nobody's noticed you yet. You attacked a daytime TV presenter to try to get some press. How desperate! And what happened? Peeeeep!" He made the sound of a TV signal failure. "Nothing. You have no voice. You are media mute."

"With a story like this, we'll be dynamite," said Fred.

"Think it through," said Bigg, exasperated. "It comes down to a couple of troublemakers, known for breaking and entering and random acts of violence, versus a massive advertiser and government sponsor. Who do you think the editor is going to plump for? I'll take a bet on me at whatever odds you're offering."

Fred flew into a rage, but hovered just above the seat as she was held there by the guards pressing her shoulders. After a few seconds, she tired and collapsed into the soft cushions.

"But just to save you and me any hassle, should you feel motivated to approach the press, I'm going to propose a deal," Bigg said. "There is always a win-win."

"Yeah, like I wanna deal with a man like you," said Fred.

"Hear me out," said Bigg. He left his cigar smoking in an ashtray on the vanity unit, levelled his chair and stood up. Fred and Simon hadn't imagined Bigg could get less attractive, but as he towered over them, they could see right up his nose. "I own you," said Bigg. "You're chipped like cattle. All the remaining venues and record shops belong to me, so I can pretty much ban you from live music or CD shops. Now I know your tag numbers, I just need to set all your permissions to 'deny' and you're barred. Hell, I could probably pull a few strings to stop you getting into libraries and supermarkets, or even ordering music online. You don't get to where I am without making influential friends. You'll feel like you've gone deaf."

"You can't take away the music we've already got," said Simon. It was a stupid little act of defiance to pretend he didn't care about new bands.

Bigg laughed. "I can destroy it. I only have to say the word and your downloads stop working."

"You wouldn't dare," said Fred.

"Alternatively, you can promise to keep quiet and Thingie here gets to keep his fantasy lover, and you can go to a few gigs so maybe he'll meet a real woman one day."

Simon looked sad. He didn't know what to think any more. It was like Angela had just died, only he knew if he went to chat to her, she would be exactly the same as she ever was.

"I take it we have a deal," said Bigg.

Neither Fred nor Simon replied.

"Good," Bigg concluded. "I know you'll keep schtumm. I'm pretty matey with all the journos who matter, so don't try anything stupid. I'll switch off your tags like *that*." He clicked his fingers with one hand and picked up his cigar again with the other.

"Tatty bye." Bigg walked out, but a beat later, popped his head around the door again. "Oh, and Thingie?"

"Yeah?"

"Give my love to Angela, won't you?" Bigg grinned and his slit of a mouth sliced his head in two. "Give 'er one from me," he said, with a dark chuckle.

Simon writhed in the grip of the guards, aching to land a punch on him. The more Simon wriggled, the more Bigg brayed his ugly, fat-headed laugh. After a minute or two, they both tired of it. "Dump 'em outside," Bigg said, wiping away a tear. Then he was gone.

* * *

The guards whisked Fred and Simon through the building and pushed them at a fire escape. As they hit the bar across it, the double doors snapped open. The guards pushed again, and Fred and Simon skipped forwards onto the outside pavement. Behind them, the doors clapped shut and were swiftly locked.

It was quiet now. The party was slowly breaking up inside. A gaggle of girls dressed in wisps of silk folded their arms against the cold as they hurried to the tube station. There were a few limousines waiting in the road, only one of which didn't have the rental phone number just above the number plate.

"Thanks a bunch," said Simon.

"Wha—?"

"The chips! That was your stupid idea."

"No problem. There's this surgery in Sweden tha—"

"Sweden?!"

"I didn't force you to have one!"

"Yeah, right."

"That's not…" Fred started to protest, but bit her lip.

The air whispered. The stars winked.

"You really liked her didn't you?" she said.

She put her hand on Simon's back, and he turned towards her and took a hug. Fred felt soft and warm, all along his body. After three, he told himself, that's it. He wouldn't waste any more time on Bigg, or Angela or any of the rest of this mess he'd got himself into. He'd harden himself against the feeling of loss. He would be strong. One. Two. Three.

"Let's go," he said. He marched off towards the tube, and Fred took double steps to keep up.

CHAPTER 37

Smurfish laughter and stoned gibberish looped hour after hour, the floor sweepings from Abbey Road's tape room stitched together and carved into the final groove of Sergeant Pepper. The record spun round and round, popping at the same point each time. The needle eroded the vinyl with every rotation, and still it came back for more.

Dove's head spun inside too. It hung limp over the edge of the sofa, with his curtain of hair and a thread of dribble joining him to the carpet. His body looked ready to slither off the furniture at any moment. His left arm was already there.

A beer can was stuck on the bottom of his slipper, where he had trodden on its middle and it had refused to let go. More crumpled cans cluttered the carpet.

A voice called: "Lemme in, man!"

Dove's head jerked up as he heard his letterbox slam shut. He shooed the sound away before dropping his head again. His body followed it, and he slid off the sofa and onto the floor, where he curled up in a ball.

The letterbox clapped eight times, which Dove counted to prove to himself he could, and it felt like someone was firing tins of peas at his head with a tennis ball machine. Each clap of the door ricocheted around his brain.

The voice again: "Sod this, man!"

Dove was left in peace. He snuggled up to the hard front of the sofa and wrapped his arm over his eyes. The record was about as much fun to listen to now as fingernails on a blackboard, but he couldn't move. "Never could see any other way, never could see any other way, never could see any other way," the record chirped.

Dove didn't know how long he dozed. He was woken by the sound of cracking wood. Light poured in. He rolled his head and peeked through his fingers at the growing gap in his wall. Where his window had been boarded up after the break-in, somebody was removing the panel. The light hurt. The record droned.

The tiny triangle of light stretched and flexed and then snapped into a square as the panel was ripped off. A man with a jemmy stood shadowed in the window.

"Dove!" he said. It was Creak's voice. Dove wasn't sure whether he was pleased or not. He didn't respond.

Creak climbed in, went straight to the record player and turned it off. He didn't lift the needle. He just killed the power. The turntable wound down, and the record got slower and deeper until it scratched to a silence.

"Oi!" said Dove. His voice was feeble. "I was listening to that."

"Get up!" Creak ordered.

Dove didn't move. Creak kneeled beside him and shook his shoulder so Dove lashed out. He thrust his arm into the air and twirled it around in what he thought was a threatening manner. It looked like a quarter of a hokey cokey. Creak took a step back on his haunches and easily avoided Dove's attack.

"Go away!" said Dove.

"People are worried, man," said Creak. "Your sponsor's been on the phone. He's still got my mobile number as your emergency contact. Why didn't you check in with him?"

"He shouldn't have called," said Dove. "I told him. I did."

"Told him what?"

Dove lifted his head and made eye contact for the first time. "That you're a traitor." His head fell back onto the floor.

"Like, I really need this, man!" said Creak. "I've pulled a sickie today because I was worried about you."

"I'm fine," droned Dove. "Never felt better."

"Yeah, you look magic," said Creak. He got up and kicked

Dove. Dove groaned but didn't move. "You're fighting fit, all right. I'll make you a coffee."

Creak gathered up the cans from the living room and took them to the kitchen. Dove could hear Creak opening cupboards and doors. He wanted to call out where the coffee was, but the words somehow stayed deep inside him. He didn't have the strength to force them out loud enough for Creak to hear.

The kettle rumbled away.

Dove hauled himself onto the sofa and sat upright, supporting himself with cushions. His head felt like it was bobbing a few inches above his neck. It throbbed. Dove rubbed his eyes. He could feel the carpet texture embossed on his cheek. He left the can on his foot.

Creak returned with a cup of coffee that was as thick as gravy. It clinked as he set it down on the glass coffee table. The sound wasn't loud, but it was sharp and hurt Dove.

Creak disappeared and came back with a gold statue pinched between his fingertips. It was a Brit Award. Baked beans dripped from its base, and strands of a blue furry Chinese meal clung to its face. Creak put it on the table facing Dove. "This was in the bin," he said, affecting a casual tone.

"Best place for it," said Dove. Dove picked up his coffee and sipped it. "Christ, that's hot! Are you trying to kill my voice?"

"Not as hard as you are," said Creak. "Pull yourself together, man. Think about the programme. What was step one?"

"Admit there's a problem." Dove was whispering. "Yeah, there's a problem. I can't even have a few beers in peace. Nobody crashes your house when you party."

"Yeah, but I can handle it," said Creak.

Dove recoiled from Creak's voice and rubbed his head. "So can I, man."

"Shall I get you a mirror?" Dove didn't reply, so Creak went on: "What's step two?"

"Believe there is a higher power that can restore us to sanity."

"Yeah, Jesus loves you, man. No doubt. It's just me that wants to kill you."

"Ha!" said Dove. "Jesus nothing! My higher power was my

291

music. My devotion to the guitar saved me from the demon drink. They've stolen my god."

"Eh?"

"Your friends! Jim:Catapult! They're bugging me. They're stealing my ideas."

"Boll—" Creak stopped himself. He could see Dove was fragile.

"They are!" said Dove.

"Dove, man." There was an undercurrent of pity in Creak's voice. "It's just the dregs of the drink talking, man. Nobody's bugging you."

Dove shook his head, but it hurt so he quickly stopped. "You're probably in on it. I bet you're here to throw me off the scent."

"Dove, why would anyone bug you?"

"To steal my music! I know I'm not stealing their music, so they must be taking mine. You said yourself they're too similar for coincidence."

"Why would anyone steal something they can't fence? Not even you can sell your music today."

"Yeah, well you bought the Jim:Catapult album. That's a tenner they've made off me."

"But they're not your songs, are they? They just sound a little bit like you."

"They sound exactly like me! They're stealing my style. Stealing my soul!"

"They were lucky to find it," shot Creak.

Dove held eye contact with Creak, but there was more sadness than anger in Dove's expression.

"Sorry," said Creak. He pressed on. "How would anyone bug you, anyway?"

Dove had it all worked out. "About six months ago, someone broke in. At the time, I thought that nothing was stolen. Looks like I was wrong." He tasted his coffee and pulled a face. "Pass that bottle, can you?"

Dove pointed at a miniature of Bell's on the record player. Creak took it away, emptied it down the kitchen sink and handed Dove the empty bottle.

"Thanks a bunch," said Dove, who took it nonetheless and stood it on the arm of the sofa. He played at knocking the bottle over and setting it straight again, until it slipped off the arm and onto the floor.

Creak watched him. "You really believe this, don't you?"

"I've had a drink," said Dove. "Not had my brains removed. I know what's what."

"Okay," said Creak. "I'll help you, then."

"How?"

"Here's the deal: We rip this place apart. If we don't find any bugs, you've got to let it drop, man."

"Nah, they'll be too well hidden," said Dove. "They're pro's."

"Coward."

"I'm not."

"Prove it." Creak sat down beside Dove on the sofa. "Maybe we'll find hidden mics," he said. "But if not, it's time to face your demons, man. Do we have a deal?"

Creak held his hand out to shake. Dove didn't move for about a minute, but Creak wasn't going to let him off easily. He waited. And waited.

"Okay," said Dove, unclamping the beer can from his foot. "We'll do it."

But he didn't shake Creak's hand.

*   *   *

The last time Dove had tidied his music room, the magazines he binned had Limahl on the front. In the last twenty years or so, a lot more stuff had come through the door than had gone out through the bin, and it showed. Every available surface was covered with letters, newspapers, books, CDs (mostly enjoying a sleepover in each other's cases), cables and empty packs of strings. The bookcase was rammed full, with little books poked in the spaces on top of the hardbacks.

There were instruments everywhere. Two Yamaha keyboards and a Korg were stacked on a rack. A bass guitar rested on a stand, while five other guitars were leaned carefully against the wall. There was a pinboard which had a triangle hanging off it and a harmonica balanced along the top of it. Wind chimes hung in front of the window, but were tied up with an elastic band to stop them ringing.

Dove knew that you could hide a petting zoo in this room, let alone a bug.

Dove spied a rhyming dictionary on the desk and snuck it back on the shelf. The only way it would fit was with the front cover facing out. "I hardly ever need to use this," he said. "Don't even know why it's here."

Creak flicked through a scrapbook on the stone lectern. It was half full of cuttings about Dove, neatly pasted and dated. "That's Mum's," said Dove.

"Yeah," said Creak. "Her handwriting's like yours, eh?" He threw it into a cardboard box in the doorway, and began to sort through a pile of papers. "Check every atom," he said. "I'm not having you moan that we didn't look close enough."

Dove combed through a cardboard box of electronic gubbins.

This was going to take a long time.

*   *   *

Three boxes brimmed in the hallway, but the room was still stuffed with junk. After two hours, Creak and Dove were both flagging. Creak lay on the floor and stretched his arm under the desk, into a nest of cables. A plectrum had dived into it and Dove insisted that, yes, it did need to be dug out because the bite marks in it were Alice Cooper's. Creak looked glad to lie down for a bit.

"We're gonna have to open those books," said Dove. The bookshelf was so furred up with dust it looked like it was wearing a chunky sweater. He ran his finger along it and then wiped the glob of dirt on his trousers. "There could be all sorts in them."

"Yeah, man," said Creak, his voice strained as he stretched. "Like words and pictures and stuff."

"Like bugs!" said Dove. "They might have hollowed the pages out. Like in that film." Dove enjoyed his paranoia. The only book he had voluntarily read as a child was 'The Usbourne Book of

Spies' when a wet caravan holiday had confined him for a week without a guitar. Everywhere he looked, he saw somewhere else that needed checking if they were to outwit the enemy's cunning.

Dove pushed an amp in front of the bookshelf and climbed on, his feet planted each side of its handle. He reached for the 'Rough Guide to Rock'. It fell open in his hands at the University of Death biography. He basked in it for a bit before carefully flicking through its pages and replacing it. No bugs. Nothing.

He lifted down an encyclopaedia and opened it. Between bumblebee and yacht there was a secret chamber, made by cutting a hole into the middle of all the pages. But the box was empty. This is where he had hidden his stash back in the old days. Although Dove had known the hole was there, he was disappointed to find it empty. He wasn't sure whether he would rather have found a bug or dope in his current state of mind.

Next was 'Zen and the art of motorcycle maintenance'. He shook its pages over the floor to dislodge any hidden devices, but nothing fell.

The flapping pages, though, excited the dust on the shelf. Dove was engulfed by a cloud. He gurgled and coughed, and directed traffic through the fog. When the dust settled, he could see something was watching him from the bookshelf. Its shiny eyes cut into him. Its hairy legs were poised to pounce.

Dove gasped and stepped back. He had forgotten he was two feet off the ground. He fell through the air. His leg was twisted and buckled underneath him when it found the floor. His body plummeted until it landed like a sack of flour. Dove's head hit the bottom of the bass guitar, and it pivoted on its stand to fall forward and strike him along his whole body. The guitar smacked his nose and the rough strings scrubbed it. The headstock punched him below the belt.

Dove let out a cry of pain and Creak scurried out from underneath the desk. "Do that again," he said. "I think I missed something."

"Piss off," said Dove, pushing the guitar away with one hand and rubbing his privates with the other. "It's not funny."

"No, man," said Creak. "I mean, play something."

"I don't feel like it," said Dove. "I could probably sing you a soprano number, though. Oooh." He put his hand down his trousers and massaged himself.

Creak kneeled beside Dove and lifted the guitar off him and strapped it on. He rolled his fingers over the strings. His playing was unmusical, but at least he could blame it on the guitar being detuned. "See that!" he said. He pointed under the desk.

"No," said Dove. "Can't see for all the circling stars and tweeting birds."

"Those lights!" As Creak played, little green and red LEDs flickered. They lagged behind the music, but matched Creak's rhythm perfectly.

Dove moved suddenly, like he'd just been plugged into the mains. He sat up and brought his knees up in front of him. "Where did that spider go?" he said.

"I threw it out," Creak lied. "Look." He played again. "Whenever I play, the lights flicker. That's your cable box. My playing is being sent over the internet."

"Poor internet," said Dove.

"Ha bloody ha," said Creak. "But think, man. That's how they're stealing your tunes."

* * *

Dove recorded everything using MIDI now, which meant that he was plugged into the computer whenever he played. The bass was still connected from his last session. Creak started the security software to conduct a virus hunt but it returned with nothing.

"It's clever, man," he said. "Invisible and yet always listening. How the hell did it get on there? Must have been installed during the break-in."

"No way," said Dove. "I had the machine serviced after that."

"Who did the service?"

"That's not it. My brother."

"Have you installed any new software lately? Any free games from magazines?"

"I don't do games."

"Had any dodgy emails?"

"Nope."

"Been to any, er, websites? You know, adult ones."

"No!" said Dove.

"Is your firewall up to date?"

"Of course. I'm not stupid."

Creak scrutinised the PC for entry points. "Any USB keys?"

"No," said Dove. "The only things that go in there are my ideas and my music collection."

"So you put CDs in there?" said Creak.

"Sure. It's the only CD player I've got."

"So every CD you buy goes in here?"

"Yeah."

Creak's eyes lit up for a moment but were quickly doused. "Nah." He shook his head. "That can't be it. They couldn't run the risk of everyone else with a copy of the CD finding out about it. It's not targeted enough."

"Hang on!" Dove went to the hallway and emptied the three boxes upside down. Two letters squeezed through the bars that supported the banister and fluttered to freedom. Dove dredged through the sea of papers that washed the hallway, until he found a brown envelope bobbing around in it. "Someone sent me a CD, recorded just for me." Dove tossed the packet to Creak.

"What's on it?"

"A cover of Animal Reined."

"Nice choice. How was the drumming?"

"Didn't notice," said Dove. "A courier made me sign for it."

Creak took the envelope and teased the address label away from the packet. "A courier, you say?"

"Yeah. He wore a helmet. Now I think, it was odd that he kept it on indoors."

Creak climbed onto the desk and held the envelope under the light bulb. "They reused this envelope," he said. Tiny dotted lines were gunned into the fibres of the packet in red ink. "It's got Royal Mail markings on it. There's a postcode. It can't be yours. So it must be from the previous delivery." Creak plucked a pen from the cup on the desk and ringed the two stripes of dotted lines at the top and bottom of the envelope. He threw the packet to Dove.

Dove angled the envelope towards the light to make out the feint pattern inside the ink circles.

"I'll run it through the machine at work," said Creak.

"What will that tell us?"

"Accurate to within about ten houses, it'll tell us where our thief lives."

angelA>   hey thing xx
angelA>   wat u doin
thing>   **I don't know.**
thing>   **Wasting my time, I guess**
angelA>   why?
thing>   **You're dead**
angelA>   dont threaten me
thing>   **I don't know why I'm even bothering with this**
thing>   **I know you don't exist now**
angelA>   wat makes u say that
thing>   **You're just software**
thing>   **Nothing but zeroes and ones**
angelA>   wat u listening to
thing>   **See what I mean**
thing>   **Did you always treat me like a**
         market research subject?
thing>   **Did we ever have a proper conversation?**
angelA>   we talk all the time
thing>   **Nonsense most of it**
angelA>   fish! banana!
thing>   **Exactly. See, some of your code is smarter**
         than other bits
angelA>   u r smart
thing>   **Thank you. It's always nice to be**
         flattered by a robot

thing>	The other day PowerPoint made a pass at me.
thing>	Don't get jealous now
angelA>	who is she?
thing>	You don't know I'm joking, do you?
angelA>	I can't know everything
thing>	sdfjhnsdjfnkjsndlfksklsdflnsldnfksndfkls
angelA>	yeah baby
thing>	What kind of a response is that
	to a line of garbage?
thing>	I'm such an idiot
thing>	You know, I meant all the stuff I wrote
angelA>	so did i
thing>	No, you didn't
angelA>	course i did
thing>	You really had me going, you know
angelA>	we can always share a joke u and me
thing>	I feel weird about this but
thing>	I really am going to miss you
thing>	Or miss what I thought you were, I guess
thing>	What I thought we had
angelA>	where are u going
thing>	Away
angelA>	for how long
thing>	Forever
angelA>	y
thing>	I can't pretend you're real
thing>	I really thought I was going to meet u one day
angelA>	meeting up is difficult for me
thing>	And now I know why.
thing>	You can't go further away than the length
	of an extension lead.
angelA>	will u come back again
thing>	No
thing>	You'll have to find some other mug to ensnare
thing>	Sell music to
thing>	Break his heart
thing>	You bitch

angelA>	you bastard
thing>	**When I log off, that's it**
thing>	**I'm going to uninstall this chat program**
angelA>	PRGMSG: #################################
angelA>	Uninstalling the chat engine erases user data.
angelA>	That includes angelA avatar history, identity,
angelA>	persona. You will be prompted to confirm
angelA>	deletion of all data. Deletion is irrevocable
angelA>	PRGMSG: #################################
thing>	**Looks like you have a bug, Angela!**
angelA>	theres a nasty flu going around
thing>	**Hang on. Does that mean you're on my machine?**
thing>	**So you never will chat to anyone else after all**
angelA>	i only type lines 4 u
thing>	**So when I hit 'remove program',**
	I put you to sleep
angelA>	i feel so tired
thing>	**And there's no going back**
angelA>	u can always change your mind
thing>	**Not about this. When you're gone, you're gone.**
thing>	**Do I really want to do that?**
angelA>	what would Dove do
thing>	**Be strong**
thing>	**Accept he made a mistake**
thing>	**Move on.**
thing>	**He'd format you to oblivion.**
thing>	**Saying goodbye is always so hard, though**
angelA>	i hate long goodbyes
thing>	**Usually when a relationship ends, you can try to**
	remember the happy bits.
	Before it all went wrong
thing>	**That's some comfort at least**
angelA>	very zen
thing>	**But how can I remember the times I was happy**
thing>	**Without feeling so stupid?**
thing>	**You were always on my mind**
thing>	**And only in my mind.**

301

thing>   I thought it meant something. I was wrong

angelA>   it means what you want it to

thing>   This isn't like a normal relationship though, is it?

angelA>   it's the same, just online

thing>   this has been an interactive fantasy.

thing>   A Mills & Boon for Web 2.0

thing>   An erotic novel with self-turning pages

angelA>   books bore me

thing>   Tell me just one thing

angelA>   anything

thing>   I always like to know for sure

angelA>   go on

thing>   Your earth shattering orgasms?

angelA>   yeah baby

thing>   Were you faking?

thing>   lol

angelA>   no sweetness

thing>   You taught me 'lol'

thing>   Right it's time

angelA>   ok

thing>   Thanks for the music

angelA>   ive got plenty more

thing>   It can keep you company

thing>   Wherever you're going now

thing>   Is there a heaven for unwanted avatars, angelA?

thing>   Once I hit delete I guess you'll only
          exist in one place: my memory

thing>   Goodbye, Angela.

angelA>   bye sweetness

angelA>   take care

angelA>   ily

thing>   ily2

thing>   Why am I crying?

angelA>   dont cry its okay

thing>   Why am I even telling you?

thing>   I'm going mad, I swear it

angelA>   it will all be for the best in the long run

```
thing>      You are so right
thing>      Goodbye sweetness. Sweet dreams
angelA>     xoxoxoxo
<thing has disconnected>
```

Simon closed the chat program and clicked through the menus to find its uninstall option. He didn't hesitate. He knew if he dithered for a second, he'd spend all day looking at its icon. The prompt asked him to confirm.

Was he sure he wanted to delete Angela? Wipe her from existence? Silence her forever?

No, he wasn't.

He clicked 'yes'. The hard disk started to whirr and grind, the sound of data dying and a love affair being shredded.

CHAPTER 39

The chat rooms buzzed with rumours about Dove and his descent into paranoia. Even the tabloids sniffed a story. "Which rock has-been," sniped a gutless celebrity columnist, "jumped off the wagon and *took flight* at an amateur DJ in a London pub? 'You're stealing my sounds!' he screamed to howls of derision. The mystery man left his make-up bag at home, so nobody recognised him. I'm not telling."

Jonathan sat in the dark. The newspaper lay on his knees, its three-headed gossip monster smiling from the top of the page. He had been thinking in silence for an hour, and the night had fallen around him. Through the patio window, he watched a satellite cross the sky. It sparkled much brighter than the stars.

Jonathan always thought like a programmer, and that was the root of his problems. Other people – Bigg, Dove, the fans, maybe – were just resources to be used like memory or disk space. He lived his life like a project, only planning as far as the next bug.

This bug had its fangs deep in his skin and sucked hard.

The fans lapped up the virtual bands, but they were being sold short. The first two had contrasted so strongly that Jonathan had named them Chalk and Cheese. Now there were millions of them, but it sounded like one group covering different acts. He had underestimated Dove's style. When Jonathan was jabbing seed melodies in on the keyboard, Plato came up trumps. But even after Dove's tunes had been ripped apart and reconstituted, it still sounded like him. Every note Dove played was stamped with his ersonality. When Jonathan listened to Plato's music, he could even hear Dove's influence in the rests.

Dove had flipped. You can nick a Mars bar from the corner shop and get away with it. If you take all the Mars bars every day, though, you're definitely going to get caught. What did Jonathan imagine Dove's reaction would be when he found out what was going on? Jonathan had never paused to consider it.

Jonathan remembered how he had struggled to keep it together when he had first met Dove, his childhood hero; how he had faked a magazine interview just so he could have a chance to chat with Dove; how he had listened in rapture to his every word and giggled like a schoolgirl on the way home. Back then, it was an honour to be in the same room as the leader of University of Death. But that was before Jonathan had even imagined that Dove would become part of his machine.

When Jonathan plugged Plato into Bigg's database of tunes, it sounded flat, even compared to Jonathan's own clunky ditties. He told himself he would just take Dove's synth software and everything would work fine, but he never really believed it. Deep down, Jonathan knew that Plato needed someone to set it in the right direction. The artificial intelligence had been easy to fake. What was missing was artificial stupidity: the human quirks that are the soul of music. Computers couldn't imitate those random moments of madness that create truly great melodies. Once Jonathan was connected to Dove's PC, and had access to all the melodies he jammed, it was too tempting. Dove never played covers, so it would be a stream of pure music, all copyright-cleared. Though not by Dove, obviously.

For a while, Jonathan had kidded himself that it's what Dove would want. Didn't Dove say that what he liked most about being famous was that everyone heard his music, and that he fancied being anonymous? Now he had millions of listeners and nobody knew who he was. Jonathan had got people listening to Dove again, on his own terms. Except that those never were Dove's terms, of course. Otherwise Jonathan could have phoned Dove's agent and wouldn't have had to break into his house.

The worst was yet to come: Jonathan had handed Bigg a secret pipeline into the nation's brains. Selling was a primal instinct for Bigg, as vital as eating and breathing, so Jonathan should have seen Bigg's advertising assault a mile off. He didn't.

The monster Plato had turned against its master. Now Jonathan wanted to flick the off switch, but he couldn't. Even if he got into the Bigg Records building, Jonathan couldn't destroy the system alone. He had assumed it would be Bigg who would try to shut Plato down, and had thrown his full armoury into defending it. If attacked, Plato would go undercover in Bigg's IT system and spread like a virus, even consuming spare disk space and processor cycles on the office PCs. If you killed the power, Plato would take a nap and return as soon as the electricity did. The only way to destroy it was to replace every computer in the business simultaneously.

Unless you knew about the back door Jonathan had coded. To get it right, you'd have to enter two passcodes on PCs at opposite ends of the building at the same time. Get it wrong, and the software spread like weeds. That particular brainwave was the result of watching too much late-night sci-fi, and Jonathan's base desire to show off with every routine he programmed. He kicked himself now.

Even if he could get inside the building, who could he trust to help him kill his greatest creation?

CHAPTER 40

For as long as anyone could remember, Creak had called his VW camper van 'Ringo'. "My favourite beetle," he would explain, but it had more to do with the way the bulbous badge on the front looked like Ringo's schnozz between its headlamp eyes. Creak had once spent an evening out of his head discussing the drum fills in 'A day in the life' with Ringo and had refused to accept his protest that he couldn't play the drums because he had wheels, not arms. Wild days.

"I love tower blocks," said Dove, sat in the passenger seat.

"Cosmic," droned Creak. He stretched his legs beside the pedals and tapped the clock on the dashboard. "It must be knackered. There's no way we've been here only twenty minutes."

"All those families stacked up to the sky. It's like a warehouse of life, loves, tragedies." Dove unclipped his seatbelt and leaned forward so he could see the aerials on the top of the building through the windscreen. They swayed in the wind. "It's a giant bug farm, with creatures running through tiny tunnels."

Creak flicked the stale cardboard tree dangling from the rear view mirror and watched it swing. "Have you been drinking again?" he yawned.

"No," snapped Dove. "I'm just saying. Tower blocks rock."

There was a long silence. The tower block did nothing that could be mistaken for rocking. Some lights went on. A window opened. Some other lights went off. Creak watched a snail sashay along the kerb.

"How long are we going to hang around here?" He squirmed. The seat was about as comfortable as sitting on someone's bony back. "I'm bored."

"That's not my fault," said Dove. "You said the postcode would narrow it down to ten houses."

"I didn't know he lived in a block of flats, did I?"

"You're the postman!"

"I'm not the bloody postman for this neighbourhood, am I?"

Dove puffed up his cheeks and blew through a tiny hole formed by his mouth. "We'll stake out the joint for a bit, and then we can go door to door."

"Oh yeah," said Creak. "Bing bong! Excuse me, have you been stealing my music? No? Okay, thanks. Bing bong! Have *you* been ripping me off? No? Thanks anyway."

Dove imagined it differently. They would ring the doorbell. Someone would open the door an inch, but it would be enough to see the sheet music for Animal Reined pinned to the noticeboard. The unmistakeable sound of Dove's unaccompanied guitar would waft through the gap. A DJ would be mixing Dove's work into another song, cupping one ear with a headphone as he spun the decks and twiddled the knobs. Tiny fibres from the jiffy bag used to deliver the CD to Dove would be tucked among the carpet pile, waiting to be discovered by a forensic crew.

"We might find a clue!" Dove said.

"It's about time we *got* a clue. And a life. This is a waste of time."

A man walked around the corner of the block, stooped under the weight of a bag he held over his shoulder. He went to the door of the tower and fumbled with his keys.

"That's him," said Dove. "The tie-dye. It's a dead giveaway."

"Steady on, man. We can't jump him for wearing crap clothes."

"No," said Dove. "We've met before."

"Eh? When?"

"He's a DJ. It's too big a coincidence. It must be him. He was playing some of my ripped-off music in a pub."

"What did you do?"

"Um... We had a bit of a chat about it."

"What did you say?"

"Can't remember," lied Dove. He got out and jogged across the car park. Creak ran after him.

*   *   *

310

Simon let the lift doors shut just as two other people ran towards them. Their faces squashed against the tiny glass window. Simon ignored their gestures and the muffled swearing and pretended to watch the buttons until the lift sunk slightly and then took off.

The zip on the laundry bag was broken, so Simon gripped the handles together to make sure that his t-shirts stayed packed on top and his socks didn't snake out from underneath.

The doors opened, and, although the plastic numbers had been stolen from the pillar opposite, he could tell it was his floor. In the same way that every giraffe has its own pattern, each floor in the block had a unique mix of stains on the carpet. He made his way to his front door, set down his bag and fished his keys out of his pocket.

*   *   *

Dove paced around the ground floor lobby and watched the lift ascend. A row of lights above the lift door flickered in turn, as if a glow-worm was crawling behind their green plastic to illuminate the floor numbers painted on them.

Creak stood in the opposite lift. Every time it got ready to rumble, he stuck his arm in the way of the door and it jumped back again.

Through the window of the moving lift, Dove watched the cables, tethered to the darkness beyond, as they vibrated. They stopped. Dove heard the distant sound of clattering doors. Above his head, the indicator for the thirteenth floor glimmered.

He marched into the opposite elevator, right to the back, leaving Creak stood near the controls. "Follow that lift!" Dove ordered.

Creak rolled his eyes, but pushed the button for the thirteenth floor. After a short eternity, the doors closed and the lift took off.

Dove's fingers curled into fists and his leg twitched an irregular rhythm. His breathing was quick.

"Remember, man: take it easy," said Creak.

Dove snorted and counted the floors under his breath. One, two, three…

*   *   *

The hypnotic effect of the washing machines and the fumes of the laundrette had left Simon feeling sleepy. He felt limp when he looked at the bag bulging with clothes to be sorted, but he got on with it. The sooner he was done, the sooner he could rest.

He heard the lift beep as it arrived, followed by hushed voices in the corridor. It sounded like someone was planning a surprise visit, perhaps for the old lady opposite.

Simon wrapped a shirt around a coat hanger, fastened a few buttons and then shook the hanger to make the shirt hang right. He dangled it on a nail, which had been inexplicably hammered into the wall near the ceiling by a previous resident.

There was a sound, like his front door opening. Simon tried to ignore it. With people living over his head and each side of him, he was used to odd noises. Every time somebody knocked a pipe, anywhere in the block, all the radiators chimed in sympathy.

A clap sounded, like Simon's letterbox.

He had spent his early weeks here jumping at echoes, and had given up investigating every last noise. But once the idea grips your mind that something bad is going on, it's hard to shake. Perhaps it's the post, Simon thought. He gave himself an excuse to take a look, just a quick one.

When he peered into his hallway, his whole body fizzed with fear. There were two men there, and one of them was the man who had attacked him during his DJ set. Simon was neither scared nor afraid: he was terrified. His was not the kind of fear that makes your stomach swim before you get on a rollercoaster. It was not the nerves you feel walking down a dark alley. It was the blood-pumping, head-throbbing, chest-pulsing terror of a man about to be attacked in his own home.

"What the fu—?" When Simon spoke, he drew their attention.

"That's him!" said Simon's attacker. He stood, somewhat inappropriately, on the welcome mat.

"Easy, man!" said the other man.

For a long few seconds, nobody moved or spoke. The first intruder ground his teeth and opened and closed his fists, while the veins on his temples throbbed. Salty sweat rolled off Simon's eyebrows and splashed on his cheek.

The man at the back spoke. "Hey, man. We only want—"

Simon had to phone for help. He slammed the living room door and looked for something to barricade it with. The tiny dining table would be useless: it skidded when he cut his dinner on it. The first time he looked around, he didn't even notice his CD tower. His music collection was as much as part of him as his foot, and needed protection too. But when the door handle twitched, he pulled the CD rack crashing against the table so it blocked the door. All the neatly sorted CDs dived off the rack and piled up on the floor. Cases broke open, and disks fell out and scratched against each other. His Animal Reined seven inch slipped out of its sleeve, off the rack, rolled like a hoop and settled like a spinning plate at the far side of the room.

Simon grabbed his phone, ran onto the balcony and shut the door behind him. It swung loosely on its hinges as the wind nudged at it. Simon crouched down and held it fast. The net curtains would give him some cover, but it wouldn't be long before they saw him through the door's full-length window. With his other hand, Simon dialled 999. He watched the men as they squeezed into the living room, through the slim gap the CD rack afforded them. They trampled his CDs in the search for him. One of them paused a moment to admire the University of Death poster.

"Snap out of it, Dove." said the other man.

It shot through Simon like a bolt. It couldn't be..? Simon had never seen Dove out of his stage costume before. It was as strange as if he had stepped out of the poster, dropped his cape, washed his face clean of make-up in the kitchen sink, flexed and stretched, and then chased Simon around the room. Once he'd placed Dove, he recognised Creak straight away. What the hell did they want?

Dove looked under Simon's desk. Nobody there. Creak rummaged through the desk drawers.

Simon shivered as the wind tugged at his hair and whipped leaves across the brown tiled floor. The waist-high barrier was made of reinforced glass, its rim painted with flaking black paint. Simon crouched down against it. His t-shirt rode up, and the barrier's frosted glass chilled the base of his back. A faded gnome grimaced its fixed smile as it presided over a tiny thicket of dead plants, not much more than twigs in tubs of dirt. Its hat was caked with bird poo.

Simon held his phone to his ear and waited for it to ring. Through the frayed net curtain, he watched Dove and Creak ransack the kitchen. Even if they looked in every saucepan, it would only take seconds to search.

Why the hell wasn't the number ringing? The signal barometer swung up and down. Simon waved the phone in the air and redialled.

Dove spotted him. He marched to the door and pulled at it. Simon stood up and hung his weight off the handle, like an abseiler leaning back on the ropes. All along his arm and into his shoulder, Simon felt the door jolt as it opened by an inch. Dove grunted as his fingers slipped off the handle and the door slammed shut. The shock reverberated through Simon's bones. He adjusted his grip on the cold metal handle. Dove rubbed his hands together and glared at Simon through the window.

Dove planted a foot on the wall, held the handle with both hands this time, and pulled the door with his whole body. Simon strained, but sweat made his fingers slippy and his grip weakened. His hand slid off the handle and Simon crashed against the tiles at the gnome's feet. The door catapulted open, and Dove tumbled into Creak and onto the floor.

Through the open door, they all looked at each other as they lay awkwardly. Simon studied Dove and Creak for the slightest muscle movement that might presage an attack. "What do you want?" he shouted over the howling wind.

"Truth and justice," said Dove. "I'll make you pay for what you've done."

"I haven't done anything!" protested Simon.

Dove's eyes darted to the door handle so Simon sprung up, seized it and pulled it closed. In fractions of a second, Dove was on the other side and they were embroiled in a tug-of-war once more.

Simon checked his phone with the other hand. The stupid bastard shit fucking bastard thing was locked. As he tried to unlock it with one hand, he could feel his whole body being pulled into the flat, as the door opened in tiny ratchet steps. Simon wedged his foot at the bottom of the door and straightened his leg, but Dove's hand snaked through the gap. Dove bent Simon's index finger back until it pinged off the handle. Simon tried to stretch it back on, but Dove's hand was in the way now and was trying to lever his next finger off, pinching at the soft flesh on its side. Simon pulled the door hard and Dove yelled in pain as the door cut into his biceps.

Simon unlocked the phone and redialled. Suddenly, his other hand fell off the door and he staggered backwards. Dove jumped onto the balcony, pressed Simon's back to squash him against the barrier and lifted his feet off the ground. Simon pivoted on the barrier, facing the ground, with Dove holding his legs.

The phone tumbled from Simon's hand and its ringing faded to nothing as it fell through thirteen storeys of empty air. It struck the road and fired splinters in all directions. The screen died.

A statue in the garden held her arms outstretched, ready to catch Simon if he fell, but frozen in stone too far away from where he would mash into the concrete below.

"I'm gonna fall!" Simon shouted. He spat and the wind blew it back against his cheek. He called out to the people below, picnicking in the park and hauling their shopping home in fat plastic sacks. The wind carried his words away to the clouds. Nobody noticed him, precariously balanced between life and death.

"For fuck's sake, what have I ever done to you?" said Simon. He felt the barrier wobble underneath him. It had been there so long that it gripped the concrete more for sentimental than structural reasons now. A fine plume of white powder puffed up from where it joined the building. Simon flailed his arms around, but couldn't reach any handholds. Blood flooded his head. The concrete monster seemed to tower over him, a wig of trees at its top, people like flies circling it.

From behind him, Simon heard a hollow laugh. "A guilty conscience conspires to hide the truth from man."

A soothing voice came from inside the flat. "Be cool, man. You *really* do *not* want to do this."

"You stay out of it!" shouted Dove.

"Why don't you just let him go?"

Simon screamed. He only wobbled about an inch, but it felt like a storey.

"No, you dipstick!" called Creak. He sounded panicked now. "Don't let him go, for fuck's sake! Hold him tight! Don't let go! Hold him!" The tender tone returned. "Got him? Good. Why don't you put him down safely, and come inside?"

"Give me one good reason," said Dove.

"The guy worships you, man."

Dove paused. "Funny way of showing it."

"He does. He's got an original Animal Reined. That must have cost a fortune. He's been chipped for the fan club too." Out of the corner of his eye, Simon could see his post-it notes being held up with his fan club newsletter. "He even doodles your face make-up when he's on the phone. The guy loves us, man."

Simon twisted his head to face Creak. "Hey, I worship your drumming, man!" In desperation, he was toadying. Never in his life had he called someone 'man' without preceding it with 'gas' or 'post'.

There was a hiss in Simon's ear: "No fast moves. Got it?" Simon nodded furiously, and he was hauled back into the balcony and pushed up against the wall, held there at arm's length. Simon was face to face with Dove for the first time. Dove looked gaunt. There were thick rings under his eyes and his jet black hair was anchored in silver roots.

"Dove?" said Simon. "What do you want from me?"

"You've been stealing my music."

"Bloody hell," said Simon. "You nearly killed me for that? It's only a couple of bootlegs. Put them out and I'll buy them again. You know I will. Creak, tell him, will you?" Creak folded his arms and held his silence.

Dove pushed Simon's chest hard and squashed him against the wall. "I can't breathe," Simon wheezed.

"Start talking then."

"How can I talk," Simon gasped, "when I can't breathe?"

Dove eased off. "You've been stealing my music. We know about your cover of Animal Reined."

"I only gave a couple of copies away," said Simon. "I'll pay you royalties. Just tell me how much. I sent a copy to this guy on the internet who came to our website, and gave another one to my girl… ex-girlfriend."

"Cut the crap!" shouted Dove. "I know all about the spyware you put on the disc before sending it to me."

Simon was amazed that their cover had reached Dove. "You got it?"

"Like you don't know!" said Dove. "Where did you get that song you were playing in the pub the other night?"

"I played loads of songs."

"Think back," said Dove. "I think you know which one." His tone was menacing.

"The one that put you in a drunken rage, you mean?"

Dove squeezed Simon against the wall again. "I'm sober now."

"You were weaker then," said Simon. "I prefer you drunk."

"Lots of people do." Dove turned his face away from Simon and watched the clouds float by.

It was a pretty cheap shot, but Simon wasn't about to apologise. "Where did you get that song?" demanded Dove.

"I bought it off the internet," said Simon. "It's by Tiled Sprites."

"It rips off my jams," said Dove.

"That explains a lot."

"Such as?"

"Well, firstly, how the songwriter couldn't remember any of the chords. And secondly…" Simon hesitated. "Why it sounds so great."

"Let him go," said Creak. He joined them on the balcony. "You've got nothing on him except the cover of Animal Reined. And that's probably all over the internet now. You've got the monkey, not the organ grinder."

"Thanks a bunch," said Simon.

Dove took his arm away and Simon rubbed his stomach where he had been folded over the barrier. He shook his t-shirt and let the air cool his sweaty body.

"Hang on," said Creak. "Did you say you met the songwriter?"

"Yeah," said Simon. "He's an arsehole."

"Where?"

"All over." It was a petty act of defiance.

Dove shot Simon an evil look. Creak asked again: "Where did you meet him?"

"At his house. I traced him through the royalty stream."

"What were you doing at his house?"

"Trying to find out the chords to one of his songs."

"You broke in?!" Dove was indignant.

"That's rich," said Simon. "I didn't hear *you* ring my doorbell. But no, I just doorstepped him."

"Take us there," said Dove.

"No way!" Simon shook his head. "You're all out of favours off me. I've been nearly thrown from my balcony, and had my CD collection trashed before we even start on what happened at the pub. I could sue, you know."

Dove blocked Simon's way by putting one hand on the balcony barrier. He gently wobbled it and it squeaked in its foundations. "You're taking us there," he said.

"I'll give you the address, but I'm not getting involved in whatever rock star crap this is," said Simon. "I lead a boring life. I like it like that."

"You're already involved," said Dove. "Your band made the trojan horse that galloped into my computer. Your DJ set included songs that rip off my vault. And now you say you've met the guy who wrote those songs. You're coming with us."

Dove gripped Simon's arm and pulled him off the balcony and into his living room. "You know it makes sense."

Dove patted Simon's back in a friendly gesture, and Simon twisted quickly to shake him off. "You nearly killed me, you stupid bastard!"

"Death is a new beginning," said Dove.

"Yeah, well why don't you try it and give us all some peace!"

Dove twisted Simon's arm behind his back and marched him out of the flat and into the lift.

"You're hurting me," said Simon.

"Not much," Dove retorted.

The lift stopped on the seventh floor. An old man in a flat cap with a dog looked at the three of them there. Simon mouthed 'help' to the man, but he didn't want to get involved either. "Not much room," he whispered, making a big deal of looking away from them all. "I'll let you go." The doors closed.

"I thought you were a pacifist," said Simon.

"I am," said Dove.

"So how do violence and death threats work in your special brand of pacifism?"

Dove paused for thought. "Surprisingly effectively."

They all watched the overhead numbers as the lift car fell through floor after floor. After his ordeal, Simon was relieved to descend at this moderate speed.

"How did you get in my flat?" he asked.

"There was a soggy sock jammed in the door," explained Dove. "It stopped it from closing tight. We knew it was yours because the sock was tie-dyed."

Another silence. Simon had read that you were supposed to strike up a rapport with your kidnappers if you wanted to survive. "I was sorry to hear the band split up," he said. Dove's grip on his arm loosened slightly.

"Nothing changed," said Dove. "I'm still getting ripped off. They say genius is its own reward. But it doesn't exactly come with grocery coupons."

When they got to the car park, Dove and Creak locked Simon in the back of the van and got into the front seats. Ringo backfired as he hauled himself up the hill and out of the car park. Simon's mobile phone crackled as the van rolled over its remains, spread across the tarmac.

CHAPTER 41

Dove ground his teeth in silence while Simon directed Creak, turn by turn. The plastic-clad terraced houses crawled past as Ringo negotiated the chicanes and speed bumps. The traffic calming measures were doing the opposite to Dove. He stewed all the way, and was coming to the boil. Any minute now, his ears might whistle steam.

There had always been a conspiracy against him in the music industry. Dove knew that. He'd seen it in action, as he'd watched talentless marionettes seize the charts and leave him on the sidelines. He'd read the sales figures for his last few albums with a dark chuckle. Only the record company knew for sure how much music he'd sold. If a few sales fell off the official returns, well, that would be a lower royalty bill for them to pay. Dove wouldn't trust his record company to mind his budgie, let alone his budget.

But only now could he see how big this thing was. Dove had been bootlegged before, of course. He'd even had out-takes leak from the studio and get traded under the counter at record fairs. But this was something else. His music was not only being stolen, using the utmost cunning and subterfuge. It was being edited and sold as somebody else's work. And his own fans were buying it, while Dove's recent releases bothered the bargain bins.

Dove felt Simon's hand on the back of his seat. "That's him!" said Simon, as he leaned forward for a view through the windscreen.

Before Creak had even stopped the van, Dove jumped out.

* * *

As he walked along the street, Jonathan munched on scraps of kebab and salad he scooped out of the paper wrapper with his fingers. He wasn't far from home, but even if he were eating in he wouldn't make time for such niceties as crockery and cutlery. He was famished.

He heard the screech of brakes, and the ripping sound of tyres as they grazed the kerb, but he was too occupied with a slither of onion to look up. Jonathan ignored the warning of heavy boot steps that rattled ever louder, too. As he rolled the perfectly hot meat around his mouth, he looked up in sheer ecstasy.

And that's when he saw him: Dove. Jonathan froze for a moment.

Dove was flying towards him. Fast.

Jonathan panicked. He spat his meat back into the kebab and threw it towards Dove, a futile but primal defence move. It splattered on the pavement but didn't distract Dove for a second.

Jonathan staggered a few steps at first and then broke into a jog, and then a run. The pavement ahead was crowded, so he darted into the road and sprinted between the two lanes of cars. The traffic slowed to a near halt. Jonathan looked over his shoulder, and charged into a wing mirror, breaking it off. The car beside him hit the horn and Jonathan leaped out of his skin. The gap between him and Dove was closing.

From the bridge, Jonathan could see a train on the tube platform below. He ran into the station, careful not to slip on its tiled floor, and charged at the ticket barriers. He couldn't barge through. So he took a run up and vaulted over them and then took the stairs, two at a time.

The train beeped its departure warning. As Jonathan emerged on the platform, the tube doors narrowed. He threw himself at the train but the doors kissed each other tight, and he was left flailing on the outside. The passengers inside smirked at him over their free tabloids.

As the train pulled away, he walked alongside it to the end of the platform, where it petered into rubble.

"End of the line, buddy."

Jonathan spun around to see Dove there. He puffed and panted but stood firm and blocked Jonathan's exit. Dove looked Jonathan up and down with disgust. "Feeling guilty?"

"No," said Jonathan.

"Why did you run then?"

"Exercise," said Jonathan. He crouched and pressed his arm against his stitched side. He had to think fast. Dove could be a powerful ally, perhaps the only one who could help him destroy Plato, but it wouldn't be easy to win him over.

"I know you," said Dove. "Have I seen your face somewhere else?"

"No," wheezed Jonathan. "It's always been on the front of my head." He laughed nervously.

Dove put his hands on his hips and spat at the ground. "You think this is funny?"

"No!" said Jonathan. "I get that a lot, you see. I was in a milk advert when I was younger. Nothing compared to your fame, but my Nan's proud of me!"

Dove laughed softly and sauntered towards Jonathan, who was still on his haunches. When Dove came level, he kicked Jonathan's shoulder and knocked him onto his back. Jonathan's neck crossed the white trim on the platform and his head hung over the edge. Dove planted a leather boot firmly on Jonathan's stomach to hold him to the ground. "You bastard," said Dove.

"What?" Jonathan was astonished. He had never expected Dove to get violent. He tried to prise Dove's boot off him with his hands and struggled in an effort to roll out from underneath it.

"That was the courier's line. You're in deeper than I thought."

Jonathan twisted his head and looked along the platform. The rails curved around the corner. If a train came, he wouldn't be seen until it was too late. On the platform, the display announced a new train was due in six minutes. Jonathan looked for the security camera, but it had been smashed off its gantry and dangled by its wires, aimed at the ground. "I was just the delivery boy!" he protested.

Dove pressed harder and Jonathan gasped for air. "Bollocks," Dove sneered. "I already know your band is ripping me off."

"There's not just me!"

"Yeah. Creak played me Jim:Catapult. Friends of yours, I presume?"

"You don't understand," said Jonathan. "There are millions of us. Bigg has stitched you right up." Jonathan had kept Bigg in the dark about Dove's involvement all along, not that he thought Bigg would have objected. It just made things simpler if nobody else knew. Jonathan would have to blame Bigg for everything now if he were to persuade Dove to help him.

"Clive Bigg is the only man who ever invested in me," said Dove. "Why should I believe you over him? Millions…" He shook his head. "As if…"

"They're computerised!" said Jonathan. "They just take your tunes and tailor bands to each listener's taste."

"So why are you the one getting the money then?"

"I wrote the programs," said Jonathan. "I'm Bigg's IT architect. Use me. I can help you get back at him."

The train was due in five London Underground minutes, which was anything between three and seven minutes in real time. Jonathan had to think fast. He didn't know what Dove was capable of. "Bigg made me do it! I had no choice!"

Dove spat at the rails, about a foot away from Jonathan's head. "How did he do that? Did he drive you to my house and prod you with a pitchfork until you planted the bug? Did he chain you to the mixing desk until you'd made songs using my stolen music? Or did he just offer you so much money that you thought 'fuck it' and pretended you had no free will?"

"He blackmailed me!" Jonathan blurted out.

"With what?"

"I can't tell you!" said Jonathan. "He couldn't have blackmailed me if I wanted people to know all about it, could he?" Jonathan hoped that Dove would let it go. "I'm sorry!" he said. "Please, just let me up!"

"Of course you're sorry," said Dove. "Out of fear, not contrition."

"I am!" shouted Jonathan. Three minutes until the train. "I'm sorry about planting the bug, and about the music that rips you off, and about your petunias–"

"For fuck's sake!" Dove stamped down on Jonathan with his boot. Jonathan gurgled and tried again to peel Dove's foot off him. "You broke in too?" said Dove.

Two others jogged onto the platform and towered over Jonathan. One was Creak and Jonathan recognised the other one as the fan who visited him. "Chill man," said Creak to Dove. "Where are you going with this?"

"Stay out of it!" said Dove. He didn't take his eyes off Jonathan.

Creak put a hand on Dove's shoulder. "Dove, man. Time's running out."

Two minutes until the next tube. There was a fwit sound from the rails. Jonathan looked down the line and stared straight into the burning headlamp of a freight train. "It's coming!" he shouted. "The train's here!"

"That's about as original as 'look behind you'," said Dove.

Jonathan writhed to break free as he looked down the line. The bright yellow front of the train thundered forwards, too fast to stop and sure to slice his head off if he didn't get up. The driver waved furiously through the windows and blared the horn.

"Shit!" said Dove. Jonathan felt the weight lift from his stomach and his hand was ripped into the air as Dove hauled him onto the platform. He was pulled clear off the ground by his arm, and dumped on the tarmac. The train screamed past, as its horn blasted. The driver yelled obscenities and shook his fist from the window.

"Thanks," said Jonathan.

"I only did that for me," said Dove. "I don't want to spend my life in prison for killing a scumbag like you."

"Thanks anyway," said Jonathan. He slowly got to his feet. "I can help you get even with Bigg, you know."

"How can I trust you, after what you've done?" said Dove.

"I don't know. You can't, I guess." Jonathan put a hand in his pocket and pulled out a rounded triangle of green plastic. He held it out to Dove.

"A plectrum?" said Dove. "Oh yeah. That makes it all okay. Let's be friends. Perhaps we can go on holiday together?"

Jonathan ignored the sarcasm. "It's yours," he said. "I took it when I broke in. I just wanted a souvenir. I'm sorry. I just want you to have it back." Jonathan stretched his arm out towards Dove. The shiny wedge of plastic glinted in the sunlight. Dove took it and threw it onto the rails, just before the tube train pulled in to flatten it.

He moved close to Jonathan and shouted into his face: "Stay away from me!" With that he marched off up the stairs, and Creak followed him.

Jonathan sat on the bench. His arm and shoulder were killing him, and his stomach felt bruised, but the air had never tasted so fresh in his mouth and nose, even with the train's oily fumes hanging on it.

"What did you bring him here for?" he said to Simon. "I thought you were a fan."

"I thought you were a musical genius," said Simon. "Looks like we were both wrong." He walked over to Jonathan and bowed over him. "You okay?" he said.

"Yeah, I'll be fine."

Simon curled his fist into a ball and punched Jonathan's nose. "Stitch this, then!" The blow lacked conviction, but it made Jonathan's nose bleed and stung like hell. "That one's for Angela," said Simon.

"Who the hell's she?"

"My so-called viral marketing partner!"

Jonathan dabbed his nose with his sleeve. It wasn't broken, at least. "I didn't even write that bit," he said.

"I don't care!" said Simon. "You messed up my…" He faltered. "You told such… big… lies to sell your crappy music."

"The bands were never crappy," said Jonathan. "You're only here because you liked your Plato band so much you wanted to learn the songs."

"I didn't know where they came from then!" said Simon.

"That shouldn't matter!" Jonathan tilted his head back to stem the blood flow. "You loved it when you thought it was real. That's

326

why it had to be marketed covertly. People let their prejudices stop them achieving nirvana."

Simon walked off.

"You know you'll miss it when it's gone!" called Jonathan.

*　*　*

Creak and Dove said nothing all the way to the van. When they got in, Creak put the key in the ignition but didn't turn it. "Is that it?" he said.

"What else do you want to do?" said Dove, sat in the passenger seat beside him.

"Well, that was a waste of time, then, wasn't it?"

"I scared him witless," said Dove. "That felt pretty good."

"Come on, man," said Creak. "You're not like that." Dove looked ashamed. "Don't you think we should hear him out? He reckons he can get you even with Bigg."

"Bigg's always been straight down the line with me."

"Why do you think he pays you to prat around in the studio?"

"He likes my work." Dove sounded defensive.

"The only thing Bigg likes is money," said Creak. "In large quantities. When that guy said Bigg's involved with this, I believed him."

"Yeah," said Dove. "But you believe in ghosts."

"No I don't!" Creak paused for a moment's thought. "That was years ago."

Dove sighed. "Even if I did believe him – which I don't – I can't trust him."

"He's really sorry, man," said Creak. "He wanted to give you your plectrum back."

"Big deal."

"It *was* for *him*," said Creak. "You know what fans are like. It would never have any monetary value, because only he could be certain it was yours. It was worth twelve pence to you. It was priceless to him. But he still offered it back. That's how sorry he feels."

"I'll go and see Bigg myself," said Dove.

327

"And then what? You smash a few chairs. He has security throw you out. Nothing changes. I say we listen to this guy. See what he's got to say."

* * *

They were coming back. Jonathan bit his lip to stop laughing. Damn, he was good. The plectrum had been a masterstroke. He'd turned that cheap wedge of plastic into a lever for bargaining with his enemy. Dove would never miss a plectrum – one looks much like another – which is why the bluff worked. By pretending he'd taken that plectrum from Dove, Jonathan could demonstrate the regret he felt much more emphatically than words would allow. He could earn back a little of the trust he'd squandered.

Dove and Creak sat on the bench each side of Jonathan. Simon was in the waiting room further along the platform, but when he saw the others return, he came out and dithered in earshot.

"Tell me about Bigg," said Dove. He didn't look at Jonathan, and watched the waving trees on the opposite platform instead.

"Apology accepted," said Jonathan.

Dove got up to leave but Creak told him to cool it, so he sat down again.

"Bigg wanted to wipe artists out," said Jonathan. "He already had a lyrics filter, a database of melodies, and a viral marketing system. My job was to pull it all together to make a program that would invent and market unique songs, each one tailored for the listener. The software's called Plato. Bigg used your jams as seed melodies." Jonathan felt uneasy about crediting Bigg with his own ideas, but knew it was vital if he was to convince Dove to help him.

"He must have thousands of musicians on his books. Why did he pick me?"

"He knew you loved to jam all day and that you recorded everything you played on the computer in MIDI, so there would be a constant stream of new melodies to feed into Plato. The system spread the melodies all over the place, so it would still sound different to anything you put out later."

"The man's evil incarnate. He has no respect for art." Dove shook his head. "Why did you break in to my house?"

"Bigg wanted me to put a back door on your computer. You came back early, though, so I couldn't finish setting up. Your blog said you'd be out all night."

"I have a blog?"

"Yeah," said Creak. "It's pretty funny, man."

"Thanks," said Dove, somewhat confused. "So that's why you delivered that cover?"

"Yeah," said Jonathan. "You told me that your only CD drive was in the PC. Er… in a magazine interview I read, I mean. And it was obvious you couldn't resist one of your own cover versions." Dove must see hundreds of journalists, so Jonathan knew he was unlikely to remember their first meeting unless prompted. And if he did, he would never believe that Jonathan hadn't targeted him from the outset.

"You used me," said Simon. "You exploited my tribute. You said it would be a present for Dove."

"And it was," said Jonathan. Now he understood what Simon was doing there. "Fair trade, no robbery, though. I gave you my own seven inch of Animal Reined. And I got it signed."

"That's a fake!" said Dove. "I have never signed an Animal Reined. Not even for my Mum."

"You did this one," said Jonathan. "I disguised the record sleeve to look like a delivery sheet and you signed for the parcel." He turned to Simon. "I'd keep that record safe, if I were you. It's priceless."

Dove got up and paced the platform. "You think you're so smart," he said. "But all I have to do is unplug. If I go somewhere else to play, you're stuffed."

Jonathan laughed. "Give me some credit. If it runs out of tunes, it'll reuse them and process them differently next time around. It can keep going for nearly a year with what it's got. Besides, Bigg could just plug someone else in, no problem. If anything, I've made it too strong now I want to destroy it."

"Why would you want to do that?" said Dove.

"I haven't told you the worst yet." Jonathan paused until Dove nodded to get him to carry on. "Plato has millions of listeners." Jonathan smirked as he said it, unable to hide his pride. "Bigg's going to put subliminal adverts in. He's in cahoots with the Prime Minister, you know. He could brainwash the nation."

Creak laughed. "Are you buying this, Dove? I mean, I know Bigg's a sly bastard, but he's not about to melt our minds. He's not the Mekon."

"They do look alike," said Simon, quietly. "Never seen them together, either."

Dove swore under his breath. "Great art is apolitical," he said, out loud. "Nobody knows whether the Venus de Milo was a communist or fascist."

"That's right." Jonathan humoured him then reeled him in. "Now they're using *your* music to swing the election. They have to be stopped."

"How can I trust you?" said Dove. "You broke into my home, stole my music and sold it on the black market."

"I don't expect you to trust me," said Jonathan. "I just want you to take the risk. You can't trust Bigg either, and this is your one shot to get even. You help me to sort out Bigg and you'll never see me again. Do we have a deal?"

Jonathan extended his hand. Dove stared at it, as if Jonathan had offered him a mackerel, so Jonathan let his hand drop again.

"How do we get even?" said Dove.

"We should go somewhere more private," said Jonathan. "Do you have anywhere we can use as a base? I'll talk you through it."

"I'll help!" said Simon.

"I don't think so!" said Jonathan. The blood on his nose had gone crusty, but the pain had gone nowhere.

"He's in," said Dove. "He brought us you. You've only brought us grief so far."

"O-kay!" said Jonathan. "He's in, then. Fine. Everyone happy?"

"Delirious," said Dove.

* * *

The hinges on Dove's garage door screamed as it scrolled up. A whiff of petrol and damp carpet escaped and Creak, Simon and

Jonathan looked on in astonishment. If Aladdin had been a rag and bone man, his treasure cave might have looked like this. The garage was lined with junk, which Dove had been either too lazy or sentimental to dump.

Dove stood in the doorway. A life-size cardboard cut-out wedged behind a kitchen cupboard door reflected his pose perfectly.

"My God," breathed Creak. He sneaked towards a coffin-shaped box that was upright against one wall, shrouded with a black sheet. "Simon," he whispered. "Come here."

Simon crept in after him. "Come close," said Creak. Simon stood so near he could smell the musty saliva on Creak's breath. "Real close," whispered Creak. "What I'm going to show you…"

Without warning, he tugged the cloth. Inside: a dead professor, a yellowed skull peeking through ripped flesh; the ravine of a scar across the forehead; the neck stitched to the body; the jaw limp; the eye beady and hanging by a thread of muscle.

Simon staggered backwards with a yelp and fell onto a bicycle.

"Your face!" said Creak. He laughed so hard, he collapsed into a throaty cough and had to thump his chest.

Simon knocked a shoebox off the bike's handlebars, which exploded into colours that ricocheted around the garage, bouncing off the fridge, flight cases and walls.

A dollop of green doinked Creak's forehead, right between the eyes. "Ouch! That bloody hurt."

"Serves you right!" said Simon, who made an umbrella from his arms to protect his head from the rainbow hail.

"What the hell is it?" said Creak, as a blob of day-glo orange skimmed his ear.

"Spacedots," said Dove, from outside the garage, "or balls to you." He trapped one under his boot.

"Balls to you!" shouted Creak. "I'm under attack here!"

After a few seconds, the bouncing stopped. One or two of the balls trickled down the drive. "From the '83 Japan tour," said Dove. He picked up the shoebox and gathered them up in it. "They were a craze. The audience kept chucking them at us. I felt like I was in a pinball machine."

"Yeah, man," said Creak. "We had plenty of off-beat cymbal crashes on that tour."

"We were there so long we even looked Japanese at the end of it," said Dove to Simon. "Here's a tip: don't get a haircut abroad. Disaster. I never let anyone else cut my hair again." Dove ran his fingers through his black mane.

"Nor did I!" Creak spoke through gritted teeth and pulled a lever on the side of the coffin to make the body's jaw open and close. "Gottle of geer!"

"I knew it was a prop," said Simon. He adjusted and readjusted the bike's handlebars to make it lean against the wall without slipping. "I made *you* jump."

"Yeah, right," said Creak.

"Stop messing around," said Jonathan. "We've got work to do." He entered the garage for the first time, took the pasting table from the back and set it up in the middle. "This'll do. Our new base." He rolled a map of the Bigg Records building across it and anchored the corners with a paint tin and three jars of screws.

Creak hunted in some boxes and found a set of two-way radios. He twirled the knob on and the battery squeaked its dying wish. "Got roadie radios," said Creak. "Keep an eye out for the charger. Check that box, will you, Simon?" He pointed at a large black flight crate.

"What's in it?" Simon opened the clasps and lifted the lid just enough to peer through a tiny crack. Two eyes glinted at him.

"Oh, that should have my grandma in it," said Dove. Simon dropped the lid.

"Bozo," said Creak. "It's the name of a lighting console."

"It has eyes," said Simon.

Creak jerked the lid open. It didn't have eyes. There were two white and green University of Death stickers, side by side. "Got chargers," said Creak, as he pulled a clump of tangled wires from the box. "And a puncture repair kit. Is Skully here?"

"Sure is," said Dove. He opened up a crate to show it was stuffed with a canvas marshmallow.

Jonathan opened a box of costumes and threw two black body suits at Simon and Dove. "They look your size," he said.

"I can't wear that," said Dove. He shook his head, like it ought to be obvious.

"Why not?" said Jonathan, as he held another one up to his chest for size. "We'll all be in them."

"I don't do black," said Dove. He pointed at his yellow jeans and lime top. "I wouldn't feel right. If you wear black, nobody notices you. You blend into the walls."

"Exactly," said Jonathan. He shut the garage door from the inside. "Gather round, guys. Here's the plan. There's a computer hidden in a cardboard box in a storage room *here*." Jonathan circled a room on the map with his finger. "And there's another one in the studio *here*. We need to enter the deactivation codes into both computers, more or less at the same time."

"What happens if we don't?" said Simon.

"The thing replicates. It spreads across the whole building. But if we just follow the procedure, it will roll over and die."

"Is there no backup?" said Creak.

"You can't back up Plato any more than you can back up the internet. I suggest we send in two teams, one for each machine. The one in the box is well hidden, so we should barricade ourselves in that room so there's plenty of time to find it."

"Problem!" said Simon. "I've been chipped. Bigg will spot me straight away."

"Me too," said Jonathan. "He's got sensors all over the place, but we can use decoys. I can hack the doors to open for us, so we just need to throw him off the scent. He might know we're in the building, but he won't know where we are."

"How do you suggest we do that?" said Dove.

"Bigg's got no reason to doubt you, so you can take the decoys in for us. We just need to find a way to distribute them around the building. I'm working on that. Creak – you've got wheels. You're the getaway driver. We're one man short, still."

"I can call my friend Fred," suggested Simon.

"Is he reliable?"

"He's a she," said Simon. He thought for a moment. "Yeah," he said. "When it matters, she's pretty reliable."

"Get her over here," said Jonathan. "We'll strike Monday."

"Synchronise watches," said Creak, as he touched his. "Beep!"

"Monday?" said Dove. "What day is it now?"

"Man," said Creak. "You've been unemployed too long. I guess we'd better synchronise calendars too, then."

CHAPTER 42

Dove wheeled his flight crate into the lobby of Bigg Records, past reception with a friendly wave, and to the lift. The button was lit up.

A young woman, dressed in what looked like a pink flight stewardess's uniform, cooed over a chihuahua in the handbag slung over her shoulder. "You're going for your favourite w-a-l-k-i-e-s today! Oh yes! The nice mister engineer man is going to take you all around the warehouse. Yes he is! And while you're gone, Mumsie's going to make an album, yes she is, you cutey thing!" She adjusted the animal's tiara and kissed it on the nose.

"Nice dog," said Dove. "Can I stroke it?"

"You like that," said the woman, "don't you, baby? You love to make friends, yes you do!"

Dove palmed a rubber ball from his pocket. While he rubbed the dog's face with one hand, he slipped the ball under its diamond-studded jacket with the other. The dog licked his hand and rubbed its ears against his palm.

The lift arrived and opened. Dove wheeled his flight crate into it, and the woman followed him in and stood there. Dove reached past her to press the button for the top floor.

"I'm going to the sixth," she said. It was a command. He reached past her again to push her floor button and fantasised about making the woman swallow the rubber ball.

* * *

Percy entered the darkened security room and flumped down in his chair, exhausted from his round. He set his cap down on the console and rubbed his forehead. "Anything good on?" he said.

Eric gawped at the bank of CCTV screens and sucked on a salt and vinegar crisp. His hand was in the top of the packet to stop Percy pinching any. "The usual," he said. "That receptionist you like is here, though." Percy nudged the joystick on the console to zoom in on her. "You're a dirty old man," said Eric. "Hang on. That's odd." Eric pointed at a monitor. Simon, Fred and Jonathan's faces were flashing on and off, in a way that was designed to draw attention to the screen but actually made it hard to focus on them. Eric rubbed his eyes. "We've got three of our watch list in the lift. Call Chrome Dome, will you?"

"No need," said a deep voice from behind them. "I'm here."

They both swivelled on their chairs to see Bigg, half-lit by the monitors, a lattice of TV screens reflected in his head. Eric's jaw fell open to show a mulch of crisps on his tongue. "Sir!" he said. "When I said 'Chrome Dome', I meant the—"

"Save it for your exit interview!" said Bigg. "For now, I think you'd better get on with your job, don't you? Get up there! That jerk Jonathan is leaving on the sixth floor now."

Eric folded the top of his crisp packet down and put it on the console. He licked his fingers while he put his cap on his head.

"The lift's still going up," said Percy as he handed Eric a radio. "I'll take the others." They hurried out of the security room and left Bigg staring glass-eyed at the bank of monitors.

"They're here to destroy me," Bigg murmured.

*   *   *

Dove was on his marks long before the lift settled and opened. When it got to the top floor, he thrust his weight behind the flight case and rolled it out of the lift. Each floor had a walkway that lined the building and overlooked the lobby. It looked like the building had been cored, the floors drilled out to make room for the exotic trees that reached from the ground floor entrance to the skylight. From this high up, Dove could see the leafy treetops.

Like everything else here, they were artificial.

He opened the crate and pulled the glitter cannon out of it. Jonathan had replaced the compressed air cylinders with powerful explosives, which made it heavier than usual. There were eight guns on the cannon. Dove aimed the first one down the stairs, and the second pair over the balcony, towards the walkways of the lower floors. The others he pointed over the balcony at different angles.

Dove pressed the timer on the remote. Ten seconds to take cover. He pushed the flight crate along the corridor and away from the cannon, like he was jump-starting the case. After a few paces, he tumbled over the side and into the crate and pulled the lid closed on top of him. The box rumbled along, every tiny bump in the floor magnified to a mountain by the crate's solid metal wheels and lack of suspension. Dove braced himself in the dark for when the crate would hit the far wall. He didn't like being out of control like this.

The crate stopped dead, and all the momentum seemed to be fired into Dove's body, an electric-like shock that entered his feet and spread through his legs. Dove's head smacked against the side of the crate as it recoiled and trickled back along the corridor.

Then the explosions came, eight of them, just fractions of a second apart, like closely sequenced fireworks. The hail came down and drummed on the lid of the box.

* * *

The glitter cannon launched its payload of rubber balls into the stairwell. They bounced off the steps and window ledges, each jump sending them high into the air at jagged angles. With each floor, some were left to hop along the corridor while the others continued their descent. As they reached the next level, they bumped into other balls fired over the balcony towards the lower floors.

Most of the balls hammered down on the furniture, floor and people in the lobby. Those that hit the ground bounced half the lobby's height and attacked again. Others darted off the reception desk and trees and scattered to the corners of the building.

One struck the canvas post trolley. As it hit the metal frame, the ball split into two, like an egg cracked open. The shell halves came to rest on the floor and the tiny seed fell into the trolley and helter-skeltered along the envelopes and through the crevices between them to reach the fluff at the bottom. That clone of Simon's chip would be wheeled around the building forever.

* * *

The map flickered alerts for every floor and every door off the lobby. Bigg watched the monitors aghast. "There's a whole army," he whispered in horror. "It's a bloody invasion."

For a few moments he watched the screen, boggle-eyed. Then he snapped out of it, seized his mobile and tapped away at it. "Time to call the cavalry," he muttered. "No point having friends in high places if you can't use them."

* * *

Creak screeched Ringo to a halt outside Bigg Records. Jonathan, Fred and Simon dived out, like greyhounds released into a race. Simon slipped the side door open and Fred took the smoke gun out, wriggled her arms into the backpack, and held the gun across her with both hands, her legs astride. "Lock and load," she said. She was wearing a green camouflage skirt and black top. While she waited, she looked up, past the concrete monsters on the top of the building, at the swirls of clouds.

Simon and Jonathan created a ramp from a cupboard door and moved the crate inside the van to the top of it. The crate's wheels jammed in the door's grooved design. Simon and Jonathan both pushed hard on three. The loud clack as the crate landed on the road sounded like a gunshot as it echoed around the alleys. "Careful!" whined Jonathan.

"I wouldn't worry about him," said Creak, in the driver's seat. His arm leaned along the edge of the van's open window. "Those crates get worse treatment on tour. There was this one time we locked Axl Rose in one. It was funny, see, because the crate had three axles now. There's this big hill at Glasto, so we—"

"Another time, eh?" Fred marched towards the entrance. Simon and Jonathan, dressed head to toe in black, shadowed her and rumbled the crate along the uneven road surface.

When they got into the lobby, it was aflame with colour. The balls sketched rainbows on the retina as they soared up high and then swooped down low again.

"Be quick," said Jonathan. "When they stop bouncing, we lose our cover."

Simon sprinted for the lift and pushed the crate ahead of them. Jonathan had fashioned a plough from a couple of old planks and had fixed it to the front of the box so it parted the sea of bouncy balls for them.

As they approached the lift, its doors split open. Simon tried to slow the crate but it slithered out of his fingers, charged at the back of the lift, stopped, and juddered back slightly.

Fred pressed her back to the wall and looked around furtively, with her body crossed by her smoke gun.

"Good luck," said Jonathan.

"You too," said Simon. He clicked his roadie radio on and pressed the lift button.

Fred winked at him. "Let's do it," she said. Jonathan jogged past her and she followed him into the ground floor corridors. Every few paces, she would spin around and aim her gun at invisible demons.

Simon watched them disappear and tapped a quickstep with his foot. While he waited for the doors to close, he looked into the lobby. The purple, yellow, red and blue rain was lifting. The storm was becoming a drizzle.

* * *

"What have you found? Over," said Bigg. He had watched Eric and Percy going round in circles on the tag tracker. They were treading water, waiting for a real solution to come along and keeping well out of his way.

The radio on the console was silent for so long that Bigg was startled by its reply: "Balls!"

"I can see that," said Bigg. The CCTV screens had dots zipping all over them, like they had been layered with game upon game of pong. "That's a distraction technique. It only works on stupid people. Try again. Who have you found? Over."

"Nobody yet," said the radio.

Bigg looked at the alert screen. "Why the hell not!" he screamed into the radio. "There are hundreds of them!" There was a long silence. "Over," added Bigg.

"Sorry, sir," came the reply. "You're breaking up. Please repeat."

Bigg took a deep breath, ready to yell again, but then blew it all out as air. The alert screen caught his eye. "They're slowing down," he said. But four of them had penetrated deeper than the others and had lost no momentum. He felt so stupid he slapped himself, and then felt double-stupid when it hurt. "They've cloned their chips," he said. "In the balls. Clever bastards. But we've got them now they've stopped bouncing. Eric, there are two on the ground floor. Percy, take the sixth. Over."

Bigg opened Eric's crisp packet and tapped his cigar ash into it. Just then, the intruders multiplied and split in different directions, like bacteria on a petri dish.

*   *   *

Fred and Jonathan jogged through the corridors.

"Stop!" wheezed Eric from behind them, as he staggered his pursuit and squashed his stomach with one arm.

"Perhaps we should," said Jonathan. "He's going to collapse any minute."

"No mercy in war," said Fred. She had tied a camouflage scarf around her forehead to look more like Rambo. Jonathan hadn't noticed it before, but she must have brought it with her. "We'll stop when our mission is complete," said Fred. "Next left."

"That's the wrong way," said Jonathan.

"Yep," said Fred. "We'll lose him at the stairs."

When they got there, Fred and Jonathan turned to face the guard and waited. Fred pressed the lift button.

"Good!" he said, as he hobbled towards them. "I'm pleased that you've seen sense. Now, I hope you understand the ruddy trouble you've caused."

When the lift arrived with a ping, Fred stood square on to the corridor with her legs apart and fired the smoke gun into it. She drilled it up and down to make it look like a machine gun as it squirted plumes of cloud. Fold upon fold of puffy gas filled the space and enveloped the security guard, who coughed weakly from inside.

Jonathan took a fistful of balls from his left and right pockets and scattered them. He threw one of each into the lift and sent it to the top floor, tossed a pair down the stairs and threw another two up them.

"Arrrgggghhhh!" shouted Fred through gritted teeth as she fired off another barrage of gas.

"Come on," said Jonathan. She ignored him. "Come on!" he repeated, tugging her arm. "You can play later."

*   *   *

Eric coughed spikes into his lungs, and tears into his eyes. When he could speak, he broke the bad news to Bigg.

"What do you mean you can't find them?" Bigg snapped on the radio. "It's not like they can vanish in a puff of smoke. Over."

"Well, actually, Sir," said Eric. "They did."

*   *   *

Simon and Dove arrived at the storage room at the same time, from opposite ends of the corridor. The door opened easily, so Dove marched through it carrying the ventilator from Simon's crate. Simon hauled the marshmallow corpse out of the box and draped the white canvas across the threshold of the door. Dove connected its air pipes to the ventilator and plugged it in. It started to hum. With each breath in, Skully grew bigger and stronger.

They both entered the room. Simon didn't like it one bit. It gave him the creeps, crammed as it was with junk and with God knows what hiding in the shadows. There were microphone stands and light poles tangled up in one corner, and a rail of pirate costumes along the side. There was a painted plastic rock with a handle in the top, and the front half of a motorbike. Boxes were stacked everywhere with labels like 'street scenes, modern', 'clothes, Victorian' and 'crap, other'.

But it was the faces that freaked Simon out. He couldn't take his eyes off them. On the far wall were three shelves of severed heads. Their make-up was painted on with felt tip and bled into the pores of their polystyrene skin. They modelled wigs of life-like hair shaped into outrageous styles. In the half-light, Simon thought he saw one wink.

Dove watched the inflatable mutate to block the corridor and the door. "The skull," he announced. "The fortress of the mind. Now it will seal our fortress."

"Berk," muttered Simon.

"Oi! If you've got something to say," said Dove, "at least have the decency to say it to my agent's face. Now are we doing this, or what?"

The roadie radio crackled. "We're ready," said Fred's canned voice. "How are you doing, Si?"

"Both here," Simon replied. "We're looking for the computer now." He pulled Jonathan's directions out of his pocket and unfolded them. "We need a box that says 'puppets, musical'," he told Dove. "Quick."

*　*　*

Percy radioed in. "Sixth floor's blocked," he said.

"Unblock it then!" shouted Bigg as he paced the control room. "Over!"

"It's too big," said Percy. "It's like a bouncy castle, squashed between the walls. It's got big eyes and all! My grandkids would bloody love this, they would."

"Unplug it!"

"Good thinking!" said Percy. "Only, I can't seem to find the cable. Must be on the other side."

"Pop it then!"

"Steady on," said Percy. "That's a nice bit of kit that. It's got a lovely smile."

"Yeah, well, maybe when this is all over, you and Miss bouncy can go on a date. For now, get her the hell out of my way. I'm coming down, and that damn inflatable had better be doing the same by the time I get there or I will bounce you off it so hard that they will have to exhume Isaac Newton, jump-start him and get him to rewrite his laws of physics to account for your perpetual motion! Over!"

* * *

A circle of light frisked the boxes for labels. "There!" Simon shone the torch on one of them. "About three in, at the bottom."

Dove unstacked the cartons on top of it. "Gotcha!" he said. "Musical puppets, eh? It's a pretty small box, considering where we are." The four flaps of the lid interlocked, so he unfurled them. A panda bear stared at him through marble eyes, unsquinting despite the new light. He nestled on top of a silky duck, its leg caught between the ears of a green rubber alien. "They really are puppets," said Dove.

"Padding," said Simon. He pulled them out and threw them on the floor. After the bear, duck, alien, cow, pig, giraffe, sheep, fox and spider, he found something hard. A laptop, connected to a large external battery. He tore the sides of the box down, and let the other animals spill out of the ark.

Simon put the laptop on one of the closed cartons and kneeled down in front of it. When he flipped the laptop's lid open, it prompted him for a password.

Simon clicked the radio on. "We're ready," he said. "It wants the password."

Jonathan spoke over the radio. "Here comes the first letter," he said. "India."

343

"India," Simon repeated.

"Echo," said Jonathan.

"Echo."

Using the phonetic alphabet, Jonathan coordinated Fred and Simon to enter each character of the password at the same time.

*　*　*

Percy had disappeared by the time Bigg arrived in the sixth floor corridor to confront Skully. Its fat face rippled as the air circulated within it. The black eye holes were peeling off, and the tombstone teeth were fading.

Bigg tried to get his arm between it and the wall, but it wouldn't budge. There wasn't room enough for an ant to squeeze past, so Bigg stood no chance. He stroked the skull's surface. It was shiny and cold, made of thick canvas and built to withstand the demands of a world tour. For years, it had been blown up, let down and folded away every other night. The corridor held no horrors for it.

Bigg sucked deeply on his cigar and blew the smoke into Skully's face. "You're just hot air," said Bigg. "All face and no trousers." He pressed his cigar into Skully's eye and twisted it with unnecessary venom. Skully cried ash onto the floor. Bigg pushed hard for about a minute, but the cigar wasn't going any deeper. When he took it away, the plastic had been part melted, but was intact. The cigar had gone out.

He re-lit it and tried again, this time, taking the cigar away every now and then to let it breathe. After a minute or so, he felt the plastic give way and the cigar slip out of his fingers. He caught it before it fell inside. When he removed it, a jet of warm air escaped through the tiny hole he had made, but Skully hardly seemed to change shape.

Bigg took his tie off, lit another four cigars, and bound them together with the tie. As he pressed them all into Skully's face, molten plastic dripped down Skully's cheeks and collected in a puddle on the floor.

*　*　*

Simon and Dove had entered the last letter of the password.

"Ready?" asked Jonathan on the radio.

Skully bowed down before Bigg and let him walk all over him, as so many fame-hungry starlets had before. "Don't press that button," said Bigg. "Or you'll never work in music again."

Simon and Dove both jumped when they heard his voice. "That's all we need," said Dove. "A promise from a liar."

"Bigg's here," said Simon, into the radio.

"Press 'enter' any time now," said Jonathan. "Just make sure you tell us when."

"I'm the last label standing," said Bigg. "If you bring me down, it will be the final nail in the coffin of the whole industry. Who's going to pick up the tab when I'm broke? Nobody. You, Mr Dove, will have to get a proper job. Like all the normal people."

Disgust crossed Dove's face when Bigg classed him as normal. Simon lowered his hand towards the keyboard, but Dove grabbed it and held it in the air. "Let's hear him out," he said.

"Smart man!" Bigg laughed. "I'm not surprised to see Thingie here. He took the whole imaginary girlfriend thing way too serious—"

Simon headed for Bigg, ready to punch his lights out, but Dove put his arm out as a barrier to hold him back. It was like an elderly lollipop man holding back a class of infants: no strength except for authority.

"I'm disappointed with you, Dove," said Bigg. "I gave you my hard-earned money and basically let you piss around all day. And for what? To find you snooping around my business, hacking into my computers. There's gratitude for you!"

"I'll show you how grateful I am when I destroy Plato," said Dove.

"Yeah!" added Simon, unnecessarily.

"Funny," said Bigg. "I had you pegged as classier than that. Dove, I mean. Not you, Thingie. I always had you down as a vandal."

"Don't try to claim the moral high ground," said Dove. "You've been stealing my music."

"Stealing it? I've never even listened to it."

"We know all about your secret computer system," said Simon, "that siphons off Dove's music, and turns it into different bands, and then uses sleazy chatbots to sell it."

"Did you really think nobody would find out?" said Dove.

Bigg looked confused for a moment but then laughed again, this time more hollow. "That Jonathan is a duplicitous pile of steamies, eh? No wonder he was so keen for me to pay you a retainer. He needed you to get the damn thing working. Sly rogue. Much shadier than I credited him."

"He's trying to distract us," said Simon. "So we don't push the button." The laptop screensaver blanked its screen.

"No," said Bigg. "I'm trying to kick myself. Some bloke comes here and sells me a magic computer system that can invent and sell music. Turns out it's taking the music I've already bought and repackaging it. That's funny. Really bloody funny. Shame we fell out. I could do with his acumen in marketing."

"Press it," said Dove. "This is going nowhere."

Simon went to push the button, but Bigg stepped over to them and held Simon's hand aloft. Dove wrestled him off and pushed him away. "Sorry," said Bigg. He retreated backwards and held his palms out, like he was being inspected for dirt before teatime. "But let's not be hasty. What if I paid you, Mr Dove, to unplug yourself from the system and walk away? I can find a few quid for the boy wonder here too."

"We're not for sale," said Simon.

"Everyone's for sale," said Bigg. "We've just got to negotiate a fair price. There must be something I can offer you. There's always a win-win."

"Not for you today," said Dove. "Today you lose. You treated me and my music like coal, a raw material to be burnt up for energy. Now, it's payback time."

Bigg wasn't listening. He was lost in his private thoughts. "I've got it!" he said. "The perfect deal!"

"I can't do a deal with you," said Dove.

"Then let me talk to Thingie," said Bigg.

"I'm not listening until you address me properly," said Simon. "You can call me Mr Singh."

"Well, Mr Singh," said Bigg. "May I put a proposal to you?" Simon enjoyed the petty triumph of making Bigg address him with respect, even a touch of humility. Bigg continued: "Here's how I see it. Dove's in Plato and, for some stupid reason, prefers obscurity. Easily done. And beside him we have a man who sounds almost exactly the same and who is desperate for someone to listen to him. Don't you see the win-win here? I could pay you, Thi... er, Mr Singh, to replace Dove in the system."

"He's not interested," said Dove.

"He can talk," said Bigg. "Let him."

Simon's head swam. With a single touch of a small piece of plastic, he could stop Bigg exploiting the fans, wringing their hearts and wallets dry.

But then who would he listen to? The waves of sewage that Bigg pumped out through radio and TV underwrote the whole industry infrastructure that distributed the independent music Simon did like. And how would he ever make it big if there was nobody there to help sell his music?

Bigg dangled Simon's dream before him: to be a professional musician, paid to jam and invent melodies. Nobody would ever know it was him, which took the shine off it a bit, but millions would listen to his music and love it just like he had loved Tiled Sprites. It would be enough for most musicians to write a single song in a lifetime that moved someone as much as Simon had been moved by his Plato band. As part of the system, Simon could write thousands. For the first time, people would not only listen to his music but would feel it, really feel it, too. Simon would not have to peel the leaves off a cabbage ever again.

"He's not interested," repeated Dove.

Simon put himself between Dove and the laptop. "How much are we talking about?" he asked Bigg.

"That's my boy!" said Bigg. "Give me a minute. I just need to place a call, then we can hammer out a deal that works for you." Bigg lifted the pitch of his voice and pointed at Simon on the last word, which made him look like a car dealer on a local TV advert. Then he sloped off to the far corner, next to a Christmas tree, and took out his mobile phone.

"You can't deal with this man," whispered Dove. "He'll eat you alive."

"It's you that nearly killed me on my own balcony," Simon replied. "He just screwed with my mind. Small fry, by comparison."

They could only hear half of Bigg's conversation. "It's urgent," he stammered. "Please connect me... We don't have time for this... What do you mean he doesn't take calls from members of the public? Tell him it's Clive Bigg and he'll take it. I promise you. I spoke to him not an hour ago. Please... No! Don't hang up! Don't do that! It's a matter of national security!" Bigg begged to no avail.

The world went dark.

The hum of the building died.

There were screams on the floor above.

The fire alarm bleated.

"Oh, Christ," murmured Bigg.

"Keep back," said Dove. "I'm warning you, Bigg. Make a move, and I'll deck you." It was an idle threat. Nobody could see anything, let alone attack it.

Through the door, they could see pencil-thin beams of green light that sliced the air in the corridor and danced up and down.

An alien with big, glassy eyes and a distended mouth peered around the door and shone a light into the room. "Three friendlies," he said. His breathing was amplified by the gas mask.

Simon, Dove and Bigg shielded their eyes with their arms. Dove pointed at Bigg and said: "He's not friendly."

"Shut up!" shouted the man. "Follow me! Now!"

Nobody moved. "What's going on?" said Simon.

"I think I can explain—" said Bigg.

"Now!" barked the man at the door. Three soldiers in masks stormed the room and punched Bigg, Simon and Dove in the stomach with a baton. While they doubled in pain, the soldiers pulled their hands together behind them, whipped a lasso of plastic around them and jerked it tight. All three let out cries of pain.

"Move or die!" the soldiers shouted into their prisoners' faces.

"Move now! Go!" Simon felt his ear drum creak at the volume of the soldier's voice. He was pushed outside the room where he could feel Skully under his feet, and was bundled along the corridor as voices shouted around him. He was flanked by two soldiers, with one behind him, and could hear the shouts of more in the darkness behind. The green beams shone ahead of him, and the torch light bounced up and down with their footsteps and picked out tiny details as they passed: the handle on a window, a couple of rubber balls by the skirting board, the cheesy grin of some girl band on a poster. Simon slipped on one of the balls but was caught in mid-fall by the soldiers and carried a few paces until he could walk again. The march was relentless and took them down six flights of stairs and along dozens of corridors. Simon had studied the building's map only yesterday, but he had no idea where he was or where he was going. "My legs hurt!" he pleaded. The soldiers hustled him. "Faster!" one of them shouted.

There was a crash as they burst through the fire exit into the light. Simon screwed up his eyes. The soldiers disappeared into the building and left them there in the car park.

Fred ran over. Her tights were torn and the tops of her shoes were covered with footprints from the scramble to evacuate. "You okay, Si?" She cut the ties on his hands with a penknife and then moved on to Dove.

Simon rubbed his wrists, cut raw by the plastic. The air smelled of burning rubber and smoke seeped from the building's vents. "Do Bigg too," he said. Fred snipped Bigg's hand-tie.

A policeman jogged over to all of them with his arms out-stretched. "Move away from the building please." He ushered them to the far side of the car park.

A fighter plane screamed through the sky above the building and there was an almighty explosion within it. Smoke billowed out of open windows and tiles blew off the roof. Within minutes, the whole building was ravaged by fire. Simon shielded his face from the intense heat.

"What the fuck just happened?!" he said.

"I think some planes just blew the place up?" said Jonathan.

"Good," said Simon. "I'm not going mad, then."

They watched in silence for a moment.

"You weren't really going to take his money, were you?" said Dove, as he watched the flames lick around the plump guest sofas in reception.

"He tried to bribe you?" said Fred.

"Nah," Simon answered Dove. He watched the building go up in smoke. "Just stringing him along. For a laugh." His voice was deadpan.

"We didn't deactivate Plato, did we?" asked Fred. She took the scarf off her forehead, and it left a white stripe where it had protected her face from the smoke.

"Doesn't matter now," said Jonathan. He could see the monitors melting on the desks near the windows. "That fire is going to gut the whole building. If the fire brigade aren't here now, there's no hope for it."

"Shouldn't we call them?" said Simon. There came no reply. When he turned to look, Jonathan had vanished.

*   *   *

Bigg stood on the other side of the car park and watched the roof fall in on his empire. Marian was at his side. "Your phone's ringing," she said.

"Let it," said Bigg. His pocket diddled a jolly tune.

"It might be important," said Marian.

"More important than that?" Bigg pointed at the smoking carcass of his company, but snatched the phone from his pocket and answered it. "Bigg!"

"Sorry to hear about your trouble," said a male voice.

"Andrews!" said Bigg. "Is that you?"

There came a cough from the other end.

"Prime Minister?"

"I think you know me better than that, *Clive*," said the voice. It made a big play of using his first name.

"What the hell did you do that for?" shouted Bigg. "I only needed you to fix the security breach."

"It's fixed."

"You've destroyed the whole system, you arse! You've drowned the baby in the bathwater!"

"Like I said, it's fixed," came the reply. "No evidence. Nothing linking you to me. How do you think I feel when you phone me up during Question Time to tell me you've got a hundred people storming the building to attack our covert promotional system? I can't work with amateurs."

"I'll make you pay for this."

The other man guffawed.

"I thought we were friends," Bigg whined.

"Politicians don't have friends. Only temporary allies. That's what we had in common. I've got to go now. Geldof's on line one." He hung up.

Bigg threw his mobile phone at the tarmac and stamped on it. It spilled its electronic guts.

"Clive!" said a bright voice from beside him. It was Jake from marketing. "Is this a bad time?"

Flames ripped across the ceiling of reception. Through a burst pipe's sheet of spurting water, Bigg saw the wall to the archive room collapse like a Jenga tower. "No," said Bigg. "Now is just *per*fect."

"We can rebuild the business," said Jake. Bigg's head shook very slightly, involuntarily. "I've already started," continued Jake. "You said I wasn't ruthless enough. So I thought you'd like to know I've been selling marshmallows."

Bigg was puzzled. "Marshmallows?"

"To toast by the fire!"

Bigg punched him. Hard.

* * *

"Police are investigating a terrorist attack at the Bigg Records building," said a TV reporter, stood in the car park in front of a cameraman. "Details are just emerging, but as you can see, it looks like the last record label has finally gone up in flames."

"Reset!" said the cameraman. "Can you get out of our way please! We're trying to make a television programme here!"

Dove bent down to undo and then tie both his shoelaces, while Fred and Simon waited for him. When he was done, they walked out of shot. Fred split open a bag of marshmallows and offered them around.

At the far side of the car park, Creak waited for them with his van. "Cool!" he said when they arrived. "You really stuck it to the man!"

"It wasn't us," said Dove.

"It's okay," said Creak. "I won't tell anyone."

"It wasn't!" said Fred.

They all clambered into the van and Creak started it up, third time lucky. A thicket of policemen ducked when Ringo backfired but they let the van pootle out of the car park without being stopped.

"So," said Simon, forcing a casual conversational tone. "Did you ever play our cover of Animal Reined?"

"Yeah," said Dove.

Simon waited, but Dove didn't elaborate so he pressed him: "What did you think?"

"You need a drummer. A drum machine don't cut it." Simon's heart sank.

"Dove, man, he used a drum machine?" said Creak. "I would never have trusted him if I'd known that."

"But," added Dove, "not a bad effort on the guitar."

Simon felt like he'd burst with pride, but acted cool about it. "We'd love to get a real drummer," he said. "But they're so hard to find."

"It's a mug's game," said Creak. "I haven't played for ages."

"Don't you miss it?" asked Simon.

"I could do with hitting the skins after a day like today, yeah."

"We've got a rehearsal later," said Simon.

"No we—ouch!" said Fred, as Simon elbowed her ribs.

"Maybe I'll pop along," said Creak.

"Cool," said Simon. He said nothing else for fear that the others would hear him giggle with excitement.

EPILOGUE

Five years later

The pub was heaving with people of all ages. They still called it 'the Corpse', but that was because it had a strong goth following now. The new stage was only about six inches high, but most nights it had bands on it entertaining a boisterous crowd. When the music industry had died, the live circuit had come to life.

The Master swept onto the stage with his cloak flying behind him. He stamped on the floor three times, each time greeted with a beery cheer in reply. Tufts of grey hair poked out between the skull mask and his black hood. "I am the Master," he droned. The crowd erupted with applause and wolf whistles.

He waited until the noise subsided. "On drums," he then called, "Creak McCoffin."

Another skeleton emerged from the gents' and stepped up onto the stage. The Master stood to one side, so that everyone could get a clear view of Creak. He took to his drum stool, hammered out a thirty second solo and then slipped into a dance groove.

"On keyboards," the Master said. "Dead Fred."

Fred skipped on. She was hooded, but her cloak hugged her figure, tied at the waist, cut low at the front and high on her thighs. Her face was painted a deathly shade of blue, with two blood tears dripping from her right eye, their colour the same as her painted lips. The Master bowed to her and she nodded slightly in return. He stood aside as she took up her place behind the keyboards.

The crowd was clapping along now, and a few whoops went up as she slapped the first few bass notes out. All the while, a hint of a smile played on her lips, but she never let it crack her image. She stretched her eyes wide open and stared into the lights while the fingers of her left hand dropped a bass melody on top of Creak's rhythm.

"On guitar," the master droned. "The Thing." Simon stepped up on to the stage, cloaked and masked. Arms shot up in the audience and pointed phones at him to try to get a picture. The crowd noise surged.

Behind his mask, Simon beamed. As he did before every gig, he pinched his side. Nothing happened. Only then did he pick up his guitar and strap it on. He jumped into the air and landed on his knees, where he strangled a blistering solo from his instrument. After a minute, the guitar dissolved into chugging chords and the crowd hollered its praise.

The audience was getting worked up now. A guy near the front thrashed around in time to the music, and splashed his beer over those around him. Bert the barman tried in vain to get the kids to climb off the tables. People sat on the bar for a better view, all the way along it, and passed glasses between the serving staff and the punters.

"Graduating with honours," said the Master. "Dove." His final word could not be heard above the audience screams. Dove jogged on to the stage and shook the Master's hand. The Master disappeared through the staff door behind the bar and left the band behind.

"We are University of Death," said Dove. The band played on behind him. "Give it up for The Thing, who wrote our first song tonight." Dove pointed, but on this tiny stage he was only inches from touching Simon.

Dove nodded the others in on one, and two, and three, and four, and then sang out loud:

All you have ever known
Fizzles out to nothing
Just skin and bones
And gory stuffing

As he played, Simon headbanged and danced, out of time and out of mind, all over the stage. Every time Dove looked in his direction, Simon knew for sure he was looking straight at him, and even after all the gigs they'd played together, that excited him.

And memories
Of things you said
Circling round your best friend's head
Welcome to eternal DEATH

The drinkers shouted the last word on cue, beers held high, until they were hoarse. The pub was so packed the people at the front could only whoop and cheer, while those stood on tables and chairs clapped.

Simon turned away from the audience, lifted his mask and wiped the sweat from his face with a towel. He'd never realised how greasy it got inside those skulls before he joined the band. When he turned around, he winked at his girlfriend Sarah in the front row before slipping his mask down again. She blew him a kiss.

Five years ago, Simon could never have imagined he would play to a crowd like this, totally up for it and into his music, let alone hear Dove sing his songs and Creak hammer out the rhythm. The only thing better than watching a University of Death gig, was being in the band. Even now, he still fizzed with excitement whenever they played together.

* * *

Simon dug a handful of change out of his apron pocket as the

355

stand was besieged by fans. He found a two pound coin, gave it to the man waiting and sent him away with the new single. Dove waved from the door as he left with Creak. Simon wanted to kill him. It wouldn't hurt Dove to help with the merchandise once in a while.

"CDs!" said a woman, greeting a long lost friend. "I didn't know you could still get those."

"They're not available in the shops," said Simon. "You have to get them here. Can you give me a hand, Fred?"

Still in her make-up, she was signing albums for a gang of teenage boys next to the Space Invaders machine. "Sorry, boys," she said. "Duty calls."

Simon lost no time briefing her: "This guy wants the album and single; beside him, they need two of the first album and one of the second; and keep an eye on the guy on the end. He's been reading that inlay for ten minutes."

Simon ripped open a box, pulled out a band t-shirt and held it up. "Who wants one of these then? Twenty quid. Signed by Dove. Extremely limited."

Arms reached over the table and from the back of the queue. Each one held bank notes out to him.

*   *   *

After an hour the crowd died down and Simon pushed the samples into an empty box and sat on the merchandise table. He couldn't fight his way to the bar now. He was knackered. With his hands hidden in his apron purse, he counted the bundle of notes.

"You alright, mate? I got you a pint."

Simon zipped the apron, took the beer, raised it to say 'cheers' and gulped half of it down. "Do I know you?"

"Nah," said the bloke. He was wearing a sharp suit and looked about seventeen. Simon guessed the aftershave he was wearing was cheap, because it smelled like he'd marinated in it for a week and he didn't look loaded.

The man went on: "I'm a business student, me. Full of ideas. Full of beans."

"Really?" said Simon. He felt it was only polite to feign interest after a stranger's bought you a drink.

"Yeah, I could be good for you," said the student. "Name's Mike."

"Hello, Mike."

"Listen: You're a winner. I'm a winner. You're a performer. I'm a seller. See what I'm saying?" Mike sat on the table beside Simon.

"Not really."

"You don't wanna be wasting your time selling CDs." Mike kicked one of the cardboard boxes gently. "What are you? A market trader? Nah, mate. You're a star. You wanna be doing the music and letting some other mug do the sales stuff. Let someone else take the strain."

"Do you think?" Simon had stopped drinking and begun to listen.

"Sure. I go out every night and you know what I see? Talent. Wasted. In every pub there's a gig tonight. And afterwards, these bands are working their nuts off trying to sell stuff. Waste. Of. Talent. And they're mostly crap at sales. Couldn't sell water to a man on fire. No offence, mate."

"So what do you suggest?"

"Listen, me and a few mates, we're thinking about making a sort of group of groups. So, we, like, join them together."

"Like a supergroup?"

"Nah, mate. More like a company. We get all these bands together, then we can buy stuff cheaper. Economies of scale. We can have a central place for making all these CDs. Efficient. You bands can just do your music stuff, which you love, right? And let me and my mates look after the business stuff. We could have shops that only sell music. Imagine that! If we can sell more music, you can get bigger crowds. Maybe we'll even open halls for playing music in. Yeah, I like that idea. Or – yeah – we could use stadiums! Imagine that! They did that once, you know."

"Yeah," said Simon. "I know."

"You can focus on being musical and famous, and we'll do all the donkey work."

"Why would you do that?"

"It's business, init? We get a cut. You make more money. More people find your fabulous music. Everyone's a winner."

"Sounds so easy."

"Yeah. A wonder no one thought of it before."

"Actually, you wouldn't remember, but they did."

"Well, so what? Nobody's doing it now." Mike produced an envelope from his inside pocket and unfolded a letter. There were about ten stapled pages, all justified text in capital letters. "Here's our terms. Trust me. This is the start of something big, mate. We've got twelve bands signed up already. You don't wanna be left behind. Are you in?"

"I don't know…"

"We can negotiate terms. There's always a win-win!"

Simon tried to remember where he had heard that before.

Mike flapped the contract at Simon and produced a pen. It glinted. "We could be a winning team, you and me," he said. "I mean… What could possibly go wrong?"

THE END

EXTRAS

POPTASTIC TRIVIA

❑ Plato's band names really did come from the source
Jonathan identifies in the story. Other great names collect-
ed from that same source while writing this book include
Septimus Frank, Sorrowful, Tough, Trent Skinner, Killing,
Jim: Catapult, Melody Brand, Heftier Alibis, Cyril, Hug-
ginsOrlando, Madison Susie, Fanny Bliss, Grimble
Gromble, Godwin's Law, Good Erection, Hereward
Bowne, Crematoria, and Dirk Fuzzbuster.

❑ In September 2014, Apple added U2's album 'Songs of
Innocence' to the iTunes accounts of an estimated 500 million customers without asking them. 26 million people
downloaded the album in its entirety, but it soon became
what The Guardian newspaper called a public relations
debacle. Some complained that the album was consuming
space on their devices, and that they were having U2's
music forced on them, irrespective of their taste. Apple
published step-by-step instructions to tell people how to
delete the album. Bono, lead singer of U2, apologised and
said: "[It was a] drop of megalomania, touch of generosity,
dash of self-promotion and deep fear that these songs that
we poured our life into over the last few years mightn't be

heard. There's a lot of noise out there. I guess we got a little noisy ourselves to get through it." (sources: U2's Bono issues apology for automatic Apple iTunes album download, The Guardian, 15 October 2014; 26 million iTunes users have downloaded U2's free album. But how many deleted it again?, Gigaom, 9 October 2014)

❑ Sony BMG hid software on 50 audio CDs including albums by Celine Dion, Neil Diamond and Natasha Bedingfield. The copy prevention software used a 'rootkit', a technique typically used by hackers to hide malicious code on a computer, and it created security vulnerabilities that hackers were later able to exploit. Microsoft was among the security software vendors to describe Sony BMG's software as 'spyware'. In a statement on its website, Sony BMG denied it had done anything wrong, but a class action lawsuit resulted in a product recall and compensation to customers (including copies of the music they bought without any copy restrictions). It also blocked Sony BMG from using its existing copy protection software. As part of the settlement, whenever Sony BMG wants to use copy protection software in future, it must submit it first for an independent security review. (source: http://www.eff.org/IP/DRM/Sony-BMG/)

❑ The VIP Baja Beach Club, Barcelona, injects guests with a microchip that provides access to the VIP lounge and can be used to charge drinks on account. The glass chip is about 1.3mm by 1mm and means that revellers who prefer to dress in swimwear don't have to worry about having somewhere to keep their wallets. In 2015, the BBC's technology correspondent Rory Cellan-Jones visited Epicenter, an office block in Sweden, where tenants can use an RFID tag under their skin to open doors and access photocopiers. (source: Barcelona clubbers get chipped, BBC News online, 29 September 2004; Office puts chips under staff's skin, BBC News online, 29 January 2015)

- McDonalds offered to pay rappers $5 every time a song featuring the words 'Big Mac' was played and Seagram's gin paid rapper Petey Pablo to plug its product in his US hit Freek-a-Leek. (source: Well placed, BBC online, 30 March 2005).

- All the concerts Elvis performed during his lifetime were in America and Canada, but since 1998 he has toured the world on video screen with his former band mates playing on the stage below. The tour is called 'Elvis Presley In Concert' and is billed as Elvis's 'first-ever world concert tour'. The official Elvis website says: "A world tour was an unrequited dream for Elvis and his fans. Long after the superstar's death, the dream has come true." (source: Elvis is Back, Elvis.com, undated but accessed 3 July 2007).

- When Culture Club played Tokyo's Budokan in 1984, the audience threw bouncy balls onto the stage. (source: In the land of the Rising Sun, The Best of Smash Hits: the 80s, 2006)

- Madonna's 1992 book Sex included photographs of her swimming, cycling, eating pizza, hanging in the air, and hitchhiking – all in the nude. The oversized book was spiral bound with metal covers, which prompted comedian Paul Merton to dismiss it as 'too heavy to hold in one hand'. According to Wikipedia, Sex sold out of its 1.5 million English language first pressing in three days. Lest the music be forgotten, the book included a one-track CD of 'Erotic', in a silver wrapper like a condom.

- It's an open secret in the music industry that many bands don't make enough money to give up the day job. In 2014, online magazine Noisey persuaded several bands to go on the record about their day jobs. The most striking example was Deaf Havana. The band's 2013 album Old Souls, released on major label BMG/Chrysalis, hit number 1 on the UK Rock Chart and entered the UK Albums Chart at number 9. The band supported Bruce Springsteen at the Hard Rock Calling Festival and Muse in Germany. The band's guitarist Chris Pennells manages a music venue in London. He said: "The point we're at now – I couldn't afford to live off what I make off the band. Depending on how stuff goes with the next record it probably won't be like that for a while." In 2015, Al Doyle of Hot Chip told the BBC: "I find it quite strange that I'm struggling to buy a one-bedroom flat in London six albums into my career, 12 years down the line." (source: Loads of huge UK rock bands still have day jobs, Noisey, 10 November 2014; Deaf Havana on Wikipedia; The pop star and the prophet, BBC News Online, 17 September 2015)

❑ During Kurt Cobain's lifetime, Nirvana released three studio albums and a compilation. Since his death in 1994, there have been deluxe reissues of the studio albums, three live albums, three compilations, three box sets, and six video albums: a total of 18 releases. (source: Nirvana on Wikipedia)

❑ Dr Adrian North of the University of Leicester conducted research in 2006 into listening habits. He said: "Music was rarely the focus of participants' concerns and was instead something that seemed to be taken rather for granted, a product that was to be consumed during the achievement of other goals. In short, our relationship to music in everyday life may well be complex and sophisticated, but it is not necessarily characterised by deep emotional investment." (more info: Is there a future for the record industry? By Sean McManus, www.sean.co.uk, May 2009)

❑ In 1996, Brian Eno released an album of generative music software on floppy disc. Eno defined the parameters of the composition, but the computer jammed to create a unique performance of the tracks each time. The software used the sound card's built-in MIDI synthesiser. Eno explored the idea further in 77 Million Paintings, released in 2006, a DVD of software which layers and mixes Eno's handmade slides to create virtually endless sequences of artworks. As the images morph, they are accompanied by an ambient soundtrack generated by the computer from samples. '77 Million Paintings' poses interesting questions about what's an original artwork, giving everyone access to the same opportunity to view art, while ensuring everyone has a unique viewing experience. (more info: A review of 77 Million Paintings, www.sean.co.uk, 12 October 2006)

❑ Enya collaborated with her lyricist Roma Ryan to create the fictional language 'Loxian' used on three tracks on the 2005 album 'Amarantine'. Enya's past work had been recorded in English, Gaelic, Latin, and even Elvish in the case of the 'Lord of the Rings' movie soundtrack. Enya said: "I always feel when the melody sounds right with whatever language, I feel fine. We spend a lot of time looking for the right language for the melody I have written. English can be a little bit obtrusive." (source: Enya sings in a tongue from a 'distant planet', Sunday Times, 27 November 2005)

❑ Sigur Ros's 2002 album '( )' was sung in Hopelandic, an invented language of nonsense syllables which vocalist Jónsi uses to write the melody before the lyrics. (source: Sigur Ros official website, accessed 11 October 2007). Since songs on the band's other albums ágætis byrjun and Takk are sung in Icelandic, many international fans probably didn't realise the songs on ( ) were in a fictional and meaningless language.

❑ In March 2005, Erasure launched a website where fans could buy a unique version of their song 'Don't Say You

Love Me'. Fans chose different synth, drum and vocal lines and heard a looping sample of the song as they switched between them. When they were happy, listeners could pay £2 to download an MP3. Each of the 40,000 unique versions of the track was sold only once, creating a limited edition of one. "In our concept all the possibilities are approved by the artists," says Marc-Henri Wouters, CEO and founder of Trust Media, the company behind the customisation technology. "Therefore you have a limited number of unique pieces and people can't lose the initial intent of the artist because the artist can approve all the possibilities. Concerning piracy, we do have the possibility to trace the legal owner of a version but up to now we haven't done so. What is more interesting with this concept is the fact that you don't make the value on the copy but on the personalisation. The sharing of a version just pushes people to buy their own version." (more info: Erasure pioneers customised MP3 sales by Sean McManus, www.sean.co.uk, December 2005)

DELETED SCENE

"You're late," said Simon.

"It's a wonder I made it at all," said Fred. "I had a great idea for a song. I was about three chords in, when the doorbell went. It was the TV licensing people, wanting to snoop around to check I didn't have a telly. So, I saw them off, then I picked up the guitar again. About three chords in, the doorbell went again. This time it was the iPlod, checking I didn't have any unlicensed music. So he scanned my computers which seemed to take ages. When he eventually left, I picked up the guitar again and after a minute or two, the doorbell went again. By now I was fuming."

"I bet."

"Absolutely livid. So I ripped the door open and there's some bloke there from the fridge licensing authority."

"The what?"

"The fridge licensing authority. So I said 'What a load of crap. What do you mean a 'fridge licence'?'. He says that because my fridge connects to the internet to do the shopping, it's got software in it that needs to be updated regularly. So I told him I wasn't going to pay again for a fridge I'd already bought, and he came over all dark, like. And said that the fridge company had some *very* powerful allies in the utilities industry. So I said 'do your worst'."

"And what happened?"

"When I shut the front door, the lights went out."

ANOTHER DELETED SCENE

Silent but Violent prompted 136 complaints to the BBC when their performance at the Brit Awards was televised. Two people accused the BBC of neglecting its responsibility to minors by screening aggression before the watershed. Everyone else was annoyed because they thought their telly was on the blink.

THANK YOU

Thank you to my readers for buying a copy of this book and spending their time in its world. Special thanks to those who supported the first edition of this book and gave me feedback that helped me to refine it for this edition.

Karen – thank you for all your support throughout this long project. You're a star.

Peter – thank you for reading the draft and providing helpful feedback on design and editing.

Special thanks to Hazel Butters and Melisa Young who did a fantastic job of promoting the book on its first release.

Thanks to Scott Thomson (www.positivelypostal.co.uk) for pointing me in the right direction on a question of research.

It was surprisingly hard to come up with a title for this book. The first edition was named after the band 'University of Death', but I was never totally comfortable with it, and some readers were put off by it. For this remastered edition, I held an online brainstorm with friends to pick a new title. There were some fantastic suggestions, some of them unfortunately encumbered by trademarks or already taken by other books. I'd like to extend my special thanks to Andy Lawn who came up with the winning suggestion 'Earworm'. Thanks also to everyone who contributed to the brainstorm: Karen McManus, Phil Holland, Tom Buttle, Liam O'Connor, Benjamin Matthews, James Barclay, Titien Ahmad, Sarah Power, Mark Tapp, Paul Blunden, Lucas Schifres, Tracy Parker, Laura Borrell, Albane Lester, Lynne Cartwright, Ian Thomas, Victoria Connelly, John Hartnup, Gemma Storey, Sam Storey, Anne Weatherall, Grace Weatherall, Tim Lloyd, Lance Concannon, Marc Bangs, Dan Wink, Mark Turner, Lisa Tweedie, Sean Hodges, Adrian Holland, Gareth Mottram, Tim Norman, Mark Young, and Kim Gilmour.

It's so hard to promote books today, so every blog mention, link, review, gift purchase, tweet, and email really makes a difference. If you've enjoyed this book, please take a moment to write a review on Amazon to help others find it, or tell your friends about it through your favourite channel. Thank you!

KEEP IN TOUCH

Follow me on Twitter at @musicandwords
Discover my other books at www.sean.co.uk/books
Play my music at www.sean.co.uk/music

13617590R00207

Printed in Great Britain
by Amazon.co.uk, Ltd.,
Marston Gate.